SUNWEAVERS

SUNWEAVERS

BOOK ONE—THE BROTHERS

CAROLYN GOLLEDGE

ILLUSTRATIONS BY: JOSHUA ALLEN

authorHOUSE®

AuthorHouse™
1663 Liberty Drive
Bloomington, IN 47403
www.authorhouse.com
Phone: 1-800-839-8640

Published by AuthorHouse   04/12/2013

ISBN: 978-1-4817-9185-4 (sc)
ISBN: 978-1-4817-9186-1 (hc)
ISBN: 978-1-4817-9187-8 (e)

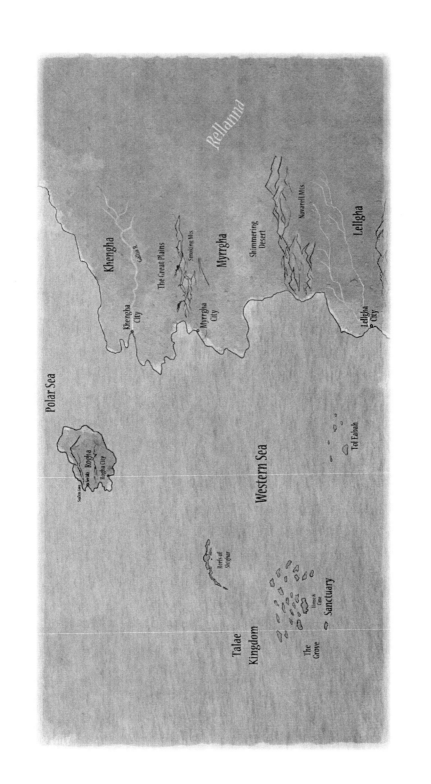

CHAPTER ONE

'Not exactly Rogha City, is it?' Kerell Lerant asked, looking around Myrrgha City's bustling, noisy and aromatic Market Square. It stood against the military barracks high rear wall, the turrets and spires of the Imperial Palace behind, and enclosed on the other side by the old city Gate that gave way to a sprawling township, covering the sun-bleached slopes above the bay and the river lined with docks and warehouses. Masts and spars blotted the white-capped blue of the bay at the river delta. More slave ships arriving with captives from Lellgha.

'No,' Parlan agreed. 'Myrrgha's sunshine and warmth hasn't touched its people. Rogha might be cold and dark, but its people are warm.'

'Some of the people I've met here are friendly enough,' Lerant said, remembering the good friends he'd made at the Military Engineering Academy.

Parlan Hollin, Lerant's brother—or more correctly, his foster-brother, looked up at him, his gentle brown eyes all dark and sad; totally unlike the Parlan that Lerant had known in their home, a coal—miner's cottage in Rogha City. That was before Myrrgha,

1

before conscription into the military. War, being a soldier, had done that to Parlan, and Lerant knew what his brother would say next.

'You've been a student, here, Kerell. Studying engineering, meeting other men who love it the way you do. Myrrgha's industries and new machines would be a wonder to me, too, if I hadn't seen firsthand what they use it for.'

'I know. I'm working to get you out.'

Parlan gave him a smile, and for a moment was again the brother Lerant knew. 'Forgive me,' he said. 'This is our only day together, free to do as we please. I'm so proud of you, Kerell, more proud than words can say. You graduated with Honors! You're a Captain of the Myrrghin Military Engineers! Celebrate!' Reaching out, he tapped the Cogs and Wheels insignia Lerant wore on his tunic jacket, over his heart, another on the left sleeve.

'Thanks,' Lerant returned the smile and gripped Parlan's shoulder before they continued on, walking side by side. He wanted to say 'I'm proud of you, too,' for he was. But he knew the words would hurt rather than please Parlan. There was no pride to be had in being a killer.

They wandered among canvas-canopied rows of stalls laden with fruit and vegetables, and spices, with fish and pork and beef, with jewelry, and clothing, and much more. Nothing there however was of any real interest to them as they searched for gifts for Parlan's wife and children, Lerant's little nephews. They crossed into the cooler shadows of the narrow alleyways that lay in a tangled maze behind the Square proper. Here were the more interesting, perhaps illegal wares, and certainly where the bargains, the black market deals were to be had.

Anger simmered, boiled higher in Lerant's blood as he saw the sadness and homesickness returning to his brother's eyes. Suddenly, he could hold back no longer.

'Damn it, Parlan!' he said, 'It should be the other way around! You should be going to Khengha to build bridges and roads, to see a new land, a free land like you've always wanted. You should be off to explore, to catalogue its plants and animals. And I should be—'

'Don't say it,' Parlan cut him off, stopping to stand in his path a moment. 'It's better this way. Knowing you're safe makes all the difference to me. You don't belong where I've been, where I'll be returning the day after tomorrow.'

'It's not better! We should be together! You shouldn't be out there . . . .'

'Killing people?' Parlan said it for him when he couldn't. 'No, I shouldn't. But it keeps Annalie and the boys safe and puts food on their table.'

That last wasn't entirely true. Annalie was a fine mid-wife and earned enough to keep them fed. But it was true that if either Parlan or Lerant had refused the 'glory' of fighting for Myrrgha, it would have been their family that would be made to suffer. Others had certainly vanished from Rogha's neighborhoods, been taken as slaves, or worse.

'And so, Myrrgha Command has its hostages,' Lerant said, suddenly weary.

'Keep your voice down,' Parlan warned, glancing about. Rumor was rife that Emperor Grouda had permitted the unthinkable and allowed the exiled Methaggars, the 'Spiders', to again lurk among his citizens, to spy and to kill those who so much as thought of rebellion.

Lerant shook his head in a sigh of annoyance and frustration. Parlan stopped to look at the wares of the next stall. Lerant didn't notice, too busy trying to figure a solution. It terrified him to think only two days away Parlan would be setting sail again aboard a steam-powered warship with the other so-called Shocktroopers, sent to sea, to track down and butcher the poor Lellghin refugees hiding in whatever island bolt-holes they could find.

'Do you think Annalie would like this?' Parlan asked, obviously pleased with his find.

'What?' Lerant looked back to see Parlan fingering a bolt of truly fine red silk, a rare luxury in Rogha but not too expensive here where it was made. 'Beautiful. She'd love it. Red is her favorite color; it suits her dark hair.'

'But doesn't really match those lovely blue eyes,' Parlan said with such wistful tenderness and fond smile of reminiscence that it cut Lerant to the bone. Parlan could die out there, cut down on some lonely beach. It made Lerant shiver despite the punishing heat shimmering from limestone walls about him.

The price was far too high, but Parlan didn't bother bartering, he just handed it over and took the wrapped package carefully under his arm. They continued on and Parlan commented, low and hard, 'I won't tell her how I earn so much—stabbing men through the guts with my bayonet and watching them bleed to death. As bright scarlet as that silk.'

Lerant could say nothing, afraid his voice would betray the depth of his pain for his brother, the gentlest of men, forced to murder. As a small child, Lerant had known what it was like to be amid a massacre, had seen his own mother's throat sliced open. What would he have done had he, too, been recruited to fight on the front lines?

Further on, they stopped at a stall full of shiny brass and brightly painted tin toys among a jumble of second-hand goods, including daggers and other weapons. Together, they hunted for gifts for little Alarn and Parla. Lerant didn't really see the things his hands picked up and put down again. All he could see was the horror of battle, of Parlan in the midst of it, killing to stay alive. Myrrgha shot any man who deserted, or hesitated to obey orders.

'I'm a Captain now,' Lerant said, wondering why he hadn't thought of it before, 'with my own engineering squad. You've had as much experience as any with mining machines. I can have you transferred.'

'They'd do that?' Parlan looked sharply up at him, hope flaring and bringing the real Parlan behind those eyes back to life.

Lerant shrugged. 'Other men get transferred. Why not you? I'll get the paperwork underway tomorrow.' Parlan nodded, held his gaze, said, 'Thank you.' But they both knew what they were not saying—getting Myrrgha Command to release a seasoned Shocktrooper when they were set for another front line battle would be no easy task.

'I'll keep at them,' Lerant promised. 'Parlan, listen to me. I'll get you out of there, I swear it. I'll get you out.'

'I know you will,' Parlan said, 'Just be careful you don't piss them off too much.'

'I know how to handle them. Your skills are needed, even they can see that.'

With that promise made between them, a dark weight of shadow lifted from the day, leaving them free to fully enjoy the exotic sights and wonders of them being here, two ordinary coal miners from icy island Rogha. Their lives there had been hard, but they'd been free, and they had their home to come back to every day, a meal shared with those they loved. Myrrgha had taken that from them with its false promises, bringing slaves to work the mines and forcing Roghinners to become soldiers. Trying to forget all that, Lerant began hunting among the tin toys on display, wanting to find his own gifts for his two small nephews.

'Little Parla will love this,' Parlan said, holding up a soft toy rabbit with a bright blue ribbon.

'And this for Alarn,' Lerant agreed with a smile, finding a bright green-painted and brass steam train amid the pile of objects on the table. He put it aside, resting his other hand on the table as he dug in his pocket for coins.

Something warm and metallic pushed itself against the palm of his right hand. His fingers closed hungrily, eagerly about it, as if they had a mind of their own. Looking down, momentarily dazzled by reflected sunlight, he saw it was the hilt of a sword, but no ordinary sword. It felt so familiar to his grip, impossibly familiar. The blade was encased in a leather scabbard incised with gilded brass designed to look like a sun, its beams spreading out in a circle that reached every edge, top bottom and sides. As he turned it over, bright sunlight blazed again into his eyes, the glare blinding him.

'What's that you've found?' Parlan asked.

Squinting, Lerant moved to block the sunlight, casting his shadow over the sword as he opened his hand to examine the hilt. It too, was fashioned with a sunburst, fanning rays like beams from a rising sun, striking downward in a semi-circle that completed the sun on the scabbard. It glowed gold even in the shadows, as if it had harvested the sunshine. Some deep part of Lerant knew he'd seen it before, as much a part of him as the hand that held it.

'How much?' Parlan asked the vendor, a skeletally thin, greasy haired old man.

'I'll pay,' Lerant protested. Meeting Parlan's gaze, he blinked in surprise—joy had returned to his brother's heart.

'No,' Parlan said and grinned at him. 'I want it to be my gift to you, to remind you of this day. That hilt looks a lot like the emblem of the Kartai, doesn't it?'

The Kartai were Lerant's tribe, from the mountain hinterland of Rogha City. There were very few left alive now; certainly none of Lerant's immediate family. 'Yes. It does, although the Kartai emblem is more about the twin moons at overlap than the sun, I think. Myrrgha won't let me wear this sword,' he said, even as he lifted it scabbard, belt and all, into his arms, already possessive. 'It's not military issue.'

'It's meant for you,' Parlan insisted, counting out coins into the old man's hand. 'High Command won't care what you're wearing on the open plains of Khengha, hundreds of miles from here. Disguise it if you must.' Finished paying, Parlan met his eyes again, a new man, fierce and determined. 'It will keep you safe.'

The dungeon cells of Myrrgha Imperial Palace were no place for a feverish man.

Worried, Marc Gerion stood close to the bars of his cell, watching Bren m'Fetrin tend his Weaver Brother in the opposite cell. Torches burned everywhere along the corridor that separated them, their wavering light uncertain but at least they gave off some warmth against the damp stone walls and earthen floor. An unusually tall man, Bren had further than most to bend down to the rock ledge that was all the cell provided by way of a bed for m'Connor. Further along the corridor at the foot of the flagstone steps that led to places Gerion would rather not think about, the guards showed no interest in whether or not one of their prisoners lay dying. They'd provided some clean straw and a few rags, a bucket of water, nothing more.

It had been some of the worst hours of Gerion's life, two days ago, waiting for his two friends to return. When they had, Bren had been carrying an unconscious m'Connor carefully, face-down over his broad shoulder, and Gerion could clearly see the same horrendous marks of torture on his back, a raw weeping-red grid spreading from the center of the back toward the shoulders and lower, burned with hot irons. They'd done the same with m'Fetrin some weeks ago—why, they didn't know. At the time, Gerion had shared the same cell. Unable to contain his fury at seeing what they'd done to m'Fetrin, Gerion had snapped the neck of one of the guards. That had earned him a whipping, a solitary cell, and a bread and water diet. He considered he'd more than won that trade-off.

'Any better?' he asked, as Bren placed the flat of his hand against his Brother's forehead.

'Yes,' Bren reported with evident relief. 'He's sleeping deeply and he's stopped shivering. That was a good sign with me, right?' he asked, the flames of the torchlight making his red hair all the more red as he looked up at Gerion. 'Taran said . . . .'

'Yes. You were fevered a good two days, too, then it broke.'

'Why!? Why are they doing this to us!?' Bren demanded, so loudly that both guards started a little and glared toward him before settling back again.

'For the same reason we wear these.' Gerion tapped the metal collar he wore about his throat. Made of methirri, it cut a Weaver away from the energy world with all the beauty and power of its varying spectrum. Gerion wasn't a Weaver, but the enemy didn't

8

know that. They just collared every male Lellghinner they captured. The females, the Magi, they . . . killed. Gerion shook his head in a futile bid to drive away the images that memory brought to mind.

'Then why don't they kill us outright? Why burn us a little at a time?'

'That I don't know,' Gerion replied, holding his friend's angry gaze and having to look up to do it. Bren could just stand straight beneath the low dungeon ceiling.

'Dead, can't be, can't be,' m'Connor mumbled, not waking but shifting a little where he lay face down to spare his damaged back.

'Dead. Can't be. Can't be,' m'Connor said.

The lifeless brown leaf covered Bren's big hand, hiding it completely. A big leaf from a big 'tree' that wasn't a tree. It was an Akkarra, a living machine housed in tree-form. AKKARRA—Automated Kinetic Knowledge and Aetheric Essence Retrieval Array. Or so m'Connor had been taught. The means by which the Magi, his people's leaders, kept their minds intact life to life, and the triggers that gave Weavers their initial ability to Weave.

Akkarra. Dead. Impossible. Bren m'Fetrin closed his fist, crushing the leaf, his fingers white-red with the force of angry grief. A paper-dry death rustle, tiny broken pieces raining down from Bren's hand, dust motes drifting on the cold breeze, every moment etching acid memories into m'Connor's heart, eating all joy, all hope, breaking him as it was broken.

'These were their energy cells . . .' Bren said, his brow furrowed as he thought it through. 'Without energy . . . maybe it's just a defensive deep hibernation?'

'Maybe,' m'Singh agreed. 'But how long can they last?'

'And how do we restore all this?' m'Akram took a shuffling step through the thigh deep river of dead leaves, and worse, in which they stood.

'This is the poison.' M'Connor shoved his hand through the red black dust that had stirred as m'Akram moved. It coated everything about them. 'It stops our Weaving, too.'

'It's like . . . a solid blackness swallowing all the light. Dense. Powerful,' Bren said.

'And deadly. Killed them in less than a day,' m'Kay warned, recalling the first shocking report they'd heard from the Akkarra of Isle Grove. Thankfully, they and their Magi were safe, and the Memory Keys each Weaver carried implanted in his mind protected their location from enemy questioning.

'Suffocated,' m'Connor said, knowing he, now their leader, must get them away from here. 'As we will be if we don't get out of here now. We can't help anyone dead.'

'And there'd be no Returning,' m'Singh voiced the horror they'd all avoided. To die and be gone forever . . . .

'We'll survive and we'll find answers.' M'Connor looked around at them, meeting their eyes, giving what grim hope he could. Only forty Weavers left alive in all the world! Ten days ago they'd been happy graduates, celebrating on Isle Grove, five hundred miles from here. A lucky escape. They'd had those frantic days of urgent sailing back here to try to deal with what the Akkarra of the Grove had told them—something had attacked and destroyed Lellgha City, butchered its people, burned its living

Akkarra-tree homes, its universities. But seeing it, smelling it, tasting it . . . . Silence cut into them in this place where music had always resounded.

Whatever had attacked might do so again. About them, towering over them, etched against a bright blue cloudless summer sky, a maze of skeletal branches, dead Akkarra. Sunlight streamed down on the Weaver Brothers, an obscene marker of a place of massacre. It should be a leafy green canopy, dappled shade, students walking along the sunny laneways between the Akkarra dormitories and classrooms.

'We must bury them,' m'Sooin said, his light voice hoarse with silent weeping.

'We should not linger here,' m'Fetrin warned. 'And we cannot bury them all . . . not as they should be buried.' The stench of death made them gag at first. Now, it was part of them, thick through their clothing, tasted in their mouths. Flies buzzed about the sticky blood that stained the leaf litter and . . . . No, he wouldn't look directly at them. The bodies, men, women, and small children, murdered, and worse, defiled with a savagery that would forever haunt m'Connor's sleeping.

'The enemy and their spider—creatures can smell your Weaving, remember that,' an older, more steady voice commanded, arriving, shoving through their ranks. Marc Gerion, a fisherman and a natural Earth, had been among the first to send the alarm and rescue a handful of survivors. Outlying villages were fleeing to the sea, to the Talae ships who had astonishingly offered to ferry them away to Sanctuary.

'Weaving didn't save them,' m'Sharral commented, sounding as sick as m'Connor felt. Behind them, in what had been the Weavers own enclave, the men and women of power, the Elder Weavers and Magi lay butchered, or gone, taken prisoner.

'They died beneath the enemy's giant dust storm, carrying their poison,' Gerion said. 'You cannot Weave anywhere near it.'

'We cannot Weave in hiding, we cannot Weave in battle!' m'Garran cried in despair. 'How are we to defend ourselves?'

'With your swords, with your bows,' Gerion said, and behind him came more men, Crafters, Fishers, Farmers, carrying axes, hammers, anything that could be used as a weapon.

'We do not kill,' m'Kay said, solemn. It was true, Weavers, experts in martial arts that also trained the mind, were taught non-violence.

'Then die, like them! Butchered!' Gerion said, pointing an arm at the rotting bodies.

'We will fight,' m'Connor said, and everyone turned to look at him in full realization; all had been changed forever.

'The enemy! They're coming back!' Weaver m'Huxley Sent from his position on sentry.

'Avenge the dead! Defend yourselves!' m'Connor ordered. As Captain of their Year, the Champion, and son of a High Clan Chief, now he must become a battle Leader.

The First Battle, it became known, later. They survived, despite the enemy's new weapon, 'methirri', Shadowstone, the Severing Stone. The invading Myrrghin soldiers wore a tiny piece of it in a diadem of metal on a band over the third eye, told it would protect them from 'sorcery'. A lie. It was its creators, the Methaggar, the Spider-Lords, who relied on those diadems. With their inhuman eyes and methirri hair-coated bodies; the Shadow thick in their very blood, they directed their commands into those bands, controlling the soldiers' minds and forcing them to a savagery they might otherwise have resisted.

The Weavers fell back, fighting to protect village after village, Shire after Shire, succeeding in giving some time to flee, more often coming too late, Lellgha dying inch by inch. The winter of the second year, their backs to the Navarell Mountains, m'Connor's Clan Lands. Blackness, Methaggar stun-poison, waking captives, Gerion and Bren chained at his side, sick through to the bone—they could no longer Sense the energy world with its infinite Song. Blind, deaf, the cold hard metal, the methirri slave collars ice about their throats.

A Methaggar Lord stood over them, its spider-eyes hungry, eagerly devouring its victory, its silky hair-covered long fingered hands stroking Bren's red hair. 'Weavers! Weaver-Slaves! March now! March to Myrrgha City, the Emperor commands a show of victory trophies!'

'Oh your feet, slaves! Get him up!'

'Leave him be!' Bren shouted at the dungeon guard close by the cell door.

'Steady, Bren,' m'Connor said, waking, and very carefully sitting up.

Bren leaned down to help him, his blue eyes dark with concern. 'How do you feel?'

'It's all right. You survived, and so will I.' The reflected shared experience in those eyes, normal senses, was all they had left now that their Sharing had been stolen from them by the slave collars. Sharing wasn't unique to Weavers; any Lellghinner could do it, born with an Empathy that conveyed the other's feeling when physical contact was made and permission given. A blessing that had become a curse in a time of such grief and suffering. It was ironic that the slave collars protected them from the full force of the memory of their torture . . . The Inquisitor with his hot irons, the agony, the smell of burning flesh. The bastard 'Pig-man, Zaraxan, claimed it was 'science'.

'Taran? You're all right?' Gerion asked from the opposite cell.

About to answer, m'Connor froze, his head cocked to better pick up the small sounds; it was hard to get used to the fact that they could no longer Sense another presence approaching. Crisp marching boots, Honor Guards, not the usual, echoed in the underground confined corridor, then halted. A sickly scent of sweet perfume rose above the odor of stinking sweat and urine, the sound of the swirl of silk over stone, and a wash of scarlet leeching into the shifting shadows of the dungeon corridor. Inquisitor Zaraxan, his bloated melon of a face twisted with cruel anticipation. M'Connor's pulse pounded, his mouth dry as sand. The day had arrived; he'd Seen Bren taken from him. Surely, forewarned meant he could change that fate?

'Be ready!' the Captain of the Guards commanded, puffing as he hurried down the stone steps into the dungeon. 'The Emperor wants to see them! He's on his way down here!'

A creeping slick of foul blackness, making the slave collar heavier, thicker, dragging at m'Connor's breathing, starving him . . . . Methaggar! The creatures accompanied the Emperor everywhere but were invisible to the soldiers who believed them exiled forever from Myrrgha.

'He wants me, Bren,' m'Connor lied, stepping forward and again oddly glad of the methirri collar that prevented Bren Reading him. 'I've Seen it.'

'What? You're still fevered,' Bren said, gently taking him by the arm. 'Keep back.'

'No,' M'Connor said, pulling free and evading Bren's questioning glance. He wouldn't let the repeated visions become reality. He could hear the Honor Guards laboring closer, carrying the aging, arthritic Emperor Grouda carefully down the dungeon's torch-lit curve of steep, uneven flagstone steps. Ahead of them came The Pig-man, High Inquisitor Zaraxan.

'I see you've recovered,' the Inquisitor purred as he saw m'Connor on his feet. 'Good. You are about to be honored far more than you deserve, slaves.'

'On your knees, slaves! *Now!*' Zaraxan ordered impatiently.

The captain's hard eyes shifted uncertainly and his hand covered his dagger hilt. If he came anywhere in reach of m'Connor or Bren while wearing a dagger he'd find himself gutted and rolling on the bloodied stones amid his own copious innards in an instant. 'My Lord Inquisitor,' he said nervously 'we enter only with a hostage.'

'I know that!' Zaraxan snarled, his blotched jowls purpling with his anger. 'Sergeant!'

Stepping down from the foot of the stairs, a burly Sergeant appeared. In his arms he carried the same small child they always used. M'Connor's stomach churned into knots. Gerion, who had three children of his own, believed the hostage to be a little girl, but beneath the dirt that caked her from head to toe and matted her long hair, it was impossible to say for certain. Her blue eyes wide

15

and frightened, she made no sound. She had long ago been taught not to cry.

'Leave them standing.' A rasping order, a snake-hiss from the shadows of the stairwell. Enshrouded in black wool, his face heavily hooded where he sat on his palanquin, Grouda was difficult to see clearly, but the shifting red of his gaze passed calculatingly over the two slaves as he was carried closer. 'These two are the champion Weavers I saw at the Victory Parade?'

'Yes, Majesty,' Zaraxan said, honey dripping in his subservient tone now. 'Naturally, for so great an honor, I have selected only the finest of our stock.'

Again, Grouda turned to examine the slaves, his narrow, shadowed eyes gleaming, mouth slightly open. 'Such strength, to fight night and day and yet overcome the great lizards in battle.'

'No,' Bren whispered, sharp as a blade against m'Connor's chill face.

'Yes!' m'Connor insisted and looked deep into the red gleam of eyes beneath the black hood, trying to force through the blocking of the methirri collar to compel the Emperor's choice.

With his Sense of Bren's Presence greatly dimmed, he nonetheless felt it, a great weariness, a Knowing, a Seeing of his Path, or the end of it. Resignation. So, he'd had the same visions.

'You don't want him, Majesty. He's fevered, burned, like this.' Bren turned about to show the scars on his back.

Taking a nervous step back from the Emperor who gasped in anger or shock, Zaraxan said, 'He might be a poor choice, at that. I fear he is . . . unwell. It takes time to heal fully.'

'I need them undamaged, fool!' Grouda snarled. 'Can you not leave off your games!?'

'Not games, Majesty. I labor in your service, in the hope of finding a . . . less extreme way of easing your pain.'

'These are the only Weavers we have and you risk them!'

'Majesty, I assure you. I am careful. As you see, the tall one is undamaged, other than for a few scars. Women love scars. The other one will survive, too. The fire I apply to them follows the same pathways as those they use when they harvest sunlight for their sorcery. That power could be ours in a much simpler, more direct fashion than the body transfers.'

'Really?' Grouda said, sarcasm dripping from the word. 'Are you and Lurghiar putting me at risk unnecessarily, then, My Lord High Inquisitor?'

'Majesty . . . You are in pain, aging. My work regarding the Sun-paths could be another year in completion. The final part—the sewing of their Blood-Seeds into our own, depends heavily on all our . . . allies can teach us.'

Methaggars, m'Connor realized, returning us to the days of growing humans to a chosen Blood Code. The means by which the Methaggars themselves had been created. The spider-thing was very close now, and without Weaving, m'Connor and Bren stood defenseless before its horrendous, chill power. Grouda sat listening to its silent instruction for long, tense moments, his eyes shifting, gleaming with dull red light. That red fire was an indicator that his mind was directly Linked to the Methaggar, making him what they termed a 'Seeker'. They did the same to create weapons with animals or men on the battle field and elsewhere as spies.

Bren tugged at m'Connor's elbow, again guiding him back a step and breaking the Methaggar spell that m'Connor hadn't been aware had begun to flick about him, tasting, testing, like a snake's hissing, forked tongue.

'That one,' Grouda said, pointing at m'Connor with one long crooked finger.

He'd won! M'Connor tried to obey but couldn't move, Bren's grip an iron band about his upper arm and his legs trapped as the Methaggar spell, certain now, locked about him. The cell door clicked loudly enough to make the guards jump in the dark shadows and flickering red torchlight. The heavy iron barred door opened, silent and smooth without its usual creaking protest, swinging back to rest without a sound against the corridor's stone walls.

The spell crawled, a teeming raw sewage over m'Connor's skin and his feet were freed. Worse, Bren's fingers were forced away from his arm, one by one. He took a pace forward. The Methaggar hadn't needed to control his body. He was ready. Bren would survive, escape . . . .

'Stop,' Bren commanded.

The word fell like sunlight on leaves, dispelling the crawling filth of the Methaggar. M'Connor stopped and blinked up at his tall Brother in disbelief. Bren's Will had broken the dual power of the Methaggar and its Seeker-Emperor?

'Take *me!*' Bren demanded, and impossibly, white light seeped from beneath his methirri collar, responding to the outpouring of the very essence of his soul. Alarmed, wary, the guards cocked their muskets, took aim. Bren's face dripped sweat, twisted with effort, but the Weaving-light vanished and he drew in a great gasping breath echoed by several sighs of relief.

'Power, so much power,' Grouda mumbled, lifting his heavily clothed arm again but this time pointing directly at Bren. 'I will take that one instead.'

'No!' m'Connor begged, struggling against the undertow, dark and light, swirling like battling storms in the confines of the underground cells. 'It's me you came for! *Me*!!'

Bren didn't look at him; his head held high, his jaw set, his expression frighteningly calm, as he allowed the Methaggar power to walk him out into the corridor while it also held m'Connor immobile.

The door slammed shut, the lock clicked and m'Connor threw himself at the bars of the cell as the Methaggar released him. 'No! Bren! *No!*'

Bren met his gaze as they led him away, calm defiance. 'You'll find me again, Taran,' he said, soft, intent. 'I know you will. Believe. Hope. Live.'

'It's near midnight,' Gerion commented from his cell. 'They must bring him back soon.

M'Connor didn't react; he just kept up his pacing, his prowling around and around his cell as he'd done, silent, all day. Abruptly, he stopped, straining to hear something or someone. The Akkarra-Bond sewn into a Weaver pair's blood made their understanding, their awareness of each other something far beyond any ordinary experience.

'Bren?' m'Connor whispered, his sun-browned face going dishwater grey. 'Bren! *No!* Don't go!' He grabbed at the iron bars set to tear them apart, grunting as if something had hit him. Then, he fell, convulsing, collapsed to the earthen floor.

Gerion couldn't move, frozen in grief. He'd seen this before.

'What's wrong with him?' one of the guards asked, coming closer.

'Careful. They're full of nasty tricks. It's probably an act, a trap, to get you in there.' The second guard took his musket from its stand in the corner of the guards' station. M'Connor's arms and legs hit the dirt with pounding thrashing bruising impact, his teeth slicing through his lower lip and his eyes rolled back, gone white. 'That's no act,' the first said.

'Get me in there!' Gerion demanded. They turned their heads, gave him a glance, did nothing. 'You stupid bastards never learn! Kill one Weaver and the other dies, too!' Fury burned through him, melting some of the icy grief that chilled his heart.

'What?' the guard asked.

'He's dying! Damn it! He's Sensed his Brother's death! You want him alive get a bloody good Healer down here *fast!*'

The guards looked at each other, looked to m'Connor whose convulsions had eased but his breathing worsened, a low agonized, eerie howl. 'Get Geddaski,' the senior guard ordered.

'He's a butcher, not a Healer!' Gerion growled. 'He can't save him. I can!'

'Open that cell,' someone said, coming down the stairwell. A tall black-skinned man with neat graying hair and trimmed beard strode into the corridor. Urgency marked every aspect of his stance, his expression, as he hurried toward m'Connor's cell. He wore a fine blue silk tunic emblazoned with the insignia of a high-ranking military surgeon and he carried a satchel marked with the red heart inside blue circle of Myrrghin medical staff.

'Surgeon-General, Sir! What are you doing here?'

'The Lord High Inquisitor sent me,' he replied. 'Something has gone badly wrong with whatever he was trying to do up there. He appears to have killed one of the prisoners. My Lord is afraid the other will die. Open that door!'

The guard regarded him, frowning. 'Sir, standing orders are—'

'Here!' the doctor said, and pulled a scrap of paper from an inside pocket. 'My Lord gave me written orders marked with his personal stamp.' The senior guard examined it, and to Gerion's overwhelming relief, pulled the keys from their hook on the wall above his station. He opened the cell door and Gerion watched, desperate, helpless, as the surgeon bent to m'Connor whose convulsing had worsened again.

'It's Severing shock,' Gerion told the doctor. 'I've seen them die like this. Please, only I can help him now.'

The surgeon spared him a brief look, but no more. 'I'll need your help to hold him,' he told the guard who'd followed him into the cell.

'No!' Gerion barked sharp alarm. 'You'll die! His Weaving is trying to reach his Brother; it'll fry you alive!'

That was true, and it stopped them, motionless. The surgeon looked again to Gerion. 'What do we do, then?'

'I can Ground him, channel the energy into the earth; drain it from him. Let me help him!' Gerion held the dark man's intent gaze and breathed again, finding humanity underlying the sharp intelligence in the surgeon's eyes.

'Get him over here,' the surgeon ordered.

'What! I mean, Sir, he's a killer! Snapped Jensen's neck like a rotten stick.'

'*Sergeant!*' The surgeon snapped so ferociously that it even made Gerion flinch. 'You read the High Inquisitor's orders! Do you intend disobeying him? What do you think he'll do if one of his last remaining Weavers dies because you delayed me?'

21

'The other one's really dead?'

'Yes.'

Gerion gasped and took hold of the bars, needing their support. Bren m'Fetrin was dead. He'd fought at the man's side for over a year, they'd save each other countless times, shared meals, patched wounds . . . laughed and sang together sometimes . . . . His eyes stung as memory after memory raced through his mind—the big red-head, taller than any Weaver and one of the gentlest men Gerion had known. 'You murdering mongrels!' he growled.

'Sir . . . .' Seeing the rage that twisted Gerion's face, the guardsman hesitated, the key in the lock but not turning it. Gerion reached through the bars, trying to snatch it but the guard pulled it away from his reach. 'Do I have your word you'll not harm us if we let you attend to your friend?' the surgeon asked.

'You have my word. But if he dies . . . . I'll come after you all one day, death in the night.'

'Fair enough,' the surgeon accepted. He looked up at the guard to add, 'Get him over here but have your partner keep his gun cocked and ready. Shoot him only on my command.'

'Sir, I warn you, he's fast, very fast.'

'Move! We're wasting time this man doesn't have!'

The lock opened and Gerion threw the cell door back to rush into m'Connor's cell, kicking off his leather sandals as he ran. He squatted down at m'Connor's side, being sure both his bare feet were planted firmly against solid dirt. 'Stand back,' he told the surgeon who warily obeyed. He closed his eyes, silently begging the earth to hear him, to come again to his aid.

'*Siviatta! Siviatta mi!*' He commanded. He shouldn't have been able to do it, not while wearing a methirri slave collar. But somehow, at a great distance, weakly, the earth, and something else . . . something of great but unfamiliar power, responded, humming into his bare feet, climbing higher toward his heart. Reaching out with both hands, he took hold of m'Connor's shoulders. Pain slammed into him, burned down through his arms, his chest, his legs, a torrent of pure fire, of grief without end, beyond bearing. His body shook, almost taking his feet from under him. Then, it stopped.

Gasping, Gerion fell forward to his knees, sweat dripping from him to dampen m'Connor's stark white face. He lay completely still now, the stillness worse than the thrashing. 'Taran?' Nothing.

'He's dying,' the surgeon said, sad, quiet.

'No!' Gerion bent low, listened, an ear pressed to m'Connor's chest. 'Don't you leave me, you bastard! Get back here now!' Leaning back, he lifted his arm and pounded a fist hard to m'Connor's chest. M'Connor grunted, gasped, breathed, color seeping back into him.

'Well done!' The surgeon put a hand to m'Connor's face, pulled back an eyelid. 'He's coming round. Help me lift him.' He glanced around the bare cell. Is there a bed in here?' Gerion pointed at the stone ledge against the rear wall where a few rags mounded as a pillow and a pile of straw marked it as a place to sleep. Unimpressed, the surgeon shook his head. 'I'll have him carried to the Infirmary.'

'No!' Gerion pleaded, alarmed. 'He needs to stay with me now.'

'You're Linked?' the surgeon asked, surprising Gerion with his understanding. It wasn't anything remotely as deep as an Akkarra Weaver Bond, but it was an emergency life-line.

'Yes,' Gerion said. 'He'll be all right with me.' Sliding his arms beneath m'Connor's armpits rather than around the wounded back,

Gerion heaved him up, the surgeon helping take the unconscious man's weight.

Gently, Gerion lay him down, hearing a moan as a hand brushed against the still raw burns. Quickly, he rearranged him onto his side, bracing him with some of the rags Bren had used to cool his brow. *Bren.* No, don't think about that now.

'Steady, Taran, steady,' Gerion soothed, stroking the tousled, dirty hair back from m'Connor's forehead. 'I'm here. Stay alive for me, stay alive for Bren, and together we'll avenge him. I swear it by all that I am! We'll slaughter the Pig-Man!'

'How many times must I tell him that burns gather infection faster than any other wound!' the surgeon cursed, patently disgusted as he examined m'Connor's back. The red marks that had begun to heal were open again and full of filth after his thrashing about on the earthen floor. The surgeon reached into his satchel and to Gerion's everlasting relief, took out clean bandaging and a jar of some kind of salve and ordered the guards to bring hot water.

Later, with m'Connor's wounds bathed and bandaged, Gerion watched as the surgeon covered his patient with a warm woolen blanket. Another blanket had been laid beneath over clean straw. 'I must go. My name's Dresin. If he worsens, give this to the Sergeant . . . .' The surgeon held up a small red-blue metal disk and showed it also to the guardsman who had sat down on a bench he'd pulled into the corridor. 'They'll know how to reach me. I'll do my best to make sure this never happens again.'

Gerion nodded, said nothing, the sergeant obviously relieved to lock the cell door behind the man. Gerion took m'Connor's hand in his and bent his head to say the Farewell to the Dead, the prayer for the Journeyer, The Ellaran. That was the only meager comfort he could find in that bleak moment—Bren would be home now; the

Akkarra would have drawn him as soon as he left his body. He'd be with his Brother Weavers and his sister Magi. But only while the last Grove still stood. If ever the enemy found it, there'd be no more Returning.

CHAPTER TWO

The twin doors were massive, beautifully wrought in gilded gold with entwining olive trees and grape vines. This had once been the home of one of Myrrgha City's wealthiest merchants. Rhyssa held no particular love for them, disliking their ostentatious pretensions and snobbery, but she strongly disagreed with the reason for their arrest and confinement on suspicion of high treason. The truth was simple enough—Inquisitor Zaraxan coveted this home, built as it was in the shadows of the Imperial palace, and what Zaraxan wanted, he got, one way or another.

Now, he wanted High Mariner Rhyssa Avenalkah. Currently, he carried out the public rituals of courting her, but she knew all too well how soon that game could turn to cruel falsehoods that would ensnare her father and her brothers if she didn't play along.

'Good morning, High Lady,' the red-liveried doorman greeted her with a graceful bow. 'Shall I take your package for you?'

'No, thank you. I can manage.' It was only a small package, wrapped in waxed paper. She always brought the same treat whenever she visited, but not for Zaraxan. Pushing down on carved ivory handles, the doorman gave her entry.

'Rhyssa!' Zaraxan greeted, hurrying toward her amid a characteristic hiss of silk over marble. The sound was unsettling, reminding Rhyssa of the warning threat of a basket of vipers. The Inquisitor's long red robes swept the floor behind him and reflected rippling scarlet in the fountain and fish pond against the far wall.

'High Inquisitor,' she nodded, smiling stiffly.

'Ahh, I see that again, you do not come empty-handed. Really, Rhyssa, you should have a body-slave to carry your packages.'

'Oh, but I want the pleasure of this day all to myself, My Lord,' she purred, making him smile and her own stomach squirm. She allowed herself the indulgence of a grimace as he bent his head over her outstretched white-gloved hand and kissed her fingers. She hated wearing gloves. She wore open sandals and a cool sleeveless shift of flowing white cotton and silk, slit from ankle to knee and laced beneath a low cut bodice. The dress was high fashion, but nothing else about her followed the current trend. She didn't own a body-slave, none of her people did.

Her title, High Lady 'Mariner' confused those who didn't know its mythology. According to the Loggia, Rhyssa's tribal line was descended from the Captains of the Sailors of the Stars. Only a few crackpots took that idea literally, although . . . there were some interesting archeological relics. The facts were the Avenalkahs had founded Myrrgha City and built the sail and later, steam ships that brought Myrrgha its wealth. They had little interest in politics; too involved with their shipbuilding business to take much notice as the Senate grew lazy and ripe for manipulation by the cunning and the cruel.

'You and your father are all alone again, I hear. Your brothers' service leave is over?' Zaraxan asked with false solicitude as he ushered her into a sunny reception room. 'I'm sorry word reached them too late to be here in time for the funeral.'

'Alas, both are now serving even further from us, somewhere far offshore in the Western Sea.' Rhyssa strongly suspected Zaraxan had had a direct hand in both her brothers' distance and her mother's slow sickening and death. 'Their absence made that awful day all the more difficult for my father.'

'Terrible thing to think our surgeons were unable to help her,' Zaraxan shook his head and pursed his lips. 'Your father is so brilliant a naval engineer! Why, his innovative designs are almost entirely responsible for our sea superiority.'

'You are too kind, my Lord,' Rhyssa said as she sat down and he poured tea. He dared not allow slaves wait on him so closely. 'I will pass on your compliment.'

'Please do,' Zaraxan said. He took a thick slab of cake and settled back in an overstuffed armchair to regard her with pale watery-blue, red-rimmed eyes. 'Or perhaps I could speak to him in person? I've been requesting an interview for some days now.'

'I know it's been months since my mother's death, My Lord, but he loved her dearly and is a broken man,' Rhyssa said coldly.

'Of course, of course.' Zaraxan waved a napkin at her, crumbs spilling everywhere and cream smearing his thick lips. 'We must give him time despite Admiral Givant's moaning. I'm most grateful for your kindness in accepting my invitation today.'

'It's a pleasure,' Rhyssa lied, hiding her anger as she bent to take a delicately shaped marzipan strawberry from the beautiful array on the tiered platter. She'd already refused his most recent invitation twice, once more and who knew, her father might be next to be buried, or more likely one of her brothers. 'Where is Bruska?' she asked.

As an aside to her studies of naval engineering, Rhyssa maintained an interest in the selective breeding of race horses and guard dogs. Zaraxan had first met her when he'd bought one of her best dogs, a big black Lalastor of intelligence and steady temperament. Bruska should by now have come bounding to greet her, seeking the treats she always brought for him.

'Oh, he's not far off,' Zaraxan said and suddenly erupted into disturbingly girlish giggles. Catching her frowning regard, he calmed to add, 'You will see, you will see. Ahh! Rhyssa, this is such a wonderful day, a memorable day! I had to share it with you.'

'I'm honored, My Lord.'

'You have no idea what I'm babbling about, do you?' he chortled, putting down his cake plate. 'But then news of that kind is not for your circle.'

Nothing that made Zaraxan so happy could possibly be even remotely good. Myrrgha City's ornate palaces and mansions housed many a savage dressed in civilized finery, and Zaraxan terrified them all, by far the most merciless creature to have won the Emperor's favor and be given one of the most powerful positions in all the kingdoms.

'You are meant to keep Bruska by your side at all times, My Lord. A guard dog cannot guard, otherwise.' The big animal's bed was still in its corner, but there was no other sign of him.

'Indeed! I have been taking him with me when I work among the slaves. You trained him well; he proved of great use. Come, I will keep you in suspense no longer,' he said, standing abruptly. 'Follow me, and you'll see.'

Lellghin slaves hurried to open a door at the back of the room. Rhyssa hadn't noticed them before, so silent and cowered were they, their heads low, and their gazes never for an instant leaving the floor. More slaves waited outside, standing patiently beside a seemingly endless line of doorways set in the left hand wall of a high-ceilinged, arched hallway. Sunlight fell in great squares from floor length windows on the hall's other side, and Rhyssa saw that they overlooked a beautifully kept garden. It was worked by yet more slaves, some of them sunburned and all looking thin and exhausted.

'Here we are,' Zaraxan said, coming to a breathless halt as he turned into a cross corridor and stopped before a step up to a heavy iron door set back into a torch-lit alcove. No slaves flanked this door; rather it was guarded by Myrrgha's toughest soldiers, the Emperor's Honor Guards in their showy gold livery. 'The High Inquisitor, Lord Zaraxan,' the senior guardsman called, coming to a crisp salute. 'High Mariner Rhyssa Avenalkah.'

'Is all ready for us, Captain?' Zaraxan asked. 'Mariner Avenalkah is keen to see my success for herself.'

'Of course, My Lord,' the man said stiffly, his expression hidden beneath the shadows of his gold plumed helm. He nodded and one of the other guards opened the door. A stirring of colder air drifted out into the warm corridor, chilling Rhyssa's sandaled feet. Suddenly, she was reluctant to enter. Zaraxan ushered her forward and she looked up at him warily. Though she wasn't tall, she was taller than he, but with him standing on the higher step, her gaze met his, level and deep. The High Inquisitor was a plain-looking man of blotchy red complexion and thinning hair, but real ugliness lived in his eyes, a shadow among shadows that set Rhyssa's skin crawling.

Glad of the dagger hidden in a flesh-colored sheath at her thigh, she stepped up beside him. She planned to kill her mother's murderer at first opportunity but hoped to use a means that would make his death appear an accident. Inside, it was darker, echoing, colder, a vaulted space with two large chairs on an upraised dais before a railed balustrade. Flanking each stood a soldier bearing a tray laden with red wine and goblets. All was brightly lit by torches in a circular sconce slung overhead. The cold draft came from the pit behind the balustrade. It too, was lit by flaring torches, but these were fitted high above in the smooth stone walls that encased the pit. Not a pit, exactly, more like a replica arena; its walls couldn't be scaled by man or beast.

Rhyssa turned to deliver an accusing frown at her host. 'I thought I'd told you I do not attend the . . . entertainment, provided in the Arena, My Lord.'

Zaraxan, busy plumping up the cushions on her chair, turned to her with a leering smile. 'Something else we have in common! I loathe the place, too, you know. It smells deplorably. Come, sit down. There will be no violence.' He patted the chair in invitation. 'I bring you here to share my greatest triumph, the great gift for which I will soon be renowned and praised for evermore. I wanted you to be first to see it, Rhyssa.' She dipped her head to indicate a gratitude she didn't feel and sat down. 'Well, second, I suppose, The Emperor was first.'

'The Emperor?'

'He's been pestering me ever since he became fascinated by the Magi witches and their rituals. He's long desired something they've flaunted before us for centuries. Watch and you'll understand.' Zaraxan took his place on the other chair, arranging his robes, pulling the folds straight about his shoulders as he sat down.

Rhyssa plastered a smile on her face and drew a deep breath, setting herself to endure this horrible room and whatever madness

31

he had in store. She couldn't wait to return out into the sunlit heat that already seemed another world entirely.

'Guards! Bring in the slave,' Zaraxan ordered. Realizing he probably hadn't been quite specific enough, he added, 'm'Connor.' Amid a clanking of iron doors from somewhere below, Zaraxan took the opportunity to lean closer and whisper, 'I know you don't relish my company, Rhyssa. I'm not a fool, for all others think me so. I tell you, when you see what I can offer you here, now, you'll be very glad I chose you. There'll be many thousands who will beg, kill, and debase themselves in any fashion just to take your place at my side.'

Rhyssa drew a slow breath, aware beyond doubt that he wasn't lying, understanding the promise and threat of his words. Whatever he'd done here, it set the marrow of her bones to ice. Only the dagger at her thigh offered warmth, lending hope.

'All these years, everyone laughing at me,—the son of a pig farmer, ego greater than intellect! Now they'll see how wrong they were; they'll rue the day they ever crossed me. No one will laugh at me again, no one!' Tugging again at his robes, he craned to look down into the pit.

Part of one wall slid open, revealing a dark-haired man stumbling inward as someone shoved him hard from behind. He regained his balance with cat-like reflexes despite the heavy iron manacles and chains that bound his wrists before him and turned swiftly, ready to exact revenge on the guard who'd pushed him. Fortunately for the culprit, the door had already closed at m'Connor's back.

Despite herself, Rhyssa leaned forward to get a better look. Everyone in the city knew the names of the Emperor's favorite exhibits, his champion Weaver slaves, m'Connor and m'Fetrin. Rhyssa's friends never shut up about the pair, claiming they were capable of the impossible. It was said they possessed supernatural senses beyond their Weaving that kept them alive despite Myrrgha bringing the giant lizards, the terraketti, from the far distant eastern kingdoms to secure Lellgha when it had seemed, for a short while, that the Weaver-led resistance was winning.

M'Connor was bare-chested, and his body bore stark evidence of some of those encounters. As he turned in a circle, examining his prison, she saw more scars on his back, these much more recent and too evenly patterned to be explained away by anything other than deliberate torture. He turned forward and looked up at his captor and Rhyssa drew a sharp breath. If Zaraxan possessed even a tenth the intelligence he boasted, he'd have m'Connor killed immediately. For this man was his death. It was there in every hard line of m'Connor's face, in all the coiled preparedness beneath the muscles of chest, arms, and legs. His cold gaze skimmed over Rhyssa, dismissing her, and targeting Zaraxan.

'I am glad to see you recovered, slave,' Zaraxan sneered, apparently unaware of his peril. 'I was told I'd killed you, taking your '*Brother*' from you.'

Rhyssa turned to look in surprise at Zaraxan but M'Connor didn't react and Rhyssa suddenly understood he was beyond caring. He breathed, lived, only to kill Zaraxan, his ferocious intelligence focused solely on finding the answer, the way to reach his objective. His keen glance settled on the burning torches high above, examining the sconces that held the pitch-soaked burning wicker brands. They were well beyond reach, yet he seemed unperturbed, calmly thinking it through. The sconces had sharp sculpted edges, the perfect spear should he only find some way to reach them.

'You seem . . . preoccupied today, slave,' Zaraxan said, cruel anticipation simmering just beneath the surface of the words. 'I thought m'Fetrin meant more to you.'

M'Connor turned swiftly, his green eyes flaring, and unbelievably, the methirri slave collar at his throat gleamed white about its edges. Startled, Rhyssa watched hopefully; even she'd felt that abrupt surge in power, that soaring heated will to kill.

It should be impossible to do that beneath methirri. It was impossible, for Zaraxan drew a gulping breath and went on living. The light guttered and died about the slave collar and m'Connor staggered, momentarily exhausted by the effort of will. Again ignoring Zaraxan, he began examining the rope belt he wore at his waist. He was weighing up the chance of lassoing the sconce with it. He simply would not quit.

'Pay attention, slave,' Zaraxan said, recovered from his fright. 'Bren m'Fetrin lives.'

M'Connor shook his head but didn't grant his tormentor any more reaction. Obviously he, a Weaver, would know his friend was dead, methirri collar or no.

'I do not lie, slave,' Zaraxan continued, 'for all that you think your so-called magic would tell you if he still lived. My craft is far greater than your superstitions.' H gave Rhyssa a snickering smug smirk of a smile. 'I do apologize, my dear. You have been most patient, awaiting your surprise gift.'

'I understand there are more important concerns,' Rhyssa said intently. She didn't look at Zaraxan but remained fixed on m'Connor, hoping he would somehow succeed, and hoping too, that he would somehow sense her intent to murder the mongrel Inquisitor given half a chance.

It was the first time she'd spoken since m'Connor had been brought in, and surprisingly, he reacted, drawn to look up at her. The expression on his face was unfathomable, especially given the circumstances. He blinked, looked hard at her, staring as if she was someone he knew and hadn't expected to see here, and then quickly looked away again.

'He is a fine specimen of the male animal, is he not, Rhyssa?' Zaraxan said. 'Young, strong, handsome in a battle-scarred sort of way, if you like him; I'll take him for you.'

'I beg your pardon?' Her attention fully won, Rhyssa turned to regard the madman in puzzlement. Was this a means for her to help m'Connor?

'What is it the Emperor most greatly desires?' Zaraxan prompted, but didn't wait for a reply. 'He's always moaning about the injustice of it—'Those heathen witches live forever, why can't I?'—and he looks to me, to *me!* to deliver it to him. Well, three days ago, that's what I did, Rhyssa! I've done it! The secret of immortality is mine! The Emperor chose his new body, m'Fetrin, and I've prepared it for him.'

'What?' Rhyssa frowned, unsure what to make of that. 'I don't understand.'

'Of course not. I haven't shown you.' Zaraxan turned again to call to the guards. 'Get him ready!' They saluted, two of them hurrying out of the room. 'The Emperor has chosen a new body, why shouldn't I? You like the look of this one.' He waved a hand toward m'Connor.

Certain Zaraxan had finally gone stark raving mad, Rhyssa hunted some reply. Was this a trap? He waited for her answer;

she needed to word it very carefully. 'A man's body appeals to a woman's eye,' she replied slowly and turned very deliberately to meet m'Connor's eyes. 'But it is his courage that wins her heart.' Making certain to flatter Zaraxan, she turned back to him. 'And it is his power and genius that excites her,' she added with a smile. That did the trick, making Zaraxan's pale eyes widen and his mouth drop open a little.

'Indeed, my dear, it is . . .' He reached out and stroked her arm with a possessiveness that made her want to slice him from gullet to crotch. 'Most exciting.'

M'Connor began tugging at the knot in his rope—belt. He was going to do it, try leaping up to lasso the sconce, hurl it at Zaraxan or use it as lever to swing up and over the balustrade. Zaraxan stood and shouted down at him. 'M'Fetrin is alive! I promise you, he's alive.'

A wolf's predatory eagerness for the kill tugged m'Connor's mouth into a hungry curve. He said nothing, his actions and that expression saying it all.

'I can prove it, m'Connor. I can have him brought before you, here, now. He's been upset. He's . . . Shall we say, not the same man he was.' Apparently pleased with the cleverness of his remark, Zaraxan spluttered a twisted, hissing laugh. 'Beg me, and I'll have him brought to you. It might make all the difference to him, to see you, know you're alive. The Weaver Bond between you is broken, but you both live. For now. He fades, m'Connor. He needs you. Beg!'

M'Connor's murderous, dark gaze slid upward again and there was something different in it, a flicker of . . . hope? A frowning shrewd assessment crossed his intelligent face, and abruptly, he dropped to his knees and lowered his head, saying, 'I beg my master. I beg his favor. Please.'

It was said as casually as he would comment on the weather and could not have been more insulting to Zaraxan, giving absolutely no satisfaction, no victory.

'Impressive, My Lord,' Rhyssa said as she realized Zaraxan was watching her, awaiting her compliment. 'I wouldn't have thought it possible to make him obey.'

'It's nothing; they are easily tamed, when you know how.' Zaraxan's tone revealed a veiled, sick pleasure at least as deep as her rage. He knew she wanted to gut him and he relished it, took as much a perverted sexual thrill in her forced subservience as he did m'Connor's. He looked away from her, back to the kneeling man. 'Not good enough, slave! Every moment you fail is another m'Fetrin suffers. Satisfy me or you will not see him! Look at me! Beg me!'

Slowly, heavily, m'Connor lifted his head and met Zaraxan's eyes. 'I beg you, my master. I must know he lives. I beg you, show me Bren lives!' With a beautiful, resonant tenor voice he poured out his heart as if he expected that m'Fetrin might be in hearing, might somehow respond. The words echoed from the vaulted roof and the high stone walls. The raw grief, the naked hope in m'Connor's shimmering eyes closed Rhyssa's throat with sympathy for his desolation.

'Oh, very good!' Zaraxan applauded, a slow, sarcastic clapping of thick, stubby hands. He turned toward the soldiers that flanked the thrones. 'He's in place?'

'He is, My Lord,' the senior officer replied.

'Excellent.' Zaraxan shifted in his seat, bending to his right. He pulled hard at a lever just beyond the line of Rhyssa's sight and abruptly, the floor beneath m'Connor began to move, sliding open. He leaped smoothly to his feet and jumped away, placing his back to the wall. The floor there remained fixed. The mechanism creaked and groaned, carrying the weight of the stone slab and leaking light that flared more and more brightly upward through the widening gap, revealing another pit beneath the first, not as deep nor as steeply walled.

An eerie, wailing sound drifted up as the sliding trapdoor came to a halt. It set the nape of Rhyssa's neck prickling. It was the cry of a frightened, lonely animal. A dog. 'Bruska?' She stood, craning to better see the second pit.

'As I promised,' Zaraxan purred.

There was no dog anywhere to be seen; just a dirt-caked, red-haired man crouched in one corner. Shallow scratches and fading bruises covered his body. His chained arms were wrapped clumsily about his head as if to protect himself from the shifting roof and the now threatening emptiness above him. M'Fetrin. The sounds of animal distress were coming from him, his eyes wild and terrified, and his entire body trembling like a leaf before a storm. Rhyssa had only thought she hated Zaraxan before, only thought she knew the depth of his cruelties.

'Bren!' m'Connor's said, a rasping fearful whisper. Then he called with full force, 'Bren!'

Overwhelming relief resounded in the cry. Rhyssa looked away from m'Fetrin in time to see m'Connor move. He judged the drop and in an instant leaped down. His expression as he looked down at his friend would be forever etched in her mind. Tears tracked his face yet a faint smile curved his mouth, his joy at his Brother's survival swamping his anxiety for his condition.

38

'Bren!' he repeated, half-laughing with relief yet wavering with fear. 'Bren! I'm here! You'll be all right now!' He took a pace forward, the chains at his wrists rattling as he lifted his arms, ready to draw his friend into his embrace.

M'Fetrin let out a howling, yelping cry and slithered further along the wall, leaving the corner, but keeping his back pressed to the stone. His hands went to the floor, and he crouched on all fours, lifting his head. His eyes were mad, white-edged, flashing terror and fury. A low snarling growl, a warning threat, rumbled from his throat. His lips drew back and he bared his teeth, ready to attack. M'Connor froze in his tracks, his chained arms still outstretched, the lines of his face altering to haggard defeat. He backed away; his hands palm outward as he made soothing, hushing sounds, those you'd offer a terrified animal that wouldn't understand words. As far back as he could go, m'Connor dropped to a crouch. All the while his gaze never left m'Fetrin's panicked face.

'Easy, Bren,' he said, weeping unashamedly, silently. 'Steady, my friend, steady. It's all right, it's all right. Hush. I'm here.'

Rhyssa tasted blood and realized she was biting the inside of her lip as she fought to control her reaction.

'What have you done?' m'Connor demanded, hoarse, cold, the promise of an open grave, as again he looked up at the Inquisitor.

'Did I hear something?' Zaraxan said snidely. He took a sip of wine. 'I could have sworn I heard someone speak. Did you hear it, Rhyssa? Oh! It's the slave!' He handed his goblet to the waiting guardsman. 'Do you dare speak to me, slave?'

'Tell me how to undo this and I'll kill you clean,' m'Connor said, steady, sure.

'Such fantasy!' Zaraxan's eyes narrowed into the yellow slits of a striking snake as he regarded m'Connor. 'Beware what you say. I enjoy you whimpering beneath my burning knives.'

Shaking his head in dismissal, m'Connor returned all his attention to his friend. M'Fetrin had settled a little, his teeth no longer flashing but his body still trembling with terror. Exactly what abomination had the Inquisitor created? Could Rhyssa provide answers for m'Connor?

'Why do you show me this?' she asked, 'If this is my surprise gift, I do not like it.'

'I do apologize, my dear! I forget, I haven't yet explained. This is my greatest triumph,' he said, indicating m'Fetrin.

'Reducing a man to trembling, howling madness?' she said, keeping her voice level and neutral. 'Surely that is the daily work of Inquisition?'

'Indeed! Yes, the outward appearance shows nothing of what I've done,' Zaraxan agreed without insult. 'But, ahh, it hides immortality! You see before you a gift every man, woman and child in the kingdom will forever, that is literally *forever*, envy you, Rhyssa. You are the luckiest woman alive.'

M'Fetrin's howling had settled to snuffling, pained whimpers. Some of m'Connor's lilting, soothing gentleness was reaching him. 'How can that be immortality?' Rhyssa asked loudly, the better for m'Connor to follow.

'While the experiment is the greatest triumph of our age,' Zaraxan continued smoothly, 'the transfer is not complete. That—' he pointed a forefinger at m'Fetrin, 'is the new body the Emperor chose and will take when he decides he's had enough of old age. What a gift, Rhyssa, to never again suffer a failing, aging body!'

Utterly astounded, disbelieving, and peripherally aware that m'Connor, too, had lifted his head to regard the Inquisitor with incredulity, it took a moment before Rhyssa could reply. 'Surely, that's impossible,' she said at last.

Zaraxan gave a half bow from his throne. 'It was, until now. Until me.'

'Won't his mind fight the Emperor's to control the body? How could that be any way to want to live?'

'None would, of course. We made certain that would not be a problem. However, he remains like this for now.' Zaraxan preened, liking nothing better than to be prompted to answer questions that would reveal his self-perceived glory, 'I emptied m'Fetrin's body but then the Emperor told me too late that he didn't want to take possession immediately. Why couldn't I hold a body ready for him? I'm afraid . . . . I had no other slave ready at hand. I do hope you will forgive me.'

Listening intently, m'Connor edged protectively closer to m'Fetrin. The man let out a terrified yelp, a sound only a dog would make. Suddenly, Rhyssa was struggling against a surge of nausea. 'You used the dog,' she said, so chilled by the image of what had been done to m'Fetrin that her voice came out a whisper of ice. 'You killed Bruska.'

Shifting back away from his tortured friend, m'Connor flinched and looked up at her, his eyes dark in his white, sickened face.

'Not killed, Rhyssa! He still lives! It's just . . . Bruska wears a man's body now.'

'And that is immortality?' she rebuked, appalled beyond belief. 'I loved that dog. Can you bring him back for me? Please?' She sniffed and drew a piece of linen from her pocket to dab at her eyes. Bracing herself and making her expression that of a forlorn

41

innocent, she repeated, 'Please? Put the slave back where he belongs and give Bruska to me as a wedding gift?'

Zaraxan's mouth dropped loosely open. 'Wedding gift? You . . . you will have me?' he managed after a moment.

'I will, when we can have Bruska to pet in our marriage bed.' The time had come. She'd kill the bastard Inquisitor; slit the mongrel's throat. Her father would have to look out for himself if he refused to escape Myrrgha with her.

'My dear, Rhyssa!' Zaraxan exclaimed, breathing hard, his face flushed scarlet. 'This is wonderful news! I intended to ask you this evening, to celebrate my triumph. I knew you'd have me when I proved I could give you immortality!'

'First, show me you can return Bruska to me, unharmed. Where are you keeping him? I hope the slave residing in him doesn't do anything to hurt him.'

'I . . . It's not as easy as that,' the Inquisitor floundered. 'I mean . . . the dog, its body, is dead, Rhyssa. I'm so sorry. The slave's essence is gone; where is a state secret.'

'You can tell me, your soon-to-be-wife, can't you?'

'I—, I would, truly I would. I can tell you this much—it's true Emperor Grouda has allowed Methaggar back into the City.' He watched her face for reaction. She shrugged; anyone with any brains had already figured that for themselves, though none dared speak openly of it. 'Yes, well, they assist my work. They made me swear.' He gave her a sickly smile. 'They captured the Weaver essence. Only they know how that part works.' He leaned forward to quickly grasp and kiss her gloved hand. 'But, come! We have our wedding to organize!'

Rhyssa couldn't find her voice, aware of the weight of m'Connor's horrified despair, echoing her own. 'You butchered a good dog. And the slave's . . . essence? The Methaggar destroyed it?'

'I have no idea. They say Weaver life-forces are automatically returned to their beloved trees. But come, Rhyssa, my dearest, it is of no concern to either of us.'

'Poor Bruska!' Rhyssa said, seeing a way to help m'Connor and perhaps m'Fetrin. 'He must be terrified down there in that pit with a stranger. How long is it since you made the transfer?'

'Four days now, I think,' Zaraxan said, frowning down at m'Fetrin.

'Has he eaten? Has anyone seen to his care? He won't be in any fit state for the Emperor to claim him without someone to take good care of the body in the meantime.'

'You are right,' Zaraxan said, and rubbed at his flabby jaw as he considered the problem. 'No one's been able to get near him.'

'He'd still recognize me,' Rhyssa suggested. 'I'll try calling to him.' She stood and went to the balustrade. 'Bruska! I have your treats for you! Where are you hiding?'

M'Fetrin straightened suddenly, his head whipping around to look for her, and he began yelping frantically, trying to reach her, leaping up at the walls and falling back. 'He'll hurt himself! Quickly! You must have him brought to me. We'll keep him with me at home.'

'I don't know . . . .' Zaraxan said, eying the huge man-dog dubiously. 'The Emperor might not approve.'

'He'll want him healthy and he needs him safe and my home is fortified,' Rhyssa reminded him, desperate to get the terrified creature away but aware she'd need help to control him. 'You can detail Honor Guards and you could visit to check on him.'

43

Wavering, he looked from the man in the pit to her. She curved her lips into a seductive smile and added, 'You'd have a reason to be with me every day. It would help with planning the wedding, and . . . everything.'

'Yes! I'll make arrangements to have him delivered to you immediately. Guards!' He turned away.

Rhyssa took the chance to cast a sharp glance direct to m'Connor and added, 'I swear, I'll take very good care of him. He'll be safe with me.'

CHAPTER THREE

'You allowed your lady friend to take m'Fetrin's body to her home,' Methaggar Lord Lurghiar accused. His flat, cold voice appeared to speak from thin air, as he stood almost invisible in the shadowy corner of the stone-walled underground laboratory. The sound made the dogs whine in their cages.

High Lord Inquisitor Zaraxan rubbed at his aching back as he straightened from again checking the Lellghin slave's heartbeat and found none. The laboratory table was too low; he must be sure to have the guards install a higher one. 'It is perfectly secure there with several Honor Guardsmen to watch over it. The creature would die without the *High Lady's* expert care! She keeps the body viable until such time as the Emperor makes his decision.'

That silenced the Methaggar at last. Poor Bruska. Zaraxan had relied on the dog, kept it close at his side, trusting its sense of smell to warn him of Methaggar, or other illicit, threatening presences. Thankfully, Rhyssa had trained another dog to serve as his private guard and was bringing it to him here today. Looking down into the blankly staring dead eyes of the young Lellghin slave, another failed Transfer experiment, Zaraxan added pointedly, 'Myrrgha must soon be shown the proof that I have gifted him with immortality! Meantime, I fear we cannot reproduce that success with these non-Weaver slaves. Not yet. Perhaps with more research . . . .'

'This creature had no training in Traveling.' Lurghiar admitted sullenly. 'Its essence is as unstable and shifting as a bubble in a lava-flow. You have failed again!'

Zaraxan felt his teeth grate together. 'You seem to forget, My Lord, *I* am not the person who made the mistake that reduced us to this farce in the first place!'

'Grouda needed his reassurance that m'Fetrin could not return and fight him for the body. We proved nothing can be retrieved from within The Lodestone.'

That was true. Privately, Zaraxan had been immensely relieved, but he couldn't resist nettling 'Lord' Lurghiar. 'You said you could do it, control m'Fetrin's essence, that it was no more than is done when your kind take possession of an animal to use it as a, a—'

'Seeker.'

The wave of menace that shivered through the thick air decided Zaraxan on choosing further words more carefully. He'd seen what the Methaggar had done to a suspected Hidden One. Lurghiar had leapt out of hiding, grasping and paralyzing the traitor all at once with poison and hooked suckers on the underside of its arms. Holding him very close against itself, the Methaggar had simply watched the man's terrified eyes and waited for its poison to slowly dissolve his muscles, making him food for certain 'Sects' of Methaggar young.

A beginning headache throbbed behind Zaraxan's tired eyes, the acrid smoke of the lanterns stinging his sinuses. He'd much prefer the new electric lighting, but apparently it was too dangerous to install here in this damp underground room. Finding the correct mix of drugs and hypnosis that would accurately recreate the altered condition of consciousness caused by Akkarra tree nectar and witches pushing a Weaver 'soul' to what they called 'Traveling' wasn't easy. Only then could Lurghiar begin wresting it away, severing the energy umbilical cord and forcing the consciousness into the methirri Lodestone. Zaraxan would then kill a drugged and prepared dog to animate the body, making it ready for re-harvesting.

How much of the ability to 'Travel', to keep the life-force intact outside the body, was inherent among 'ordinary' Lellghinners? No one knew. Zaraxan planned a test of the Weaver 'circuitry' with the one named Gerion, later today and had already sent the guards for the prisoners. Having m'Connor present as well was critical to checking for any energy transfer that might be triggered between the two when he applied the hot irons.

'A message from his Majesty, Emperor Grouda!' the Honor Colonel of the Imperial bodyguard announced as, followed by two subordinates, he pushed open the door. 'He commands your presence and yours, My Lord Lurghiar.'

The solid iron chains and manacles clanked ominous threat as they were thrown onto the cell floor. 'Out!' The Captain of the Guard ordered, looking sidelong at his Sergeant who held the child hostage. She cried out as the Sergeant, impatient, twisted her arm.

'Leave the little 'un be!' Gerion snarled. 'Me?' He stepped forward and bent to pick up a set of manacles whose long chain would lock to the irons he wore about his wrists and ankles.

'Now why would I throw two sets in there if I wanted just you?' the Captain said, sneering. 'You know the routine. Both of you; be quick about it. His Lordship's waitin'.'

No. Not again. M'Connor met Gerion's sickened expression, knowing the same horror must show in his eyes. 'I guess it's my day to be branded,' Gerion said, utterly calm.

'No, not today, not ever,' m'Connor told him quietly, certain, despite knowing that torturing Gerion was precisely what Zaraxan had in mind.

The Captain gave an eager snigger as he exchanged a hungry, lusting look with the two guards who stood with muskets ready. M'Connor wanted to gut him right here, right now, hostage or no. The click of the lock on the wrist and leg-irons made m'Connor's stomach twist with the memory of being forced to watch as they'd strapped Bren to a table and . . . .

Looking inward, m'Connor found Focus, tapping into the great ocean of calm that would fuel his will and compel his speed of attack. He and Gerion—and Bren—had been through many a battle together where the odds against them had seemed insurmountable. But they'd won regardless. With Gerion sharing the same cell after Bren had been taken, they'd had their chance to discuss every detail of their plan—they would question and kill Zaraxan and escape. Somehow find the Hidden One network and get to Bren. Then, they'd take him home, to Sanctuary and Grove Isle, where the Akkarra would be holding his soul. They hoped.

Once inside the torture room, they'd drop, duck under the musket fire and take a guard each to the floor with them, use the chains to entangle them, snap their necks, and then take the Sergeant who would rush inside to Zaraxan's call, his arms full of struggling child. The white hot coals of the braziers used to heat the branding irons would be turned to their aid rather than torment, the source of heat to melt through the manacle chains if the keys could not be found. Visualizing it, gave m'Connor the strength to follow his friend, both of them hobbled by their chains, slowly climbing step by step up to the underground tunnel that linked the cells to the Inquisition Tower. 'Enjoy,' the Sergeant said, leering at them as they reached the torture room door. 'I'll keep the brat safe until you get back. Nice 'n safe, won't we, eh?' he added, speaking to the silent, terrified child.

'You there! Captain!' a woman's voice called, startling everyone and breaking m'Connor's murderous concentration. He turned his head and saw a woman striding toward them from the farther end of the corridor, a huge shaggy brown and black dog loping at her side. Just behind her came two Honor Guards, heavily armed. 'High Lady?' the Captain said.

'I'm to deliver this new guard dog to My Lord,' she replied, 'he asked me to meet him here.' As she stepped clear of the shadows, m'Connor recognized her as the same woman who'd promised to care for Bren. 'Here?' the Captain echoed, puzzled.

As she drew closer, m'Connor's eyes were drawn not to her but rather to the two gold-cloaked Honor Guardsmen flanking her. The way they walked, the way they carried themselves, and something else . . . something that tugged at the methirri collar at m'Connor's throat, as if trying to connect with him through its shadow. *It can't be.* 'Taran?' Gerion asked.

'Inside's no place for you, My Lady,' the Captain was saying.

'I've seen my Lord's work, first hand,' she replied crisply and gave the man a sweet smile—a snare, as deadly dangerous as Gerion's polite manner. 'You forget, I have the results of one of his experiments living under my roof.'

'Oh, and so you do, My Lady. Pardon, I'd forgot.' The door came fully open, the guard coming out to ask about the delay but falling immediately silent as he saw the woman.

'Then, you'll stand aside and let me in, Captain,' she said. M'Connor hadn't been paying much attention to the exchange, his eyes fixed on the two Guardsmen. He couldn't make out their faces in the shadows and the protective edges of the helms that came down about their eyes and noses. Suddenly, both drew small pistols and fired—shots that made no sound.

M'Connor ducked away, but it was the Captain who fell, a red-tipped dart embedded in his face. He didn't move, unconscious in an instant. One of the guards had gone down in the same manner to the other's fire. As Gerion attacked the door guard, M'Connor snagged the second musketman with his leg chains. Bringing him down, he got his chained arms about the man's throat, snapping the windpipe and leaving him strangling for breath. He stumbled to his feet to attack the Sergeant and wrest the child away from him, but the Honor Guard Captain had already stunned him, and placed the child on the floor by the door. 'Come on, inside, move!' the helmed man ordered and joy surged through m'Connor's veins.

'M'Garran!? M'Sharral!?' he exclaimed.

'Yes,' m'Garran replied, 'quickly now, follow the woman.'

She was already inside. 'She's your hostage?' Gerion asked.

'No—' m'Garran began, but was drowned out by a ferocious growling as they all entered the torture room. The woman and her dog had the last guard backed into a corner, the animal snapping, threatening the man's genitals. He'd been disarmed, surrendered, and had one hand in the air and the other guarding his lower body. Disappointingly, there was no sign of Zaraxan.

'Taran! Marc!' m'Sharral greeted with a beaming smile, pulling off his helm. 'We're getting you out of here!'

'She's a Hidden One?' m'Connor asked.

Likewise taking off his helm, M'Garran shrugged. 'You could say that. High Mariner Rhyssa Avenalkah. She's—'

'You know she's got Bren? How do we get to him?'

'I said, where is he?!' the woman demanded, so cold, so deadly sharp that m'Connor turned away from his friends to see what she wanted.

'Who?' the guard stammered.

'The bastard Inquisitor!'

'C-called away. The Emperor, an urgent conference 'r somethin'.'

'Where do they meet?'

'I don't know!'

'Bite!' she commanded and the dog lunged forward.

'I swear! I don't know. They don't tell us!'

'Shit!' the woman cursed. 'My dog's hungry for Pig-blood.'

'She's trained it to rip out Zaraxan's throat,' m'Sharral explained and, forcing open the lock, began exploring a wall cabinet behind the torture table.

'Move and your dead,' the woman warned her prisoner. Leaving the dog slavering eager watchfulness, she turned away to ask, 'Can we wait for the Pig-man to return?'

M'Garran shook his head. 'Bren is our first priority and the tide won't wait.'

'Damn, damn and damn!' She sighed. 'Hopefully they're having their cozy little meeting somewhere here in the Tower and will be killed, regardless.' She bent to pull something from the satchel she'd carried over her shoulder, clothing by the look of it.

M'Connor had known shock, but never of the pleasant kind. 'We walk out of here as your prisoners?' he asked, assuming that was the plan.

'No, we march as an Honor Guard duty squad,' m'Garran said. 'Here are the keys to those manacles. Get the chains off and switch clothes with the Captain and the Sergeant. Be sure to pull the jacket lapels high enough to hide those cursed collars. They can't come off until we're home with the Magi and the Akkarra of the Grove.' At m'Connor's startled joy, M'Garran grinned, the great wolfish grin m'Connor remembered from the battlefields of Lellgha. He engulfed m'Connor and then Gerion in huge back slapping bear hugs. He gave over the keys, watching his Brother examine a cabinet full of vials and bottles. 'Anything?' he asked.

'Not yet,' m'Sharral said.

'A particular drug he's working on to try to break our Keys,' m'Garran said by way of explanation of the search. 'We had hoped to question the bastard.'

'That I'd have enjoyed!' Gerion growled.

'It was going to be a highlight for us all,' m'Garran agreed and bent to work, stripping clothing from the two unconscious prisoners. Looking up as he tossed the Captain's uniform jacket to m'Connor, his eyes dark with sudden sorrow, he said, 'I'm sorry we didn't get here before they took Bren.'

'So, we go get him now,' Gerion said, pulling on the Sergeant's stripe-seamed trousers. 'And the Akkarra will have his soul. He'll be back.'

'Yes, he will. But you don't need to go get his body; we already have it aboard ship.'

'What? What ship?' m'Connor demanded, one arm entangling in a sleeve in his surprise.

'*My* ship,' the woman answered. Straightening, she gave him a smile and m'Connor knew, knew it as sure as he knew his own face—something had just changed forever in his personal life, changed for the better. 'The fastest in the harbor, though we needn't worry, we won't need to outrun anyone. She already has clearance from the Harbor Master. He's expecting to see her sail this afternoon—the crew taking her for a sea-trial.'

'Without you, however,' m'Sharral said.

'Right. I'll be dead,' she agreed, and twisted her shoulder-length dark hair into a knot that she shoved beneath the leather militiaman's cap she now wore.

'Excuse me?' Gerion asked, pausing as he put on the Sergeant's jacket.

'They've all seen me come in here; they know I have a new dog for him. I don't leave, the Tower burns to the ground. I'm dead,' she replied in rapid summation.

'Clever,' Gerion agreed.

'Yes,' she said, and straightening, met his eyes to add, 'Keeps the rest of my family alive, too, I hope.'

'You're leaving with us?' m'Connor asked, finished with dressing.

'It's my ship and my crew.'

'What about him?' Gerion asked, jabbing a thumb at the cowering guardsman.

'What about him,' she said, unconcerned. 'He won't be telling anyone anything.'

'P-please,' the man begged.

Gerion casting the man a murderous glance. 'You think your 'please' can sway us?' m'Connor asked, low and tight, meeting the man's terrified eyes. 'I used the same word, several times, to beg you to stop burning my Brother before my eyes.'

'They did what?' m'Garran whispered and m'Sharral froze, his search halted. M'Garran fired and the stun dart brought the man down, the dog standing over him, looking up at Rhyssa who signaled it to return to her side.

'Let him burn with the rest,' m'Sharral said. 'This will make sure of it.' He held up a glass vial full of some yellowish liquid. 'Embalming solution,' he said, 'highly flammable.' He drained half the bottle around the room and trailed more out into the corridor. 'What are we doing with this poor little kid?' he asked from outside.

'Home. With me,' Gerion said. Out into the dark corridor, the toddler still sat, afraid to move. No, these Myrrghin guards had not earned mercy. 'It's all right, now, it's all right. No one's ever going to hurt you again. We're taking you home.' Gerion continued soothing the child but she cowered away as he gently scooped her up in his arms. 'I'm wearing the bastard's uniform,' he said with sick realization.

'I doubt it would make any difference if you were still a prisoner,' m'Garran told him softly. 'Come on, let's get out of here and don't forget to keep your jackets pulled up over those cursed collars.' As m'Connor and Gerion checked each other, he added, 'The Magi have figured how to get the things off now; something the Akkarra were able to help them with even though they themselves can't tolerate the stuff being anywhere near them.'

'Good!' Gerion said, so bright with relief that it made the child flinch and pull away from him. 'Hush, it's all right,' he told her, settling her more comfortably and securely in his arms.

'I'll lay the fuse to give us time to get out, but not enough for anyone to find it and stop it; move fast,' m'Sharral warned. He pulled a long line of black powder fuse from beneath his tunic and began unraveling it up the hall. At m'Connor's questioning glance, he explained, 'My Lady tells us there's a munitions store third door down.'

M'Connor nodded and turned to follow the others. A free man. It felt more than good.

With an Honor Guard Captain leading the way, they met no opposition within the building and certainly it was no strange sight to see a Sergeant carrying a small child hostage. Outside, in the wide white graveled marshalling yard, the only problem for the former slaves was the glare. Blinded, they were forced to a standstill until their eyes adjusted. The feel of sunshine and a fresh sea-breeze on his face was something m'Connor knew he would never forget.

'Through that stone arch-tunnel,' m'Garran directed, 'the compound gates lead out to the town market. Let me do any talking, but . . . if our timing is good everyone will be too busy to notice us. You might need your arms free, Marc.'

'Here,' Rhyssa offered, and hunting inside her satchel, pulled out the long scarf she'd been wearing when dressed as a woman. Quickly, expertly, she made a sling that firmly secured the squinting child to Gerion's back, She, too, had not seen the sun in many long months.

They'd gone only a few yards into the tunnel when m'Connor felt it—the methirri collar about his throat growing heavier, colder, like ice burning at his throat. The dog growled, a low threatening rumble. 'Methaggar,' m'Connor said quietly, his hand going to his sword.

'Hiding here somewhere,' Gerion affirmed, the others stopping, preparing to fight. The Methaggars would sense the methirri about m'Connor and Gerion's throats.

'Kill!' Rhyssa told the dog and it leapt willingly into the darkness of the shadows toward the far end of the tunnel. A garbled scream mixed with the dog's low snuffling as it pulled something down, a struggling figure that as quickly stilled.

'There's another one, somewhere . . . .' m'Connor warned.

The dog left its kill to track it down, but the second Methaggar struck first, it and the dog going down in a tangle. The dog yelped in pain but continued fighting, Rhyssa racing toward it.

'Stay back!' m'Connor said, trying to pull her back as he drew his sword.

'*You* stay back!' she returned and pulled away. Her right arm came up, a dagger hilt in her fist. She aimed, threw.

A hiss of pain from the shadows and the Methaggar looked up at them, her dagger embedded in its face, its spider eyes reflecting red in the dim light. Abandoning the dying dog, the Methaggar flung its long poison-sucker tentacle arms toward Rhyssa. M'Connor hacked, sliced off an arm. The creature snarled and hurled itself at them. Mid-flight, m'Sharral brought it down with a solid swing of his blade. The thing's head bounced on the cobblestones and Rhyssa bent to retrieve her knife.

'Gotta take the bastards' heads off,' m'Sharral reminded m'Connor with a grin. They were free and fighting together again and, even if unable to use Weaving that would draw every Methaggar in the city, it felt damn good. Behind them came a monstrous whump and a roaring explosion. The tunnel suddenly lit with flaring firelight and radiated warmth. 'There's our distraction,' m'Garran said. Clapping m'Sharral on the shoulder, he added, 'Good work, Brother.'

A pang of grief cut m'Connor at the sight, knowing the Sharing the Brothers would feel, the Sharing he'd felt so many times with Bren on the battlefield.

Fire alarms sounded everywhere about them, people scrambling, fleeing or heading to grab buckets and fill them from the yard's central well. 'Follow me,' m' Garran instructed. 'Remember, I'm your commander.'

At the gates, the sentries gave them no more than perfunctory checks, too busy avoiding a horse-drawn fire wagon that came charging through the archway. Outside, suddenly, m'Connor found himself surrounded by an ordinary civilian market place, so alien and vibrant after so long underground, a prisoner in a world close by yet so far from life beyond the walls.

'This way,' m'Garran directed. 'We have a wagon waiting.'

'Hurry! His Majesty does not like to be kept waiting,' the Honor Guard Colonel urged as Zaraxan, puffing for breath, lagged behind. A steep flight of stairs further along connected the Inquisition Tower level to another maze of tunnels and stairways. The War Ministry building and other official edifices of Senate Ministries were on the other side of the Imperial Citadel complex that stood on the highest point above the sprawling city and its harbor. With a Methaggar Lord present, this meeting must be held in utmost secrecy and would not take place in any of the Palace chambers with their magnificent views and comfortable furnishings. They'd find the Emperor in a windowless room hacked out of the rock beneath the palace, the direction from which the Methaggars had returned in stealth to the city. Their females were able miners, with serrated edges on their powerful pick-shaped arms rather than poisonous suckers. It was debatable which sex was the more dangerous when attacking.

Outlawed after the War of the Geeahm Sects centuries ago, they'd been forbidden to live anywhere other than in the Smoking Mountains two hundred miles beyond the city. Now people spoke in frightened whispers, saying the Spider Lords were back. But even in whispers they dared not voice their opinion that their Emperor himself was harboring the creatures.

'Failure!' he snapped, firing a glare at his Chief Inquisitor. Hunched and skeletally thin, Grouda sat in a cushioned, comfortable armchair that eased his twisted, arthritic limbs. He wore soft velvet slippers on feet he had propped on an equally well-cushioned foot-stool. A small table stood to one side, complete with wine decanter and pain medicines. Coming down here to these dank cold chambers couldn't be helping either his mood or his suffering.

'We succeeded with m'Fetrin. The young strong body is ready for you whenever you choose, Majesty,' Zaraxan promised. 'Today's experiment was not a total loss. We now know it is useless to work with any Lellghinner who has had no training in so-called 'Traveling. We must use fully-trained Weavers, or find a drug that will emulate the process.'

Grouda regarded him a long, tense moment through bloodshot, rheumy eyes and said nothing. His expression said it all. Both he and his High Inquisitor knew this was not good news. 'Fully trained Weavers,' he repeated acidly. 'And exactly where do you suggest we 'procure' them, My Lord Inquisitor? There are no longer any to be found in Lellgha; they've all run off with their pirate friends!'

Then, it might have been best not to kill so many during the initial invasion! Zaraxan wanted to snap. But two years ago they had not discovered how their abilities could be harnessed. 'I can and will, naturally, use those two we are currently holding. First, as you so correctly point out, it is a more urgent matter to find a means of overcoming the so-called Keying of their memories that has thus far prevented them revealing where the surviving Weavers and Magi are hiding. With that obstacle at last removed, our naval forces will no longer search islands at random but can harvest all the Weavers we want, direct from their main refuge.'

'So, High Inquisitor, all your efforts with the Transfers are at a standstill until such time as more Weavers are captured?'

'Well . . . no,' Zaraxan hastily back-pedaled, 'my work continues on various drugs that might strengthen and hold the slave's life-energy until—'

'The secret lies in the power of the methirri,' Lurghiar interrupted before Zaraxan could correctly lay blame for failure at his feet. 'The Lodestone almost captured the slave's essence this morning. Double the power of the Lodestone, and I'm certain we need no longer concern ourselves with a supply of Weaver slaves or of new drugs.'

'Yet, My Lord, you report that not just any methirri suits your purposes?' Grouda asked.

'No, Majesty. Only the rarer more dense methirri and in larger pieces has proven strong enough to attract and imprison a Traveling Weaver.' Slinking forward a little from where he'd been standing, Lurghiar repeated, 'Double or triple the power and it will drag in even the more ephemeral of untrained life-forces.'

59

'Every scrap of methirri we find goes to the military,' Zaraxan said with an accusing side-long look at the Methaggar.

'Our new methirri-coated battleship will deliver Weavers to you the sooner, Lord Inquisitor, if you break the Key mind-codes!' Grouda shouted. Exhaling a long, rattling sigh, he settled back again. 'Fortunately, I have more hopeful reports from General Rusark.' He leaned toward the Colonel who quickly handed over a ribbon-bound tube of papers. Opening it, the Emperor held up what appeared to be a map with various red ink lines and marks. Below the map was a neat hand-drawn key and graph, signed *Captain Kerell Lerant.*

'Only yesterday, we received this survey report from an engineering officer in Khengha.' Grouda waved the Colonel to display it for Zaraxan and Lurghiar.

Eagerly, Zaraxan spread the papers on a nearby table. 'You've found methirri!'

'Not just any methirri, the report shows the stone located is of the highest quality.'

'So much,' Lurghiar murmured, startling Zaraxan who hadn't realized the creature had moved around behind him.

'Yes,' Grouda nodded, his small round eyes feverishly bright. 'Enough to arm our soldiers, cloak our ships, *and* solve our Inquisitor's problems with his experiments.'

'A long way from the coast,' Zaraxan mumbled, aware several supply ships had been lost to attacks from Talae pirates in recent months.

'Our engineering teams are building bridges and roads, and there is a navigable river,' Grouda said, a satisfied smile leaking about the edges of a wrinkled, determinedly sour mouth.

Zaraxan had to bite his tongue to keep from demanding why this wonderful news had not been mentioned sooner. Reading that expression, Grouda's expression became a malicious leer. He'd been stringing Zaraxan along, watching him sweat, knowing Zaraxan feared competition from the military and the Methaggars.

'Good!' Zaraxan said, plastering a pleased expression on his face. 'With both Weavers and high-grade methirri, I am certain the m'Fetrin success can easily be repeated.'

Grouda waved at the Colonel to come help him to his feet. 'I have work to do, negotiating with the Khenghin King to allow us build fortresses to mine methirri in the lands of his troublesome nomadic peoples, and to—.'

A tremendous explosion shook the underground room, thundering in the confined space and terrifying Zaraxan. An Honor Guardsman rushed in, saluted, and reported, 'The Inquisition Tower, Majesty, under attack! Hidden Ones!'

'Oh, no!' Zaraxan remembered in horror. 'Rhyssa!'

CHAPTER FOUR

With most of the crowd heading the other way to gawk at the fire, the escapees and their rescuers were soon in empty streets and not much further on had reached the docks.

'There she is!' Rhyssa said proudly, jumping down from the wagon to the timber wharf.

The yacht was bigger than m'Connor had expected, and much more luxurious, portholes showing from what could only be several passenger cabins. She had three masts and carried a lot of sail, all of it furled away as she seemed also to be fitted for steam propulsion, and set to go if the black smoke streaming from a tall funnel was any indicator.

'A steam ship?' Gerion said, impressed.

'Yes. We still need the tide to clear the bar, but we can do without wind or the need to worry about its direction,' Rhyssa said, smiling up at two crewmen who stopped their work to greet her with evident relief.

'We were beginning to worry,' one of them called down.

'About me?' Rhyssa laughed and it hit m'Connor with a surge of more than pleasure.

'It went well? Ahh, yes, I see you have them. Good, we can cast-off,' the bronze-skinned man said, and bent to tend what m'Connor realized must be an anchor chain winch. They were really going home! Impatient to see him again, to judge how well he'd been cared for, he wanted to ask where Bren was.

'My Chief of Sail,' Rhyssa introduced. 'Kumar Jamal.'

'Our very great thanks,' m'Connor called up to the lean brown-skinned man who wore a white turban style headdress and a smile to match.

'My pleasure,' he replied. 'Hurry now, climb aboard and we will be underway.'

'I do like the sound of that,' Gerion said, eager. He walked up the gangway carrying the child who seemed to be asleep in his arms, m'Garran and m'Sharral following.

Rhyssa spoke to another of her people who stood ready to cast off the heavy ropes wound about the bollards. M'Connor waited, and as she turned to him, he said, 'I need to thank you. I owe you a very great debt.'

'You owe me nothing,' she told him. 'Seeing . . . what happened the other day, made me realize it was past time I left Myrrgha permanently. Rhyssa Avenalkah,' she said, extending her hand to him and giving another of those heart-warming smiles. 'It's an honor to have you and your friends sail with us.'

'Taran m'Connor,' he said and took her strong hand in his. An immediate feedback flooded him despite the collar, dampened but powerful, like a wave of recognition . . . and something deeper. 'Maybe there's no debt between us, but I will never forget what you did for Bren. If he'd still been with the Pig-Man . . . .'

'I know. Come on, the others are aboard and you and Gerion need a hot meal under your belts and real beds to sleep in. First, I'll take you to the cabin where we have Bruska . . . Bren.'

'That's the name of your dog?'

'Yes. Best we continue to use it as the animal recognizes nothing else right now.'

M'Connor nodded and followed her up the gangway. She led the way through a hatch and down a companionway, and then along a corridor lined with beautifully finished glossy timber panels that glowed under the soft yellow light of low burning lanterns.

'That's yours and Gerion's cabin right here,' she pointed out. 'Mine is opposite. Bruska-Bren is next along, but I've had the internal bulkhead removed so he can always see me and know he's not alone.'

'Good thinking,' m'Connor said, his heart thudding. His last sight of Bren had been harrowing. How were they to deal with him? A big strong man's body controlled by a dog spirit.

Perhaps reading his expression, Rhyssa paused at the cabin door to touch his arm and say, 'It's not so bad now. He's much calmer and has been eating, happy enough in the familiar surrounds of my home. The problem, if any, will come when he wakes here at sea.'

'I understand,' m'Connor told her, just to say something reassuring, knowing she felt the same uncertainty.

'He's sleeping, heavily sedated,' she added, 'He shouldn't wake before dawn.' She stepped into her dimly lit but spacious cabin, fitted with a single bunk and shelves lined with books and an interesting-looking collection of bits and pieces, he supposed, collected from her various travels and studies. At the foot of the bunk atop a locker, were odds and ends of what could only be some kind of engineering repair.

Seeing the direction of his gaze, she said, 'My father and I, always tinkering with how to make a better engine . . . I'll miss him.'

'Will he know, I mean, that you're alive?' m'Connor asked, suddenly better appreciating all she had given up to help them.

'Yes. He said he was glad I was getting away before I got into any more trouble.' Her lips half-curved into a soft smile and the loneliness left her eyes. 'My brothers . . .' She shrugged. 'It will be up to him to decide what and when to tell them the truth, if ever. They're . . . . very loyal to the Myrrghin military.' She indicated the empty space where the interior wall had been removed and the next cabin was in deeper shadow. 'Your friend's through here.'

M'Connor found he had to bite down against a surge of overpowering emotion as finally he found himself looking again at the man who was his Weaver-Brother. Bren's face was composed, serene in sleep, his red-haired head comfortably pillowed. 'You found a bunk big enough for him,' m'Connor commented, not knowing what to say. 'Bren always complains about the beds being—' He cut himself short, realizing he could no longer control his voice, relieved and terrified all at once. *The Akkarra will have him,'* he told himself silently, firmly, but doubt nonetheless gnawed at him. *What if they didn't? What if the Methaggar . . . ?'*

'Would you like to sit with him a moment?' Rhyssa asked. 'I must go help my crew get underway.'

That was almost certainly untrue; m'Connor was fairly certain her crew could sail perfectly well without her instruction, and he was immensely grateful for her understanding of his need for privacy. 'Thank you, yes,' he managed.

A moment later, he was alone with his sleeping friend, or so it seemed. But Bren wasn't there. Somehow it hurt even more to see him like this, looking the way he always had, and knowing, knowing . . . . 'Bren, oh, Bren,' he sobbed, covering his face with his hands as he sat on a chair thoughtfully left by the bunk. Bracing himself, he looked again at his friend's body, knowing he'd seen something odd, out of place, amid the shock of that first sight. Bren shifted in his sleep, moving his head on the pillow and m'Connor realized what it was. 'You're not wearing a slave collar! The bastards took it off!'

That was good news. He, Bren and Gerion had been forced to witness a 'demonstration' of what would happen if they tampered with or tried to remove their collars. He didn't want to remember, to see it again, but it was seared indelibly into his mind, bringing a surge of nausea. The collar growing hotter, burning, the man's screams cut short as finally, mercifully, the thing exploded, killing him. Forcing away the image, he told Bruska-Bren, 'At least we don't have to worry about you, there.'

He took his friend's big hand in his, but Bren, or rather the dog inside the man, tried instinctively to pull free. He put the hand down again quickly, that one short exchange near breaking him—there'd been not the least hint of the Bond that once existed between them. Bren would know it was him even in the deepest sleep. 'The Akkarra will have you,' he said aloud, 'it'll be all right.' Maybe somewhere, Bren could still hear him.

'They will,' Gerion said, entering quietly and making m'Connor start. It was a difficult adjustment to make despite having worn the collar for months, of not being able to Sense other presences, 'Sorry, didn't mean to creep up on you. How is he?'

66

'Heavily sedated.' M'Connor found he had to clear the lump from his throat. Gerion gripped his shoulder a moment in sympathy which only pushed m'Connor closer to weeping. 'The child?'

'Poor lil' mite's hungry. One of the crew carried some food for her to our cabin. They're fixing up a cot for her, too.'

'Good,' m'Connor said, his attention all for Bren.

'He'll be all right,' Gerion said with calm reassurance. 'There's only one place he'd go when he left his body. The Akkarra would draw him like iron filings to a magnet. You know that.'

'Thanks, Marc. He, or the dog, Bruska, pulled away when I touched him. Best we keep our distance, I suppose, until we reach Sanctuary.'

'Right.' Gerion let out a great sigh of weariness and released strain as the ship shifted, her engines pounding, leaving the docks. 'Can you believe it? Free! We're on our way home, Taran! *Home!* I'll see Katya and the children again!'

'And the little one we rescued?'

Gerion nodded. 'Number four. Katya won't mind, she always said Alicia needs a sister.'

'She and the children will welcome her,' m'Connor agreed, feeling an easing of his mood. Gerion and Katya and their brood of three-four with the pending adoption, always warmed his heart, one of the first families to flee to safety at Sanctuary's Home Cove.

'Did you notice this?' m'Connor asked, touching his slave collar and then indicating Bren's bare throat.

'No collar!' Gerion said in pleased astonishment.

'I suppose . . . . After . . .' m'Connor said, heavy and grim once more, 'there was no need.'

There were footsteps, a woman's light tread made deliberately loud. She was giving them warning, being sure not to intrude on any private conversation. 'We're underway,' she reported. 'If you're hungry, there's hot food waiting for you in the galley.'

'If we're hungry, she says!' Gerion turned to her with a smile that faded to intent gratitude. 'Thank you, My Lady.'

'Rhyssa,' she said and held out her hand.

'Rhyssa,' Gerion repeated, shaking hands. 'You got Bren aboard unseen? Surely he was heavily guarded in your home?'

'Four of those filthy Honor Guardsmen,' she said. 'That's where m'Garran claimed the Commander's rank, swapping clothes after he and m'Sharral felled the bastards.'

'Heh,' Gerion snorted, 'that's m'Garran all right.'

'Actually, we had to make some quick adjustments; the uniform was too small for him. But, it's fortunate he and m'Sharral are big men—it required strength to carry Bruska out and into the prepared wagon.'

'How is he likely to react when he wakes?' m'Connor asked, still looking down at the sleeping dog-man.

'Hard to say, but I've taken the necessary precautions to prevent him bolting and falling overboard.' She lifted a corner of the blanket by the foot of the bed, revealing a metal cuff and chain about one ankle. 'I have a chest harness for him, too, so he can be exercised above deck.' She sighed and met m'Connor's gaze. 'He had calmed down fairly well, familiar with me and my home. I had him eating again and steady enough, if confused when we insisted on clothing and grooming him.'

M'Connor flinched; sick to the stomach at that image. 'I can only be most grateful you were there and willing to take him in. I remember . . . some of the answers you got out of the Pig-man that day. Again my thanks for that.'

'My pleasure. Hopefully, he'll settle in here, too. The extra large bed and the double cabin gives him some room to move, although I fear he'll hit his head when he stands. That stupid bastard, Zaraxan, thought the removal of the bulkhead was done to accommodate our marriage bed.'

'I thought I heard something about a wedding, but . . . .'

'Yes. It got him to agree to having Bruska-Bren held in my home. Marrying into my family is the only way Zaraxan could ever claim aristocratic standing and an avenue to the Senate. He's the son of a pig farmer.'

'We knew that last,' Gerion said. 'Calling him Pig-man always scored a direct hit.'

'It would,' she said with a keen-edged twist of her mouth. 'I'll give him that much; only his depth of cruel intelligence could have made it from there to High Inquisitor. I hope that fire trapped the mongrel, otherwise . . . .'

'If he's still alive,' m'Connor said; certain sure, 'you, me, Marc and Bren will come back and slit his belly.'

'Sworn and set,' she said, holding her hand palm upward for his thumb print, the Myrrghin fashion of sealing a deal. He touched her hand and again felt a strong connection. 'So you see,' she concluded, 'it was no great tragedy for me to leave Myrrgha. The Pig-man had already poisoned my mother. I was planning to kill him . . . but, there were my father and brothers to consider.'

Leaving them to digest that, she bent to pull the blankets more warmly about m'Fetrin . . . Bruska. She no longer wore a Myrrghin militia man's clothing but had changed into a neatly tailored trouser suit, suitable for work aboard ship. It was the first time he'd really noticed her appearance fully, and realized suddenly that she was beautiful, a wild fierceness and sharp intelligence balanced by a deep gentleness in the soft smile of her full lips. Strength of purpose showed in the dark eyes, her light brown face framed by waves of jet black shining hair. She had washed quickly; he could smell rosemary and lavender soap.

'He won't like all these Myrrghin uniforms about him,' m'Connor commented as she straightened up again.

'No. He seems to have a heightened sense of smell,' she said, eyeing their Methaggar-blood-splattered and dust caked uniforms and wrinkling her nose. 'There's hot water and soap in the wash room at the end of the corridor, and fresh clothing for you both in your cabin.'

'Hot water . . . .' Gerion said with wonderment. 'A bit of a change from our former quarters!' he added with a smile for m'Connor who was feeling the same sense of overwhelming, pleasant disorientation.

'Meet me with your two friends in the galley when you're done,' she said, giving them both a smile. 'I can answer any questions you might have.'

'The bastard's soldiers got there before us!' Lurghiar snarled in disgust. 'Grouda will have his new methirri mine heavily guarded and we'll get only as much as he wants to allow us.'

As by far the most junior member of this secret meeting of Methaggar Lords, Varasaghir remained silent. He was not of the Upper Sect, was the only Subordinate, or more scathingly, 'Underling' of the group and had few of the distinguishing physical features of his two Superiors. He'd been recruited initially as a kind of glorified assistant and baggage handler to ensure Superior

Apomerghia arrived safely in Myrrgha City. Lurghiar had been the spearhead of their people's stealthy return beyond the lands of their exile, and it wasn't hard to sense his resentment at being pushed down to second in command.

'Perhaps,' Apomerghia agreed. 'Thus we might live the longer.'

That was true. Methaggars had done all they could with their breeding program to protect against the slow poisoning of methirri, but as one generation followed another, they'd become more dependent and more susceptible rather than less. Now, Apomerghia was the eldest of them and he was no more than fifty years old.

'I'll be lucky to live to thirty five and I'm half way there now,' Varasaghir thought gloomily. He waited and listened for his Superior to turn the discussion around to speak of what they must surely know was by far the better plan than trying to re-harvest the bodies of the few remaining male Weavers, Wilder, or otherwise.

'The humans knew they were condemning us to slow extinction when they exiled us to such polluted lands! They knew we'd have to retreat to the volcanic caverns or die!' Lurghiar returned angrily.

'Of course they knew,' Apomerghia agreed again.

'They want us dead, but we'll outlive them all.'

'We could be as immortal as the Magi if—' Varasaghir dared speak up.

'The human child Seedling escaped us more than twenty years ago, and there's been no trace of him since,' Apomerghia said kindly enough, using his rear set of eyes to look around.

'Dead, more than likely,' Lurghiar sneered. 'Fanciful dreams are no use to us, Varasaghir! We have no time to waste on someone who no longer exists!'

It was not Varasaghir's place to reveal his Superior's exciting news, such vital news, holding tremendous potential, it had been necessary to carry it here in person.

'However, young Varasaghir might yet be proven correct. I have seen—She still lives,' Apomerghia put in, at last making the announcement, 'She is in fact showing signs of improvement, of waking from her hibernation.'

'She' was the tiny female Akkarra tree that was the Methaggars' greatest secret, grown from the seed found, buried deep in methirri, two hundred years ago. No female Akkarra existed anywhere else, the Lellghinners having mourned them as lost during the Crossing—and lived with less than half their full power ever since. Then, less than thirty years ago, the Methaggar had succeeded in forcing the seed safely open and compelling it to release its cargo—the blood energy codes of a male Magi and his two female Weavers. Still viable, they'd been successfully imprinted to form embryos. Unfortunately, during a volcanic eruption and earthquake, the children and many other prisoners, had escaped.

'Why was I not told?' Lurghiar demanded.

'I just did,' Apomerghia said. 'This information is to be most closely guarded, and could only be carried here in person. None of the humans must ever know of it.'

'Are you saying the human Seedling is still alive and his Akkarra awakening?' Lurghiar asked, skeptically.

'Perhaps. There are other possible causes.'

'Still, it might be wise if we redouble our efforts through our Seekers,' Lurghiar said.

'Redouble!?' Apomerghia rebuked quietly. 'You cannot redouble zero effort.'

'He'd be about twenty four years of age now?' Varasaghir asked, trying to tamp down his excitement. *Not much older than me.*

'Yes, and that's what worries me,' Apomerghia said. 'How is it that a male Magi could have grown to such an age and *not* be located by his own people and their *'trees'?*

'Precisely.' Lurghiar returned to his sneering attitude.

'If he and his Weaver pair exist and can be returned to us, we need no longer continue this farce with Grouda,' Apomerghia reminded him. 'Our power would be unassailable. Varasaghir will resume watch for the Catalyst Blade. It alone may have caused Her awakening.'

'If we do recapture him . . . .' Lurghiar said, his long tongue curling about his thick lips as if in anticipation. 'We taught him from the cradle to hate his Akkarra, to believe they drink human blood. It shouldn't be too difficult to coerce him into 'freeing' the other male Magi when we find more seeds. What an army that would create for us!'

'So we plan. The Seedling child escaped with his mother first into Khengha and would now be a young man. It is there we will resume the search. Varasaghir will watch through the ancient slargapent-Seeker, and we two will search with creatures of the air and the land.'

CHAPTER FIVE

For once, Parlan, I'm glad you're not here.

Kerell Lerant strained to listen for the least sound, wondering if the carnivorous reptile could attack him from the rear. All he could hear was the gurgle and hiss of green-brown river water eddying and flowing over rock and sand. After the clinging heat of a Khenghin summer night, the dawn air was surprisingly chill here on the floor of the narrow ravine. He must be ready to move when the small slargapent came for the bait he'd tethered beneath the unfinished bridge. Shifting his weight fractionally, he tried to ease his cramped legs. Hiding among a damp clump of towering bulrushes had seemed a good idea, but left him shivering and squatting uncomfortably in the slimy, stinking mud.

Unable to sleep after witnessing yesterday evening's attack on one of his troopers, he'd gotten up and taken his Sergeant's heavy-gauge musket, determined to kill the reptile. His boot-heels made a squishing sound as he shifted, sinking deeper into the mud. He glanced down at the black, knee-high leather he'd once prized for its polish. If he had a body-slave like most Myrrghin officers, there'd be nothing to looking immaculately groomed, as he'd been told more than once. But it was against all his independent Roghin instincts to own a slave.

He sighed heavily, adding a white puff of breath to the already gloomy fog drifting in swathes over the river, catching the pearl-gray, glimmering light just before dawn. Like low-lying clouds, the columns of fog seemed to take on shape, reminding him of the superstitions of the local tribes who believed in wraith-like, 'Traveling', Lellghin Witches.

He should have told his sergeant he was coming down here, but Fallon had managed to find some sleep and Lerant hadn't had the heart to wake him. Orders from General Rusark required the bridge finished in a ludicrously short time and was pushing them all hard. Myrrgha needed this supply route established badly and it wasn't for more coal for their warships. Lerant had helped draw up the surveys himself—it was the deposits of methirri that Myrrgha lusted for out here on the endless prairie grasslands, the *tierdrun* as the Khenghin nomadic tribes called it.

Mercifully, Lerant's little bridge had been deemed too small a project to send the extra men needed to guard a work-gang of Lellghin slaves. More likely, High Command didn't want any chance of word of the newly discovered methirri reaching the ears of the Lellghin sympathizers known as The Hidden Ones.

He knew he would have only the one shot from the musket; there'd be no time to tamp down another ball and wad in the black-powder. Clumsy weapon, but better than a sword for this job. Nonetheless, he was glad he had his as back-up. His left hand caressed the engraved hilt, the silver sunburst insignia warmly familiar, repeated larger on the leather scabbard. To Myrrghin Command it was a dangerous symbol of ancient beliefs and potentially divided loyalties. Out here, so far away from prying eyes, he hadn't bothered with disguising it.

The sun would be rising above the ravine rim behind him soon. He could see the bait clearly now, tethered above the waterline on one of the lower wood and iron braced cross-beams. The slargapent would have to lumber up out of the river to reach it, slow and awkward on its four stumpy, clawed limbs, a perfect target. There! A circle of ripples moving toward the bridge, against the current. Twin slits, yellow eyes set beneath bony protuberances just showed above the waterline.

Holding his breath to steady his aim, Lerant slid his thumb up to cock the hammer on the musket, wincing at the too-loud seeming click. The slargapent's long, narrow snout with its overlapping, hooked teeth nosed at the stonework. One forepaw then the other clutched at the crossbeam and it hauled itself, awkwardly, slowly upward. It took the bait in its jaws, tossing its head, trying to break the tether.

Gun at his shoulder, Lerant fired, the noise shattering the silence with resounding shock. Water-birds burst upward in startled flight as the recoil set Lerant down on his heels, his left hand flung out through the reeds and sinking deep into the mud. When he steadied himself again he found the slargapent twitching in its death throes.

Leaving the empty gun propped against the bulrushes, he splashed out into the cold shallows. The current tugged at his booted ankles, making the hidden, rocky bottom treacherous. He crossed safely to the lower bridge girder and gave a satisfied nod when he saw he'd hit his target dead center despite difficult conditions. He took a knife from his belt and sawed at the toughened tether line, then tossed the body securely higher on the bridge framework. He couldn't have done that with one of the much bigger slargapents native to Rogha. He bent closer to the water to wash as much of the mud and muck from himself as he could before returning to camp.

'Captain?' Fallon called from above the riverbank. 'Is that you making all the noise down there?'

'Under the bridge!' Lerant replied. 'I got it!'

The river erupted, a sinuous explosion of bronze-scaled muscle and gleaming, scimitar teeth. Yelping in terror, Lerant stumbled, falling on his back across the iron girder and the stone pedestal. Giant jaws snapped loudly shut on empty air, just missing him. Water fountained as the monstrous creature fell back into the river. It eyed him hungrily, its hooked teeth grinning.

An impossibly giant slargapent. Their eyes locked, the slargapent's cold as death, bright as blood-lust. Beneath, even more chilling, Lerant sensed a malevolent intelligence.

He scrambled backward, aware dimly that the world about him was hazed blood-red, the sky crimson. Fallon was calling to him, wondering at the mighty splash, laughingly asking if Lerant had fallen into the river. He couldn't see what was happening beneath the bridge.

Lerant opened his mouth to scream at the man to get the gun. But his throat was paralyzed by terror, and he knew the weapon was empty, useless. He fumbled with nerveless fingers for the sword-hilt that burned painfully against his hip and it smacked hotly into his grasp, suddenly seeming to arc with liquid fire. Gasping, he scrambled to his knees on the girder just as the monster lunged a second time. Its dark, wet form blotted the red sky with massive shadow, its razor-edged jaws agape. Bracing his arm against the girder, he twisted his face away. The creature's

77

teeth snapped so close that Lerant would swear they'd parted his hair.

The monster fell, impaled on the sword blade, jolting Lerant's arm all the way to his spine and sending blood splattering hotly over him. He lost his grip on the hilt, but the sword remained embedded even as the monster's enormous tail lashed about and its muscles convulsed.

Grabbing clumsily at a cross-girder, Lerant sat gasping, his chest heaving, his lungs burning. He stared in utter disbelief, cold sweat stinging his eyes, his heart hammering. The thing could have swallowed him whole, a nightmare come to life, many times bigger even than a Roghin slargapent.

With one final, shuddering breath, the monster stilled, its yellow eyes glazing over, clouded and empty of threat. The river fog gathered about it, seeming to rise from it, then coalescing above the massive, scaled corpse. Rapidly, it took on shape. A human figure? Cloaked in a coweled robe, dark as night, reaching for him—

'Kerell!' Fallon shouted, his voice hoarse with alarm.

The figure broke, swirled away.

'Kerell!'

Keep moving!

Weary after its long journeying, the giant Seeker-slargapent tried to resist Methaggar Varasaghir's direction. *Keep going!* Hunger pangs swamped him, feedback from the slargapent. He hated this part of his duties the worst, even more than the way the shifting, murky images he received from the creature made him nauseous and often left him with a headache as well. At least while it was underwater, there was no bright light to hurt his eyes.

Crack!

Musket fire!

Track! Varasaghir ordered, suddenly fully attentive. Sullenly obedient, the Seeker swam upstream, a loud splashing directing it toward the riverbank. *Blood!* Energized by the promise of food, the slargapent honed in on the hind section of a tiny Khenghin slargapent floating dead atop the water, something anchoring its upper body to what appeared to be a partially-built bridge.

To the surface! Watch! Varasaghir ordered and braced against the appearance of a dawn sky as the slargapent lifted just high enough to see above the waterline. A young human male waded into view and climbed a bridge girder to claim his prey. Fair haired, he wore a shirt embroidered with a Myrrghin military insignia. As Varasaghir tried to focus more closely on him, something flared intensely bright and hot from about the man's body. The radiance of it forced Varasaghir back with a cry of pain and dismay. It was no ordinary light, but rather something that seemed somehow aware of his Seeker-Link. Aware and intensely hostile, it battled to sever him. Cursing, he fought back. The light lanced deeper into him, a reddish-gold halo, spreading outward in the form of . . . .

The Catalyst! The Superiors had said it would look like this, a miniature sun, golden beams radiating from the energy form created eons ago by the Akkarra to fight Methaggar.

Overwhelming hunger, blood-lust, an urge to feed, to cut, to rend, to kill . . . . *Wait—No!*

Too late, the creature launched itself at the man, jaws agape. Startled, Varasaghir concentrated, focused on forcing it back.

Ahh! Damn! Blinding, hurting him, the cursed Catalyst cut sharply into his mind-form. He couldn't maintain control of the Seeker-slargapent and it attacked again, a great, driving upward lunge meeting an explosion of pain that sliced deep into the slargapent's chest. The Link broke and Varasaghir's energy-form lifted clear of the dying Seeker and hunted the man's Presence, eager to claim information, if not the man himself, for The Superiors. The Blade fought him and pain intensified, climbing higher. Desperately ignoring growing agony, he forced the human to look toward him.

Now! I have you!

The Catalyst lunged back. Blazing radiance exploded in the small cavern room, sucking at Varasaghir with killing intensity and forcing him to cower down, arms over his head, whimpering with the pain in his eyes. He must release the Link, he had no choice. He let go and the radiance recoiled, disappeared, a soft, gentle darkness closing about him in its place. He sat long moments, shaking and gulping cool air.

'What has happened here?' Apomerghia demanded, entering the cavern room at a run.

'Kerell!'

Fallon sounded panicked, something Lerant would only yesterday have declared impossible. The veteran master Sergeant was completely unflappable. He looked from the giant slargapent to the scarlet spray covering Lerant's chest and grunted in shocked horror, almost falling in his haste to climb the bridge lattice-work down to him.

The sword-blade lost its glow as the sun hid behind low clouds and the sky changed from red to clear blue. A cool breeze stirred, rifling the river water and lifting sweat-streaked hair from Lerant's eyes. Somewhere nearby a water-bird called.

Gasping, Fallon came to a halt and collapsed to his knees at Lerant's side. He reached trembling hands to pull back the bloodied shirt.

'N-not mine,' Lerant managed to croak.

'Are you sure?' Fallon patted him down, shaking his head and casting a strained glance at the monster. 'You're not hurt?'

'Fine,' Lerant said, his voice squeaking. He cleared his throat, said again, 'I'm fine.'

'How did you know that thing was hidin' out there?'

'I didn't.' Lerant hunted along the girder with unsteady hands and found the smaller slargapent's tail. He heaved it clear, gave Fallon a shaky smile, and said, 'I shot this one, see?'

The Sergeant grunted. Singularly unimpressed, he spared no more than a cursory glance for Lerant's prize.

'That's the one got Hawson?' he asked and Lerant nodded. 'Lucky it weren't that monster.' They turned in unison, awed, to look at the dead creature.

'We can't let the men see that,' Lerant said at last. 'They'll never come near the river again.'

'I might just second 'em there.' Fallon sighed, his bare chest heaving.

Lerant suddenly realized the man was wearing no weapon other than his belt-knife and must have stumbled from his bed half-dressed when he'd heard the shot. 'You came down here unarmed?'

Fallon eyed him bemusedly. 'Someone seems t've stolen my musket. You wouldn't've seen it anywhere, would you, Sir?'

'Oh,' Lerant said, suddenly remembering. 'It's over there, in the reeds.'

'Good thing y' didn't try huntin' with that piss-weak pistol they've given all you officers. Anyone'd think they want you all dead. You could 'ave been killed coming down 'ere alone. Next time, take some help,' the veteran growled. As a distinct afterthought he added, 'Sir.'

'I don't plan on a next time, I'm swearing off slargapent hunting for the rest of my life!' Lerant declared, earning a somewhat grudging chuckle. He staggered as he tried to get to his feet and Fallon lent him a firmly steadying hand. Lerant nodded thanks and asked, 'Do you think we can weigh that thing down and sink it somehow? Or would the current carry it far enough away from camp if we got it started?'

Fallon shrugged. He was shorter than his commanding officer but more stockily built, his shoulders rippling muscle. 'I hope there are no more like it 'ereabouts,' he said. 'I'm not sure I want t' go back into that water.' He regarded the dead animal grimly a long moment, then added, 'I don't care t' touch it. That thing is no ordinary slargapent. Ensorcelled, I'd say.'

Lerant blinked. 'What?'

'Created by those Magi-witches probably,' Fallon surmised, rubbing one hand over the other. 'Though I can't figure why they'd be huntin' in Khengha. There was a mighty show of light coming from down 'ere, part of their spell, I suppose.'

'Bullshit!' Lerant snapped. 'The sunrise was red. There's nothing magic about it, except what your superstitions give it.'

He bent to retrieve his blade and found he had to strain to heave it clear of the beast. It seemed reluctant to leave its victim.

'From where I was standin', it looked like your sword glowing fit to blind me,' Fallon insisted.

'The scabbard is designed to do that, useful in battle, distracts the enemy.'

'If you say so, Sir.'

Suddenly, the dead creature trembled and its outer hide flowed liquidly to crumble inward as if molded from sand. In moments, only the skeleton remained. Then, just as quickly, it too melted away leaving no more than a pile of ash. Ash and something else, something very small that glinted metallically in the sunlight—methirri? The breeze grew stronger, eddying up from the river-surface and the ash and metal evidence disappeared, swirling away. There was no proof the giant beast had ever existed.

'That settles it, then. Cursed Magi filth!' Fallon spat at the damp mark where the slargapent had lain. 'You are one very lucky soldier. That thing should've 'ad you dead to rights.' He frowned, and then decided, 'Must have been the iron in the bridge put it off. Methirri would've been better. Where's your band?'

Dazedly, Lerant rubbed at the spot above the bridge of his nose where the diamond-shaped piece of red-gray methirri should have protected him from a Magi or Weaver's attack. He hadn't worn it in days, none of them had. Who'd suspect a Lellghin witch and her Weaver-warriors would attack out here in this empty wilderness of wind-swept, sun-seared grassland a thousand miles north of their homeland?

'Where's yours?' he countered, glancing at the scarred ridge on Fallon's wrinkled face. It was a distinctive mark, an upraised welt left by a methirri band burning in reaction to a Weaver's attack. Such was sure sign a soldier had met the enemy in battle, a badge of courage. Most young troopers envied that mark. Not Lerant.

Fallon merely scrubbed at the welt and said nothing. Silence reigned. Finally, a waterhen called to its chicks, and the mother came paddling into view, her tiny, speckled babies strung out single file behind her, looking innocently content.

'She thinks it's safe enough to come out now!' Fallon declared, his mouth twisting in a wry smile.

The sudden return to such a mundane image after the sheer terror of moments before was too much. Weak-kneed, Lerant leaned heavily against a crossbeam, his hand shaking embarrassingly about the sword-hilt. 'You're wrong. Magi can't . . .' He lifted his free hand unsteadily, sure he was about to be sick, '. . . . take on animal form. No one can, it's not possible.'

'They don't take on the form, they use the animal to find and attack. Surely you've heard of Seekers?'

'Only in tales to frighten children.'

Fallon eyed him shrewdly. 'Scared you good enough.'

Lerant managed to drive the sword home into its scabbard with a satisfying hiss of steel over leather. 'It was a rogue creature, poisoned into madness and already dying. There's no magic in it, only cruelty.'

Fallon rubbed at his grizzled chin. 'Think whatever you want if it'll help y' sleep better,' he said. 'Come right to it, I might adopt that version meself.' He moved closer and put a hand to Lerant's shoulder. 'Here, son, you're white as death 'n chilled to the bone. Best get you back to camp.'

'I'm fine,' Lerant repeated, adding pointedly, 'Master Sergeant.'

Fallon just grunted, reached out and hauled Lerant's arm over a wonderfully warm, muscular shoulder. 'I'd be surprised if you ain't pissed yerself, Captain. Lucky yer breeches're muddy and I can't tell.' Stooping down, he handed up the small dead slargapent, gripping it by the tail. 'Here, don't forget your prize. Trooper Hawson will be pleased.'

Lerant reached out for it, and had to shift a foot to balance himself quickly as dizziness and fatigue swirled through him.

'Best I carry the damn thing,' Fallon said, frowning a little in concern before he heaved it up over one shoulder.

Together they made their way carefully along the crossbeam to the place where they must reenter the water to regain the shore, if they were not to climb all the way up the bridge lattice-work and Lerant was too unsteady for that.

'You comin' back covered in blood won't do the men's nerves any good,' Fallon observed, studying the scarlet and crimson splashes soaking his officer's white shirt.

'Right. Good thinking.' Lerant pulled it off over his head and splashed hastily through the shallows to climb up onto the embankment. He shoved the bloodied shirt into the reeds and collected the Myrrghin gun and offered it to its owner with a rueful look. 'I've been too complacent about the methirri bands. I'll re-issue orders for them to be worn at all times.' He snorted. 'Immediately after I've put mine on again!' Realizing Fallon already had enough to carry, Lerant hefted the gun himself.

'Slargapents,' Fallon spat as he stepped clear of the ravine rim. 'Cursed creatures. It's a bad omen.' He mouthed a sudden foul oath and slapped at his forehead. 'Almost forgot! It weren't your shot that woke me. A message came in for y' over the Connector, relayed all the way from Myrrgha City Command. They're waitin' for y' to respond.'

Lerant's curse echoed his Sergeant's feelings. 'Might've known they'd be after me as soon as I reported the bridge was near completion.'

'Shouldn't 've done that.' Fallon muttered sagely, 'Never let your superiors know when you're ahead of schedule.'

Lerant arched an eyebrow. 'Oh? Is there any other advice you've forgotten to pass on to me, Sergeant?'

Spluttering sudden laughter, Fallon slapped him on the shoulder and they strode onward toward camp.

Clear of the gloomy ravine at last, they met a sea of waist-high, thin, blue-green grass stirring in the breeze and flowing down slope before them, flooding out across a rolling landscape. These wild, free plains bred an equally independent native race who resented their aging king's willingness to ally them to Myrrgha by marriage to the Emperor's young niece. Khengha wasn't as safely neutral as Myrrgha pretended.

At the foot of the hill, a group of weather-beaten, dirty-white tents circled a rough timber pole from which waved a red standard marked in its center by two black crossed swords, the symbol of Myrrghin domination, defying the otherwise unbroken expanse of Khenghin tierdrun. Almost invisible in the distance to the south, a hazy smudge marked the border where lay Myrrgha's Smoking Mountains. The river Gallia, over which Kerell Lerant's team worked to construct a bridge ended its journey at the sea, far to the west, at Khengha City. Only a few miles beyond the tents lay a sheltered, farm-cleared valley guarded by a stockaded Myrrghin fortress that had been Lerant's home base for the past few weeks.

He still found it all so incredibly different from Rogha island's icy confinement and isolation.

He turned about, facing the eastern horizon, relishing its warmth and light washing over his face. A new day, a newly-returned life. It felt good, even if there was Myrrgha Command to face.

As soon as they entered the camp proper they drew a small crowd of interested observers, mostly troopers, and some bronze-skinned Khenghinner native guides who left off tending the line of hobbled cavalry horses behind the tents. He carried the dead slargapent to the medical tent, wanting a report on Hawson's condition and thinking the man might like to see revenge had been served.

'Could be they just want the usual term report at the Embassy,' Fallon commented as Lerant paused uncertainly at his command tent flap. 'You're overdue.'

The Sergeant was referring to the Myrrghin Embassy in Khengha City. Lerant had been assigned there first as a liaison officer and only later been sent out onto the tierdrun where his engineering knowledge was needed.

'I hope you're right. Myrrgha City . . . .' He pushed back the canvas flap and stooped to step inside. 'It's not my kind of place.'

Following, Fallon cocked an eyebrow and flicked him a curious glance. 'The Imperial Capital? Most people can't wait to see it.'

'I've seen it before. And I'm not like most people.'

'So I've noticed.'

Fallon watched as Lerant caressed the Sunburst sword-hilt in absent-minded gratitude before unbuckling it and laying it atop his bunk. The covers were undisturbed; reminding him he'd never bothered to go to bed last night and provoking a yawn. He moved to the rear of the tent where a small, folding canvas and wood camp table held the patiently flashing Connector Stone. Regular beats of yellow and green light illuminated the shadowy tent interior, indicating a message awaiting a reply.

'I sure don't want none o' their kind of officer up 'ere takin' your place.' Eying the device warily, Fallon shook his head and his expression became uncharacteristically sullen.

Surprised, Lerant turned and regarded the man. 'Are my Roghin ways so obvious?'

'Well . . . .' Fallon avoided his young Captain's gaze and turned to rummage about the boxed shelves where rations were stored. 'I wouldn't put it like that, exactly.'

He found the bottle he wanted and turned back with a nervous smile.

'All I know is the troops like workin' for you. You're fair-minded, reasonable, and most important, you care about 'em. You've earned their respect and their loyalty.' He snorted, and then uncorked the whiskey. 'You should hear what they 'ave to say about the officers who came before you. There were no tears when Meeren took that arrow, let me tell you.'

Lerant didn't realize he'd sat down suddenly on his bunk until Fallon pushed the metal cup of liquor into his hands.

'Down that, Sir,' the Sergeant advised, sipping at his own cup. 'It'll clear yer head t' speak t' those idiots.' He nodded at the Connector Stone.

'Idiots, Sergeant?' Lerant fought a smile. 'Is that your carefully considered opinion?'

'Damn right it is.' Fallon saluted him with the cup. 'I hate t' tell you this, Sir, but you're right about that recall to Myrrgha.'

The cheer washed from Lerant's mood and Fallon dropped his gaze guiltily.

'It was part o' the original message,' he confessed. 'But you were in no state t' hear that when I found y' by the river with that . . . thing, damn near swallowin' y' for breakfast.' He looked up at Lerant from under graying eyebrows. 'Sorry.'

'It's all right,' Lerant said. 'I understand.'

Suddenly angry, he slammed the fist of his free hand on the bunk beside him. 'Curse them! They could at least have waited until I finish this bridge! First they tell me to hurry, now they drag me away!'

'Well, about that . . .' Fallon said slyly. He hooked a three-legged camp stool to himself and sat down astride it. 'Maybe you could negotiate more time . . . tell 'em about the slargapents. Tell 'em you suspect Magi involvement. It's true enough.'

Lerant nodded and reclaimed his drink. 'I like the way you think, Sergeant.'

Fallon winked. 'We make a good team, we do. Shame t' break us up.'

Lerant snorted a laugh and coughed, choking a little on another mouthful of raw alcohol. 'Then I'd best get this over before I change my mind . . . or get drunk.'

'Do some of m' best thinkin' drunk,' Fallon muttered, his expression unhappy again as Lerant got to his feet and turned back to the Connector Stone.

A small, irregularly-shaped translucent lump that resembled melted glass, or Amber as the Lellghinners called it, none knew precisely of what it was composed, only that is was Magi made. Convenient, the way Myrrgha outlawed all forms of 'sorcery' yet plundered Lellgha for any of its more useful inventions. He passed his hand over the device to stop its flashing and indicate his readiness to reply.

This Connector, now gone clear as it awaited Lerant's voice, was not particularly powerful. The message would need to be relayed all the way to Myrrgha City via the larger, vastly more powerful device installed at the Embassy in Khengha City. That might give Lerant some chance of delaying, of winning a longer stay here on the tierdrun. Clearing his throat and flicking a hopeful glance to Fallon, he spoke up. The Connector immediately flashed golden light in time to each of his words.

'Captain Lerant reporting from Gallia Bridge, as requested.'

There was a pause during which the Connector light faded and became immobile but did not entirely vanish. Then someone could clearly be heard to mutter, 'About time.' The man sounded none too happy, and Lerant wondered if he'd won any bargaining points by testing his superiors' patience.

'Captain Lerant,' the voice continued, setting the Connector Stone to flashing again. 'Corporal Sallik, here. I'll call Chief Commander Davers. He's been waiting for you since before dawn.'

Davers was a stickler for punctuality and obedience to the letter of the law, no matter how absurd. Lerant groaned and resisted the urge to swallow more whiskey. Fallon was under no such restraint. 'Davers!' he swore succinctly and sloshed more liquid from the bottle to his cup.

Lerant did his best when at last the Embassy Chief's irate voice erupted from the Connector, sending much brighter light flaring about the tent. Clearly, he was in no mood for tales of giant slargapent attacks or any other 'half-witted, hastily concocted excuses'. Lerant's heart sank further with each word, a leaden lump in his stomach.

'Those are your orders, Captain. Three days to get your work on the bridge finalized and instruct your replacement. Then you are to set sail for Myrrgha City and report to General Rusark at the War Ministry inside the Imperial Palace. He made it very clear he needs further survey assessment and supply estimates, and he needs them now.'

'Looks like Myrrgha has big plans for Gallia,' Davers concluded. 'Don't fail the opportunity, Captain. Your work on the bridge has been noticed and appreciated. Forget any hysterical talk of so-called 'Seekers'. Out.'

The light vanished abruptly as the connection was cut at the far end.

'Damn,' Lerant swore.

'He sounds jealous,' Fallon said. 'I'd say you're in for a promotion, Sir. Congratulations.'

It was no comfort whatever . . . . Unless, it might help him earn more say in having Parlan transferred from marine front line duty to be placed safely under Lerant's command. So far all his requests had been denied or ignored.

Reclining back on the bunk and stuffing a pillow beneath his aching shoulder, Lerant finished his drink in silence, enjoying the warmth spreading through his veins. His gaze roamed about the tent interior, tallying the things he'd need to pack. Maybe he'd even find Parlan on shore leave in Myrrgha City.

Idly, he ran his fingers over the Sunburst sword-hilt, drawing solace from its now familiar touch. *It will keep you safe.* Parlan had been right. It had saved his life out there today, he thought, listening with half an ear while Fallon vented his opinion of Myrrgha Command. But he couldn't take the sword with him to

Myrrgha City; he'd have to ship it back home, entrusted to the care of Parlan's wife, Annalie, back in Rogha City.

'I'll be back,' Lerant told Fallon. 'You heard. They're planning on expanding up here and they need my so-called expertise. There'll be more bridges to build, count on it.'

CHAPTER SIX

The weather held fine for the first two days, Rhyssa's ship steadily pushing itself through gentle swells, heading due south-west. The third day found Gerion, m'Connor and m'Garran sitting shirtless and barefoot, their legs hanging over the side, catching the bow-sprit wave as they tried fishing with cast-nets. M'Sharral was more interested in the workings of the engines and was below deck.

'Come on, Bruska,' Rhyssa said, firm but gentle as she stepped clear of the hatch, one end of a chain attached to a chest harness held in her hand. 'Watch your head now!' She guided the big man up onto deck, aware he had missed the sunshine, too.

Hearing her voice, the other men turned to watch her progress. She'd introduced each of them to Bruska and he'd accepted them warily but calmly enough in her presence. M'Connor couldn't bring himself to look, could bear to see the body only when it was asleep.

'There you are! Well done! Plenty of sunshine to enjoy and maybe a fish for lunch!' she told Bruska as he settled down, crouched on his haunches on the blanket she'd left for him. She bent to secure the lock of the chain to a solid iron ring set into the deck by the hatch. The man-dog regarded her with something she recognized as Bruska's happy grin. It was difficult for her, too, seeing some of Bruska in familiar patterns of behavior, and somehow seeing his spirit in the man's otherwise blank hazel eyes. If she found it difficult, every glance must destroy m'Connor.

'How much longer until we rendezvous with your friends?' she asked the Weavers who welcomed her with smiles and made space for her to sit with them.

'Two or three days,' m'Garran replied. 'They'll be looking for us at the co-ordinates I gave your Captain.'

'Good,' she said, accepting a fishing net that m'Connor handed to her. Meeting his eyes, she felt warmth flare through her body. It made no sense, but she couldn't deny she was attracted to him and not just the usual physical attraction. There was something about him . . . somehow familiar, something she could trust absolutely.

'The Talaers don't normally allow we 'Soil-Bloods' aboard their ships?' she asked.

'No,' m'Connor said. 'But Lellgha established an alliance with them that goes back centuries.'

'Then,' Gerion finished, 'when they saw what the Myrrghinners had done, they volunteered their ships, since Myrrgha claimed most of ours.'

'You were a trawler fisherman?'

'Yes, and a damned good one, too,' he said with a wink that didn't entirely mask the pain of loss in his dark blue eyes.

'It's good to see Bruska getting a bit more used to ship life,' Rhyssa said, looking back to where the man-dog had sprawled out full length, basking in the warm sun. 'He'll need to accept another change when we transfer to the Talae ship.'

'It'll be much, much smaller than your yacht,' m'Connor warned.

'How many days will we need to travel with them to reach Sanctuary?' she asked.

'None of us really know, exactly,' m'Garran told her, reminding her that amazingly enough, none of them knew precisely where Sanctuary lay.

'I'd judge no more than another five days or so,' M'Connor said. 'Rendezvous is usually half-way.'

'They'll take us to Tol Eabah first,' m'Garran said, 'a refugee clearing station.'

Rhyssa frowned. 'How suspicious will they be of me, a Myrrghinner?'

'We have the Sharing to take care of that,' m'Connor met her eyes with swift reassurance. 'Allow them to shake hands with you and they'll know beyond doubt of your intent. You can't lie to a Lellghinner, and they'll soon enough recognize you for your courage.'

'You'll probably be feted as a hero!' Gerion told her with a grin that faded to gentle sincerity as he added, 'And rightly so.'

Rhyssa laughed, making m'Connor's eyebrows climb in surprise before a smile blossomed on his strong-jawed face. She'd never seen him smile so freely. 'I don't know which rattles me the most, heroine or intruder.'

'None will think of you as intruder,' m'Connor said, his hand brushing hers as he helped her straighten the net ready for casting.

She kept any remaining doubts to herself. The very fact that these men's minds had been . . . altered somehow to prevent them revealing the whereabouts of their home was more than unsettling.

Seeming to understand where her thoughts had wandered, m'Connor said, 'Keying isn't so bad. Myrrgha city uses what you call electricity for lighting and such, doesn't it?'

'Only in the Imperial Palace and its surrounds. It's all very new science,' Rhyssa said, 'a discovery that arose from the use of steam-power.'

'Keying uses a similar form of energy to shut away dangerous memories. The lock will be released when we reach home. Any hidden memories will be returned as soon as the Akkarra restore them through an energy Link.'

'My people call that sorcery,' she said, avoiding looking at any of them as she concentrated on getting the net into the water without snagging any of theirs.

'There would be Lellghinners who'd label your electricity the same way. People fear change, are wary of anything different,' m'Garran said. 'It just takes spending time within a culture until you discover it's all based on science . . . it's impossible for it to be otherwise.'

'I suppose that's correct,' Rhyssa said, giving him a half-smile. 'But . . . I wouldn't like someone making decisions about what I could and could not remember.'

'It keeps our people alive,' m'Connor said, very quietly. 'That's all that matters.'

'And your friend, Bren; these Akkarra beings will have his . . . soul, his life-force and memories intact?' Rhyssa found that impossible to believe despite their assertions.

'When a Weaver dies, that's where he goes,' m'Connor explained. 'To await rebirth. But in Bren's case . . . .'

'His body still lives, I see,' Rhyssa said, unable to resist looking over her shoulder to check on Bruska-Bren. 'But if the soul still exists, wouldn't it naturally be drawn back to the living body?'

M'Connor flinched, and she wished she'd kept her mouth shut. But it worried her to think they all were relying so much on what, to her, seemed logically impossible.

Gerion explained. 'Both the Akkarra and Bren would have assumed he's dead. When the life-line was severed, the Akkarra would automatically reclaim and Hold his soul.'

She shook her head. 'Obviously, I have much to learn before I can begin fitting in with your people.'

'All of us are deeply indebted to you,' M'Garran said, looking over Gerion and m'Connor to meet her gaze. 'There won't be any problems, you'll see.'

Two days later, the Talae ship emerged from a sea-fog, coming up right alongside them, silent and swift. Rhyssa and her crew were astonished to find that it was indeed true that these amazing ships carried a living skin . . . . Sea creatures that gave her a sleek finish that was impervious to rot and cut water-resistance to almost nothing. Every tiny detail of construction came from the sea—railings made of coral, cabin windows, oddly shaped, and made of some kind of translucent living shell that changed with the changes in daylight. The sails were the most wondrous of all, scallop-shaped and able to sense the least change in wind, adjusting without thought.

To Rhyssa, the Talaers themselves appeared forbidding, silent but for brief words in a deep and strange language she didn't know. Their skins were heavily tattooed, blue stained, and their yellowish eyes regarding her with some suspicion although they greeted the

Weavers, and especially m'Connor with an open, child-like joy that moved her deeply.

Bruska however, was deeply unsettled and in the end, she found she had no other option but to use sedation. They'd keep him asleep and below decks in a secure cabin as much as possible for the next few days.

It was quickly decided that given they had no 'unknowns' aboard, and in their concern for Bren, they would bypass Tol Eabah and go directly home, something that she could see immediately lightened m'Connor's heart, easing the grim lines from his expression.

'Four days, they tell me,' he said excitedly, giving her one of those heart-stopping open grins, as he strode toward her. 'Their ships are faster than you will believe. We'll soon be home!' He looked toward Bruska-Bren and she knew he was seeing his friend, whole and healthy, as he'd known him bare weeks ago.

Those days passed faster than she'd have credited, with so much to see and learn about Talae life, their ingenuity in finding all they needed for life without ever stepping foot on land. Their means of sailing, their supreme knowledge of the sea, made her title of High Mariner an embarrassment. She knew no more than a Talae infant by comparison.

'There! The Gateway! Grove Isle and Sanctuary! We're home!' m'Garran called from above decks on the fourth day.

Knowing Bruska was heartily sick of being held below decks, Rhyssa carefully lead him up on deck where he took an immediate, happy interest, finding the smell of land on the breeze.

Taking out her Seeing-scope, Rhyssa found The Gateway was little more than a tower of bleached coral surrounded by a milky blue lagoon edged with the white froth of an ocean determined to smash its way inside. She was certain there was no passage for any ship, no matter how shallow-keeled. But the Talaers, again, reduced her to open mouthed admiration as they expertly navigated the shoals.

'Someone's come out to welcome you,' m'Garran yelled down from up in the rigging. 'There, see, standing along the beach.'

'May I?' m'Connor asked, holding out his hand for Rhyssa's Seeing scope. She gave it over and he put it to his eye, straining to make out any details. After a moment, he lifted his head. 'Oh, no.'

'What's wrong?' Gerion demanded, coming to stand at his friend's side.

'Katya and the children,' m'Connor said, making Gerion frown in an expression that said, So what? Sounding sick, m'Connor added, 'And the Fetrins. They won't have been told.'

Gerion paled, his mouth tightening. 'Damn. What do we do?'

M'Connor held his friend's gaze for a long moment, before finally he said, 'There's no way of breaking this to them gently.'

'But they'll know the Akkarra have him.'

'They'll have been told he's dead,' m'Connor explained. 'They'll see him on deck, or think they do.'

'Oh, flame it!' Gerion cursed. 'I'd not thought of that.'

'Nor had I until now.'

'Too late to hide him, they've spotted him,' m'Garran said, immediately understanding the dilemma and climbing down to them. Bruska stood on what to him were his hind legs, stretched to his full height, the better to see, as he leaned against the coral hand railing.

'They had to see, sooner or later,' Gerion said, noting Rhyssa's dismay.

'I'll go ahead and explain,' m'Connor said. Before anyone could say anything, he vaulted the railing, diving smoothly into the dark blue seas.

'Swims like a fish. Or a Talaer,' Gerion told her, the admiration in the words swamped by a deep concern—how could Bren's fate be explained without terrible shock and grief?

'Taran!' the calls resounded about m'Connor, full of joy, absolutely elated.

Dierna, Sean and Flynn Fetrin raced toward him, outpacing Gerion's family with his much smaller children, all splashing through the warm sandy shallows. Dierna wept with joy at the sight of her returned son, her joy cutting m'Connor to the bone. Her smile faded to puzzlement as Bren didn't react to his mother calling to him. Rather, Bruska cowered away, huddling up against Rhyssa.

'You've come home!' Dierna Fetrin shouted above the others, her skirts clinging wetly to her as she waded out to embrace him. Sean and Flynn, Bren's two brothers, one almost a man, the other still a small boy, leapt through the waves, stopping briefly to slap him on the back in welcome, but their gazes, their heart-breaking smiles, fixed on their brother who drew ever closer as the sleek Talae ship wound through the shoals.

'No, wait!' m'Connor tried to tell them. 'It's not Bren!'

Sean spared him a glance that said, 'that's not much of a joke' and ignoring m'Connor's warning, charged on, diving into the sea and swimming toward the ship. So much for warning.

Dierna, Bren's mother, knew m'Connor better, Sensing his truth, his words hitting hard.

'What do you mean, it's not Bren?' she asked, all the color drained from her face. Somehow, she'd already Sensed her son's Presence was nowhere on the approaching ship. 'The Magi told us they thought they'd felt his collar removed. But they assured us he must still be alive and hidden beneath methirri because the Akkarra didn't have him.'

'But . . . they must have him,' m'Connor began, shock slamming into him. 'He has to be with them! There's nowhere else.' He couldn't get out the beginnings of any kind of explanation, sickened as he watched Sean and Flynn clamber eagerly aboard the Talae ship.

'They don't have him, Taran,' Dierna said, gently insistent and looking at him as if she thought his mind had been affected by his time in captivity. 'So he can't be dead. And if that's not him over there then he has a twin brother I knew nothing of!'

'Dierna . . . .' M'Connor blurted as she looked, whey-faced back to him. 'The enemy, the Methaggars, somehow forced his soul from his body, from his *living* body. I brought it back because I was sure the Akkarra would have him.' He caught her as the shock hit her, taking her to her knees in the gentle warm seas of Home Cove. He could no longer see her expression through the tears stinging his eyes.

'But . . . ' she said, looking up at him, pleading, desperate, 'he *will* find his way back home to us, to the Akkarra? He must!'

M'Connor tried to say yes, of course he will. But she'd have known his doubt and he couldn't speak for the desolation that filled him. He could only hold tighter to her as they heard her sons' anguished cries.

'Mama?' Flynn's plaintiff question sheer agony, 'What's wrong with him? He's scared of us. What's wrong with him?'

Sean's reply, a wall of sorrow. 'He's not here, Flynn. He's not anywhere.'

Kerell Lerant downed the last swallow of grog from his battered tin mug and reached across the cleared area on the wooden deck to collect his meager winnings.

'I'm out,' he said with a yawn. 'Gonna get some sleep.'

A chorus of disappointment arose from the Khenghin merchant sailors sitting sprawled about him in the crew's quarters below deck.

'Hang round, Cap'n. Give us a chance t' let yer win back some more!'

Lerant laughed. 'This'll do me, you keep the rest.'

'One more round?'

'I've been playing hours!'

'All night, in fact. Shade your eyes when you get up on decks—the sun came up an hour ago,' the oldest man advised with a kindly smile.

'You lot are used to working odd hours.' He yawned hugely again. 'I'll need to be . . . . all ship-shape and squared away when we reach Myrrgha City.'

They groaned at the bad pun and threw game-pieces at him, and he was grinning as he stepped out into the hatchway, pleased to have made friends and left them laughing. He had been finding the journey from Khengha to Myrrgha aboard a sluggish merchant ship most relaxing, until yesterday. He just couldn't stay still, felt queasy in a way that had nothing to do with sea-sickness. Unable to figure it, he'd sought to distract himself in the mathematics of the card games and been here ever since.

This was the tenth day of his enforced break from duty as the ship made its laborious way south, clinging to the coastline, wanting to avoid pirates, though Lerant doubted any would be operating so close to Myrrgha. As an officer, he had a private cabin, and he was glad of the seclusion and peace it offered. He opened the door and fell onto the bunk bolted to the bulwark, intending to get up and wash and undress before sleeping. Drowsiness enveloped him in a comfortable cocoon and he allowed it to take him, drifting off to the soothing rolling motion of the ship under sail beneath a fair wind.

'So beautiful . . . ' Sleeping, Lerant smiled and rolled over, hearing Parlan's voice. His brother stood on a ship's deck, looking toward shore, admiring the view of the dazzling blue waters of a coral lagoon surrounding a lushly foliaged, hilly island.

A sudden, shocking blast, then another, shattered the peace. Cannon fire.

'Take the Weavers alive! Kill everyone else!'

Lerant moaned and grimaced, tossing to his other side as the dream abruptly became Parlan surrounded by other Shocktroopers, ready for battle.

'Surrender! Please!' Parlan begged, utterly desperate as he watched the villagers onshore, children among them, scrambling from their burning huts. 'I don't want to hurt you!'

'Be ready!' a voice barked.

'Kerell! Help me!' Parlan cried. 'I can't do this anymore!'

'Hang on, Parlan! I'll get you out of there!' Lerant answered. Frantic, he pushed himself to his brother's side, struggling to change the course of the familiar nightmare, somehow aware he was dreaming but helpless to stop. He reached out to drag Parlan to safety, but his hands were empty air.

'I can't do it, Kerell. Not even for Anni and the boys. Not even for you'

'I'm coming for you! I'll get you out of there,' Lerant promised. 'I'm coming, Parlan.'

Parlan fell to his knees and dropped his musket, and suddenly it was very real, different to all the other times. Lerant could feel the sand shifting beneath his boots; he could smell the smoke, hear other voices shouting and screaming close by, taste the salt on the sea breeze.

'I can't do this anymore,' Parlan cried.

'You *must!*' Lerant shouted, terrified for him. 'Listen to me, Parlan! Keep going, just one last time!'

'No.' Abruptly, Parlan was looking directly into Lerant's eyes, except he wasn't just Parlan anymore, he was something far greater. 'I *won't* do this anymore.'

'No!! Please! Don't!' Lerant pleaded.

Parlan smiled, transcendent calm enveloping him. He turned his head away, drawn by something white and gold, waving in the breeze off to one side. Flowers.

'Don't!' Lerant screamed, powerless to stop him and more afraid than ever, and now not just for Parlan. 'Come back! Stay with me!' Parlan walked away from him, slowly as if in his sleep, his gaze fixed where Lerant dared not look. 'Don't touch it!' Lerant begged, feeling certain it was their death, and worse, that waited there.

Unheeding, Parlan bent and picked one of the blooms. He straightened up again, holding the flower out to Lerant.

Dreading, drawn against his will, Lerant looked down at it. White petals, gold centers. Ice teeth sliced into Lerant's spine. Beautiful. Deadly dangerous. Forbidding. His future. He would not do this again, he had promised himself, never again.

'Annalie? You love daisies,' Parlan said softly, no longer seeing Lerant, but smiling down at the bloom. Carefully, he tucked it inside his tunic pocket, over his heart. He drew a great breath and let it out. Terribly grim and pale, he looked back to the battle. Then, he lifted his gaze to the bright blue sky.

'That's it,' Lerant urged. 'Please. You don't have to hurt anyone. Just come back to me.'

Parlan staggered, choked, fell. Blood spilled from his lips and his hands flexed, trying to close about the arrow impaling his chest.

'No!!!' Lerant screamed, his voice breaking to a wracking sob.

A loud, repeated banging. Muskets? No, a fist pounding on Lerant's cabin door.

'Noon! Chow time!'

Lerant sat up on his bunk, gasping, covered in sweat, a sour sickness rising in his throat.

'Are you all right in there, Sir?' Geadra, the ship's captain, called worriedly from the corridor.

'Y—' Lerant tried to say and threw himself across the tiny cabin, reaching the washstand just in time to avoid throwing up all over himself. The floor and the overhead reversed places and he fell with a resounding thump, dizzy, heaving and shuddering.

He'd had nightmares like this before, seen Parlan dead a hundred times, a hundred ways. He'd always been wrong. Parlan had always been alive. It had just been fear or grog creating terrible images in his mind.

Lerant's head pounded with ferocious pain and he clamped his hands over his ears, still hearing the sickening crack of bone, feeling the sharp pain in his own chest where the arrow was striking his brother. The taste of blood filled his mouth and he choked on it as he heard Parlan's last gargling breath and saw the red stain on Parlan's lips, felt and heard the thump as his dying body hit the ground.

He knew deep inside himself, this was not a nightmare. This was real.

CHAPTER SEVEN

The slave collar had been removed. He'd come home almost three weeks ago. The Akkarra and the Magi were out in the Void again, searching for Bren. It was time he got his Weaving back so he could help.

Sunlight streamed through pine needles, verdant green against a deep, clear blue autumn sky, taking the damp from the mossy lawn of Isle Grove and making the sea-breeze soft about his face. Sitting cross-legged and shirtless, silent and completely still, m'Connor sought the Lock within his mind that allowed that sunlight access to the Weaving pathways in his arms and torso.

His shoulder-blades itched with the feeling that someone or something might attack him from behind. His mind knew his ability to sense when others were near had returned to him, but his body had yet to be convinced. Closing his eyes despite the tension within him, he slipped into the beginning of his Focus, and began hearing the correct harmonics to trigger the Lock.

The hardest part of trying to Weave again wasn't the struggle to overcome the deeply ingrained crippling of methirri. It wasn't the trying to remember the complicated musical steps needed to trigger the Lock. It wasn't even the needing to relax and drop his guard enough to properly enter Focus. It was the giving up on waiting and hoping, and hoping some more. To Weave alone was an admittance that Bren might never be found, that they'd never Weave together again as they'd always done, as they'd first learned to do here in Isle Grove.

Taking a deep breath and letting it go slowly, he tried to return to the state of mind he'd enjoyed before the war. Next, he ran through the musical steps of the Unlocking Progression. They should be as familiar to him as breathing, but it was a deliberately complicated harmonic sequence, designed to prevent someone with beginning ability burning himself alive while trying to Weave too soon. He and Bren had thrived on the challenges of learning this same process, and many others, in tandem with their Magi and through her to their Akkarra-mind sewn into the living fibers of its giant tree. Then, they'd been allowed to try it alone and the feeling was overpowering, all-consuming, exhilarating.

If only you were here with me, Bren. We'd sing this harmony together as always and walk away laughing about which one of us had been worried.

The happy memory wavered, became Bren cowering down in a dungeon pit, howling in terror, his eyes those of a wild animal, his soul cast so far into the Void that the Akkarra had as yet been unable to locate it. A place of chill black nothingness between life and death, the Void was familiar to m'Connor only from the brief moments of his and Bren's Traveling in Ea-form from one place to another in Link with Magi Silsun and their Akkarra, Genoh. They'd been terrified of what it might be like to lose their Link and remain lost in that awful place forever.

Where Bren probably was right now.

Grief tore at m'Connor's self-discipline, but sitting and weeping wouldn't bring Bren back. There was no one to see and probably no one to hear him, but still he looked around self-consciously, embarrassed to realize he'd need to actually sing the Lock Progression aloud to get it right. The gradual tonal vibrations would reach into his mind and trigger the Lock open. Steeling himself, he began to sing again in a lower key, up the scale, then changed to a minor key and climbed back down in half-steps . . . With great relief he found The Progression pouring back into him as if it had never left.

Fine; but Unlocking was the first lesson taught a sixteen year old Apprentice. What would happen when he needed to actively Weave? Without his Akkarra-Brother, Weaving was like trying to see with one eye or run on one leg. How was he supposed to go on like this, missing half of what he was? *Please be out there somewhere, Brother! I beg you. Be there!*

Fueled by his despair and urgent hope, his voice lifted, carried despite his wish to keep quiet. The pine trees about him seemed to blaze with sudden, brighter life, the air about him hummed, the sea crashed on the rocks below, harmonizing, the very earth joined with him, their essences blending . . . . The Weaving-Lock triggered and released. Pure warm energy flooded into him, carrying with it the usual joyful affirmation: Life will always find a way. Let it be.

If Bren was out there, they'd find him. Or so Magi Silsun said, knowing he could Read the doubt in her mind as well as she in his. This was the third time in as many weeks. No Weaver had ever been permitted to Travel the Void at length. He'd argued and they'd countered that even disregarding that rule, his Ea was too disjointed after his long time a captive, that the effort of trying would certainly kill him. He hadn't cared about that, and that was precisely why they'd left him waiting here.

He'd had a restless night, wanting to be part of the search, frustrated and angry he hadn't been included, terrible images of what Bren could be enduring filling his mind. Understanding, but exasperated with his tossing and turning, Rhyssa had finally gotten up, stirred the coals of the fire and made tea for them both. Rhyssa . . . . Her touch had warmed him more than the tea, though she claimed she had none of his people's Empathy.

As the humming sense of the sun's energy began to fill him, the Now of Trance settled within and he let his mind drift . . . .

The horrible odor of burning flesh filled his nostrils. Sickness soured his mouth. His eyes clenched shut, but the glow of the hot irons came closer, closer . . . . Shuddering, and breathing great, gulping breaths of pine fresh air, he forced away the memory of his torture. The stinging, burning pain in the scars on his back persisted and he realized with some alarm he'd allowed the sun unchecked access to his body. Quickly but carefully, he sang the Lock shut again. He scanned himself for injury, sighing embarrassed relief that it was no worse than minor sunburn, affecting the sensitive skin of the scars on his back. A stupid, basic error and one for which he'd be justifiably chided. He hoped Magi Silsun wouldn't comment, though of course she would know. Maybe they were right, maybe he was . . . unwell. Any first year Apprentice would be given a thousand retraining drills for so basic a mistake, let alone m'Connor, a Weaver and a commander, with many lives depending on his judgment.

Sea-salt and sweat trickled over the sunburned scars and he scooped cool, clean water from the basin of the Grove Fountain and tossed it over his back. Within the cool liquid he felt the vibrating essence, the background singing of the Akkarra minds, directing their giant tree roots to deliver water here to the top of the Isle cliffs from who knew what underground source.

'This is great! This is the best!' Bren declared, surveying their shared dormitory room, made just for the two of them now they were senior students of Lellgha City University.

Listening happily to his friend, m'Connor could only agree as he ran his hands over the room's beautifully polished, russet-gold living Akkarra-wood walls. He was as amazed as Bren at how the Akkarra had formed itself precisely to produce a space exactly right for them. Not too big, not taking more of the Akkarra's heart-wood than was their share, but giving more comfort than he'd ever expected even given his being the son of the Connor Clan-Chief.

'Look!'

Smiling, m'Connor watched as his very tall friend jumped up and down, demonstrating that he still wasn't hitting his head on the ceiling. Bren walked quickly, straight and upright, not hunched down, as he entered and re-entered through their doorway—much to the bemusement of their passing fellow-students—then finally threw himself down on his huge bed. A bed whose frame, formed by the Akkarra just for him, was at last big and strong enough to comfortably support his much larger than usual body.

Needing the comfort of the sight, m'Connor lifted his head to look at the giant Akkarra trees, towering above the pines in front of him. They'd formed the ancient dormitory in which their human Magi partners lived here just as had the Akkarra of Lellgha created the University Halls and dorms. It was almost impossible to accept that Isle Grove now held the only living Akkarra in the world, all male, for the females had been lost in the migration across the stars more than a thousand years ago, leaving no chance of beginning a new generation from seed.

Twenty, only twenty. If the enemy ever reached the Grove . . . .

Abruptly, m'Connor sensed his Magi's presence, released from her exhausting Search in union with the Akkarra and her sister Magi. Reunited with her body, awakened, she was already on her feet and coming toward him from inside the Grove. M'Connor couldn't bring himself to step back into the Grove proper, not without Bren at his side. Silsun's full-length tunic glimmered against the backdrop of the sorrowful dark shadows of the Akkarra as she walked toward him, her hair now as white as her sun-bleached robes, her face lined with a grief and weariness that revealed her great age.

He knew the answer, but desperate hope forced him to ask the question regardless. 'Anything?'

'No. I'm sorry.'

Inhaling sharply, m'Connor had to look away from the agony in her eyes. He'd expected the answer, but not the finality he felt in her mind. Had she given up all hope, too, like the others?

'No, Taran, you know I won't.'

'I know,' he murmured, finding his voice rough and hoarse. She allowed him to feel her terrible exhaustion, enough that he would have been unable to stand beneath a similar weight.

'We sought him long and far, almost beyond returning.'

He turned back to her. 'I knew you would. I feared you would . . . .'

'You won't lose me, too.'

He might, if the enemy couldn't be stopped. He felt the tremor of sadness as she Read that feeling from him. Their Sharing wasn't thought to thought, not without permission, although that was rarely needed in a Triad. Except theirs was no longer a Triad.

Silsun's mind recoiled away from that ugly memory, looking for something, anything to distract her. It took less than a moment for her to find what he'd known she would. 'Your scars are hurting. What . . . ?'

He flinched more at the concern in her mind than the sound of her heavy sigh as she realized the reason for his minor sunburn. She took a pace forward, then halted, knowing as did he, that Healing was impossible between them just now. Any physical touch would be unbearable, trebling their agonizing empathy for Bren's loss. He opened his mouth to tell her, no, she was also too drained for a psychic Healing, when he realized that of course he'd already told her. He'd worn that damned collar too long, was still relying on speech where none was needed.

They stood, unmoving a long moment, just watching each other, reluctant to part with such hollowness between them. Other Triads had lost someone to battle, but the Ea, the soul, remained in sight and would someday Return. Never had a Triad suffered . . . this.

Laughter broke their grim mood with as much surprise as relief for m'Connor. Together they turned to watch proceedings down below on the tiny pebble beach where Marc Gerion was, with some amusing difficulty, trying to safely disembark and organize a group of very young children come to The Grove for their weekly lessons. Gerion pretended to hate getting wet and the Wavedancers who towed the small boats knew it.

Provoking the children to helpless fits of giggling, the marine mammals deliberately splashed the man, using their tails to smack the seawater up in small waves about him, then flipping and corkscrewing away, delighted with their prank. Two of the 'Dancers slid briefly up onto the pebbles, seeking the children's patting hands, squealing and chattering deafeningly. Shaking his head, Gerion sent water droplets flying from his dark hair. M'Connor had seen the Gerion of the battlefield use the power in his broad shoulders and thickly muscled forearms to kill a charging armored boar with one punch to the throat. Now, that power was belied by the gentleness and tenderness with which his hand clasped the tiniest child's shoulder, keeping her from falling into the choppy swell. The child he'd rescued from Myrrgha dungeon. The others, too, would have been scarred by the burning of their homes, the butchering of family . . . .

Gerion swiped seaweed from his short beard and threw it back at the 'Dancers who snapped it midair with obvious glee. The children's laughter reached a crescendo and m'Connor smiled, grateful and almost surprised that he could still enjoy such simple fun. Gerion was playing it to the hilt, although he didn't raise his voice, something he knew would upset the traumatized children. He splashed back, stomping his bare feet in the shallows. He'd done this enough times to know to keep his boots tied over his shoulder. A deep affection welled in m'Connor's heart for his friend.

'He's good with them,' Silsun murmured at his side and his happiness multiplied in hers.

'The best,' m'Connor agreed, craning to see if Gerion's other children were among the group. Yes.

'Hush, now! Hush!' Gerion commanded and gradually, as the merriment on the beach stilled, he added, 'Listen and you'll hear them greeting you.'

'They're so big!' one of the youngsters exclaimed excitedly, craning her head backward further and further to try to see the highest Akkarra branches. Gathering themselves into a more or less orderly file, the children began climbing the steep, winding track up the cliff. Pulling on his boots, Gerion followed, both he and his small companions serene in the knowledge that should any one of them slip, the Akkarra would prevent them falling. The beautiful, knotted and curved waist-high balustrade constructed from their living roots saw to that, its handrail gleaming under the morning sunshine, polished by thousands of hands over hundreds of years.

Primona, currently the only Journeyman Magi of the Isle, took charge of the breathless children as they reached the top of the track. Not yet fully trained, she hadn't been permitted to join her Sisters in their searching of the Void. Quietly, she ushered her small students away.

Gerion hurried to him, but m'Connor was unable to meet his friend's gaze, Reading disappointment and sorrow in Gerion's heart. Even though he was not a Weaver, Gerion knew he would have felt m'Connor's joy if Bren had been found.

'Still nothing?' Gerion asked and m'Connor's chest tightened anew for the desperation beneath the words.

'No,' Silsun replied softly.

Gerion grunted as if he'd been hit and m'Connor looked up in time to catch the raw grief in the man's dark eyes. His pain was as much for m'Connor and Silsun as for himself.

'But how?! How can they not find him?' Gerion blurted the frustrated, angry question m'Connor had wanted to hurl at the Akkarra but hadn't because he feared he knew the answer. 'We have his living body over there!' He waved an arm back across the bay toward Home Cove. 'How can they not sense him holding to it? Aren't they supposed to be aware of every soul existing anywhere, anywhen?!'

Her calm fraying beneath her great exhaustion and sorrow, Silsun snapped, 'You know very well they are! You've been there with them many times!'

'Between lives!' Gerion threw back at her. 'So I don't remember! I'm not a Weaver!'

'But I am,' m'Connor interrupted quietly. 'And I do.'

Gerion ran a hand through his already wind and sea tangled hair, made darker by the water that dripped from the strands he brushed back from his brow in annoyance. Sighing as he met m'Connor's gaze, he asked, 'If he's not trapped in The Void, and he's not on the Other Side, then where is he?'

'Bren is gone,' the answer rumbled in all their minds.

M'Connor was accustomed to the overwhelming presence of Genoh, his and Silsun's Bonded Akkarra, but Gerion was not. He paled a little, but as ever pragmatic, recovered quickly to demand, 'Gone where?'

M'Connor flinched, dreading the answer.

'Gone. Like our Brothers . . . Like our Sisters.'

'Or hidden!?' Gerion exclaimed. 'You couldn't see the enemy on our doorstep, how can you be sure Bren is gone!? We can't see anything the way we used to!'

'We Search. All the Ways,' Genoh said, and abruptly, his presence left them.

The giant's terrible loss echoed raw pain through m'Connor. Silsun dreaded the same images of Bren, locked away forever, aware, but beyond reach, beyond hope, until it drove him insane . . . if it hadn't already. Puzzlement and frustration flooded the Akkarra's presence, adding to the thread of impossible hope that kept m'Connor going. Never had a soul gone beyond reach of the Akkarra. *Any* soul, let alone that of one of its Bonded sons.

'Bren isn't gone,' m'Connor whispered, 'He's here!' He put his fist against his chest, over his heart. Silsun brushed his mind and he knew she agreed. Knowing this moment would bring comfort, not pain, m'Connor dared to reach out and place his hand over hers. Conviction, immense, undeniable, flooded through them both. They would find him, impossible though it seemed. They must find him.

'Myrrghin people tell me they still feel their limbs long after they've been hacked off,' Gerion said flatly, bringing m'Connor sharply back from the Sharing. Their enemy was a savage race, not least in their means of so-called 'medicine.'

'Because their limbs *are* still there, in Ea-form,' m'Connor reminded him.

'Ea-forms can never be severed from the Akkarra, Taran. So where is he?'

'Somewhere, Marc. *Somewhere.* And I'll find him. *We'll* find him. I swear it.'

Turning and reaching out his free hand, m'Connor caught Gerion's and brought it up to join his right where it rested over Silsun's. His point made, m'Connor bent to pick up his shirt and sword. 'But for now, we have a Legion to train.'

'Your Arc hits more targets dead-on than any others, Sean,' m'Connor congratulated his youngest Lieutenant with a hearty shake of the man's thin shoulder. Their Legion was a company of one hundred men, divided into five Arcs of twenty. 'Well done.'

Sean Fetrin merely grunted acknowledgment and m'Connor heaved a weary sigh understanding better than any just how hard

Sean had been hit by the news of the repeated failure to find any trace of his brother. 'They work hard,' Fetrin responded, turning his head to deliver a stiff smile, no doubt Sharing his Captain's pain. 'They'll be pleased you've noticed.'

'I have,' m'Connor said, glad of the Empathy evidencing a bond that held Lellgha together despite exile. He gave the shoulder another grateful squeeze and let go.

They walked side by side down the sand dunes toward the mangroves, heading to the village for a hard-earned noon-meal. Most of the other men and women of the Legion had chosen to eat where they were on the training field, or close by, avoiding the heat of midday and relaxing in the rock pools by the bay with its magnificent view of Grove Isle. Leaving the dunes and stepping into the welcome shade of bordering trees, both men ducked low to avoid a thickly leaved branch hanging out over a well-trodden jungle track that was nonetheless overgrown with long clumps of saw-grass. The late summer rains were torrential and m'Connor remained astounded at the rapid regeneration and greenery of the tropics, so unlike the turning seasons of his home's snow-capped mountains.

Invisible from the sea, Home Cove was one of the smaller villages at Sanctuary Bay, its huts and lodge constructed beneath the protection of a cliff wall that rose into one of the island's towering mountains. Here were gathered the families of those Weavers and friends associated with Magi Silsun or the Connor and the Fetrin and other mountain clans—prime targets for the Methaggar.

M'Connor veered left to avoid the mangrove swamp and lagoon around which the track circled and into which ran a small fresh water stream that tumbled in a series of cascading waterfalls, born high above in the central plateau. Closer to the water source stood massive hardwood trees overgrown by tangler vines and adorned with an ever-moving rainbow of parrots playing noisily among vivid flowers. Drunk on nectar, the birds happily gorged on any fruit the villagers couldn't reach or didn't want.

The bow and matching quiver slung over his shoulder and across his back made m'Connor itch beneath his loose shirt and lizard-leather vest and he adjusted its hang. He needed to wash off in fresh water rather than salt. He'd taken a quick dip in the sea to rid himself of the sticky sweat and smell of a long morning's combat training, but the humidity had him sweating anew, making him all the more glad one of the Healers on the training ground had seen to his sunburn. The steamy air was thick with the promise of another downpour despite yesterday's monstrous storm. His stomach grumbled, reminding him he hadn't eaten. Noon-meal with the Fetrin family had become a daily ritual.

Beyond the bordering jungle, the track met a well-made path inlaid with stone that kept it from becoming a muddy quagmire and allowed the villagers easy access from one home to another and to the central lodge. Old m'Hallon called greeting to them as usual from where he sat cross-legged on the porch beneath the low-slung palm fronds of his thatched hut. His gnarled, sinewy hands busy repairing a fishing net and his age-creased face was as always, adorned by a cheerful smile. He'd once been Silsun's Chief Weaver Captain, but now, bent and partly crippled by both age and wounds, had been retired but was a source of constant useful information.

'More fish for dinner!' the old Weaver commented with a grin. 'What I'd give for some wheat bread, cheese and cow's milk!'

The memory of being starved in the dungeons of Myrrgha was too raw for m'Connor to find comment, but Sean happily agreed fish was becoming monotonous. Lellghinners would not eat flesh from another mammal, so the wild pigs on the island were of no use to them. But they'd proven a life-saver when it came to feeding Bruska who'd been brought up on beef and pork.

A desire for privacy rather than any sense of shame had dictated the relative distance of the Fetrin's home, tucked behind an abutment of cliff and a cluster of trees. Their neighbors offered only solid support and respect of their great courage. But, they disliked the smell of stewing meat, not to mention seeing m'Connor and Sean delivering the bloodied carcasses of whatever wild animals they'd succeeded in hunting down on the vast island.

'They're disgusted because it's Bren's body doing the eating,' Sean commented, Reading m'Connor's reaction to the talk with m'Hallon. 'Lots of people kept dogs back home.'

'Dogs that ate fish and fowl. Bruska is a Myrrghin dog. He likes his red meat,' m'Connor countered, impressed at his young friend's perception. Or then again, how much was m'Connor projecting? He had to remember things he'd once taken for granted, like the etiquette of Shielding the depth of private emotions. He now had a much better understanding of why Myrrghinners were nervous around Lellghinners.

Watching the living body of the man he and Sean both loved more than life reduced to drooling at the smell of raw meat, leaping on it and ripping it while using those powerful, once clever hands like paws . . . . Bren had been able to coax the most intricate of melodies from his lyre, a beautiful musical instrument he'd made himself and now sat unused in a corner.

'They don't like their children seeing Flynn walking him on the beach, either,' Sean added heavily.

'It's a dog spirit. It adores children and enjoys playing with them.'

'But when they laugh, their parents don't know where to look.'

'They're afraid,' m'Connor said. And he couldn't blame them for that; Bren m'Fetrin was walking proof of a fate they all faced. 'Sorry,' he added quickly, giving Sean a glance in apology for the blunt emotion he'd been unable to Shield.

Sean shrugged. 'It's hard, I know.'

Fetrin's home came into view as they rounded a clump of red-flowered bushes draped with squabbling parrots. Sean left his bow and sword hanging on their hooks under the palm-fringed eaves by the door. Squaring his shoulders and giving m'Connor a solemn regard, he ducked low under the lintel of the open front door. Divesting himself of his own weapons and hanging them well clear of the damp, m'Connor shifted from foot to foot, weary, wanting to sit down on the low bench by the door, but holding back and wanting to give Sean a moment's privacy to gather himself after being greeted by Bruska rather than Bren.

'Taran?'

He looked up to find Flynn, only nine years old, watching him uncertainly from the doorway. 'He knows you're here. He's whimpering. Will I let him out?'

'No. I'll come in. Thanks, Flynn.' He gave the boy a smile and a quick ruffle of the gold-streaked red hair that was the Fetrin family's unofficial banner. 'I saw you both on the beach earlier. He's looking well. You're doing wonders with him.'

The boy flashed a great grin that tore at m'Connor's heart, reminding him vividly of the Akkarra-Brother he'd lost. 'Did you bring Bruska his treat? He's missing Rhyssa's cakes, she's late,' Flynn asked.

'I have something else he'll like, but Rhyssa will be here soon,' M'Connor assured and patted the pocket inside his damp linen shirt; he still had some of the bread and cheese he'd taken with him to the training ground.

Rhyssa was indeed late. M'Connor had been unable to Sense her presence as he approached the house. He wondered what could be keeping her. She looked forward to these meals, a time of getting together with the only family she now knew—with the exception of Gerion, Katya, and their children, this was her only place of unreserved welcome. She was respected, she had come to be trusted, but she was still a Myrrghinner, and the refugees who had suffered at the hands of her people understandably kept their distance.

'Hello, Taran,' Dierna Fetrin greeted, busy with tending pots and pans on the hearth stove and blotting the beaded sweat from her brow. It was even hotter in here.

'Hard to believe I'd want more rain after yesterday's storm, but as long as it doesn't drown us all or bring the roof down again, it'd be good to break the stickiness out there,' m'Connor commented, stooping low to add the usual kiss to her cheek.

'It'd be nice to be able to breathe again,' she agreed, leaving off fanning her flushed face to accept his greeting. It both touched and embarrassed him a little, the way she insisted he regard himself as another of her sons. There were only a few ingots of red in the solid silver of her hair now, he noted, and her round, kind face showing lines of strain and exhaustion. He couldn't imagine how she managed.

She patted his arm in understanding. 'It's all right, Taran. Don't fret so much. You're home. It's better than . . . before.'

M'Connor merely nodded, going along with the lie. The long months of their capture, of not knowing their fate, would have been an agony. But this . . . this was worse.

The small, circular room was heady with the aroma of a very heavy handed use of cooking spices. It still couldn't completely mask the odor of the hunk of wild boar that Dierna was stewing for Bruska. Chunks of meat bubbled in the big black iron pot on its hook over the glowing coals of the hearth fire. The storm had washed away the outside kitchen. He and Sean and Gerion would finish rebuilding it for her tonight.

'Hrowf?' Bruska growled low, a sound of joy and impatience m'Connor couldn't ignore any more than he could the body's towering presence. Although he wasn't standing straight and tall as had been Bren's habit but stooped a little. The dog wasn't used to standing on two legs.

Plastering a smile on his face and bracing in case the man-dog tried to leap at him in excited greeting, m'Connor turned around. 'Hello! Did you enjoy your walk?'

'He did,' Flynn answered for him. 'Wave-Dancers came out to play with him in the water.'

'Ahh. That explains the wet hair.' M'Connor's smile eased into more genuine pleasure as he saw Flynn's simple happiness. 'He's gaining weight,' m'Connor said to Dierna who was taking time out from cooking to watch them.

'A little,' Dierna agreed, returning his smile with affection.

'He's eating like a horse!' Flynn said proudly.

'Or a dog,' Sean muttered under his breath, eying the bowl of cooked boar meat distastefully.

Ignoring his elder brother, Flynn handed the bowl to m'Connor, both pretending they couldn't see the man-dog beginning to drool down his chin. 'Now we know what he likes best, he eats well,' Dierna said, joining the tacit disapproval of Sean's comment.

Accepting the bowl and the duty of trying to train Bruska to eat with his hands, if not a spoon, m'Connor sat cross-legged on the reed matting that covered the earthen floor by the cooking fire. Seated on a cane chair by the table, Sean nodded thanks as his mother gave him a bowl of grilled fish, griddle-bread and steaming vegetables picked from the little kitchen garden behind their home. Keeping his balance, m'Connor held out a strip of meat, refusing Bruska's attempt at snatching it with his teeth and forcing him to lift a hand palm up.

'That's it!' M'Connor congratulated as the dog-man took the meat with fingers rather than teeth and lifted it to his mouth.

Bruska gulped a second strip of meat and looked at them with a great panting grin. It wasn't Bren's smile, but rather the happy lolling grin of a dog that knew it had pleased its masters. Unable to bear it, m'Connor looked away, using the pretext of collecting more food and in the process catching Dierna's tear-filled eyes. She missed her son's smile, too. Renewed hatred for Inquisitor Zaraxan burned away m'Connor's appetite.

'Thank you for hunting for him,' Dierna said, approaching with m'Connor's dinner on a tray which she placed on a low table to his right. 'Eat. You must be hungry after working with the Legion all morning. I suppose Rhyssa will be here soon?'

'Thank you, Dierna. She'll be on her way,' M'Connor said and commented, 'Sean's Arc has the best archery score by far.'

'Really?'

'Absolutely.'

Dierna returned to the hearth, smiling as she collected boiling water for their tea and filled the pot. She carried it to the main table, put it down and gave Sean a hug. M'Connor was amused to see his young Lieutenant blush and squirm like a small boy at his mother's attention.

Bruska gave a low barking whine indicating he didn't like being made to wait, and those once articulate fingers pawed clumsily at m'Connor. Still, it was a major improvement on the way the dog-man had eaten when he'd first returned home, snarling and snapping at everyone until Rhyssa arrived to calm and feed him. He'd barely eaten a single full meal until she'd insisted the Fetrins break the Lellghin cultural taboo and kill and cook red meat for him. It had been eat beef or starve when they'd been slave-prisoners in Myrrgha City. He hadn't had the heart to tell the Fetrins that in fact Bren had grown to prefer red meat.

'The Wave-Dancers like hunting for him, too,' Flynn put in, adding kindling sticks to the cooking fire. 'It's fun! You should see them playing and splashing together! They have a wonderful time of it!'

'You do well to look after him so carefully,' m'Connor complimented sincerely and was rewarded by a blush that matched the boy's russet hair.

'It's a dog, they like dogs!' Sean muttered.

'Sean!' Dierna rebuked. 'Stop it! Your brother will return some day, I know it.'

'Then you know more than the Magi,' Sean countered mutinously. Understanding the source of his anger, Dierna brushed his head with a gentle touch before returning to her work, saying no more.

Flynn's former happy expression was gone. 'What did they say?'

M'Connor held the boy's earnest gaze. 'They won't stop searching.'

'Yet in all this time, not even the Akkarra have found a trace of him!' Sean exploded, pushing away his plate and standing. 'While we go on living with this! It's blasphemy to so defile my brother's body. Let him go!' Leaving his meal, he stormed from the room, as he'd done several times since m'Connor's arrival with the thing that had taken the place of his brother.

Flynn came closer and whispering, asked, 'He doesn't mean that, does he?'

'Of course not. But hope . . . hope can hurt. Bren will find his way back to us, I know it. He won't give up and nor will we,' m'Connor said, being very careful to Shield his doubt and hoping Flynn didn't yet have Sean's Talent.

'He's half-way home and the rest will follow,' Dierna told him with a kiss to the top of his head. Then, looking across at where Bruska had curled up on his blankets, having successfully gulped down all the meat from the plate, she added, 'He's finished; Taran. Come to the table and eat with us. I'll keep some hot for Rhyssa.' She returned to the hearth to collect some more flat-bread that was close to burning.

Flynn, following m'Connor's gaze to Bruska, noticed the dog-man's drinking bowl was empty. He got up and collected the earthenware bowl and went to the basin to fill it from the pitcher and take it back. A shadow fell across the room as Sean returned to stand looming in the doorway. 'Rhyssa's here,' he announced.

Distracted, Flynn turned sharply to look at him and lost his grip on the bowl. It fell, shattering to shards on the hard clay floor. Shuddering, m'Connor tried to fight back the images filling his mind, taking him back—

'On your feet, slaves! Stand!'

The earthenware dinner bowl fell from m'Connor's hand, spilling the nearly raw meat of his daily ration, mixing it with the shards of broken pottery flying across the stained stone-slab floor of the cell he, Gerion and Bren shared.

'Kneel before me!' Inquisitor Zaraxan ordered, adding to the Captain of the Guard. 'The two younger ones. I'll work with them today, I think. Yes, the tall red-haired Weaver, the perfect beginning. I'll soon find the source of their power.'

'Come after him and die,' m'Connor warned, and bent to collect a razor-edged piece of pottery. Then, he heard a child's scream, heard Zaraxan laugh, looked up to see them threatening the little child.

'Steady, Taran. We'll take the bastard next time.' Bren's fingers closed like girding talons about m'Connor's right arm, holding him back.

He tried to tug free and the grip became a much softer hand but just as insistent, the voice Rhyssa's . . . . 'No, Taran. Don't. Come now, stay with us. Steady . . . .'

He sagged, cold with sweat, trembling from head to toe, glad he'd been sitting down when this assault from his past had hit. It'd been worse than the others, longer, clearer . . . . He pressed the heels of his hands into his eyes but could still see the resignation and farewell in Bren's expression as the Methaggar took him away.

'Breathe, Taran,' Rhyssa urged, her hands gently but firmly kneading the trembling muscles of his forearm, steadying him. Sean and Dierna stood at m'Connor's other side, called there by the agony of his reliving, their hands holding firm to m'Connor's shoulder, Sharing too much of the pain.

Obeying, M'Connor took a deep breath, focusing on the sound of the parrots chattering away happily beyond the open window, the scent of corali flowers thick and heady above the fainter salt tang of the sea breeze. Bright sunlight, streaming through the doorway, bathed the earthen floor in a rectangle of gold and highlighted the bronze skin of Rhyssa's bare feet in her open sandals.

Lifting his head, m'Connor caught sight of Flynn watching, wide-eyed and afraid, not understanding, the dog living inside his eldest brother whining distress beneath his petting hands. Bruska always seemed to be dragged back into the memory along with m'Connor. Once, it had given them hope that the odd Linking might help them find Bren. But nothing had come of it other than terrifying Bruska.

Steadying himself on the table and nodding thanks for the support, m'Connor got to his feet. Flynn was crouched on the floor, and, glad of the excuse with his legs still shaking beneath him, m'Connor went to his knees beside the boy, Rhyssa crouching down, too. Gently, he squeezed Flynn's arm before aiding Rhyssa who had bent closer to the man-dog huddled on a mound of blankets on a wooden pallet in the corner.

'It's all right now, Bruska,' she soothed. 'It's all right. It's over. They won't touch you again. I swear. It's over, be easy . . . .'

Gradually, the man-animal's trembling ceased, its eyes never leaving the reassuring promise in Rhyssa's regard. Eventually, Bruska accepted the cake she'd brought for him and settled back to its doze. Standing, m'Connor looked to the family who were pretending to finish their meal. Sean had returned to his plate, and Flynn had cleaned away the broken pottery and was looking for another bowl for Bruska's water.

M'Connor returned to them with a murmured word of apology that Dierna refused, giving him a swift hug that ended with wary advice. 'Why don't you let the Magi help you? They can stop this pain.'

'And stop the memories with it!' m'Connor snapped more sharply than he intended. 'I might see something I've missed.' He gripped the edge of the table, feeling his knuckles go white as he looked down at Bren's sleeping body, Rhyssa still watching over him. Asleep it looked like nothing was wrong. She came to m'Connor to wrap her arms about his waist in a hugging embrace made all the warmer as he opened his arms to draw her close against him.

'Bad?' she asked. He nodded. She'd seen him go through this before.

A surge of a grim resolve, a melancholy-triumph flooded the Sharing her touch brought to him. Dipping his chin to look down at her, he guessed, 'You've found it!'

'Yes. Up in the cliffs, about three miles from here, hidden by overhanging jungle. Taran, it's enough, it's more than enough. It could reclaim your homeland.'

'That explains these scratches?' Gently, he rubbed his thumb over a shallow scratch on her cheek and another on her chin. There were more on her bare arms, too. She wore only a sleeveless tunic and trousers in the heat.

'You have to climb down a bit and push aside the brush to find it. But there it is, a huge, bright yellow band! And, handily, it's close by the saltpeter in those caves.'

'You've found the sulfur?' Dierna asked with a smile.

Rhyssa nodded and Flynn cheered but Sean only commented sourly, 'Fine. Now all you need do is talk the Council into using black-powder to kill.' It was true their Leaders might veto the entire plan, and m'Connor couldn't help but share his young Lieutenant's pessimism.

'There are ways of using explosives that can aid victory without killing,' Rhyssa said, and m'Connor realized she hadn't been deflated by the comment. She'd expected it, and in her usual thorough manner, was working on finding a solution.

'Let the Council try to stop *me* defend my family! They won't take us meek and mild like they did before,' Dierna snapped sharp and sure. She bent to pull a blanket over Bruska who was sound asleep, drained by his sensing m'Connor's reliving.

'You'll need a lot of iron and a smelter to make the cannons,' Sean said, just as dismissively. This time, he earned a swat from his mother, but again, he was right.

'Sometimes you don't need cannons,' Rhyssa said very quietly.

'You're all scratched. I have some salve you can use,' Dierna said as she put another platter of hot bread and grilled fish on the table. Rhyssa nodded and added thanks for the food.

'I'll tend to you . . . later,' m'Connor promised with a sly smile that matched the caress of his thumb over her long, smooth brown throat.

She stood on tiptoe and kissed him, the taste of her lips sweet against her gritty determination to do what was needed. She was much more an exile than any Lellghinner at Sanctuary and her discovery would kill her own people, not just the hated Methaggars, but possibly her two brothers. With Bren's soul-less body on the floor at his side, m'Connor could feel little pity for the enemy, but his stomach knotted for Rhyssa's conflict.

'After, I'll show you the sulfur,' she said, as ever full of purpose.

That night, Rhyssa jolted awake, darkness thick about her, the warmth of m'Connor's body at her side gone as he sat abruptly upright. 'What?' she demanded, a knot of sour fear already telling her the answer.

'The Magi call for aid. Tol Eabah,' he said. 'Under attack.'

'Oh, no! Magi Liraith is in charge there?' Rhyssa remembered the kind little woman, the first Magi she'd ever met, who'd welcomed her to Sanctuary and who had since volunteered to help with the refugees at the way station, several hundred miles closer to the mainland.

'Yes. And m'Singh and m'Akram. They can't hold against so many.'

Against the glimmer of starlight that spilled through the small, open window of their beach-hut bedroom, she saw m'Connor stand and pull on his trousers. She swung her legs from the bed and lit the lantern then flung a robe about herself to follow him into the small living area. He didn't stop there but threw open the front door and strode out onto the porch to lean onto the balustrade and fix his gaze across the silver-spangled black of the water between Sanctuary and Grove Island.

'You're going over there?'

'No time,' he said curtly and turned to look back up the beach-track toward the tall shadows of the mangroves on the other side of the low dunes.

'Isn't Tol Eabah Shielded?'

'It was, but the bastards found it somehow. Silsun suspects Methaggar masking their ships.'

The sound of running footsteps drew Rhyssa's attention to the track. A disheveled Marc Gerion appeared and in a few strides came up the steps. Rhyssa blinked at him, standing there in the starlight that danced from the sea behind him and from the dew that gleamed on the palm frond roof overhead. His bare chest heaved and he wasn't wearing his boots. It could still startle her, the way he and m'Connor, through their Magi, could communicate telepathically.

'Marc will pull me back if I go too far,' m'Connor told her quickly, turning to give her what he must hope was a reassuring regard.

'Go? Where? You said—'

'Travel. The Magi of the Grove have summoned all their Weavers. We're to Channel to support them.'

'Channel? I don't—'

'Marc will explain.'

With that, m'Connor sat down cross-legged on the bare bamboo floorboards. In the darkness, she saw the flash of white as his eyes rolled back but he remained sitting straight and tense, his right arm extended toward the Grove.

'It's a Travel-Trance,' Gerion told her and moved to stand close at m'Connor's back. 'He'll see and hear along with the Magi and their Link will carry his Weaving energy to strengthen them when they reach Tol Eabah. Don't worry; I won't let him give them too much.'

'Give them too much what?'

'Of his *Ea,* his life-energy.'

Rhyssa stared at him in sudden fear. M'Connor made a low grunting sound, as if someone had punched him. His fingers stretched, reaching, trembling, straining . . . . She couldn't see it, but she'd have to be dead not to feel the energy that thrummed about him. Then, faint but growing brighter, tendrils of green light wound about his bare forearm. She swallowed over a dry throat.

She'd never seen that before. He'd been advised against what they called 'full' Weaving until he was fully recovered.

'I thought they told him he wasn't strong enough for this?' she said, rubbing her arms against the chill of the sea-air.

'He's ready and they need all they can get. Don't move between him and his line of sight with the Grove,' Gerion warned unnecessarily. Then, he added as casually as if they'd met for dinner. 'Might as well get comfortable, this could take a while.'

CHAPTER EIGHT

'Help us! Cannons blasting the wall! Enemy soon ashore!'

At the Magi Home on Isle Grove, Primona, too, came suddenly awake with Liraith's desperate cry resounding in her mind. As yet only a Journeyman Magi, she wouldn't normally have heard such a long distance summons. Liraith dared Send from The Void to reach The Grove so urgently. Primona Sensed the Grove's Superior was already moving, leaving her room, heading for the Great Hall.

'Everyone to me! We Travel!' Silsun commanded from outside in the corridor.

Everyone? Excitement and trepidation rippled through Primona; Journeymen were permitted to Travel no farther than their home surrounds, not enter The Void. This would be her first time back there in this lifetime. Knowing a Travel-trance would make her cold, all the more while wearing only a sleeveless night-tunic, Primona took her blue woolen cloak from its wall hook, her bare feet silent on the terracotta tiles and the warmer green and gold patterned wool rug that ran the length of her beautiful room. Its living Akkarra-wood walls began to glow softly, lighting in response to her need. Her Akkarra-mind, Hilea, had shaped and colored her room to her wishes, including a pretty flower vine-entwined opening for a window that gave a glorious view to the sea.

'How did they find Tol Eabah?' Another Magi asked the question Primona hadn't dared voice.

Primona came to a breathless halt in the diminished ranks of her Magi sisters. High Lady Silsun strode into the Hall to regard the few remaining, the lines of her thin face grim and stern, her blue eyes dark with urgent calculation.

'There are at least two Methaggars, Liraith believes. Call your Weavers to Link to you immediately!' she commanded. 'We have no sunlight. We need all the Ea-strength they can Channel for us, and more. Be warned—to accept and relay such a potent Link, you must remain in physical contact with your Akkarra at all times.' She eyed Primona sharply as she repeated, 'At all times! Your Akkarra are ready to assist. Hurry! Outside! We Travel instantly. There will be some Tearing but there's no time for the usual progression.'

The gathered Magi murmured understanding and small green-gold spheres blossomed from the glowing palms of their hands to lessen the darkness outside. With no one on guard—a task Journeymen or Weavers were usually given—oil lanterns would have been a danger to anyone in Traveling Trance. The Hall's great, carved twin doors swung open as their housing Akkarra responded.

'A moment, Primona,' Silsun ordered.

'Yes, High Lady?' Primona halted to turn to her Superior nervously.

'I don't like asking The Void of you so soon. But, we need all our Magi . . . .'

'. . . and we might be about to lose Liraith,' Primona Read the rest clearly.

'I'm going with you.'

Silsun nodded approval. 'Good. You won't go unguarded, nor as quickly—follow the usual Progressions. Captain m'Connor will help you.' She Sent, *'Taran?'*

'Here. Liraith can't hold,' she heard him tell Silsun. *'Can we Summon any Wave-Dancers in the area? They can help the younger children swim down into the sea caves.'*

'Good thinking. Elena will call them. Help Primona prepare. You know what she'll see.'

M'Connor would indeed know, better than any. Grounding him, Primona could feel the unique power of Marc Gerion. He wasn't a Weaver but was a natural Guardian, an ally of the Elements, and had somehow managed to keep m'Connor from dying, or worse, Fading, when his Weaver Bond with m'Fetrin had been so savagely cut in the dungeons of Myrrgha City.

Primona lowered her personal Shield and Sent, *'Captain?'*

'You'll be all right. Hilea can draw us both back instantly if need be,' was all m'Connor said by way of greeting. His mind was preoccupied, so much so that he couldn't conceal a trace of annoyance at being shunted to the 'baby-sitting' duty that kept him from more closely protecting Silsun. He was worried, too—had his time with Myrrgha lessened his ability as a Weaver?

Primona hurried out of the Hall beneath the high vaulted arch with its beautiful and ever-changing rainbow image windows. Outside, she ran down the ancient stone steps and on into the Grove, finding the sea breeze cold and redolent of salt and fish. Distant from the dark ocean, tiny gold points of lantern-light glimmered from the Talae ships returning from their fishing. Any Talae allies closer to Tol Eabah would already be hurrying to the rescue.

She drew her cloak closer, stumbling a little on the last step, unable to resist looking high into the vast leafy canopy overhead. Towering, shadowed sentinels against a star-strewn sky, graceful and silvered by moonlight, the Akkarra tree-bodies dwarfed their human kin. Primona gave a quick touch to her forehead in respect, the soft, bright green moss floor cool beneath her bare feet as she ran lightly between the other giants to go to Hilea and sat down with her back pressed against the tree trunk—the physical contact necessary for Traveling.

'The cursed methirri weakens me! They're coming!' Liraith cried.

'We Travel! Now!' Silsun commanded.

Shutting her eyes and feeling very nervous, Primona tried to remember the exact sound she needed to reach the higher level of consciousness to exit and follow her sisters.

'Like this,' m'Connor said, allowing her deeper into their Link the better to hear the correct harmonic sequence he was using. He had a truly fine tenor voice, steadying and energizing her all at once. She hummed the same progression, her deep contralto carrying her Ea into blending with the sounds and following m'Connor deeper into Hilea's Presence. Safely cocooned, she allowed herself to drift swiftly up and away, exasperating m'Connor as she rushed his 'go' chord.

The thrill of flying swamped any other emotion as the three of them soared higher and higher, Sanctuary's beaded string of islands dark specks on the glittering sea. A little way ahead, shining against the black and silver of a starlit sky, Primona could see the blue-white orbs that were her sister Magi, moving forward and up like sparks from a fire. Trailing about each were the shimmering gold-dust threads of their accompanying Weavers.

'Now!' Silsun commanded. *'Together! Tol Eabah!'*

She and her sisters vanished. Hastily, Primona and m'Connor leapt after them into the Void, its nothingness of cold and dark closing around them. Primona might have been afraid but for m'Connor's sure Link with Silsun. Its glowing line drew them unerringly onward, unbreakable other than by the horrifying and incomprehensible hunger of methirri.

Golden sunlight suddenly streamed through a pin-point portal ahead, breathtakingly beautiful amid the dreadful dark. Silsun had safely found the correct Focus for them all, as was her duty. Daylight drew them with a fierce, joyful magnetism and the small, green island of Tol Eabah came whirling into view, spinning dizzyingly far beneath in a brilliant blue ocean speckled with whitecaps.

'I can't kill again!'

The distressed male voice yanked Primona painfully down and sharply away from her sisters, tearing at hers and Hilea's presences like a strong wind hitting a smoke spiral and completely severing their Link with m'Connor. A black wall of filth rolled up about Primona, blinding, as slick, thick and foul as sewage and mud.

'M'Connor?!' she Sent in alarm, Seeking and finding nothing. Her Link with Hilea, though strained, wasn't broken, but where was the Weaver?

This madness must stop!

Who? Where had that cry come from? Whatever its source, that voice was her only anchor in sudden black fear and it drew her despite her effort to keep her distance. It wasn't a Magi, it wasn't a Weaver, it wasn't even a Lellghin villager at Tol Eabah. There was a stain of Severing-Stone about it . . . .

A Myrrghinner, an enemy! As with all his kind, he wore a tiny piece of methirri on a leather band about his forehead.

'Go to him,' Hilea ordered, swamping her with relief as his Presence suddenly fully enveloped her once more.

'What happened? Where were you? Where's m'Connor?' Primona demanded.

Her blindness vanished. Sunlight dazzled her, dancing from the white-frothed tips of dark green ocean swells splashing about her Ea. A rust-gray barnacle-encrusted metal wall loomed above her, the hull of a steam-driven Myrrghin warship, completely buried in Shadow. So much methirri! It should be impossible that she could see the ship and hear the voice that came from within it, somewhere below decks.

'You must go to him,' Hilea repeated, ignoring her puzzlement.

'Where are the others? Is m'Connor safe?'

'Your sisters have called him to aid the children. He fears for you. I cannot reach him. None can see or hear us so close to . . . that. You <u>must</u> go to the soldier.'

'How!? I can't get through that!' Her very Ea trembled before the threat of so much Severing-Stone.

No more! The soldier's terrible despair sliced into her mind as strong as the Calling of newly found Weaver to Magi, yet different.

She was meant to be here, to Link with him. The tiny amount of methirri in the diadem he wore would never protect him against a Magi's power, though he'd been told it would. A sudden shove from something unidentifiable swept her through the methirri wall and into the ship without so much as a faint brush against the Shadow.

Her Ea melted into the stranger's mind and she was there, behind his eyes, feeling his trembling, smelling the terror in his

139

and his companion troopers' acrid sweat beneath the sharper odor of vomit. He was hot and cramped, other bodies, more troopers, pressing against him on either side. His breathing was rapid, laboring in the thick air of the enclosed quarters. He sat among other red and black coated and armored men below decks, his shaking hands covering his ears against the deafening sound of cannon fire.

His name was Parlan Hollin and he would give anything to be anywhere else.

Blessed silence fell as the cannon barrage ceased, but the respite was brief. A strident blaring horn, a call-to-arms, brought the soldiers to their feet. They charged up the stairs in a thunder of boot-heels and clanking armor to cover the warship's fore-deck, like spiders spilling from an egg.

Reluctant but resolute, Parlan checked the straps of his sword and musket, and followed. Beyond the gloomy hold the glare of searing tropical sunlight momentarily blinded him. He took his place in the assembled ranks, standing rigid at attention, facing a red plumed-helmed and cloaked Myrrghin commander. In the shadows further aft, Primona sensed the implacable, cruel will fueling the others' kill-lust. Methaggar Lords, two of them, their loathsome essences searching, probing like daggers through the aetheric wash of minds, seeking mutinous emotion or thought.

Parlan must have expected the test. His mind went suddenly still, focused on the one thought . . . *So beautiful.*

He had great aesthetic sensibility, capable of escaping into the loveliness of what was to him a most unusual, lush, tropical beauty. He concentrated on the view of the dazzling blue waters of the coral lagoon surrounding the densely foliaged, hilly island. Colorful parrots and white-grey gulls, startled by the cannon fire, circled agitatedly, their cries carrying on the sea breeze. The pang of joy at what he saw was as painful as a wound for a man who noted every fresh bud, every seed-head on wild grass, every birdsong. The battleship, steam-engines silent, glided under black sails as smooth and sure as any predator creeping to the kill.

Satisfied with the obedience if not the loyalty of the troopers they'd Scanned, Primona felt the Methaggar Send their orders through their minions.

'Kill the Magi!' The Myrrghin Commander repeated. 'But take the Weavers alive! Hear me! Take the Weavers alive!'

The ranks moved, scurrying down thick rope nets into longboats where blue-coated sailors manned the oars. Fully-loaded, Parlan's boat moved off and they were ordered to check their methirri bands. 'Fix bayonets!'

Parlan obeyed, had killed with it before, seen men die, struggling, impaled and bloodied by the long, triangular blade, and wanted nothing so much as to never do that again. The beach was closer now and through him, Primona could see the burning thatched huts of the Lellghin refugee village. Dismayed, she saw that even the palm trees about them were ablaze and the once sturdy encircling stone wall shattered by the cannon barrage. Crimson flames and black smoke lunged, whipped by the sea breeze, as eager as the Methaggar to consume, to devour.

'Surrender! Please! I don't want to hurt you!' she heard Parlan's silent plea.

The ranks stood, balancing uncertainly in the rolling boats. With the soldier's desperate emotions slipping free of his control, Primona caught an impression, a feeling of a powerful bond between him and someone else, also in the Myrrghin army, but serving somewhere far away. His brother . . . .

'Kerell, help me! I can't do this anymore!'

Primona tried to see his 'Kerell', aware Parlan clearly could, but to her, the image remained veiled despite the overwhelming intensity of his cry and the strength of their love.

Hang on, Parlan! I'll get you out of there! The memory of the promise he was holding to came to him, shivering through her, as deep as the bond between Akkarra Weaver-Brothers.

'I can't do it, Kerell. Not even for Anni and the boys. Not even for you.'

The long boat lurched, its wooden keel grating on a gravel and sand bottom in shallow water, making the soldiers stagger. They clambered out, climbing awkwardly over the sides, some slipping and falling, earning snarling rebukes from their officer as they struggled to avoid dampening the powder charge in their muskets. Parlan and some others managed better, splashing awkwardly through thigh-deep sea-water onto dry, white sand. There, he braced himself and aimed high, firing one loud, smoking blast from the musket. Relieved to be done with it, he didn't pause to reload. He refused to use the bayonet, either, removing and replacing it into its storage slot along the barrel.

Hanging the gun from a looped strap about his shoulders, he drew his sword. Arrows, spears and Woven-fireballs came searing about him. Ducking away, he tripped and stumbled over a dead Lellghinner, a young man with curly hair and sun-burned face. Ugly, raw wounds made a ragged mess of his chest and abdomen. Parlan lifted his head and glanced forward toward the thick of the battle.

Able to see only as he did but far enough away now from the methirri wall, Primona at last traced her comrades, though they remained unaware of her, masked as she was by Hollin's Presence.

Most of the Magi and their Weavers were Linked with Liraith, defending the village, but some, m'Connor and Silsun among them, were gone, presumably to aid the escape of the children.

Liraith, m'Singh and m'Akram, fought desperately, Weaving the Akkarra power inherent to them and drawing more from those Channeling to them from Sanctuary. The emerald light of the unified Weave to Parlan appeared as a high, burning wall just ahead of him, its green flames leaping up as apparently lethal barriers. His methirri band hummed and gleamed warning and he yelped in pain. The front rank hesitated. The Weaving was strong, the illusion of killing heat frighteningly real, and growing stronger as their fear fed into it.

'Charge! Go through! It's not real! They don't have the guts for killing!' The officers bellowed but nobody did more than edge a little sideways.

A spearing black-violet storm of lightning slammed into the ground beneath the Weavers. Methaggar power! Knocked unconscious by the thunderclap of displaced air, their faces gashed and bloodied by stone fragments, m'Singh and m'Akram toppled limply into the shallow crater caused by the explosion. The wall of fire vanished. Sickened, Primona was helpless to intervene.

'Take them!' Parlan barely heard the order over the ringing in his ears.

Sprinting forward and clearly marked by his red-plumed helm, an officer ran to claim the prizes, methirri slave collars and chains swinging and jangling with ugly threat from a strap at his waist. Eager for reward, other soldiers hurried to help, scrambling down behind him into the rough hollow.

'No!' Liraith's terrible pleading cry tore through them, ferocious in its awful grief. She dared open the Shield of the village lodge in a frantic bid to gather her Weavers safely to her before they could be collared. The Methaggars blocked her thrust in an explosion of clashing power, sending sprays of green and purple light flaring haphazardly over the battlefield. Seeking to enter through the narrow breach in the Shield dome, and drawing on the massive store of methirri in the battleship, the thin grey forms of the two Methaggars flickered ever closer.

Forced to abandon the Weavers she loved, Liraith's grieving fury became a stronger Shield and repulsed the enemy but the Weavers were enslaved, their throats encircled by dense, powerful methirri collars. Primona wanted to weep, watching with Parlan, as amid much cheering by his fellow soldiers, the unconscious Weavers were roughly hauled back to the boats.

'We've got what we came for!' the commander turned to tell his men proudly. Then, his jaw setting grimly, he relayed the Methaggars' new orders, 'Leave no one alive! Take no slaves! The Weavers are our prize money! Kill the others! Kill them all!'

Parlan froze in shock. Fierce fighting erupted as the villagers advanced in the hope of rescuing their Weaver Captains. Armed only with rough spears and knives and backed by Liraith's anger, they charged, a handful of Lellghin archers appearing from nowhere to cover them. They'd been away helping the children escape, Primona realized. But only the older children who could swim or be helped to swim by the Wave-Dancers, could have reached the caves hidden now by high tide, protected by the sea-water that Methaggars couldn't penetrate. The smallest infants remained with the very old and the badly wounded back in the lodge.

For them, these valiant, once pacifist farmers fought with all they had. Arrows hummed overhead, protecting them but flying like lethal hail into the Myrrghin ranks. Parlan's fellow soldiers cried out and began falling, dying. He ducked into the shelter of a fallen tree. Despite its uncompromising savagery, Primona wanted to cheer. Her people were gaining ground on the officer and his group of soldiers dragging the unconscious Weavers toward their boat.

A swift, murky red shadow passed overhead and Parlan looked up fearfully to see a fiery red cloud descending about the Lellghinners. A Methaggar creation, this fire was real, erupting to set the villagers aflame and burn them alive. Parlan looked away. Cheering, his fellows hurried forward to kill those who had survived.

'Kill the Magi!' the Methaggar snarled, furious that such a pitiful defense could have delayed them.

Getting up and stumbling forward on leaden, unwilling legs, Parlan looked toward the new target. Beneath a great, shining green-gold dome of shimmering energy, the lodge was only just visible. Parlan gasped with awe, the Shield reminding him of the magnificent canopy of his favorite giant leafy tree, its limbs and summer foliage glimmering as if under sunlit water.

The Woven Union created the strongest Shield Primona had seen. It held, keeping the Methaggar at bay although trembling under the strain.

A deafening, grating crash resounded from behind him and Parlan pivoted sharply about. A huge boulder lifted free from amid the wreckage of the stone wall that had encircled the village and, levitated crudely and clumsily by the Methaggar, it floated toward the Shield dome.

The disembodied Magi of Sanctuary could do little other than to direct their Weavers to aid them by Channeling still more

Ea-power. Astoundingly, Liraith's Shield dome managed to grow thicker and stronger; sprouting what Parlan saw as more leaves, incredibly vibrant and beautiful. But, with so much methirri so close by to block them, and working from so great a distance, Primona knew it was too much to ask that the dome would hold.

Inextricably Linked with the soldier despite her fervent wish to aid the defense, she struggled to break free and return to be with her sisters.

'Be calm. I am here,' Hilea steadied her.

'We must help! Let me go to them!' Primona begged.

'Help Parlan! He is the answer!' Hilea commanded, uncharacteristically frantic.

The boulder shimmered with heat, rippling with colored waves of energy as the massed Magi fought to repel it. Caught between the two forces, it hovered then fell, exploding into molten hot fragments. The lodge walls disintegrated with a burst of blue-green light—Liraith's Ea leaving her dead body amid a swirling mass of other disincarnate souls. The Link to Sanctuary snapped, hurling Magi and Weavers back into the Void, and leaving a terrified Primona alone, stranded but for Hilea.

'You want me to go to a murderer?!' Primona sobbed. *'Our Sister is dead!'*

'But not lost, and Parlan grieves with you.'

Parlan pushed himself to his knees, shaking his head, and struggling to clear his vision. A twisted wreckage of bloodied and broken bodies, dead and wounded Lellghin men, women and children lay all about him, thrown outward by the explosion. Myrrghin soldiers too, lay dying, caught in their masters' uncaring murder. Whooping joy more for the knowledge that they were alive than for the victory, the surviving soldiers charged, bayonets and swords at the ready.

Shocked, Parlan remained on his knees, and suddenly, Primona horrified, saddened, saw what he was seeing—two small children, boys, the elder with an arm still about his infant brother. He'd chosen death rather than leave the little one who would have been unable to swim to the sea-caves. Both faces were unmarked, peaceful in death. Only the trickle of blood at ears and nose betrayed how they had died, killed by the concussion of the explosion.

Parlan began to weep.

'Are you hurt?' a trooper asked urgently, stopping to bend over him.

'They look like my sons,' Parlan said, hoarse with tears and smoke. His gaze remained fixed on the dead children a moment before he looked up into the other man's eyes, finding them wild in a gore and smoke-stained face.

Primona felt it, a deep, certain calm, settling over Parlan as he recognized his Path. The other man saw it too, blinking in puzzlement as he witnessed the dawning transformation.

'I can't do this anymore,' Parlan told him. He let his sword drop and sat back in the sand, repeating with an edge of anger that burned through his calm, 'I *won't* do this anymore.'

'That *will* be your boys if you don't get moving!' Someone screamed in agony and terror from somewhere ahead, making the soldier flinch and jump. Snarling, he bent and hauled Hollin to his feet with one hand, slinging his own weapon to collect Hollin's abandoned sword and shove it back at him. 'You know what the Spiders'll do if they think you're holding back. Come to your senses or it'll be your family, too!'

Weary, Parlan turned away from the butchering of the wounded. Not far to his right, a small, waving mass of delicate white shapes caught his eye. Flowers, growing in a neatly tended garden plot, all that remained of the thatched home that burned behind it. To Parlan they were simply daisies, something that reminded him yearningly of home. Primona recognized the gold-centered, white-petal blooms with pleasure as the symbol of Lellgha's long lost champions, The Sunweavers.

A sudden, urgent wash of foreknowledge flooded through her, a crucial warning that the fate of many teetered here, among these flowers. They beckoned to Parlan, making him smile, reminding him of the gentle life he'd once known. 'Annalie . . . .' As tender as the way he said her name, he reached out to touch one tiny curve of petals. 'You love daisies.'

In his memory, Primona saw his wife had wavy, long dark hair and a winning smile to match the bright intelligence and compassion that lit her blue eyes. She cradled a small son in her arms and at her side stood another boy who was the image of his father with unruly chestnut curls and hazel eyes.

A terrible weight of sadness enshrouded Parlan, dragging his vibrant spirit into black despair. The Myrrghin Empire didn't forgive. His only hope lay in the whispered mention he'd heard of the Hidden Ones, who were said to rescue and protect the families of deserters. He'd been planning desertion for some time, Primona realized, but was delaying for some reason . . . the promise his brother had made. *'Hang in there, Parlan. I'll get you out.'* His 'Kerell' hoped to free him with a transfer from the front lines, letting Parlan and his family keep their home, but Parlan could wait no longer.

His vision blurred by unshed tears, Parlan bent and broke off one of the white-gold daisies and very carefully folded it into a pocket of the red tunic beneath his padded jerkin. Then, stooped by more than fatigue, he lifted up his sword again. He had no intention of using the weapon but needed it to make himself appear a threat to the defenders.

To make himself a target.

He turned and took a step toward the battle where the Lellghin archers were still holding their ground, protecting a few ragged huts on the slope of the hillock that hid the children's escape route. Calm and serene in the knowledge that this was the only Path left to save his family and refuse to become a murderer, Parlan walked on. Appalled, Primona understood the best he hoped was to be badly wounded and sent home.

With Methaggar Lords fueling and feeding on their blood-lust, his fellow soldiers were ruthlessly slaughtering the wounded or surrendering villagers. Parlan couldn't bear the sight. He walked closer to death, uphill, and looked away to its crest at the infinite reach of an impossibly beautiful, peaceful blue sky. The birds no longer circled, either returned to their homes, or gone to find another nesting place.

'Now!' Hilea broke in urgently. *'It comes. Be ready.'*

A bone-shattering impact to Parlan's chest drove him staggering back and he grunted a shocked, strangled breath. He fell to his knees and Primona gagged with him as the metallic tang of blood flooded his mouth. Dying, Parlan blinked in disbelieving shock at the arrow shaft embedded in his heart. Their Link broke abruptly and Primona snapped free, recoiling sharply back, up and away with the force of it. Parlan Hollin fell dead, his sightless gaze turned to the sky he'd so admired, one more corpse among the many.

'Now,' Hilea repeated, and the usual tranquility of an Akkarra voice again trembled with something rare, a shining triumph totally at odds the tragedy about them. *'Together, we Greet him.'*

'Together!?' Primona could barely form coherent thoughts, the idea was so shocking. Never had an Akkarra touched the mind of an untrained mortal, let alone an enemy.

'Yes,' Hilea insisted and brimming joy vibrated in his tone. *'I must Hold him.'*

'Hold?? But . . . He's . . . You can't!' Beyond shock, Primona could only splutter protests as Hilea firmly drew her into obeying his impossible intent. To Hold a Myrrghinner? To keep his memory alive? *'He won't understand!'* Primona refused. *'You'll shatter him!'*

'I know what I do,' Hilea responded, sounding a little unsure nonetheless.

A misty light swirled over the man's dead body and Hollin's Ea drifted free amid a signature shimmering of rainbow lights that bore evidence of a history of hardship and great compassion. The rainbow quickly reformed to a sphere, a wispy whirl of soft golden-white light. If it had belonged to a Lellghinner it would have remained in that form. But, from a land that didn't train its people to understand where and what he would return to, Hollin's Ea immediately shifted, taking on the shape he'd carried in life. The ghost-like reflection of his body wore not a trooper's uniform but rather a Roghin coal-miner's simple trousers, shirt and vest.

'Welcome, Parlan,' Primona spoke soft greeting as his Presence wavered in bewilderment. *'You're free at last. If you wish, I will show you The Way.'*

Unusually for someone with his background, Hollin didn't seem startled to find her there watching him, a young woman, a spirit, dressed in blue and white. He nodded calm acknowledgment and turned to regard his lifeless body.

'I'm dead, aren't I?' he stated more than asked, sadly looking down at his old self.

'Yes,' Primona confirmed, and moved a little closer. *'But you are not ended.'*

Again, surprisingly, he merely nodded acceptance. Reassured by his calm and by Hilea's confidence, and knowing time was in short supply, Primona set herself to go immediately onward with Hilea's plan. More worryingly than her sisters' reaction, even with his consent, she knew they could kill Hollin far more finally than any corporeal death. It had never been done before with an outsider and an unprepared one at that. Too, she could feel her own distant body's growing weakness. She had little power remaining to accomplish such a feat.

'Are you certain?' she asked Hilea one more time.

'Yes! Hurry or They will find us.' No Akkarra would ever use the word, 'Methaggar'.

She gathered herself to try to explain to Hollin. *'You must come with me.'*

'A moment,' he said and bent down to his body to retrieve something from its uniform pocket. Surely even he understood that he couldn't carry anything of the physical world with him into the spirit realm? *'No, wait, it's here.'*

Straightening up and turning to face her again, he slid his ghostly hand inside his equally insubstantial vest. A light bloomed brightly from high on his chest, at about the same place the arrow had entered, and immediately over the place he searched. Power radiated more and more intensely, becoming a dazzling red-gold. He drew something from within the beams of light, something round and with curving, delicate edges, something stained with his blood. The flower?

Cradling it in the palm of his ghostly hand, hesitantly, he held it out to her.

'Here,' he said softly. *'I wanted it for Annalie, but . . .'* All his pride and joy in the gift vanished into a shadowing grief. *'I'll never see her again, will I? Or our boys.'*

'I—I'm not sure,' Primona stumbled, not knowing what to tell him.

Normally she'd have all the answers. She'd shepherded lost human spirits onwards many times before, though admittedly they'd all been Lellghinners. If Hilea wanted to Hold this particular Ea, he should supply words rather than leaving her standing speechless. Her Akkarra seemed distracted, preoccupied by something to one side. For a moment, Primona thought she heard another male voice.

'Thank you,' Primona said as Hollin insisted on placing the glowing flower on her upturned palm. Startling energy and hope poured through her, revitalizing her tiring Travel-form and, in her mind's eye, she caught a vision, a fair-haired man wreathed in red and gold, standing at an entry-way. Sunset colors leaped high about Primona amid the astonishing tide of Hilea's unbridled ecstatic recognition. Then, abruptly, cold daggers of shadow stabbed at the fabric of the light, trying to tear a way inside and making the flower shape shudder and recoil as if struck. Primona closed her fingers protectively about it and pulled it back toward her.

'Parlan!' Hilea shocked Primona further by speaking to him directly. *'You cannot remain here. Come with us! Primona! Quickly! With me! Home!'*

Waiting no longer, Hilea's whirlwind rainbows swept them both into the Akkarra's powerful Presence and in an instant she and Parlan were Traveling back to Sanctuary.

'Primona!' m'Connor cried aloud, sounding desperate, frantic. 'Primona! Answer me!'

Marc Gerion cursed, turning away from trying to see the Grove and its island across the starlit bay to frown at m'Connor who was seated on the porch floor beside him.

'What is it?' Rhyssa asked sharply.

'I'm not sure. Sounds like trouble.' Gerion reached out a hand to his friend, but it was too soon, would break the Link with Magi Silsun and through her to others at Tol Eabah.

'Go! Go!' m'Connor urged suddenly. His body strained, his arm trembling with Power, reaching toward the Grove on the island that rose from the dark waters directly ahead. His eyes were closed but constantly moving, flickering beneath the closed lids, seeing a battle frustratingly beyond Gerion's Sight. Gerion was here only because Bren m'Fetrin couldn't be, to try and protect m'Connor, to somehow Ground him should he try to Channel too much of his life-energy. That was looking more and more likely by the moment.

'You can do it! Come on! To the caves!' m'Connor gasped, gulping great breaths, his fingertips straining, reaching, reaching . . . . Trying to aid who? What? At his other side, Rhyssa sat, watching, listening, and hoping. Like Gerion, she feared what could happen when a Weaver, desperate to save lives, disregarded his own mortality.

'How much longer?' she asked Gerion. 'I can see the pulse jumping in his throat. He can't—'

'Nnno—'! The despairing word died, cut short in a gargled choke and m'Connor collapsed, falling to his side on the bamboo floor of the porch, his arms and legs jerking, his whole body convulsing.

'Taran!' Rhyssa called and moved toward him.

'Stay back!' Gerion warned. 'The Link is broken! They've lost Liraith!'

Kneeling, he reached out with both hands toward the thrashing body. He couldn't touch him, couldn't call him back, not yet, he realized over his building panic. This had to be done exactly right or he could kill his friend as easily as save him. Gerion closed his eyes, sought Focus as he'd been taught and shut out the sound of m'Connor's limbs striking the floor with bruising force, his breathing an agonized high-pitched wheeze.

Concentrate, Gerion told himself. Let go. It will be there . . . . A deep soft silence flooded him and he knew he had found the Source of the earth. Now.

Opening his eyes, he bent over m'Connor, reached down and grabbed each arm, found the wrists, and held on despite the muscle spasms shaking the man from head to toe. It was a tricky position from which to Ground properly; he should by rights be standing, the Power surge that had caught m'Connor would then more easily be directed outward. Gerion sat back on his haunches, allowing the energy clearer access to the earth for which it hunted. It flowed like fire through his arms, his chest, his legs, and out through his bare feet. Anyone else would have been burned to a cinder.

M'Connor's thrashing stopped. He groaned and his eyelids moved as he fought to wake. 'Steady, Taran. Steady,' Gerion urged and waited, making sure all the back-lashing power was drained away from the Weaver.

'Marc?' Rhyssa asked, uncharacteristically afraid, badly shaken.

'It's all right. I've got him,' Gerion assured her, his own voice thin and dry, his body reacting to its ordeal and becoming terribly fatigued.

'Can I touch him now?' Gerion nodded permission. He braced himself, preparing to lift his friend and carry him inside. They must get him warm; he'd lost too much of the Essence. 'He's so cold!' Rhyssa cried.

Gerion grunted, straining as he heaved m'Connor up and partly over one shoulder. He staggered under the weight a moment before steadying, weakened after having called the earth to him. He ducked through the low, palm-frond fringed doorway and cooling dew spilled from the branches down his bare back. There'd been no time to dress properly when he'd been called here so urgently and there was the full stretch of the mangrove track between their homes.

Inside, it was shadowy, the lantern burned low, and he squinted, trying to remember where the sparse furnishings stood. The room brightened suddenly as fire flared from the hearth where Rhyssa had stirred the coals to life. She hurried into the bedroom and quickly returned with an armload of bedding. 'Put him here,' she said, spreading the quilted blankets on the rough planked flooring before the fire.

'Lost them . . .' m'Connor rasped, a low broken whisper of breath against Gerion's ear as he lowered him to the floor. 'Tol Eabah has fallen . . . .'

'Primona?' Gerion asked, afraid he already knew the answer.

'Not . . . sure . . . .'

Rhyssa looked away from m'Connor, shocked, meeting Gerion's eyes. 'I thought I heard something. Did you see anything?' she asked.

'Suddenly, there was just . . . nothing,' Gerion said quietly. Rhyssa bent to pull the blankets warmly about m'Connor. 'The children?'

'The 'Dancers saved most,' m'Connor said, his voice a terrible echo of weakness, nothing like his usual self. He opened his eyes and shivered, wrapping his arms about himself and sit up. 'I lost her,' he said. 'I had her, then . . . methirri . . . . A great black wall of it. And Methaggars.'

Rhyssa reached for a gourd of water by the hearth and filled the black iron kettle that hung on a hook close by ready to swing out over the fire.

'M'Singh and m'Akram are prisoners,' m'Connor said and scrubbed a hand over his eyes.

Gerion swore, gripping his friend's shoulder hard. They both knew, all too well, why the enemy needed Weavers.

'Good. They're alive,' Rhyssa said firmly. 'We can get them out. They'll take them to the Citadel. We got you both out of there. We can do it again.'

'Only because the bastards didn't suspect you,' Gerion told her with a hint of a smile for the memory. 'Unless you know another Myrrghin Lady who wants to give up her soft life and rough it on a fish diet?'

'Oh, there are some compensations,' she said, smiling at m'Connor and Gerion could have cheered for the light that returned to m'Connor's eyes, but if faded too quickly.

'They're collared,' m'Connor said bleakly, closing his eyes, closing himself away from them. 'Damn it!' He slammed a closed fist hard into the floor once, then twice.

Rhyssa caught his hand with her right, her other hand coming up to turn his face to hers. 'They're alive,' she repeated firmly.

M'Connor let out a great, heavy sigh. 'Primona. I don't know if the enemy has her or—'

'I'm here! I'm safe!' The Sending was broadcast so widely and with so much power that even Rhyssa reacted, startling. M'Connor's tired, strained face eased. 'She's back! She did it, somehow.'

'You see,' Rhyssa chided. 'There's always hope. You didn't lose her.'

M'Connor cocked his head to one side and listened a moment, the tension easing from his body. 'I can hear Silsun, too.' The firelight picked out the tears shining in his eyes as he whispered, 'Liraith is dead. The Akkarra have her.'

'She'll come back to us someday,' Gerion reminded him.

'If there's anywhere to come back to.' M'Connor turned again and looked hard into Gerion's eyes. 'There's only Sanctuary now. If they find The Grove . . . . There'll be no more Magi, no Akkarra, no Weaving. Lellgha will be gone forever.'

CHAPTER NINE

Lerant stood waiting to disembark in Myrrgha City, absorbing himself in watching the mooring procedure as he leaned on the merchant ship's port railing. Below on the dock, stevedores hurried about catching and securing lines, their blue-striped shirts stained with sweat. Lerant had gone as half-naked as the crew during the voyage, but had reluctantly donned his Myrrghin red surcote and accoutrements as the ship sailed into harbor.

He turned about to study the other vessels crowding the waters of the most prosperous city in all the southern kingdoms. Low over the bay, looking blood-red and angry, the sun was setting, shimmering and huge in a glassy sky choked by smoke; distant volcanic mountains competing with the city's iron foundries. Soot-dark brick walls and furnace chimneys were an uncompromising backdrop to the Myrrghin warships at anchor by the naval base. The gunboats' black-iron cannons caught the last of the day's light, seeming to run red with the smeared blood of their victims; the sea-birds' cries echoing death screams.

Again, he saw the blood spilling from Parlan's lips, and heard his last, choked cry. A ghostly chill walked skeletal fingers down Lerant's spine. How he wished these terrible visions would leave him be! The dream of Parlan's fate was only the latest, if by far the most horrific in a long series of precognitive experiences that had never served to help anyone.

'Still feverish, lad? Grog and a landlubber's legs don't mix too well.' Geadra, the garrulous ship's captain, was watching him quizzically. The portly man's grizzled chin and worn shirt were stained by the run-off from the ever-present wad of tobacco he chewed.

'I'm fine,' Lerant assured. 'And I do thank you for your nurse-maiding.'

"T'were nuthin'. Took ye worse than t'others.' Geadra nodded toward shore. 'Most north'ners crane their necks fer that view. Seen it before then, have ye?'

'Shouldn't you be watching your crew rather than worrying about me, Captain?'

'Ahh,' Geadra spat a thin line of black liquid over the side and into the narrow band of oily water between the ship and the dock. 'The lads could do this in their sleep.'

'They're good sailors.' He shouldered his carry-bag, extending his free hand in farewell as he saw the gangplank being lowered.

Geadra gripped Lerant's hand within his meaty palms, and said, 'Ye play a clever hand at slates n' stones. Use some o'ye' winnings t' buy yerself a slave. Never seen a Myrrghin officer without one.' He shook his head reprovingly, 'Carryin' yer own bags 'n all! There's a sales-yard further up the dock and yonder is a slaver ship just arrived from Lellgha. Move fast 'n y'll get the pick of their haul.'

'I want nothing to do with slavery!' Lerant snapped, sunset-light blinding him and adding to the power of his glare.

'Suit yerself.' Geadra blinked and took a pace backward. 'Cursed sorcerers brought it on 'emselves. Gotta employ 'em somehow.'

'Those who survive,' Lerant muttered and strode onto the gangplank.

Climbing the steep street from the waterfront, Lerant turned around to see the bay flooded by a final burst of red-gold light spectacularly highlighting masts and sails. The Eastern Sea washed a crimson tide against the black granite walls of Myrrgha Citadel, the point from which the city sprawled out into open, hostile desert. Enameled spires and marble domes shone gold in the dying light, marking the heart of the Myrrghin Empire.

Walking downhill again, the stench and noise of the packed streets spoke more clearly of the City's nature, an unpleasant contrast to the fresh, open grasslands of the Khenghin tierdrun. Which reminded him; he needed a Myrrghin military regulation haircut. It wouldn't do for his commanding officer to catch him going native. He was eager to reach the fortress, anxious for word of Parlan and determined not to leave it another day before he used all his savings to bribe whoever into getting his brother transferred out of the Marines. Khengha City had been too far removed from the heart of power. Here, he had a real chance to succeed.

Hold on, Parlan, he pleaded silently. *Hold on just a little longer.*

'Sorry, Captain', the thin, lanky Duty Sergeant repeated rather irritably—he'd already checked twice. 'There's no mail for you from Trooper Hollin.'

Lerant scowled disappointment and scratched at his itching neck. The scraping of the barber's blade had left it raw beneath a very short haircut. 'But there should be something. It's been months!'

The Sergeant sighed gustily, making the papers on his desk flutter. 'A Marine Shocktrooper, you say?' Lerant nodded, looking encouraging of further information. 'What ship did his squad usually sail with?'

'Umm, his squad doesn't stay for long with any one ship.' Lerant frowned, searching for the latest name, 'The Blacksword. No, The Shadow, that was it!'

'Oh.' The Sergeant's face set, lips thin, squinty eyes shifting. 'They're gone from port.'

Lerant gripped his Myrrghin-issue sword-hilt tightly, wishing he could grab the Sergeant's throat instead. 'I already know that.'

'Some important mission or other. Supposed to be secret 'r something.'

'Oh.' Lerant's stomach knotted. The memory of the bloody light drenching the ships' cannons didn't help.

The Sergeant frowned at him warily. 'Sorry I can't help you further, Captain.'

'No matter. I thank you for your time.' Lerant turned to a small table by the door and awkwardly gathered up the tied bundles of parchment maps, engineering sketches and supply scrolls he'd placed there as he entered. If anything had happened to Parlan surely Annalie, if not the military, would have let him know, and there was no mail from her either.

Burdened by his awkward load and a little dizzy, he stumbled outside, the oppressive heat assailing him even though it was almost full dark. Oil-fueled lanterns were everywhere, radiating more heat and making the back of his neck itch worse than it had inside. On the far side of a white-gravel parade ground, a towering black granite wall lit by more flaring sconces separated the compound from the Palace grounds.

He must report to General Rusark in the War Ministry offices, after which his orders were to take up his old post at the Khenghin Embassy some miles away, liaising between them and the Palace. Fine by him. There were too many Lellghin slaves here for his liking, trotting after officers, skeletally thin, their eyes hollow sockets of despair.

He crossed the parade ground quickly and entered a small, sheltered portico where the sentry checked his identity. He was directed through a gate and into a cream-pink marble-faced and columned courtyard full of fountains and greenery that made a pleasant change from the barracks' harsh surrounds. Clutching his maps and tally-sheets, he headed through a white rose-arbor arch and climbed the flagstone steps of the War Ministry building.

Inside, he paused, momentarily overcome by his fascination with the latest miracle of science, a series of small electric lamps that lit the domed lobby. Beyond him was a maze of corridors. He asked directions from yet another sentry, in flashy gold Palace Honor guard livery. He turned a corner and was alone in a long, marble-floored hall, his boot-steps echoing hollowly.

Suddenly, he was engulfed in icy air, the shock almost making him drop his charts. He took another pace and was surprised to immediately re-enter warm air. Checking, he found the deathly cold emanated from this one spot in the hall. He looked below then above and to the side, expecting to find some vent that brought air up from a hidden cistern deep beneath the flooring. The walls were smooth and unbroken, a nearby tapestry unmoving. A strange hissing noise swelled and roared up behind him. Dropping his papers, he whirled about, his hand on his sword-hilt. But there was no one, nothing.

Then, he saw it. Leaving a shadowy alcove he hadn't noticed before . . . *something,* a misty blue dust-whirl, spinning higher, it disappeared through the ceiling. The terror and the cold went with it and warm, stale air rushed in to take its place. The wall was seamless, not the least gap allowed a draft let alone a mini-storm. Quickly, he bent and gathered up his bundled documents, glad there was no one about to see him behaving so oddly.

At last he found Rusark's section, entering a room busy with officers working at desks or checking messages coming in from Connectors. 'Engineer Captain Lerant?' someone called irritably. Rusark's aide—or so the sign on his desk proclaimed. 'You're late.'

'Sorry. I had some trouble finding the right place,' Lerant replied. 'I have all the requested documents, and—'

'Yes, well and good,' the middle-aged man shook his head. 'But the thing is, the battle is over and the General is busy following the reports that have finally arrived from the front. I don't know how long it might be before he can see you. Take a seat and make yourself comfortable.'

'Battle?' Lerant frowned. 'I hadn't heard . . .'

'Well, of course not! It was classified top secret until only a few hours ago!' The aide gave him a pained look. 'You must know how readily the cursed Magi witches seem able to uncover our plans?' A faint smile escaped his sullen expression. 'But this time we did it! Found one of their island refuges and took them completely by surprise.'

'Oh, good.' Lerant's throat was suddenly dry and he was sure he was about to throw up. He swallowed and asked, 'My brother is a Shocktrooper who might have been in the thick of the fighting. He's assigned to the Shadow. Was his ship there?'

'Everyone will know by now,' the man said casually. He shuffled the files littering his desk and pulled out one sheet of parchment. 'Yes, The Shadow, specially modified for this mission, left port some weeks ago with the rest. All available Shocktroopers were dispatched with them, heading for the battle at an island named Tol Eabah, more than five hundred miles from Lellgha.' His dark eyes flicked up to Lerant's face and he doled out another smile. 'But not far enough. We'll soon round up all those who escaped. We might even get a day off, there'll be a victory celebration, I'd think.'

Lerant took a step back, not wanting to hear anymore. His heart hammering in his ears, he asked, 'Losses?'

The man snorted dismissively. 'No specifics as yet. But we really caught them napping. Captain?' he asked with sharp concern as he looked up at Lerant again and got quickly to his feet. 'I'm sure your brother is all right. The savages rely on primitive weapons—Steady!'

Weight dragged Lerant down, the weight of a dead body falling, the taste of blood making him gag. He knew one arrow had struck home.

Jabbing low with a wooden practice sword, m'Connor pivoted to swing at the trainee soldier behind his first strike. 'You won't have time for fancy steps when those Myrrghin bastards come at you. Butcher them as hard and fast and bloody as you can and kill another before they cut you to pieces. Tol Eabah fell because they were slow to kill. Strike hard! Here, here, and here!' His wooden blade made contact at throat, armpit and groin and his opponent went down in an ungainly heap. 'You won't be dancing in neat pairs when you face the Abandoned. Watch now. All of you, charge me. Come on!' He swung at the boy who ducked under and parried correctly but everyone else shifted about uncertainly. 'Attack me, you stupid bastards!'

Dust choked the air, sweat blinded vision, and lungs burned. M'Connor's sword arm ached with the strain of warding off and delivering so many strikes. Blood roared and pounded in his ears, his harsh breathing drowning out all else. Like The First Battle, with Bren protecting his back . . .

'Easy Taran, easy,' Gerion's resonant voice soothed, his bulky figure blocking m'Connor's path. 'Unless you want to try to take my head, too?' he added with a familiar eager twinkle in his eyes as he hefted his practice sword.

'No thanks, not today.' M'Connor dropped his wooden sword to flex an aching hand and push his sweaty hair back from his brow, pleased to see his knuckles and forearms were cut and bruised. His Legion was beginning to get the idea.

Come to me. M'Connor froze, listening, checking for more from his Magi. About him the Legion reacted, able to feel it to some degree, but only a Weaver would hear the words and recognize the voice. *Bring your Retha,* Silsun's bell-like mental voice continued. *The Akkarra call for a Testing.* 'Retha' was the Old Word, the Magi word, for Grounding Lieutenant.

'I've been called to a Testing,' he told his Legion, noticing Sean Fetrin had moved closer to stand frowning at him. 'All the Weavers must attend. It seems the Akkarra have uncovered some clue at Tol Eabah that needs further investigation.' Sensing their anxiety, he displayed his cuts and bruises and said, 'Well done. Your hard work shows. Your training ends early today, enjoy a swim, do some fishing. You've earned it.'

They called thanks and good luck, already dispersing toward the beach, but Sean marched purposefully forward. 'Gerion is to go, but I can't?' he asked, unable to mask his disappointment both at that fact and deeper, that his own Magi hadn't as yet been found. This was becoming dangerous for Sean, on the brink of feeling the first push of Weaving in his blood.

'I don't know why,' he answered truthfully, knowing there was no point in anything else. 'I will tell you when and if I can. Right now all I know is I'm to prepare to be Tested.'

'The Akkarra don't ask for such an ordeal without reason,' Sean countered worriedly.

M'Connor sighed. 'Likely it'll come to nothing for me. They're Testing us all.'

'This time it's different!' Sean insisted. 'You know it as well as I do! The Akkarra are excited, we can all feel it. They've found something, and what they've been looking for is Bren.'

'Not just Bren. The Akkarra look to find many things . . . including how to prevent us all being massacred like everyone at Tol Eabah and Lellgha City.'

Sean shook his head in frustration. 'If they know something that can help my brother . . . . If this has anything to do with him, I should be there.' He cast an understandably resentful scowl at Gerion. 'Gerion isn't a Weaver.'

'Nor are you,' Gerion said, unperturbed.

'I will be soon! I only need my Magi . . . and my Akkarra-Brother.'

166

M'Connor shook his head and straightened up from collecting his sword. 'Gerion is my *Retha*, my Ground, and I need someone there with me.' Very gently, looking Sean in the eye, he added, 'And we all know your Magi isn't at Sanctuary; we've looked. You can't help me, Sean. You don't have the skills for a Testing yet.'

After a moment, Sean said quietly, 'Take care, both of you. I know there are other broken Triads but they're Weavers without Magi, or Magi without Weavers. Not . . . .'

'We'll be careful,' m'Connor promised. Finished buckling on his sword belt, he extended his hand, leaving the choice of Sharing with him. Sean took his hand, making the truth of m'Connor's words undeniable and flooding m'Connor with a better understanding of the depth of the younger man's loneliness, confusion and frustration. Overriding all was an impatient, desperate need to be able to do something, anything.

'I'll ask them about your Magi,' m'Connor promised. 'Just remember, none of us can Weave when we stand before the Severing-Stone. It's all changed, Sean. It's all changed. Weaving . . . counts for nothing.' It was the coldest of cold comfort, but it was all he had to offer.

Sean withdrew his hand, but m'Connor could still sense the mounting fury, not at m'Connor, but a need to strike back at those who had taken everything from him.

'They haven't got methirri everywhere,' Sean said, the defiant light in his eyes reminding m'Connor painfully of Bren. 'They don't value their women and children or even their foot-soldiers. Where would Myrrgha be without them to do their dirty work or provide hostages to obedience? If we . . . got rid of them . . . . It would be no more than they've done to us.'

M'Connor nodded, feeling the same blasphemous urge to use Weaving to murder, to burn and slaughter without mercy. 'If it comes to that,' he agreed. 'I must go.'

Fetrin stood silent, gathering himself a long moment. Finally, he said, 'We need hope, Taran. Bring us hope.' He slung his bow over his shoulder and marched away toward his home, returning to the shell of his brother. He didn't look back.

By the time m'Connor and Gerion stepped out of the Wavedancer-towed boat onto the rocky shoreline beneath the Grove Isle's craggy cliff-face, long shadows were cast as deeper blues across the wind-riffled surface of the bay. Their boot-steps crunched on the yellow-brown pebble-strewn beach, draped now in the pale purple twilight. Together they climbed the Akkarra stairway, its living timber resonating, humming, with something indefinable, something he'd never felt from it before.

At the top, m'Connor braced himself to enter the Grove proper without Bren but when it came to it, he found he couldn't. He stopped and Gerion stopped with him. The breeze stirred through the pines. Waves crashed on the rocks below.

'Come on,' Gerion said matter-of-fact and took him by the arm, pulling him forward. The touch, the Sharing and the Grounding made the difference, reminding m'Connor he wasn't going into this alone—as much as it felt that way for him. Then, the support, the weight of that Sharing doubled and redoubled, then trebled and re-trebled. Standing in a semi-circle before him at the edge of the Grove were all the Magi and Weavers of Sanctuary.

He'd come home. Not the way he'd wanted to, never the way he'd imagined, but he'd come home, something that had only been a dream in the depths of Myrrghin enslavement and the horror of a methirri slave collar. Swallowing hard, m'Connor dipped his head in acknowledgement, again having to remember that he didn't have to voice his gratitude, they'd feel it in him just as he was feeling their combined empathy.

The semi-circle broke apart, reforming into groups of three but for Primona who stood somewhat apart from the rest.

'You're right,' m'Connor told Silsun after bowing to her in formal greeting, then looking up at the giant Akkarra whose beautiful ever-changing leaves fluttered like spinning gold coins against the lowering sun. 'There is something . . . different about them tonight. A tense anticipation.'

'Yes,' she agreed. 'And something else, too. I swear, I could almost Sense . . . .'

'There's someone else here,' Gerion said, coming back toward them after stalking around among the deep shadows under the giants' canopy.

'Someone else?' m'Connor turned swiftly about, looking. Gerion regularly amazed him, Sensing things that were beyond the usual parameters of either Magi or Weavers. It seemed to be a Talent unique to the man, most useful and something m'Connor had grown to trust with his life. 'Where? I can't see—'

'He's not visible,' Gerion cut him off. 'And he's not . . . . here. Exactly.'

'Well, that makes it easy,' m'Connor said sourly.

'He?' Silsun asked, her keen eyes studying Gerion's expression and her mind and spirit reaching out to Read him. But Gerion was a puzzlingly difficult man to Read at the best of times.

Gerion rubbed at his bearded jaw as he considered the problem. 'Definitely male.'

'And a friend?' m'Connor asked, though it was more statement than question. No one entered here without permission.

'Well, he'd have to be wouldn't he? But . . . it doesn't feel like . . . damn it, I just can't pin it down! It's frustrating. Whoever, whatever, it is, it keeps shifting about.'

'I think Primona might have some answers,' Silsun told him quietly.

'Primona?' Gerion looked toward the slim, dark youngster standing apart from the others.

'That's where whatever it is, is.' Gerion frowned. 'I think.'

Intrigued by the mystery, m'Connor turned to go take a look for himself. Gold and green light suddenly arced between the Akkarra, their signal that they were ready to begin.

Aleath, one of the elder Magi, stepped forward, waving for Primona to come along at her side. They made a striking pair, dressed like all the refugees here in unmatched odds and ends, but proudly displaying the embroidered sashes of their respective Color Training. Aleath had skin near translucent with age, her hair pure white and streaming down in long waves about her shoulders and back. Primona was shorter, ebony-skinned, very young, lithe and light on her feet. Her tightly curled, coal-black hair was cropped close about her face, highlighting beautifully sculpted cheekbones and jaw. Her eyes shone, hazel and bright, alight with life. She wasn't shy and seemed nervous more of the situation than of her own ability to handle it.

Aleath Sent silent greeting to the Weavers and, remembering Gerion's presence, said aloud, 'Many of you have not met our newest Journeyer, Primona. It was her experience at Tol Eabah that caused us to call you to this Testing so suddenly.'

She stepped back and indicated the younger woman should take her place on the grassy high spot in the center of the Grove. Primona cleared her throat and took a deep steadying breath before beginning. 'I experienced a most unexpected Link at Tol Eabah with a Roghinner, forced into the Myrrghin army.'

A murmur of reaction rippled through the Weaver Captains, but it was Gerion who said aloud what they were all trying hard not to think at her, 'A soldier!'

'I did not Link with him precisely of my own volition.'

'Your Akkarra, Hilea, Sent you to him,' Aleath explained when Primona fell silent a moment, perhaps listening to him.

'He did,' Primona agreed. 'And . . . . he did not. If it was a physical situation rather than aetheric, I'd say something else both pushed *and* pulled me through the methirri to the soldier.'

'We don't yet know all the Methaggar might be capable of. Two were present. Could they have . . . ?' Weaver Captain m'Kay suggested darkly.

'I wouldn't be here if so,' Primona told him, sharply certain.

'None of us have ever known anything like it, but we know it has no methirri contamination,' Aleath agreed. 'Whatever it was, it made it possible for a great gift to be carried to us. Primona?'

'The Roghinner's gift is extraordinary,' she said. 'First, you should see him as I did. I'm sorry Lieutenant Gerion.'

Gerion waved away her apology. 'Taran can describe him for me later. Best I leave you all to it for a while, I think.' He moved away a few paces, returning to his tracking of whatever mysterious presence lurked among the Akkarra. Surely they must know exactly what it was?

Silsun murmured silently in his mind, making him aware that whatever it was, it was no threat and he should give full attention to Primona.

The young Journeyer's memory pressed at m'Connor's Shield, and giving assent, he opened himself to her past sensory intake as had all the other Weavers. The mutilation of his Ea, the amputation of Bren's Presence, stood stark and sharp against the inaudible buzz as four sets of Akkarra-Brothers prepared themselves.

Primona Shared the Roghinner's moment of rebellion and revelation, the soldier's Ea form exuding fierce compassion, the type of man who was never going to survive on a battlefield. But this hadn't been his first battle, and he had killed before . . . . A deeper love had been holding him obedient. He was a father. To spare them all the shock of the sudden separation at the moment of the man's death, Primona broke the communal memory, returning to verbal communication as Gerion circled back to stand at m'Connor's side.

'A deserter?' m'Kay asked Primona.

'No. He knew they'd murder his family,' Primona answered, grim and sad. She understood that m'Kay well knew the answer but had asked for Gerion's sake.

Watching the exchange, Gerion asked, 'Still, he wouldn't kill?'

'To freely choose death rather than murder is the most valiant of all acts,' Primona continued, speaking now for them all, finishing the story. 'A Lellghin arrow took him through the heart; he died instantly.'

M'Connor plainly felt the shudder of repressed revulsion that ran through some of the older Magi who had trained Lellghin children in their pacifist tenets for generations. For that reason, m'Connor knew the same Magi found it difficult to be with him for any length of time as they inadvertently shared the ugliness of his intent to use the violence necessary to protect them.

'Perhaps because of his gentle courage, he was able to give us a very special gift after he died, when his Ea-Form had taken on a ghostly reflection of his old self,' Primona concluded. 'Remarkably, the gift, a flower, transmuted from physical to aetheric to be carried here and then returned to a physical, yet . . . most unusual form.'

Astonished questions and disbelief ran like a firestorm through the Weavers' minds. Nothing physical could Travel through the Void. Could the Akkarra have changed it to bring it here? Impossible.

Made dizzy by so radical a notion, m'Connor shook his head and Gerion grabbed at his arm as a potent mix of disappointment and disbelief warred with a growing, unstoppable sensation of hope. That last came more from the Akkarra than from any mortal among them. Ignoring the tumult of empathic emotion tangling about them, m'Connor turned and met his friend's eyes, hope losing the battle on the personal level. Whatever it was it would lead them no closer to Bren.

'A dead soldier carried some artifact here? Huh, maybe that's what I've been sensing. Not much though, to get the Akkarra all edgy,' Gerion said quietly, close to m'Connor's ear.

Suddenly all the hair stood up on the back of m'Connor's neck. Someone else was present. Someone who wanted dearly to speak to him, someone held back, pulled away from him abruptly by one of the Akkarra like a parent would pull an infant away from a blazing hearth.

'Did you feel that?' Gerion asked, astonished.

'Yes, I—'

'Perhaps we should let the evidence speak for itself?' Silsun said, her familiar tone of reproof calling them all to order but her piercing gaze connecting with m'Connor in a way that told him she'd felt the presence, too. He had the distinct impression she knew exactly what it was but wasn't saying. She turned back to Primona and asked, 'If Hilea will allow?'

'He is ready,' she confirmed.

Moving away for a moment, Primona bent and collected something that the Akkarra had apparently only now presented, unfolding a small aperture in part of his massive buttressing roots. Straightening back toward the group and standing as tall as possible, she uncurled long slender fingers from about the object that bled a soft, warm golden light against the darkness of her skin.

M'Connor gasped, startled.

A single, living white-gold starflower, shining like a miniature sun. Entwined in a woven thread through its brilliant mesmerizing gold, a line of blood red formed a perfect spiral beginning in the heart of the flower and spreading ever wider to breach its outer edge. The Tanortha! The male Magi! The Sunweavers!

'Beautiful. Reminds me of something . . . .' Gerion said, impressed more by m'Connor's stunned reaction than by the object itself, unaware of its import.

'Impossible, yet here,' m'Connor murmured, swept by the recognition that surged among the Akkarra who'd been eager to share their secret. A male Magi emblem—where was its matching female seed? The other eight Weavers, equally astounded, closed in a tight circle about Primona but avoided jostling her outstretched hand.

'Where have I seen that before?' Gerion muttered.

'A Starflower, a real living Starflower . . . .'

'Living?' Gerion exclaimed, bumping against m'Connor as he craned for a closer look. 'But it can't be!'

M'Kay stood aside for him, smiling. Only then did m'Connor realize he'd been seeing the flower as much through the group mind as with his own eyes. He stepped up alongside his friend and saw more clearly the glowing golden-white petals with their red spiral seeming to pulse like a vein of still-vital blood.

'Emblem of the male Magi, the Tanortha, and their Sunweavers, gone with the destruction of their starship,' Silsun said even as m'Connor felt the memory flood his friend's mind with amazed elation.

'This is no ordinary bloom,' Primona continued, as proud for the soldier who had presented it to her as she was pleased by their reaction, 'It began, as you saw, as a simple daisy, nor is it a standard Tanortha emblem. The thread of scarlet, the Roghinner's blood, remains as reminder of his sacrifice. It will never fade and has somehow passed through the Void. It can be no coincidence that the spilling of his blood has resulted in so perfect a recreation of the most famous of all Starflower Emblems.'

'A blood spiral!' Gerion whispered and m'Connor turned to him in shared amazement. 'Tanortha d'Rellan!'

The Sun's Heart, the Shining One. A legend they'd all heard from the cradle—the one male Magi who was born to be not only a philosopher, but a warrior, a leader who carried life onward through the direst, coldest dark.

'Your turn, Taran,' Silsun said, carefully taking the flower from an awed m'Kay and placing into m'Connor's grasp.

'Careful,' Gerion said warily. 'The very stones about us are shaking with its dangerous power.'

'We'd hoped you might feel something we can't, Marc,' Silsun said, intrigued by his reaction but her eyes and mind never leaving m'Connor. 'Your unique perspective is invaluable. Later, we'd like you to tell us more about it.'

Gerion shrugged, but m'Connor could feel his pleasure and basked in it. The two of them, odd men out, hadn't been allowed here simply as an act of kindness after all. Silsun sighed heavily, unnecessarily adding to the strong sense of exasperation she projected in reaction to the thought.

M'Connor ignored it, so engrossed was he in the indefinable something radiating up his arm and into his heart from the beautiful, glowing starflower. It was almost as if the thing was trying fervently to tell him something. Certainly, beyond all his resistance, it rekindled an ember of real hope for Bren. If a living flower could somehow travel beyond the paths of time and space to reach them from a long since forgotten world . . . . Or had it come from *this* world, from beyond the veil of methirri? Could Bren likewise be trapped? Was the flower a clue as to how that wall could be breached and its prisoner safely returned?

'Why would this come to us through the means of a stranger's death?' one of the Weavers demanded. 'Shouldn't it have come to us through the Akkarra? Can we be certain it's not a trap?'

'Nothing is certain anymore,' another murmured in grim response.

More comments were made, but m'Connor lost track, mesmerized by the starflower that warmed his hand and renewed his strength. Something deep within him insisted this beautiful thing hadn't been crafted by the enemy. Here, at last, solid, irrefutable, here at last, was hope.

'Do we know any more about this Roghin soldier?' Gerion asked and, with an effort of will, m'Connor looked away from the starflower to rejoin the discussion.

'I saw only his wife and children clearly,' Primona replied quietly. 'But he also has a brother, another soldier, somewhere far away.'

'Many questions remain unanswered, but this much is undeniable,' Silsun told them. She drew a deep breath, and m'Connor sensed urgency and trepidation competing in her thoughts. 'This starflower, living, eternal, given here to us, is proof despite all contrary evidence that our Brother Magi and Sister Weavers may yet return to us.'

'But—surely,' Weaver Captain m'Gavaskari voiced the group skepticism as politely as he could. 'The Tanortha died millennia ago, lost inside the female Akkarra seeds.'

'No seed, no male Magi,' Captain m'Suooin summarized bluntly. 'Even if Tanortha d'Rellan walked among us again it's no guarantee of help. We all remember our last failure despite his leadership.'

'Tanortha d'Rellan, The Portent of Doom, that's what my father used to say,' Gerion muttered.

'Our failure? Our old world is gone, but we live. Not such a failure, perhaps,' m'Connor said, lifting his voice and making no attempt to Shield his feelings. 'Perhaps this has come to remind us that the ancient battle is not so lost as we thought.'

'I recall many valiant deeds,' Aleath said in verbal agreement with the sentiment, 'Such deeds are not vague but as clear as present events and are understood and held more closely by we whose memory continues on through many lives.'

177

M'Connor reverently handed back the flower and Primona carefully returned it to the special niche Hilea had created for it.

'The Methaggar seek it,' Primona reminded them all as Hilea's body closed protectively about the starflower, again hiding if from view. She looked directly at Gerion who started a little at the unexpected attention. 'Can you sense the flower's presence now, Marc?' she asked.

M'Connor felt Gerion concentrate hard then wonderment fill him. 'No,' he answered. 'The stones, the earth, everything was singing to it, but now, it's just . . . gone.'

'Good,' she said with a relieved smile.

'It appears this special flower can travel the paths of time and space,' Silsun added. 'We feared it wasn't safe anywhere or anywhen. But, if the earth no longer carries its presence, and we all can't sense it hidden here . . . . Hopefully, it is secure.'

'Hopefully?' Gerion repeated in surprise. 'But this is The Grove!'

'Yes,' Silsun responded sadly. Then, lifting her voice to address them all again, she continued. 'The flower brings us a remote, perhaps forlorn hope that this man's death might yet bring the Tanortha to return to us. Let us pray this Testing will reveal the right Path by which we might trace them—should they exist.'

'It is Time,' she commanded sternly, gathering the Captains back to their stations by their various Magi and Akkarra.

'Could the spiral link the dead man as distant family of the Tanortha? Do we have his name?' Gerion asked, watching with grave concern as m'Connor began moving toward Genoh, Silsun's and his Akkarra.

'There is always purpose in the means of revelation,' Silsun reminded them all. 'The future is continually altered by each moment of decision by all living in time's flowing—and splitting—current. More knowledge of the soldier's identity at this time could cause us to approach in haste and error.'

M'Connor looked up sharply at his Magi, his mind carrying the same impression to her—she knew something more, they all did. They knew the man's name, and more of his family. Silsun couldn't deny it and her thoughts veered away from the Shield she'd constructed about the information. M'Connor knew she would tell him when and if the time was right.

Chapter Ten

Gerion had never been present during a Testing before, though m'Connor had described it in detail. Or rather, he'd described a Testing he'd undergone with his Akkarra-Brother at his side, and one that had taken place during a time of peace. Gerion had never liked the sound of it, of a man's soul being drawn from his breathing body and cast into the often chaotic Paths of Time, reliant upon his Magi to guide him safely back again. Only Weavers could Travel and correctly carry back impressions of the future. Magi, ironically, were too adept at it, and thus too prone to contort the Path into one of their own making and so relay false images.

Even should Tanortha d'Rellan exist, who was he really? Flesh and bone like them all, just a man. Could one man truly make such a difference, alone? He would be mortal, had been killed before, could be killed again, *would* be killed again if the enemy found the least trace of him.

'We know that one of you, perhaps more, holds the Key to open the locks to the Paths that will carry us onward to learn more of the fate of our Tanortha,' Silsun told the nine Captains. 'As you see, all has been prepared.'

She indicated the ritual drinking bowl placed on a moss and lichen covered gray stone pedestal atop a grassy mound beneath the waiting Akkarra's outstretched limbs.

The other four Magi who would take active part in the Testing had already chosen the one Weaver of their pair who was to Link to their respective Akkarra and enter trance with him and the Magi while the second Weaver stood watch, keeping the bodies safe and warm. Vibrant gold streamers of energy swirled about the magnificent giants who, in preparation, were drawing an extra harvest from a gold-purple twilight sky. More and more silver sparkled amid the gold as the stars appeared one by one in the gaps in the Akkarra's glossy canopy. The day was passing into night.

Were the Tanortha and the female Akkarra trapped out there on another world somewhere amid those glittering stars? Could they direct him to Bren?

'Let the Testing begin.'

Sweet and fiery, the Akkarra nectar was smoothly potent as m'Connor drank it down, taking his turn as the scalloped bowl was passed around the kneeling circle of Captains. The Magi had distilled and prepared it from the giants' offered blossoms, knowing that this Testing would require a deeper trance than usual and the nectar would aid transition out of the body and into the Akkarra Mind. One by one the Captains sagged, consciousness altering, and their Brothers bent to gently help them lean back against the sure support of their Magi's Akkarra. It was essential to remain in physical contact for the duration of the Testing.

Eyes closed, drifting, m'Connor relished the sense of sheer exultant freedom as his Ea lifted free of the prison of the flesh.

This was the one part of Testing that made the rest of it almost worthwhile. Almost.

Before the war, back in Lellgha City, the Weaver Captains would all have been dressed in formal uniforms, their shoulders bearing their color cloaks to signify their particular strengths in Weaving. Now their only adornments were the Akkarra and moon-emblem embossed sword hilts, catching the first of the rising twin moons to shine as molten silver as their owners' freed souls.

Bring us hope, Taran, he recalled Sean Fetrin's desperate plea.

Genoh waits, Silsun chided softly, bringing him back to full Focus.

M'Connor Sent acknowledgment and acceptance to their Akkarra and immediately his Ea melted like a raindrop evaporating, absorbed by a sunbeam. Enveloped in a golden mist, warm and brightly welcoming, he entered.

Genoh greeted him, calling his name, and accepting him as a candidate for Testing. Abruptly, M'Connor stood in what seemed to him a magnificent cathedral. Ethereal light spilled down from above, gilding each of Genoh's immense buttressing roots. This indeed was a sacred realm. Here the very Light of the creative source itself was harvested, the Light of all the souls ever born or yet to be born. Here time ceased to exist. Thus all Paths were laid open. Past, Present, and Future were one.

A human mind couldn't encompass such a concept, and Genoh, knowing that, shifted perspective. To m'Connor it seemed he moved forward, crossing the cathedral floor to stand before three tunnel-like openings cloaked in swirling rainbow-colored mist. He must enter and experience each in turn. Sending acknowledgment, he moved to the left tunnel, the past.

A creeping slick of foul blackness, swallowing the light . . . The slave collar heavier, thicker, dragging at m'Connor's breathing, choking him from the inside . . . Methaggar!

'No,' Bren refused, gripping m'Connor's arm and holding him back.

Not this again. He, Genoh and Silsun had already examined this memory a hundred times from every perspective, trying to find some clue they might have overlooked. Please! M'Connor begged of the Akkarra. He wanted this over before he saw again the sad farewell in his Brother's eyes as Bren turned and looked back at him for the last time.

Sensing his pain, Genoh and Silsun pulled him back. The Akkarra murmured comfort and again offered hope; they had found real hope. Gently insistent, Genoh sent him onward.

The middle tunnel, the recent present.

Dierna, Sean and Flynn, raced toward them, splashing through the warm sandy shallows, Dierna weeping with joy at the sight of her returned son. Her expression even now, removed from its full power by his reliving, cut m'Connor to the bone. That smile, fading to puzzlement as Bren didn't react to his mother calling to him.

'Mama? What's wrong with him? He's scared of us. What's wrong with him?' Flynn demanded.

'He's not here. He's not anywhere.'

M'Connor resisted the Path and Genoh helped him, aware there was nothing here of use to them. He could feel the ageless Mind studying, appraising his spirit and approving of his reaction to his life's Testing. For himself, m'Connor was sure he'd failed all those he loved. The final, most difficult tunnel waited. The future.

Centering himself, m'Connor warily obeyed Genoh's urging to continue onward. He drew comfort from the knowledge that

Silsun, though not consciously present, was still Linked with him and would guide him back to his body when the final test was done. Nonetheless, as far as they knew, this was the first time any Weaver had ever entered a future Path without his Akkarra-Brother to supply the aetheric safety rope that could be followed if for whatever reason, the Traveler was lost.

The third rainbow mist swirled up and over him and he was falling, tumbling into its depths. All the colors ever known spun about him, dizzying him as they sped him down and down into a vortex of light. A sudden wrenching jolt told him from brutal experience of past Testings that he'd been thrust forward in time to join with his body of the future.

An immediate rushing flood of sensory detail threatened to overwhelm and drown him in its tide. Time moved much faster in unison with the millennia-aged Akkarra, his mind couldn't keep pace. Sharp and clear above it all was pain, fiery pain burning molten and bright through his right leg. Then came cold; intense, killing cold. A snarling face, half-spider, half-man lunged at him, fangs trailing saliva, dark eyes gleaming from gaunt sockets, thin gray flesh pulled taut over a skeletal, death-mask skull. A flash of seemingly reversed images—a town wall, high and ancient, topped by uneven, crumbling stonework. Beneath it a river, shimmering in icy twilight, its rippling surface revealing a small boy's face, mouth agape in terror, lips forming a silent scream and huge brown eyes running with tears that were the river's eddying. The water dissolved into a snowfall whose white flakes turned red and dripped blood as they fell, melding into a curtain, a cloak, a sneering voice. Zaraxan.

M'Connor's very Ea was dissipating, merging into that scarlet blizzard. He struggled to pull free.

Red-gold light exploded, engulfing and lifting him like an autumn leaf before a gale. Then, abruptly, all was still. The gold halo became an oval shape, a man's face. Piercingly intense blue-gray eyes regarded him, glittering like winter ice. Lightning flickered between those eyes and flared upward into a blade-like flame, expanding, widening, climbing, becoming a radiant sun.

Unable to resist, m'Connor was drawn into the fire, speeding upward only to be spewed out into chilling silence.

'I tell you something's wrong with him!' m'Connor heard Gerion growling in an accusatory tone that said he was badly scared.

There was warmth at m'Connor's back and he knew he'd returned to his body, was leaning against Gerion's supporting chest, no longer in contact with the Akkarra's gnarled trunk. It'd never happened like this before, he'd always followed the ritual, said a formal farewell in Genoh's cathedral halls where Silsun arrived to guide him home. There'd been no guiding Magi, no memory of anything beyond the last tunnel.

'You shouldn't have moved him!' Silsun admonished, the fear in her sharp words even worse than Gerion.

'I didn't move him! He started to convulse! The others are all awake and gone long since,' Gerion continued, sounding more concerned than m'Connor could recall him being in a long while. 'Wasn't he supposed to come back with you? You ask too much of him!'

M'Connor tried to get his tongue to move to say, 'Steady, Marc,' but couldn't.

'He is awake,' Silsun said, the words almost lost to a great exhalation of relief.

Her cool hand came to rest on m'Connor's brow. She Sent power and it poured forth in a healing wave of golden light that entered through m'Connor's third eye. The darkness receded and m'Connor saw Silsun's white face hovering above him. Unsteadily, he tried to push himself to his feet.

'Be still,' Silsun urged at the same moment Gerion said, 'Steady!'

'You've been hard-tested,' Silsun told him, her river-blue eyes dark with a concern that brightened suddenly as she added with pride, 'And done well! Genoh has relayed your Seeing to us all. Some of those images will lead us where we need to go, I'm certain.'

'I have?' m'Connor muttered with a tongue thick as sheep wool. 'I don't remember them,' he added, not sure if he was glad of that or not.

'Of course you won't, you know it doesn't work that way,' Silsun reassured him.

Gerion bent closer, his foggy breath clouding m'Connor's sight. 'How do you feel? Do you remember me? More to the point, do you remember you?'

'Who could forget your ugly face, Marc!' M'Connor managed a weak smile but when his attempt at gripping Gerion's arm missed, his friend's relieved expression faded back to stern worry.

'Take him to the Weavers Lodge,' Silsun instructed. 'He'll need to sleep and eat before he's strong enough to return to Sanctuary.'

'I can see that for myself!' Gerion snapped. He slid an arm beneath his captain's shoulder and began propping him up.

'Wait,' m'Connor protested. 'What about all those future visions? What did they mean?'

'Rest. We'll hold your visions for you, and when—if—the time comes that you're Called to walk this Path, together we'll unravel the meaning of your Seeing.'

'Come along,' Gerion urged, hauling him up. 'Your legs are all askew like a newborn colt. Lean on me.'

'But . . . .' m'Connor said dazedly, 'I must ask what . . . if . . . I mean . . . .'

'You don't know what you mean, and you won't know what you mean until you rest. The Magi will call when they have need of you, of that you may be certain.'

Gerion grunted, half-carrying him forward and down the slope toward the gray stone lodge whose glow-moss lit windows gleamed through the surrounding trees. The night air was chill, the grove dark, the Akkarra silent. Low above the lodge and its leafy backdrop, one of the moons hung softly yellow amid gray-white ghostly clouds.

Had he been in trance so long? He thought he remembered a face . . . .

Gerion had the room too warm for m'Connor's liking. He'd lit a small fire in the huge open hearth at the far end of the rectangular lodge and kept it blazing all through the two nights m'Connor had been recuperating. It wasn't anywhere near cold enough to warrant a fire, but such was life living with a coast-man unused as he was to winters in the highlands that carried snow to bury the windows and block the doorways. Seated alone at the lodge's long wooden table, m'Connor shook his head and took another spoonful of his lumpy breakfast porridge, watching with disbelief as Gerion added another log to the fire.

'I'm not the only one thinks it's cold,' Gerion grumbled, reading m'Connor's expression rather than his mind. 'And Silsun insisted I keep you warm.'

M'Connor waved a stalling hand. 'I'm not complaining, am I?' Satisfied, Gerion turned back to tending the fire. 'But we'll be leaving as soon as we're done eating.'

Gerion looked over his shoulder at him. 'You don't know that yet. You still look a little white round the gills to me.'

M'Connor snorted and picked up another piece of hot bread. 'I don't have gills. You're confusing me with our friends the Talaers.'

'They don't have gills either; they only swim like fish.' Gerion straightened up, his mood darkening as he returned to his meal. 'I hope they were able to find the children of Tol Eabah. Poor little mites.'

M'Connor sighed heavily and pushed away his plate. 'The Wave-Dancers would lead them to them.'

'Oh, that's right,' Gerion frowned at m'Connor's half-eaten porridge. 'Eat.'

'It's as well they had the sea caves to hide in,' m'Connor murmured and dutifully, scraped every bit of porridge onto one huge spoonful and downed it with a grimace.

'You didn't finish your bread,' Gerion pointed out, indicating the half-eaten slice with his laden spoon.

'Yes, mother.'

Gerion looked away from his breakfast as the lodge's heavy wooden door opened admitting a breath of blessedly cooler air.

M'Connor took the opportunity of his friend's distraction to stuff the remaining bread inside his shirt; Bruska would enjoy it.

'Good morning, Magi,' Gerion greeted.

'It is, thank you, Marc,' Silsun agreed, closing the door. She carried a small, embossed box in one hand and put it down carefully on a spindle-legged table to the left of the door. She turned to eye m'Connor shrewdly. 'You look better than you did yesterday, Taran,' she observed.

'I'm fine,' he said, standing to go to her. He touched his fingertips to his brow in traditional greeting then smiled. 'Or I will be if I escape this furnace.'

Silsun puffed a laugh. 'It is a little warm in here. He slept well?' Silsun asked Gerion, making m'Connor roll his eyes and feel as if he were ten years old again. 'Ate well?'

Gerion, much to m'Connor's relief, came to his rescue. 'Snored all night, and I've had to guard my share of the food.'

'Mmm,' Silsun said, lifting a hand and running it, testing, a few inches above m'Connor's chest. She studied the energy feedback from his Ea a moment and then said, 'You're a free man.'

'Good. I need to get back to my Legion.'

'But . . . .' Gerion looked from one to the other, frowning. 'Is that it? Don't we get to hear more about . . . . how it all worked out?'

'The Akkarra believe Sean's Magi must be too young and probably is still on the mainland.'

'Oh, well, that's some news,' Gerion said, 'but . . . .'

'There's nothing to report as yet,' she told him, m'Connor having already Sensed it. 'There were many visions from all the Captains. We're still sorting through them.'

189

'The others were let go straight back to Home Cove after,' Gerion pointed out, not buying that for a moment. 'Whatever he saw, it totally flattened Taran.'

'It did not 'totally flatten me',' m'Connor scowled and turned away to collect his sword belt where it hung on the bunk bed post. They were avoiding mentioning he'd been only half a Weaver when he'd gone in.

'Looked that way to me,' Gerion said cheerfully and went to gather his own things from the other bed.

'It has never been an easy road for you,' Silsun said softly. 'There is always pain.'

'Pain?' Gerion turned so sharply that he tangled with the trailing loop of the sword belt in his left hand.

'You had to tell him that?' m'Connor complained.

'Then you do remember it?' Gerion asked.

'A little of it is coming back.'

'The pain?'

'Nothing. The past.'

'Oh and I believe that.'

'Come on, Marc, you can't go up against Myrrgha without getting a few scrapes and bumps, you know that.'

'Uh-huh.'

'All will be revealed should the Akkarra decide you are the right Weaver for this Path,' Silsun said tartly. 'Until then it's probably best not to dwell on it.'

'I could say it,' m'Connor said, strapping on his sword, 'but I won't.'

'I should follow my own advice,' Silsun sighed. 'I know. It's just . . . hard, sometimes. And this time, well, none of us have Seen anything like it. There is so much to be unraveled. That alone will take many days and only then do we begin to work on sorting the various possible Paths. Choosing this time . . . it carries much more than ever before. We need to be very, very careful.' She looked down at her hands, clasping them together as if to hold something closer. 'Sometimes, I wish there was another way.'

'I understand,' m'Connor said softly.

'They won't let me go,' Silsun admitted. 'The Akkarra are forbidding any Magi to leave Sanctuary.'

M'Connor flinched, knowing just how difficult that would be, how much he himself would hate it. Gently, he enfolded her hands and lifted them to his heart. 'We're always together,' he said simply. But Bren's absence stood silent agony to that lie, a great gaping emptiness that roared a constant dull ache between them. Thinking of that reminded him of Sean Fetrin. Bring us hope.

'There is hope, Taran. The Akkarra are certain and The Tanortha are not just empty myth.' She paused, lowering her gaze, avoiding his eyes before she said, 'You saw something. Someone . . . . Remember the stories of your childhood.'

Before he could comment, she turned toward the door. 'I have something for you to take back to the Fetrin family, or rather, the Akkarra do. It is their gift, they created it.'

She picked up the small box she'd left on the table by the door and carried it across to him, gathering Gerion with her glance, urging him to come closer. As if he needed any urging; he'd been brimming with curiosity since he'd seen her carrying something. Silsun traced gentle fingertips over the inlaid lid of the box. Solemnly, she handed it to m'Connor. 'Here.'

'The Akkarra have created a gift?' Gerion asked, bending forward a little the better to see it. 'I've never heard of such a thing before.'

'It has seldom been done before,' Silsun said, and m'Connor could feel her studying him intently, not looking away to Gerion.

'The Fetrins will be honored,' Gerion said.

'They've earned it,' m'Connor reminded him heavily.

'The Akkarra are as distressed over their sorrow as are we,' Silsun murmured sadly. 'They feel they have failed us all, being unable to locate Bren.'

If nothing else, m'Connor might at least meet Bren in death. It didn't bear thinking that his Brother might exist for all eternity bound in a Void of Zaraxan's making. Or that his soul had been utterly destroyed, even the sanctuary of death stolen away from him. And from them all if they should fail.

'What do I tell them, Magi?' he asked softly, frowning down at the small box cradled in his hands.

'Just give them that, along with the Word of the Akkarra.'

'Which is?'

'They haven't forgotten their promise, and they've found the beginning of the Path.'

He looked up at her again. 'The Path to Bren?'

'So it may be.'

'May be.' M'Connor sighed and turned his head to regard the sea gleaming blue and silver beyond the fringe of dark green pine needles that overhung the partly-shuttered window of the Weavers' lodge.

Silsun reached out and pushed the box gently against his chest. 'Open it.'

He frowned from it to her. 'But it's not for me.'

'It is for the Fetrin family,' she said chidingly, 'And are you not Bren's Akkarra-Brother?'

He remained doubtful despite that truth, but his fingers had a life of their own, working their way under the box's rim. He stopped short of pushing against the clasps.

'The Akkarra ask that you open it. Now. Can't you feel it?'

'I can,' he answered with surprise, suddenly aware of their keen, hopeful and perhaps a little nervous anticipation. 'They're like . . . .'

'Like parents eager to see their child's face when a very special gift is given them,' Gerion finished for him, looking wonderingly toward The Grove.

'Yes. And they are as eager for your reaction as for Taran's.'

'Me?' Gerion's eyebrows climbed to his shaggy hairline. 'Well, then,' he rubbed at his bearded jaw and elbowed m'Connor in the side. 'What are you waiting for? Come on, open it!'

Carefully, m'Connor did so. As the lid lifted, gold light spilled over his hands. Inside, nestled on a bed of simple blue linen, was the loveliest most exquisite shape of delicate curved petals, symmetrically arrayed around a pitted center. He had seen it before, the original, first in Primona's hands, then his own. But this flower had been poured from Akkarra blood and shaped by their craft and their will in pure golden amber.

When he was sure of his voice, m'Connor asked, 'A copy?'

'Yes.'

'It's so beautiful,' Gerion breathed, awe-struck, his dark eyes reflecting the light that radiated from within the box.

'It is a treasure, a rare carving from their very life-essence. Proof of the blood oath wrought in their promise to you and to the Fetrins.'

M'Connor found he had to swallow hard against a suddenly tight throat. Hope flickered back to life somewhere deep inside where he had thought despair had forever rooted it out. He lifted his head to share that discovery with Silsun. He found her eyes shimmering with emotion. She said nothing but touched her hand from her brow to his heart.

'Sean will say it's only a flower,' Gerion said bluntly.

'It also carries a promise that he cannot deny,' Silsun pointed out.

'True enough,' Gerion admitted. 'But he's a hard case to convince.'

'His heart is broken, Marc,' Silsun said softly. 'It takes much courage to dare to rebuild.'

'Indeed,' Gerion agreed, casting a grim glance at m'Connor. 'Indeed it does.'

Silsun hadn't looked away from m'Connor's face. 'What does your heart tell you, now that you see it?' she asked.

'I . . . I'm not sure.'

'Touch it,' she suggested.

He obeyed, very, very gently brushing one forefinger against an upturned petal. And suddenly, just as in the Grove before the Testing, he felt it again. A Presence reaching out, seeking him from some vast distance, then forced away by something much more powerful, a snapping recoil, like the rebound from an overloaded ballista. It burned his fingertip, making him pull away.

'What was that!' Silsun exclaimed, taking a step back.

'The same as the Presence I felt?' Gerion asked.

'No,' Silsun answered for m'Connor.

'I don't like mysteries,' Gerion grumbled. 'Whatever it is, why can't it make itself clear?'

'Something or someone is holding it back,' m'Connor suggested grimly.

'Bren?' Gerion asked sharply.

M'Connor sighed and rubbed a hand over his brow. 'I don't know; it was impossibly far away.'

'The Void?' Silsun dared speak the unspeakable horror.

'Further.'

'There is nothing further than the Void,' Gerion stated, watching m'Connor worriedly.

M'Connor merely grunted and closed the box. He placed it back on the table while he went in search of the sword, scabbard and belt he'd left hanging on the bedpost. 'We won't speak of this to the Fetrins. I fear . . . . I fear it's only my wanting it to be him that deceives me.' He strapped on the belt and settled the sword and scabbard at his hip. 'We will not speak of it to the Fetrins,' he repeated, eying Gerion.

'You don't need to glower at me like that,' Gerion huffed, also busy with his sword belt. 'I would not give false hope.'

'No,' m'Connor agreed, remembering Gerion's strength in the dungeon cells after Bren had been taken from them. He walked to the man's side and gripped his shoulder. 'I know you do not.'

Gerion nodded. 'At least we're not going back to Sean empty-handed.'

'No.' Straightening, M'Connor clapped him on the shoulder. 'Come on, I Sense Rhyssa waiting.'

'Oh, good,' Gerion brightened, 'She's probably made some of that special spiced rice thing for us.'

'You can't still be hungry!' m'Connor spluttered disbelief, left floundering in his friend's wake as Gerion strode outside.

CHAPTER ELEVEN

'You're late!' Rhyssa greeted m'Connor with mock scolding, drawing back from his engulfing hug. He held something in his hands, a small wooden box that had dug into her back as he held her hard to him. 'I missed you,' she added and reached up to cup his cheek and caress his face, picking up signs of tension. 'Are you all right?' There had been something different in his embrace, a desperate hunger as if they'd been parted for more than just a few days. 'They kept you a day longer than the others? The Testing was difficult?'

'I don't remember much of it,' m'Connor said, frowning down at the box in his hand.

'Silsun says they have a lot to unravel,' Gerion put in, shadowing m'Connor.

'Is that good?'

'Probably not,' m'Connor admitted.

'What's this?' She indicated the box.

'A gift for the Fetrins, from the Akkarra, a token they want delivered along with their message.' He looked away toward the track that led back to the village. 'I promised Sean I'd go straight to him.'

'I haven't seen Bruska yet this morning,' Rhyssa said firmly. 'He'll be waiting for me.'

'He likes those honey cakes,' Gerion said, taking the two steps to pick up the package Rhyssa had left further up the beach, clear of the tide.

They fell into step side by side, Rhyssa in the middle. M'Connor tucked the box inside his shirt and held out a hand for hers, then drew her close so he could wrap an arm about her waist as they walked over the sand and into the mangroves. Morning light slanted down in misty beams of gold through the glossy olive-green leaves. It was unusually quiet, the parrots gone elsewhere to feed, or still in the tree hollows. It was as if all Sanctuary waited for something, and Rhyssa had a strong feeling that something was carried in the little wooden box.

'The Akkarra have given a token? Is that usual?' she asked.

'It's most unusual. They're worried about Sean,' m'Connor murmured. 'So am I. They couldn't give us any real information about a Magi or Brother.'

Rhyssa nodded and squeezed his hand. 'His grief has become anger.'

'I know how he feels,' m'Connor muttered.

'Is there any hope?'

They had reached the top of the low rise that overlooked the village. M'Connor stopped and gave a great, sighing breath. She waited for his answer, sensing Gerion just as anxious though surely he must know more than she. Gerion shrugged, catching her worried glance as m'Connor remained silent, standing frowning toward the palm thatched huts where people were stirring, going about early morning chores, gathering firewood or carrying fruit and water.

'I don't know,' he said at last. 'The Beginning of the Path, they called it, but how long a path? How much longer can they endure?' He turned away and looked down into her eyes. 'I don't want to give false hope.'

She freed her hand to grip his forearm and give it a little shake. 'Hope is hope. We've come this far. We can make it the rest of the way.' He held her gaze, searching. A slow smile dawned first in his eyes, then spread to curve his lips. He nodded.

'Good,' she said. 'Now, come on. I want to see what's in that box!'

As a High Mariner Lady of Myrrgha City, Rhyssa had lived a privileged, comfortable life. She'd worn rare jewels and walked ornate hallways adorned with treasures from around the known world. Yet she'd never seen anything as truly lovely, as perfect and exquisite, as the carved amber petals glowing in the morning sunshine and glowing, too, with some inner light of Akkarra magic.

Sean and his mother thanked m'Connor and Gerion for the gift and set food before them, Bruska already happily munching on the honey cakes Rhyssa had surrendered to him as soon as she entered. M'Connor delivered the message as they gathered about the box and opened it, but the words had little effect. The Fetrins were politely grateful, gave sincere praise for the flower's beauty and rarity, but hadn't been particularly impressed by the words.

The message changed nothing for them here, now. Finished devouring the cakes, Bruska came closer to sit on the floor and nudge Rhyssa's arm until she stroked his head. Seeing the body of the man who'd been his Brother behave in such a fashion made m'Connor flinch and turn away, as did the Fetrins. The day grew older, another day in which they must care for a man they loved who didn't recognize them, couldn't speak to them, and didn't know how to feed or clothe himself.

'But, it's just a flower,' Flynn said, echoing his elder brother's disappointment. He frowned down at the amber sculpture resting on the blue cloth inside the box he held carefully in his cupped palms.

Watching him, a small red-haired boy, the image of his brothers, standing there with tears welling from his eyes and his mouth trembling as he tried not to cry, Rhyssa wanted to gather him into a hug, but he put the box back on the table and ran outside.

'Oh, no,' Dierna murmured, ready to go after him.

'Something else has upset him?' m'Connor guessed, looking worriedly to Dierna. He moved away from the breakfast table and the open box that sat among the fruit and bread bowls.

'The Talaers arrived back with the children from Tol Eabah yesterday,' Dierna said quietly.

'I found Flynn coming back from speaking with them,' Sean explained grimly. 'Some of them are wounded, all are terrified, some can't talk at all. You know how it goes.'

'Damn!' m'Connor swore under his breath and rubbed a hand over his face. It would have been a terrible shock for Flynn, to see the evidence of the violence that haunted them all but from which he'd been thus far successfully sheltered.

'He'd have to meet them sooner or later,' Dierna said. 'He'll be all right.' She was right, he'd survived the shock of Bren's condition, and he'd handle this, too. But not right now.

'I'll speak with him,' M'Connor offered, touching his hand to Dierna's arm as if for permission.

'Take the flower,' she said, surprising Rhyssa with the confidence that rang in her voice. Obviously, something she couldn't sense had transpired between the two. Usually, Rhyssa found her inability to follow these silent communications immensely frustrating and annoying, but this time she could only be glad of whatever reassurance m'Connor had been able to convey.

Rhyssa waited a moment before quietly following him outside. She found m'Connor on one knee at Flynn's side, his hand on the boy's shoulder, man to man. 'It's a very special flower,' m'Connor was telling him. 'It's made from their heart-amber, their blood. It has great power.'

Flynn shook his head, his tears tracing his face with lines of silver in the morning light. 'The Tanortha is just a story for babies.'

'The Akkarra have given you their token,' m'Connor said, quietly insistent. 'They have given you their blood-promise.'

'I know. But . . . .'

M'Connor slipped an arm about the boy's shoulders and said nothing. At first Flynn resisted, but gradually the tension eased from his small form and he surrendered, moving into the embrace and burying his head against m'Connor's chest. Rhyssa heard a few snuffling sobs. She could well imagine the firsthand accounts of butchery, of merciless savagery, the boy would have encountered. And her people were responsible for it all. Somehow, someday, they must rid Myrrgha of the Methaggars and their henchmen who warped ordinary minds to murderous rage.

'They say . . .' Flynn lifted his head a little, gulping back his sobs and wiping an arm over his nose. 'They say they'll come here, too.' M'Connor wisely said nothing for the moment. He merely nodded, unable to deny the possibility. 'They killed the Magi and, and captured the Weavers!' Flynn blurted out the news that had most unsettled him.

'I know,' m'Connor said quietly. The boy held his gaze a moment, then m'Connor drew him back against his chest and let him cry a while longer.

Dierna stood in the doorway, watching them, her eyes moist and her face pale. Bruska appeared, crouched at her side, whining a little as he sensed their distress. He adored Flynn. Hearing him, Flynn held out an arm, beckoning him to come to him.

'Steady, Bruska!' m'Connor warned. 'Steady now!'

'Slow, Bruska,' Rhyssa commanded softly, and the man-dog glanced at her.

Bruska for once managed to gather himself and remember his much greater size. The dog-mind continually forgot that it no longer inhabited a body less than half the size of a man, let alone a man taller than most. He slowed, shaken by the depth of Flynn's grief. As he crouched on all fours, Flynn wrapped his arms about Bruska's neck, and Rhyssa could see m'Connor was glad that the boy had someone else to care for, someone to draw him away from his fear.

'Go inside now, Bruska,' Flynn instructed in a suddenly much older sounding voice. 'I'm all right. Go, have some porridge.'

Bruska looked back to the door and Dierna waved him to her, somehow finding a watery smile. It should be Flynn's eldest brother standing there with him, not this thing Zaraxan had created.

'Will Bren ever come back to us?' Flynn asked m'Connor with a plaintive hope that tore at Rhyssa's heart.

'Yes,' m'Connor said, sounding as if the revelation surprised him as much as Rhyssa. 'The flower might help me find him.' He held the boy at arm's length to look long into his eyes. 'I don't know how, I don't know when. But it will happen.'

Flynn nodded and hugged him as hard as his thin arms could manage. 'You're going away?' he asked.

'Yes. Likely I will.'

Flynn said nothing for a moment, struggling against a fresh bout of tears. 'Will Sean and Rhyssa go, too?'

'Sean . . . .' m'Connor considered. 'No. Rhyssa, maybe.'

'Gerion will, though.' That was more statement than question.

'Yes. He's . . . . he's looking after me until Bren comes back.'

'And your Magi will go?'

'No. The Akkarra have ordered that the Magi are not to leave Sanctuary.'

'I'll bet she didn't like that!' Flynn declared with a sniff.

'No, she didn't. But it's best this way.'

Flynn nodded. 'We need to keep them safe. We mustn't lose any more.' He sounded so grown-up, so gravely certain they would all do what they must to survive that Rhyssa had to look away.

'If you go . . . . out there,' Flynn said uncertainly, getting to the heart of his fear at last. 'Could they catch you again?'

'I won't let them,' m'Connor assured as best he might.

Suddenly, Rhyssa was horribly afraid for him. What had he seen during the Testing? What did the Magi and the Akkarra ask of him now? Surely he'd already suffered enough? But for Bren . . . . for Bren, she knew, he would do all and more than the impossible.

'They might,' Flynn whispered.

'Then I'll get away again, like I did before.'

'What if . . . . Could they follow you back here?'

'They can't,' m'Connor said, and this time it was without hesitation, absolutely certain. 'They couldn't follow when we brought Bruska back. It's a maze of islands out there, Flynn. You can get lost just looking at them all. Even if they knew we were out here, they couldn't find us.'

'Only if someone told them exactly where to go?'

'No one will,' m'Connor replied with the same certainty. 'No one *can* tell them.'

'Because of The Keys?' Flynn asked.

'Right. The Akkarra won't let any of us go out without first erasing any memory that would help the Myrrghinners. Sanctuary is safe, Flynn. I promise you. They won't come here. I swear it.'

'Will the Key stop you remembering me, too?' Flynn asked wistfully.

'No, I won't let them take that memory. There's no need and I need you, Flynn. You, Sean, your mother, Rhyssa.'

'Because that's home?' Flynn asked.

'Because that's home. Yes.'

'Good.' Flynn flashed a wide, open smile. 'But I hope you don't have to go, anyway.' Bruska whimpered from inside the house. 'I know you'll keep us safe,' Flynn said, explaining the smile. 'You came home.' Hearing another whimper from Bruska he hurried inside.

Heaving a weary sigh, m'Connor got to his feet. He opened his arms and she walked into his embrace. 'It's true?' she asked.' The Keys can't be broken?'

'It's true.' M'Connor rested his chin on her hair, leaving her with her head against his chest. She loved to feel the rumble of his voice as he spoke. 'The energy, the light, that blocks the memories is a complex Weave that only the Akkarra can undo.'

'Without killing. It scares me,' she admitted and shifted to look up at him.

'There is hope here,' he said, bending to the little box sitting on the ground before him. 'I don't understand it, I'm not even sure I believe it. But there is hope here. You can feel it.' He held the box out to Rhyssa. 'Touch it.' She blinked at him in surprise. 'Go on, it's all right. Touch it. I don't know how, but it seems to carry memories of Bren, at least for me.'

Rhyssa frowned but took the open box. 'You think the Akkarra might be trying to give us some clue?'

M'Connor scrubbed a hand over his face. 'Maybe.' He looked to her with desperate hope bright in his dark eyes. 'I have to find him, Rhyssa. Even if only to be sure he's safely dead.'

'I know.' She leaned forward and kissed his mouth and it became a long, lingering sharing.

When they drew back, m'Connor smiled. 'That helped,' he said.

'Good.' She traced the palms of her hands over his chest. 'It was only a sample.'

That made him laugh, as she'd hoped it would. Then, nervously, she sat on the bench and reached a fingertip to touch the flower. 'Wait,' m'Connor said suddenly, gently taking her hand before it could make contact with the Akkarra amber. She looked at him questioningly. 'I'm an idiot,' he said.

'Well, we all know that,' she said teasingly over her puzzlement.

He snorted, but the moment of humor was short-lived. 'Your memories of Bren are . . . painful.'

'You know as well as I that it is no coincidence this flower comes to us here today. They would know I would want to see it, and they know how we met,' she reminded him.

He sighed, his gaze full of tenderness and remembered sorrow, softening to darker forest green. 'That's my thought, too,' he admitted.

'All right, then,' she said firmly. 'Perhaps we'll find some clue we overlooked the first thousand times.'

'We didn't miss anything,' m'Connor said bitterly.

Those first days after arriving here, full of hope that the Magi and the Akkarra would at least be able to track the whereabouts of his friend's soul, had been pure agony for m'Connor. Time after time the Magi had called him to announce only another failure. Sometimes she wondered if he would have brought Bren's body back here at all if he had known his Brother would continue such an humiliating existence among his people. The lingering fragment of hope that he might still be found was torture for them all, but worst for m'Connor.

'Rhyssa,' he murmured, 'Something happened in the Grove. I didn't want to tell the Fetrins because, well, I'm not sure it was anything other than my own wanting it to be so, my imagination.'

Her heart jumped, her pulse suddenly running with the same excitement she felt him struggling to suppress. 'The Akkarra do not allow false touches in The Grove,' she told him, using his own words.

'I know.' He looked away from her, his eyes following the rapid flight of some parrots emerging from the giant trees against the foot of the red-brown cliffs. 'But, this . . . . This was different. Even Silsun couldn't help me with it and her memory reaches back through centuries.'

Her fingers tightened about his. 'You think it was Bren.' It was not a question; she could sense it in the pounding beat of the blood in his veins.

Slowly, he turned and met her eyes. 'Not him, exactly, but something Linked to him. Yes.'

'Taran!' she cried, and bit down over an upsurge of emotion.

'Now, wait!' He held up his free hand, gently tracing its palm against her cheek, cupping her jaw, his thumb stroking her face. 'I haven't admitted it even to Gerion. I can't begin to describe how impossibly tenuous and fleeting a touch it was.'

'But, Bren,' she said, annoyed at the tremor she heard in her voice. 'The least touch, you would know.'

'Exactly right. So you see why I doubt.'

'Zaraxan said the Methaggar were involved . . . .' Rhyssa's mind raced, analyzing every clue afresh, m'Connor hanging on her every word. 'How many times have you said that everything, *everything*, is different since the coming of The Shadow Stone. It killed the Akkarra in Lellgha who should have been able to see it coming. The Methaggars found some way to hide their weapon beyond the paths of time, didn't you tell me so?'

'Yes, that's right,' he agreed, continuing to caress her face. 'Keep going, I think I see where you're heading but I want you to verify it independent of my influence. I've never known anyone who can figure things quite the way you do, Rhyssa. Nor as quickly.'

'Flatterer,' she said and turned her head to bite his thumb gently. But she was pleased by the compliment nonetheless. If the dog spirit had much to learn of living in a man's body, Rhyssa had had a thousand times more to learn in the first weeks of her new life among her lover's strangely, frighteningly, gifted kin. He'd tried to teach her all he knew of the ways of the Akkarra and the Magi, but much of it remained mystery, even to a Weaver who relied on it.

'So,' she picked up the thread of her analysis, her body's instinctive response to the by-play distracting her. 'If they could hide their methirri stores and their plans from the Lellghin Akkarra until it was too late for them to defend themselves, they could as easily hide Bren's soul from the Akkarra of the Grove. The question is, how, and where . . . . or more precisely, when?'

'That's my thinking. But not when or where,' m'Connor jumped in, unable to contain himself a moment longer. It was the first time she'd heard him speak with any hope since the Akkarra pronouncement that they could not locate Bren's soul.

'It has to be one or the other, or both,' Rhyssa corrected. Then, catching the gleam in his eyes, she asked, 'Doesn't it?'

'What if . . . . 'He looked away again, toward the rising sun, toward the east, toward the place he had last seen his friend. 'What if somehow the methirri and the Methaggars' methods, have created a place beyond space and time?'

Rhyssa frowned. 'The Akkarra are able to enter the Void.'

He looked back at her. 'Another Void, separate, different somehow.'

'And you think Bren somehow contacted you from this place?'

His shoulders heaved in a massive shrugging sigh. 'I know, it sounds crazy. Maybe . . . . maybe I *am* going mad without him.'

She broke free of his grasp to lift both hands to his face and turn his gaze to meet hers. 'You are the sanest man I know.'

'No hope for the rest of them, then!'

She shook his head a little, let go and looked back down at the flower that reflected sunlight into her eyes. 'Everyone is saying they've never seen the Akkarra in such a mood. You think they've sensed or suspect the existence of this place, too?'

'Maybe. But it could be just this crazy belief they have that they've found The Tanortha d'Rellan.'

'Flynn says that's just a story for babies.'

'It was true once,' m'Connor said quietly. 'He was our leader, the oldest and the strongest, the man primarily responsible for our survival. He made the way here for us.'

'But he himself didn't survive?'

'No. No male Magi can exist without a female Akkarra.'

'And all the female seeds were destroyed in the Crossing,' Rhyssa finished for him, adding with a smile, 'See, I remember your lectures.'

They sat together, silent, watching the amber flower gleaming in the morning sunlight, as if somehow it held all the answers. 'This is a replica of an Akkarra flower that can only be produced by a female seed?' she asked.

'Not quite,' he corrected, looking up at her. 'It's a Starflower, symbol of the male Magi. But this one's different. If you look closely at the center, see the red spiral? It indicates the Firstborn, the Warrior Magi, the Tanortha d'Rellan.'

'But he can't exist without a female Akkarra,' Rhyssa repeated. 'Which means the Akkarra have seen their females somewhere in our future, but they can't tell us yet.'

M'Connor frowned. 'That's impossible . . . . The seeds were destroyed before they could reach this world.'

'Taran, everything we think we know about time and place, and what we think we know has happened and will happen can no longer be trusted. Maybe they're right about the Warrior Magi.'

'He existed once long ago, on another world,' m'Connor said slowly. 'They tell me I knew him and my heart knows it's true.'

'Something happened during your Testing. Then, they send this here, the emblem of the Firstborn Warrior. The Beginning of the Path, they call it.' Taking his hand again, she said, 'We've never had a Path before, or anywhere to start searching.'

'Yes, but a Path toward what?'

She moved his hand toward the flower. 'Let's find out—together.'

'Together.' He touched his lips to hers in a fleeting kiss and at the same moment she felt the cool, smooth amber under her fingers bringing memory flooding into her mind. Again, sharp and clear as crystal, she was looking into m'Connor's desperate gaze, hearing Bruska howling from below her in the pit. Shock hitting her as she saw the sound was coming from the body of the big red-haired man m'Connor had named, Bren. Together, they listened again to Zaraxan's answers to her questions, hunting down any clue.

'First, show me you can return Bruska to me, unharmed. Where are you keeping him? I hope the slave residing in him doesn't do anything to hurt him.'

'I . . . It's not as easy as that,' the Inquisitor floundered. *'I mean . . . the dog, its body, is dead, Rhyssa. I'm so sorry. The slave's essence isn't there, it's—well, it's a secret.'*

'You can tell me, your soon-to-be-wife, can't you?'

'I—, I would, truly I would. I can tell you this much—it's true Grouda has allowed Methaggar back into the City. They captured the Weaver essence. Only they know how that part works.'

'—Rhyssa!' Flynn called, 'Bruska wants to come out to you. Should I . . . ?'

The boy's voice brought the present world crashing back into place. Sky, sun-laced treetops, hut roof, walls, ground, spun around her and she fell from the bench to land rump first in the mud with a thud. 'Rhyssa!' Flynn repeated in alarm.

'I'm all right,' she assured him. 'Taran?' she asked, overcome by another wave of dizziness as she turned to look up at him.

M'Connor sat, swaying a little, but still upright, his head buried in his hands. She assumed that he, as she, was battling vertigo. But then he lifted his head and she saw that he was weeping. 'Oh!' she cried, and lurching upward, sat at his side to wrap her arms about him.

'I was wrong,' he said, gulping a breath and steadying.

'Rhyssa?' Flynn approached warily. 'Taran?' M'Connor held out an arm to the boy and managed a reassuring smile that didn't fool him. 'You look sick,' Flynn said. 'Is it from the Testing?'

'No.' He ruffled the boy's hair. 'I ate the Magi's porridge.'

'Eww,' Flynn's mouth screwed up. 'Do they really put weeds and grubs in it?'

M'Connor huffed a laugh. 'No. I'll be all right. Go; I can hear him whining. Give me a moment to talk with Rhyssa, then let him out and we'll all go for a walk on the beach.' Flynn nodded and disappeared happily back into the hut.

'You were wrong?' Rhyssa prompted immediately.

'The Methaggar have him somewhere. I shouldn't have brought Bruska here. If we'd waited, if you had spied for us, maybe we'd—'

'All be dead,' Rhyssa snapped. 'Don't second guess it now, Taran. We could not have stayed and survived, you know that.' She grabbed at his arm and shook it. 'If they have Bren, we'll find him.'

He remained silent for several long moments. 'Even if that's possible, finding him might not help save him. The Akkarra believe only a male Magi can counter Methaggar work.'

210

'So,' she said, unperturbed. 'We'll just have to find a male Magi. What did you call him—the Tanortha d'Rellan? The Warrior Magi?'

He sighed. 'I haven't believed in the Warrior Magi since I was six years old!'

She bent and picked up the box, tucking the flower back into place using the linen, and carefully avoiding touching it. She held it up to m'Connor. 'And when you were six would you have believed a dead Myrrghin soldier would bring this to us?'

Chapter Twelve

Returning from a business luncheon with the merchants and craftsman who were supplying and installing the modern materials for his new bath-house, Zaraxan stepped out of his palanquin onto the colonnade at the rear of the palace and followed it down into a courtyard.

'My Lord, my Lord!' the panicked, familiar voice of his second officer, Lanras, hailed from the covered portico, 'Come quickly! I fear the Weaver slave is dying!'

Unleashing a foul oath, Zaraxan shuffled as fast as his long robes would allow to step up beside the man. 'I left instructions he wasn't to be disturbed until I returned! He needs time to recover between sessions.'

'No one touched him, My Lord!' Lanras backed away a little. 'I found him struggling to breathe when we carried food down to him. I took the liberty of having Surgeon-General Dresin see him moved to the Infirmary. It seemed wise when—'

'Lead on, then, man! Hurry!'

Sweating and wheezing, Zaraxan followed until they reached the two-storied sandstone building that was the barracks Infirmary. He had asked that Grouda build a similar facility for the Inquisition complex, but had been refused; there were too many other buildings needing construction or repair after the disastrous fire begun during m'Connor's escape.

'My Lord?' Lanras called, turning back as he realized Zaraxan was lagging, puffing up the stairs to the second floor. 'He's over there, on the bed in the corner by the window. Dresin is working on him. I thought it best he helped rather than wait for—'

'Yes! Yes! I see!'

Zaraxan crossed to the indicated bedside. It was indeed the collared Weaver-slave, m'Akram, on whom he'd been experimenting. Zaraxan sagged under crushing disappointment. All that work! As the slave struggled for breath, Dresin-Zaraxan's personal Physician no less!—bent over him, listening to the heartbeat and doing little else.

'Lanras!' Zaraxan snarled. 'You should have realized! It's an allergic reaction to my new drug. We'll need to mix the specially prepared antidotes. Move!'

Terrified, Lanras paled and muttered, 'I'm not sure how to do it, my lord.'

'Then bring them here and I'll mix them! Move!' Zaraxan lifted a closed fist in threat. 'Collect all the vials from the cabinet beneath my . . . Oh, you know where they are!'

Lanras scurried away as fast as his skinny legs would carry him. But the laboratory was on the other side of the Ministry buildings from the barracks; he'd never make it back in time. Zaraxan felt sure his blood would boil in sheer frustration. He glared down at the dying slave.

M'Akram's mouth twisted in agonized search for air but his eyes were open, as sharp and annoyingly intelligent as ever. Seeing Zaraxan hovering, helplessly enraged over him, his eyes gleamed knowingly and a faint smile touched his lips despite the pain. He knew his death would rob Zaraxan of a great prize. He managed to turn his head to look up at the sky beyond the window, no doubt attracted to it after the airless darkness of his dungeon cell.

'We must keep him breathing until I can mix the correct antidote!' Zaraxan snapped at Dresin.

Already reaching for a breath mask brought by an orderly, Dresin paused to give an irritated glower. They both knew it was too late. The slave's mouth and cheeks were tinged blue, his eyes losing focus. A shaft of red-gold light suddenly played over his face, lighting his eyes with a golden radiance. A little startled, Zaraxan looked up to see the day ending amid a typical desert sunset of flaring clouds burnished with bands of spectacular color.

'The poor fool believes his spirit will return home with the setting sun,' Dresin said.

Zaraxan snorted contemptuous dismissal and glared accusingly at the sky. 'Myths! Legends! That's all these primitives care about!'

'He's dead,' Dresin announced, giving up his attempts at resuscitation.

'I know that! All my work, wasted!' Zaraxan tugged at the scarlet robe of his office, pulling it hard about the yellow under-tunic. 'Have the body carried to my chambers. Perhaps I can find some answers if I examine the internal organs. The Emperor will not be happy. This is hardly fitting news to take into the month's ministerial conference! None of you have any idea how difficult it is to work with these savages.'

When the day of the Ministerial conference finally arrived, rather than being anxious, Zaraxan found time dragged as the ministers of each department reported in turn. Grouda didn't seem particularly entertained, either. The Emperor slouched on his throne at the head of the long polished rosewood table listening without apparent interest to reports of an uprising in Lellgha City that had been savagely put down by the occupying troops. News of local politics was just as callous.

Zaraxan took a certain malicious satisfaction from General Rusark's embarrassed admittance, that yes, Tol Eabah had in fact been a small settlement, and his agents had yet to locate the main Lellghin outlaw base. Nor had Givant—who was absent, under house arrest pending an inquiry, pinned down the ever-moving Talae fleet, the only opposition of any kind to his steam-powered warships. Smugly complacent, Zaraxan settled back to enjoy the military men's discomfit.

'Well, Lord Inquisitor?' Grouda snapped, his narrow, red-shot gaze instead settling on him. 'It seems total victory would be ours but for the failure of Inquisition efforts to provide the necessary means to break the Lellghin mind-codes. Have you made any progress in that area?'

Zaraxan stood, happy to remind him that it was the military that was blundering and failing him badly. They'd failed to guard valuable prisoners, allowing m'Connor's escape with what was left of m'Fetrin, and leaving Zaraxan with no Weaver slaves to work on breaking the Keying. Admiral Givant would never have stumbled across Tol Eabah without Methaggar aid and yet, the entire aim of the exercise had been lost due to his interfering stupidity! Wanting all the glory for himself, Givant set out to question the captured Weavers aboard ship rather than wait until they could be safely delivered to Zaraxan. M'Singh had died under his clumsy torture, leaving Zaraxan the survivor who was already failing, suffering from the effects of a suddenly severed Weaver Bond. Fortunately,

Zaraxan had found another pair of young would-be Weaver slaves among the captives taken during the latest uprising in Lellgha City. He was working on them as well, despite the information and the type of Keying they carried being out of date by comparison to m'Akram.

'Lack of healthy captives are the source of the problem,' he concluded. 'Our work was showing rapid success until the military let our first Weaver subjects escape and failed to protect our much better equipped facility.'

'But the fact remains,' Rusark interrupted angrily, 'you can't find your way into the savages' minds any more than can my officers!'

'Silence!' Grouda barked, startling them with the force of will from so frail a frame. 'I'll not have my commanders bickering among themselves! All I've heard tonight are excuses, not solutions. There will be no further incompetence! If there are no better reports next month I'll find minds of greater ability to replace you! Is that clear?'

'Yes, Majesty.' White-faced, grim, everyone about the table nodded submissively. All but one. Khenghin Ambassador Mancire remained unmoved, serene and steady as ever, his strong, bronze-skinned hands relaxed on the armrests of his chair. Zaraxan sneered, it was easy for him, an Ambassador from a neutral, sovereign country and therefore beyond reach of punishment. Or rather, of official punishment. Zaraxan knew of many means by which the man might yet meet with disaster. His lips curved up at the thought.

But he needn't have worried; Grouda didn't spare Mancire criticism, either. Coal supplies from distant Rogha were being delayed in Khenghin ports where the ships laid over to take on

216

more supplies. Zaraxan listened avidly as Mancire stood to reply to accusations his people were to blame.

'On the contrary, Your Highness,' Mancire said, bowing graciously, and causing Zaraxan to huff irritation at his confident, smooth manner. 'I believe the reports I have here,' he produced a sheath of ribbon-tied parchments, 'will prove that the problem arises in Rogha Harbor.'

Zaraxan quickly lost interest in the details, his attention returned only by Grouda's sharp complaint that Rogha was 'full of sympathizers' and his ordering Rusark to 'cure them of that disease', using 'every means available.' Something about that convinced Zaraxan that the Methaggars were now working with the General as well as Admiral Givant. He would keep a close eye on that development, too.

It was late evening when Ambassador Mancire finally left the hated palace and returned to his Embassy. Tired as he was, he knew he wouldn't sleep tonight; not after he'd heard the High Inquisitor's horrific description of the Weaver Brothers' deaths and the experiments made on the new captives.

At present, he had more pressing problems. He must insure he kept his position within the privileged Ministry where he was the only man able to access vital information for his Hidden One contacts. To do that he must succeed in solving the problem of Rogha's disappearing coal shipments. He'd been ordered to find someone to go investigate what was happening in Rogha Harbor. Grouda didn't trust Rusark, Givant and Zaraxan's continual infighting. So, he had demanded that Mancire find and assign someone removed from their influence, someone from the Khenghin Embassy, yet someone whose loyalties were all for Myrrgha. Not an easy task.

Portfolio under his arm, Mancire strode briskly toward his office. As he rounded a corner he collided heavily with someone going the other way. The portfolio fell open, its pages scattering across the tiled hall.

'Can't you watch where you're going?' Mancire snapped and crouched down to collect his work. He glanced up angrily to find the other man, a young, red-coated Myrrghin officer, getting to his feet, hastily tucking something that looked like a letter into his tunic pocket. He'd been reading that, then, and wasn't paying attention to anything else.

'Sorry sir. I didn't mean to . . . Yes, sir,' the youthful officer blurted, his fair face flushing. He crouched down and began helping collect the scattered documents. When they were all accounted for, he handed the neat pile back to his superior.

Mancire's angry retort died on his lips as he met the other man's expression. Grief and loss were deeply etched into the weather-beaten face whose gray-blue eyes were liquid with unshed tears. He was much younger than he carried himself, only a closer look revealed him to be no more than twenty five or so.

'Here,' Mancire said softly, 'What's wrong? Bad news?'

'Sir.' The officer nodded stiffly, avoiding his eyes.

Mancire studied the lean jaw, the firmly set mouth, and the intelligent eyes beneath a high brow and neatly combed sandy-brown hair, his face deeply tanned by exposure to sun and wind. He wore a Myrrghin Military Engineer's insignia on tunic and sleeve.

'Lerant, isn't it?' he asked, fairly certain he had the right name. 'Captain Kerell Lerant? Finished that bridge assignment up at Gallia?'

'Yes, sir. Several weeks ago now.'

'Why don't you come into my office and have a drink?' Mancire suggested, knowing he at least wanted one for himself. 'Myrrgha City can be hard on the nerves after the *tierdrun*, and you look like you've had a nasty shock to top it.'

The blue eyes widened and flicked toward his in grateful surprise. 'I could use one, sir. Thank you.'

'Here, sit down.'

Mancire handed over a crystal goblet swirling with the famous Khenghin brandy, golden lagmeld. Lerant took a swallow and sat in the green leather chair facing the desk, his expression revealing surprised appreciation of the quality of the liquor as some color returned to the ashen pallor beneath the tan. 'Now, do you want to tell me about it?' Mancire leaned back in his armchair.

Lerant's jaw set hard against any further show of emotion. 'Not much to tell, sir.'

'Then it won't take long.' Mancire tried a smile. He'd been hastily reviewing his knowledge of this particular liaison officer and recalled efficient, prompt results from a skilled engineer who'd rapidly worked his way up through the ranks, all the more of an achievement for someone not native to Myrrgha. 'Not that you have to tell me anything. I just thought you might need a sympathetic ear.'

'Sympathy is a rare commodity around here,' Lerant said sourly, his fine brows lowering into a gloomy frown.

Mancire drew a deep breath and let it out in a long sigh. 'Sadly true.' He collected his glass from the desktop and sipped at the liquor. 'You're not Myrrghin-born, are you?'

That had been the wrong thing to say, putting Lerant instantly back on guard. 'No,' he said. 'But Myrrgha has been good to me and is deserving of my loyalty.'

'Of course,' Mancire agreed smoothly, liking at least the man's direct nature. 'So, that letter, a death in the family?'

'Worse. It's the approval to have my brother transferred to my staff. Three days too late.'

'I can see that, in your job, you'd want someone whose loyalty is absolutely certain.'

'He was a miner, already a trained sapper, perfect for an engineering squad.'

'Was?'

'He died at Tol Eabah.'

'I'm sorry. A married man, with children?'

Lerant's eyes narrowed in a shrewd, wary regard. 'How did you know?'

'Most Shocktroopers are. Myrrgha can control them that way, no matter how murderous the orders. I am truly sorry the transfer came too late from Command.'

Lerant fidgeted with his glass. 'This letter is from my marriage-sister, Annalie Hollin. She writes to tell me . . .' He drew a deep breath, fighting to steady himself, 'Parlan was killed in battle. The best brother . . . .' Tears brimmed in his eyes and he repeated the words in a husky whisper. '. . . the best brother a man could hope for.' He lifted a hand and hurriedly wiped at his eyes.

'More?' Mancire refilled Lerant's glass. 'I'm sorry.' He'd offered those words in similar circumstances many times before, but was feeling it more sincerely. Like sympathy, such a show of honest grief was rare in Myrrgha. He waited a while, then curious, asked, 'Parlan Hollin? But you're not a Hollin?'

'My foster brother,' Lerant said quietly, looking down at the liquor. 'I have no blood kin living. They were all killed in a massacre when I was about five or six, they think. My new parents wanted me to keep my own name.'

'I see.'

'I wish I'd known sooner. It's been weeks. Apparently, the military powers that be didn't realize we were brothers, because of the names.' Lerant took another gulping swallow of lagmeld. 'I only knew for certain when I received this letter today.'

'But Tol Eabah was, what, more than two months ago now?' Mancire said.

'Yes, sir. Something like that. It's just . . . If I'd known. I wasn't even there for the funeral. Annalie has no one else and her sons are but infants.'

Mancire knew the body would not have been sent home, but a memorial service would have been conducted. 'The mail shipments are notoriously unreliable. Where did it come from?'

'Rogha.'

'What a coincidence!' Mancire straightened in surprise. 'I was just taken to task because of delayed coal shipments from Rogha Harbor.'

'Rogha is my home,' Lerant said with all the longing of one desperately homesick.

'A long, long way from here. A vastly different climate.'

Lerant snorted. 'It's an ice-chest! And that's summer!'

Mancire chuckled and leaned back again, sipping thoughtfully at his drink. Lerant had proven a competent officer and knew much of logistics and supply to distant bases. More importantly, he displayed personal qualities Mancire wanted in an envoy. 'Perhaps,' he said slowly, waiting until Lerant looked curiously up at him before continuing, 'perhaps we can help one another. I take it you'd like to return to your home to aid the widow?'

Lerant leaned forward, his eyes brightening. 'I was hoping to ask for reassignment, but General Rusark needs . . .'

'Forget Rusark,' Mancire waved a casually dismissive hand. 'I have a higher commission—from the Emperor himself. You want to go home, and I need someone to go to Rogha and oversee coal shipments. I've been given the authority to use whatever means necessary to fix the shortfall. Up to and including stealing away Rusark's officers. What would you say to a promotion to Commander and a posting to Rogha Garrison?'

All the somber grief left Lerant's face, making his youth apparent. 'I . . . you're serious?'

'Never been more serious in my life. Well, not often.'

That at last earned a small smile. 'Then I accept, with thanks.'

'Glad to have you aboard, *Commander* Lerant.' Mancire stood and extended a hand and Lerant came to his feet to take it in a firm grip, his shy smile becoming more evident. 'Another drink to celebrate?' After refilling their glasses a third time, Mancire was surprised to see Lerant frowning, lost to somber brooding. 'Something wrong?' he asked. 'Changed your mind already?'

'No, of course not.' But Lerant seemed suddenly very evasive. He drew a breath and said, 'This is very fine brandy.'

'Naturally, it's from my own vineyards.'

'Truly?' Lerant's gaze met his in admiring surprise then flicked away again.

'Out with it. What is it about this assignment that you suddenly don't like?'

'The coal,' Lerant muttered after a moment.

'The coal?' Mancire must have sounded as puzzled as he felt because Lerant dared to explain.

'Well, to be accurate, the mines. Or rather . . . the slaves who work them.'

'Ahh . . .' Mancire put his drink to one side and tented his fingers on the inlaid desktop. 'You're a Roghinner and your people weren't happy when Myrrgha promised to employ your workers then broke their word and went ahead and used Lellghin slaves instead?' Mancire waited patiently, realizing the day's shock combined with the potent brandy was making a muddle of a normally sharp mind, and was also making the young officer more candid than he might otherwise have been.

Lerant swirled the liquor in his goblet. 'I prefer bridges, open air, freedom. Slavery turns my stomach.'

'Mine too,' Mancire said fervently, trying to drive back the images carried by Zaraxan's report. 'Mine too.'

'Then you understand, sir.' Lerant looked up, his eyes a little unfocused, blurred by the liquor, 'As much as I want to return to Annalie and my nephews. I've heard the slaves at the mine are half-starved, near frozen, worked to death.'

Mancire slammed his fist down on the desktop, making the liquor decanter jump and startling Lerant who flinched back into his seat. 'Then by all that's holy, let's you and I do something about it, shall we?'

Frightened into sobriety, Lerant frowned. 'I didn't mean to give the impression of disloyalty to Myrrgha, Ambassador,' he said, wary now.

'Naturally not,' Mancire agreed smoothly. 'But tell me, Lerant, where's the disloyalty in you and I doing all we can to increase labor yield from the coal mines? You're an engineer, you can redesign the machinery. My personal estates are vast. I can send you all you require to better feed and care for the slaves. There'll be no need to requisition Myrrghin supplies.' He lifted his drink in salute and asked bluntly, 'Are you with me, Commander? After all, we'll only be obeying Grouda's instructions to increase coal shipments.'

Lerant's boyish smile reappeared and he added, 'You remind me of a Sergeant I knew in Khengha. He and I made a good team, too. I accept your commission, gladly.'

The crystal gave a melodic ring as Lerant reached out and the two goblets touched.

CHAPTER THIRTEEN

'You're dripping,' Gerion pointed out as Lieutenant Sean Fetrin arrived in a hurry from over the dunes and down the mangrove track that wound through the trees to Sanctuary Assembly Lodge. Late again, out hunting . . . alone, again, and dripping wet after a hurried wash.

'Be thankful it's only water,' the boy replied, meeting and matching Gerion's gaze without hesitation.

'*Mostly* water,' Gerion corrected, swiping his fingers over a bloody patch at the back of Fetrin's head. 'It's dangerous hunting wild animals, alone. What did you do—climb *into* the carcass this time?'

'The damn dog-thing got excited when I came home, jumped at me! I lost my balance and hit my head.' He gave Gerion a sharp glance, his bitterness palpable as he added, 'Wild beasts are dangerous, especially the ones under your own roof!'

'Don't hunt alone,' Gerion said, refusing to be drawn off subject. 'Have one of the Healers close that cut before the blood brings the flies.'

Irritated, Fetrin touched the sore spot and then looked at his blood-sticky fingers. 'Time our leaders saw the blood on their hands, too! They should have done more to protect Tol Eabah!' He rubbed the blood off on his trouser leg, his mouth twisting sourly as he muttered, 'Hunting alone is a lot less dangerous than sticking to archaic traditions! It's time they woke up and saw we'll *all* be butchered if they don't act and act now!'

'This isn't the time or place for this conversation,' Gerion said, tilting his head toward where m'Connor and Rhyssa were coming into view, negotiating the slight incline and the twists in the path to the Lodge, made to accommodate the roots of the trees that shaded it.

'It never is,' Sean replied, voice low, torn between anger and his respect for m'Connor.

'Later,' Gerion promised him. 'And keep your Shield up, damn it!'

Sean took a deep breath, schooling his emotions. He gave Gerion a single nod of acknowledgment before moving past him through the open doorway to take his place with the other three Lieutenants of their Legion. Gerion watched him a moment more, knowing a seething kettle when he saw one. One wrong word and someone would be scalded to the quick.

'Bloody bugs!' Rhyssa and m'Connor were close enough now for Gerion to hear her muttered curse as she swatted at the midges buzzing around them in the humid night. It made m'Connor smile, at the same time that he reached out to put his hand on the small of her back, guiding her steps safely while her gaze tried to track her tiny foes.

'Sean made it in time?' m'Connor asked Gerion.

'Just. Still wet from sluicing off the muck.'

Shaking his head, m'Connor frowned toward the doorway. 'He's so close to Weaving power. He should have found an Akkarra-Brother by now.'

'Taran . . . Broken Triads are already sharing out. Things have to change. Why can't they let him train with them?'

M'Connor turned to meet his eyes. 'Because Silsun and the others can only go by what they see through the Akkarra, you know that.'

'Know, yes. Understand, no. The earth carries our need tonight, you can feel it. Sean's right.'

'His anger is . . . bottomless, just now. We've all offered to help him train. He refuses.'

'The Circle is changing. They accepted my help. He'll see,' Rhyssa said quietly.

'Everyone else is inside,' m'Connor said, his hand stroking the length of Rhyssa's bare forearm. 'Ready?'

Taking a deep breath, Rhyssa shrugged. 'Ready as I'll ever be.'

Gerion had no great talent for empathy, but he'd be made of stone not to feel her tension. 'No fish dinners tonight. Katya's roasting the traditional chicken . . . well, waterhen, anyway.'

'She's a good cook,' Rhyssa agreed, the taut lines about her mouth and eyes easing. 'My first Silvernight. I've heard some . . . *interesting* stories about old rituals and such.'

'Now, who would be telling you such lurid tales?' Gerion said, well aware of the old traditions of fertility rituals and Silvernight. Rhyssa's smile became an eager hunger that melted the introspective frown from m'Connor's eyes as he looked up at her.

'Silvernight was Bren's favorite festival,' he said.

'Randy bugger,' Gerion said with a smile, trying to keep m'Connor from dwelling on the thought of Bren's lyre sitting alone and untouched on a night that should be alive with music.

'I've heard that he was a very good . . . singer,' Rhyssa said primly.

M'Connor's lips twitched with a smile as he looked back at her. 'I'm better.'

'I'll look forward to the proof of that, maybe even more than the chicken,' Rhyssa returned and twined her fingers with his.

'Maybe?' he yelped, playing along in a manner that cheered Gerion no end.

Stepping to one side, he waved the couple forward so they would enter the bamboo-walled military 'headquarters' first, as was proper. He followed them inside. Rhyssa led the way to their Legion's four Lieutenants all of whom came to their feet in a gesture of respect. Each Legion sat before the insignia they'd chosen to represent them. Gerion could wish m'Connor's Legion had chosen something other than a naked flame that not only added to the heat but also carried very bad memories. The brazier burned low, its small flame barely flickering, but Gerion sat as far from it as possible. M'Connor, the stubborn bastard, pretended not to notice. Rhyssa already knew these men and Gerion could sense her relax a little as they called their welcomes.

'Did the Circle give you any hint as to what they're planning?' Fetrin asked. Word had reached him about her having at last been invited among their leaders.

'They asked about our work with the black powder and how it might be used against the Myrrghin navy,' she replied.

'What good will that do? We can't fight a naval battle, we don't have any ships!'

'We have the Talaers,' Captain m'Kay put in from across the aisle. 'They do well.'

'Because they're fast and they know where to run and hide,' Fetrin countered flatly, leaning forward and around Lieutenant Kaitlin the better to see the Weaver Captain seated among his own circle of five officers. 'If the Myrrghin bastards find us, what? Run . . . *again?*'

'Running has kept us alive long enough to fight back,' m'Connor said. Knowing they were set to argue, he shot his arm out like a knife above the small flame in the oil-filled brazier, gaining their attention and making Gerion flinch. M'Connor's Fire-Breathers, they'd been called by the other Legions. 'Fire is our emblem,' he told them. 'It gives and takes life. Guard your words tonight. They carry the power to shape our future.'

'We're going to battle?' m'Fetrin demanded, reading the edge to m'Connor's statement.

A stirring at the front of the enclosure where it adjoined Leader Cantrell's private quarters announced his arrival and everyone stood in salute. A lean, tall man with a sharp-boned angular face and thinning gray hair, Cantrell stood studying them all for a long moment, testing their mood. How aware was he of the developing rift among his men? Did he understand just how close it was to tearing their exiled community apart?

'It's time we take action to protect our people,' the old Leader announced as if he'd heard the silent question that hummed in the very ground and sizzled in the humid air. 'The Circle has heard our need and spoken. We go to battle.'

'Yes!' Fetrin said, a soft, keen affirmation that vibrated through all present like a gust of cooler air after a storm.

'As you know, we have begun making our own black powder. Recently, our Hidden Ones in Myrrgha have provided us metal, enough to create our own version of cannon shells—

It's time we use fire against fire or perish.' Cantrell's stern expression didn't alter a whisker before the surge of amazement among the ranked officers.

'At last!' Fetrin said, his loud elation echoed by some but also contrasted sharply by other mutterings of shocked dismay. M'Connor shifted uncomfortably and Gerion cast him a wary glance. There was something he knew Fetrin wasn't going to like.

'So armed, we begin to make plans,' Cantrell said when the outcry had settled. 'We will take the attack to the enemy though not before much careful preparation. Our aim is to destroy the Myrrghinners' fuel source. However, our new explosives will be designed to save lives, not take them. The ships will be shattered but we will capture, *alive,* their human cargo.'

'Alive!?' Fetrin snarled, so heatedly that Gerion flinched. 'They're murderers!' Others in the room certainly shared his opinion but hadn't voiced it so adamantly that it drew Cantrell's full attention.

'Lieutenant Fetrin? You have something to say?'

'Sir!' Jumping to his feet, Fetrin didn't bother to rein in his emotion and Gerion knew the youngster hadn't bothered Shielding. This wouldn't be pretty.

'We're to shatter their ships but not put a scratch on the butchers of Tol Eabah?' Fetrin demanded. 'Why?'

'I was hoping you in particular, my Fire-breather Legion, would be with me on this plan, Lieutenant Fetrin,' Cantrell replied, unfazed.

'I am, Sir! We are! On the first part! We don't intend to be defeated by—'

'What you *intend* is that we should rain fire on the enemy without warning, to kill without mercy, to take no prisoners. You intend to ask our Weavers to become the very murderers you despise.'

'I ask they do their duty and protect us! We have no place for prisoners. We can barely feed ourselves let alone them!' Fetrin admitted, stone-faced and unrepentant. 'I say we do to them what they do to us!'

A loud, buzzing tension and murmuring drowned out anything Cantrell might have said as he walked the few steps to the waiting table and its burden of maps. He placed his hands hard on its edge and leaned forward, his lean frame hovering like a bird of prey over its bickering fledglings. Sensing his stern disapproval, everyone fell silent again.

'Fetrin speaks of our physical survival. He doesn't see beyond that,' Cantrell said quietly. 'Oh, yes, to make war as Myrrgha does would leave us breathing, would return to us our homeland.' He straightened up to sweep the room with a burning gaze. 'But the stain of murder in our souls, in our minds, carried forward with our newborn children, would leave us forever changed. Is this not so, Lieutenant?' he asked, returning his focus to Fetrin.

Fetrin drew a deep breath and Gerion could Sense the stirring promise of Weaving power in the youngster's boiling blood. 'Have you seen what used to be my brother, today!? This isn't about living or dying anymore! They annihilate us—*forever!* Just like they did my brother!' For all his defiance, Fetrin's eyes shimmered and the last word quavered.

M'Connor reached out and squeezed Fetrin's arm in silent support, his own breathing tight. Defiant, blazing, Sean looked so like the Bren of the battlefield guarding their backs as massive numbers of enemy came at them, that it stole Gerion's breath.

'They will annihilate no one without fuel for their ships,' Cantrell argued.

'We take them alive, then what? Let them go to come back and murder us aboard new ships? Months, a year, it doesn't matter! They won't stop!'

That hit home. Cantrell turned, his chin lifted proud and determined, he left the dais and strode forward until he stood immediately before Fetrin. 'We will stop them *permanently* at sea, Lieutenant. They won't be back. Not these men. There is much of this plan that I cannot reveal here tonight.'

'Sir, is there to be no justice for the children of Tol Eabah? No justice for Bren? Why should these men be allowed to go free even if we could be sure they wouldn't be back? Why! What else is left for us but justice?'

Set with stony grief, overlaid with furious anger and sustained with courage and pride, Fetrin was the embodiment of Lellgha. Watching him, Gerion felt his eyes sting.

'It's true Zaraxan and the Methaggar Lords who control the soldiers are butchering murderers,' Cantrell agreed. 'Against them, and against any Myrrghinner found to have murdered without compulsion, we will seek justice. But vengeance and hate, Sean, believe me, harm only the bearer. If Bren cannot be returned, you must live for Flynn and for your mother, your friends. As we all go on for those who remain.'

Cantrell's face suddenly became so shadowed with grief and compassion that Gerion looked away. The elderly Leader's entire family, targeted by the enemy, had been killed in the early days of the Myrrghin invasion. Cantrell made an open-handed gesture, asking permission to Share but Fetrin ever-so-marginally leaned back, and the hand lowered.

'I know, Lieutenant. I know. We seem lost. Yet we are far from it. Don't close your heart, I beg you. What else is left for us?' He lifted his voice to them all. 'Hope. Love. And eventually, victory. The Grove Circle has found new hope and given us new weapons. Now, we must find new faith and the strength to be sure we kill only at need.'

'At need!?' Fetrin echoed in agonized disbelief. *'At need!?'*

Slowly, his own eyes bright, the aging Leader lifted his hand again, this time leaving it, palm out, a short distance from Fetrin's chest, above the heart, offering a complete opening of himself to Fetrin's Empathy. It was proof he had nothing to hide, and everything to give Fetrin in support.

'I had the very great honor to know Weaver-Captain Bren m'Fetrin,' Cantrell said quietly. 'I give you my Oath, Sean. I swear to you, we won't stop fighting until we find Zaraxan and your brother's Ea has returned to us.'

'Returned?! It no longer exists!' Fetrin exploded, his fury only emphasized by the tears that stood in his eyes. 'Why can't you all accept that?!'

'If we fight on their terms, if we murder our prisoners, Lieutenant, we become them!' Cantrell returned to the map table raised on its low platform, the better to begin unfolding parchment sketches and maps. The first, a diagram of the workings and design of a Myrrghin warship, had been drawn for him earlier that day by Rhyssa, Gerion knew.

'I might just have killed my brothers,' she'd told he and m'Connor, making Gerion flinch for her agonizing choice. But the savagery of Tol Eabah, the first-hand accounts of merciless butchery she'd heard from the mouths of small children, had decided her at last.

'Our explosives will hole the Myrrghin escort ships close by the sea-cliffs of Khengha as they seek to protect the coal carriers.

Those are manned by Khenghinner merchantmen, neutrals. We capture them. This plan won't destroy the entire Myrrghin fleet, but it does deprive them of access to fuel for some time. The combined effect should be enough to double the workload on the remainder and hinder their search for Sanctuary. The holed ships surrender to us, or . . . .' He sighed heavily, plainly hoping the Myrrghin Admirals would have enough brains not to let it come to that. But Gerion, seated so close to Fetrin, felt the savage hope that surged in him at the image of dead bodies tossed onto those same rocks by the surf.

'Our honored friend, High Mariner Rhyssa Avenalkah, has agreed to train special teams to precisely target the vulnerabilities in the enemy ships. Our Talae friends, are as ever, ready to back us to the hilt and are looking for the best place for an ambush. Too, they are willing to reveal to us an approach route down the west coast of Rogha. We can thus add the advantage of a surprise outflanking to our plans.'

'And then what, Sir?' one of m'Kay's Lieutenants asked before Fetrin could find voice. 'Fetrin is right—we can't feed and house so many prisoners.'

Cantrell sighed. 'Another problem we are working on, Lieutenant. As it stands, we intend to return to their homes those who are no danger to us.'

Fetrin's muscles bunched, preparing to launch himself to his feet, but m'Connor grabbed him and held him back with a whispered snarl, 'In private, Sean, *in private!*'

'Now—High Mariner Avenalkah? If you would be so kind as to show us how we might achieve the crippling of the battleships?' Cantrell waved a hand to indicate she should approach the plans and diagrams she had prepared for him earlier.

'It's just Rhyssa, now,' she said smoothly and stepped forward.

'Those who are no danger to us!?' Sean repeated in disbelief. 'There are no innocents! Taking them prisoners is stupid! They must be killed!'

'In cold blood? Rhyssa's family possibly among them?' Gerion asked when m'Connor remained silent.

'Yes! You think they'd hesitate to kill us?!'

Gerion said, irritated. 'We're talking about not killing them after we take them prisoner, Sean! *After!* Can you look a chained man in the face and shoot him in cold blood?'

'No one will have to do that if we make sure they're all blown to pieces by Rhyssa's bombs!' Sean returned furiously.

M'Connor cast Rhyssa a wary look, expecting any moment that she would erupt. But he could feel no anger in her, only weary resignation of her duty, risks and all.

'M'Connor?' Cantrell called as he escaped the animated conversations of the men and women still lingering inside the meeting place. 'If I might have a moment with you?'

He replied and, looking back at Sean, said, 'I promise you this, Sean, I *swear* to you—when the naval battle is won, you, Rhyssa, Gerion and I will go back to Myrrgha and cut the truth out of that mongrel, Zaraxan, and his Methaggars.' Sean stood frowning at him, saying nothing. 'Promise me you'll wait until I get back, if I'm called away. If we've not found Bren by then, I'll train you in Weaving myself and the four of us go back to Myrrgha.'

Slowly, hoping, m'Connor extended his arm for Sharing, overwhelmingly relieved when Sean accepted. M'Connor's affection and caring hit Sean first, the new hope m'Connor carried for Bren caused some irritation, but equally came acceptance—M'Connor would go on hoping and searching until the day he died, and beyond. Feeling Sean's wariness become affection and pride that he might stand at m'Connor's side where Bren had once stood, m'Connor nodded. He'd stand as Sean's Brother, and do it gladly, if no one else was found. They had a pact.

When they were properly alone, Cantrell drew m'Connor further aside to say, 'Magi Silsun tells me that your Testing has uncovered the Beginnings of a Path that might lead to . . . shall we say, some rather unusual and powerful allies?'

'The Tanortha, yes, sir.'

'Well,' Cantrell said, straight-faced despite the skepticism m'Connor could feel thick about him. 'All well and good, but they tell me the Path begins in Rogha and it seems likely you and Gerion will be Chosen to follow it.'

'Such is my feeling,' m'Connor admitted.

Cantrell rubbed slowly at his jaw and frowned down at the maps spread in disarray across his table. 'Currently we've just the one contact stationed in Rogha City and his information is less than reliable. I'd have you make an assessment of the man, then with or without him, seek out other possible Hidden Ones. We will need support to investigate a means of establishing an escape plan for our people enslaved in the coal mines. To that end, The Magi have compiled a list of names of forced Myrrghin recruits, similar to the poor man Primona Linked to, who would likely desert and return to Rogha to set up a Hidden One network if their families were protected, brought here to us. I'd like you to meet with those families and prepare them for the possibility. Get some of them out while you're there, if you can.'

'The list includes the name of the soldier who gave us the flower?'

'No. He died to earn his family the right to stay in their home; the Magi prefer we leave them be. Local law forbids the wearing of swords inside Rogha City walls; you and Gerion will carry Stingers, stun darts, should you need to later ask your target questions.'

'I'm grateful for any assistance, Leader,' m'Connor said over his wariness. 'But, as regards the plan to attack the coal shipments, it seems to me we must destroy their methirri-cloaked destroyers, too. Only they can take us without warning.'

'I'm aware of that, Captain. However, the problem remains that we've no means to compel them to come to us, away from their search in the Western Sea. If we rob them of their fuel,' he shrugged. 'It will be some time before they recover.'

'But they *will* recover,' m'Connor said, grimly. 'The Testing gave me an idea how to take them but I need to gather some more information first.'

Cantrell nodded. 'I'll be pleased to hear what you've come up with, Captain.'

'Marc and Sean have gone ahead,' Rhyssa told m'Connor when he left Cantrell. 'What was that all about?'

'He needs someone to verify the integrity of our Hidden One in Rogha City and set up a complete cell.'

She sighed heavily and leaned her head against his shoulder. 'Oh, good. I'll be sure to pack my warm woolens.'

'Rhyssa . . . .' he pleaded. They'd already been over this at least a dozen times.

'Maybe the Testing didn't show you it all! Maybe I *am* there somewhere.'

'Maybe,' he conceded. 'If so, you'll be called along with me when they decide.'

'When *the Magi* decide,' she said bitterly, disliking Magi ritual and his reliance on their judgment. He sighed and she added in unspoken agreement to leave the matter rest, 'This is my first SilverNight. Tell me more about it.'

'Well, you already know the part I like best . . . .' he said, and tucked her close against his side. She wrapped an arm about him as they headed toward the foot bridge that linked the smaller village of Home Cove to Sanctuary proper.

'The food,' she said teasingly, more than glad when he laughed.

He'd told her about an ancient belief that lovers' souls would be permanently linked if they made love in the open, under the moonlight of SilverNight. It was the only night of the year that the two moons were in full phase together, eventually overlapping, making love after a long search and chase, according to the old myth. But, the human lovers' souls could be permanently united only with the addition of music—a song created by the man for his lover alone.

With the first, smaller, of the twin full moons only just risen, the twilight purple sky blazed with fiery white and gold stars and the evening air was heady with the scent of night-blooming tropical flowers. The entwined bamboo-log cottages of Home Cove looked snug and welcoming with their overhanging fringes of woven palm thatch and circular windows softly agleam. Her mouth watered as she caught the aromas of spice, roast tubers, and grilled waterhen.

As was Lellghin custom on Silvernight, communal campfires were being lit and gold and blue garlands of glowstones were strung from low tree branches. The first notes of a lovely piece of lyre-music came to them from beyond one of the blazes, quickly joined by strummers and a woman's voice lifted in song. M'Connor inhaled sharply and came to a standstill. The sound of the lyre would remind him of Bren. Uncertain what to do, she watched him a moment. He slipped his hand inside hers and squeezed gently, no doubt sensing her sympathy.

'It's good . . .' he began, but had to clear his throat, 'good they're not giving up their music. We need it.'

A magnificent flute joined the other musicians, blending with more of the lilting voices for which Lellgha was justly renowned. It was a heart-stirringly beautiful song, calling yearningly for a lost home and it brought tears to her eyes. She blinked them away, refusing to think of the happy home she'd known before her mother had died, before her brothers had been dragged into the war.

'Hey!' Marc Gerion called, laughing from some distance down the path, 'Are you two going to take time out to eat? My beloved Katya is not happy. She says a festival meal takes much preparation and should be eaten hot.'

An odd, low humming sound brought Rhyssa awake from a deep sleep. Lifting her head from the warmth of m'Connor's shoulder, she tracked it to a spinning orb of pure light hovering at the foot of their bed. Sometime ago, m'Connor had described this means used to Call a person to a special task. 'Taran!' she whispered, hoping he would tell her it was all a dream.

He was already awake, his dark eyes wide with a mixture of pride and sadness. He sat up to touch his lips to her brow, 'I see it. Wait. Be still.'

The slowly spinning sphere was the purest, whitest, loveliest light she had ever seen. 'It's so beautiful!' she couldn't help but acknowledge in an awed whisper. As if it had been waiting for her to speak, the miniature moon ceased its spinning and moved gracefully closer. It hovered a moment before m'Connor's eyes, then, as he nodded and closed them again, it darted up to touch his forehead.

Rhyssa watched, enthralled, and dreading all at once. She heard a high sweetly musical note which she, according to him, meant the timeless Akkarra Light had Linked to his mind and will. He would accept whatever they asked of him. And with that, abruptly, the sphere vanished. All exactly as he had described.

'It's as we guessed,' he said simply, turning to regard her with quiet intensity. 'I must go to Rogha.'

'Alone?'

'Marc will come with me,' he answered, looking away as if in sudden pain and she saw the gleam of tears on his face in the darkness of the moonlit room.

'There's something else,' she realized with fresh dread. 'What else did it reveal?'

'Word reached the Magi earlier tonight,' he admitted brokenly. 'We can wait no longer. M'Akram is dead.'

'Oh, no!' She wrapped her arms tight about him, wishing somehow she could spare him further pain. 'And . . . his Ea?'

'Safely home with m'Singh and Liraith.'

Giving him a moment for his silent grief, she asked, 'Zaraxan?'

He nodded. 'Someday I'll gut that mongrel.'

'Not if I get to him first! But why would he murder m'Akram if they need their Weavers alive for the soul-transfer experiments?'

'He was trying to get inside m'Akram's Key, find Sanctuary.'

'But he failed?'

M'Connor was silent, considering it for longer than she liked. 'This time, yes.'

Suddenly, Rhyssa was cold through to the marrow of her bones. She knew Admiral Givant had had the other Weaver tortured to death, not understanding neither man could tell them what he wanted, blocked by their Keying. She could only hope that Givant and Zaraxan were suffering Grouda's retribution for losing both Weavers; so many had died at Tol Eabah so Myrrgha could capture them.

Unable to stand the tension, she climbed out of bed to pace from it to the window and back again. 'If the Keys aren't safe it's madness to send you out there again!'

'It's our only hope,' he said softly. 'You know it better than any. We must destroy the Myrrghin fleet or they'll be here before another year is out.'

'Then I go, too,' she said firmly. 'I can guard your back.'

'Not this time, my love. Your presence would upset the Path's destined unfolding.'

'The Path! Destiny!' she snapped. 'Listen to yourself! We needed neither to out-think Zaraxan and the Methaggar and escape!'

'This is different.'

'How? Why! Because the Magi say so? How can you put so much faith in the hallucinations they fed you along with some tree sap?'

His jaw set, holding back the anger she could see flashing in his eyes. 'The Akkarra are not trees! They are . . . knowing, intelligent keepers of the light of all creation. Their Testing casts you forward in time. It is not hallucination.'

'How can you be sure?'

'I'm a Weaver.'

He stood and went to their washstand. He went still, his eyes closing then coming open sharply to glow with an inner light like sun on the leaves of a summer forest. He held his hands out, close to either side of the ceramic water pitcher. Green light shone in the veins of his forearms, then emerged like radiant vines, winding about his arms, then disappearing, diving into the bones at the back of his wrists. Twin white orbs appeared, hovering close to his palms. Rhyssa could feel the warmth of them even from the other side of the room.

So, his Weaving strength was fully returned. That was something, at least, if they expected him to go out again. She'd almost succeeded in making herself forget about her lover's dangerous, and to her, unnatural, abilities. The ewer began to glow red at its base. Steam wafted up and she heard the bubbling of boiling water. She turned away to watch the shifting fronds against the bright night sky as the breeze moved the palm trees beyond the window. Moonlight and starlight silvered and gilded the edges of the dew-heavy leaves.

'Weaving is real. The Magi are real. The Akkarra are real,' m'Connor said, flatly insistent. 'And the Testing reveals a real, possible future.' He came back and wrapped a gentle pair of arms about her from behind and drew her, unresisting, back into his embrace.

'Rhyssa,' he said softly. 'What I saw, what I felt in the Testing, was as real as this.' He bent and, as she turned in the circle of his arms, he kissed her. She tasted the salt of both their tears on his lips, unaware until then that she too, had been weeping. 'I know you fear the Keying,' he said, darkly grim and intent. 'So do I.'

'Then why let them do that to you?' she demanded, her anger easily re-ignited. 'You said it leaves you feeling like you're walking around with a head full of holes! How can you possibly think clearly and react fast enough to survive in enemy lands like that?'

'It's the only way to keep Sanctuary safe.'

'You told Flynn no one could find their way through the maze of islands out there. And you're right, even my brothers couldn't navigate through all those twisting channels and hidden reefs. There must be hundreds of atolls and islands and sandbars between us and the open sea. Why do you need Keying when we have that?'

'Because I didn't tell Flynn the full truth,' he admitted. 'Because the same something in my blood that lets me do that—'He jabbed a thumb toward the water ewer,'—gives me an exact awareness of the position of the stars and the navigation coordinates. A Weaver always know where he is in relation to where he's been and can give someone else the coordinates on how to get there, too. The Magi use it when they create the Ambers . . . Connectors, and when they Travel like we did to Tol Eabah. I could bring the enemy direct here, *if* the coordinates were still in my head. After I'm Keyed the Talaers won't wake me until I'm a long way beyond these waters.'

Appalled, she tried to follow the import of all he was saying. 'You won't know your way home. You'll have to wait for the Talaers again.'

'It'll be faster. They'll know to look for me.' He broke their embrace and moved back to check the water in the ewer. 'It's still hot,' he said. 'Want a wash? Or will I make tea?'

'The Talaers are never Keyed,' she pointed out, 'and they know the way back here better than you do!'

'They could never explain it to a Soil-Blood, even should they want to. None of us understand their terms of reference. They've never stepped foot on land, they don't have maps—'

'I've heard it all before!' she snapped, interrupting him.

'Then I don't need to explain, do I!'

Suddenly as angry as she, he went to the big wooden chest that rested at the foot of their bed. He knelt and threw back the lid. 'I best sort through my clothes.'

'I can't let you go back there, Taran,' she whispered. Aware she was trembling, she wrapped her bare arms about herself, under her breasts. 'I can't,' she repeated.

'This work will eventually free our people in the mines of Rogha. It'll take days for the Magi and the Akkarra to figure all the intricacies of our Keying. I won't be the only Weaver going out, but I will be the only one going to Rogha. The others have the more dangerous mission. Me . . . they're giving me the easy stuff these days.'

'Easy! You've have to be joking.'

He looked up with a grim smile. 'Nope. Rhyssa . . .' He got to his feet, the better to look into her eyes in the dim light of pre-dawn. 'We can't quit now. If this Path brings all it promises, maybe, just maybe, we'll have a future, a home, children.' He gathered her into his warm embrace once more. She nodded, unable to speak for the emotion that tightened her throat. He held her for a long while, silent, strong, his hands moving in soothing patterns over the tight muscles of her back and shoulders. 'It'll be all right,' he murmured.

'You cannot know that.'

'I know it's our only chance to make it be all right.'

'If only we could go back together, if I could know what was happening . . . . Staying here, waiting, relying on the Magi for word . . . .'

'They won't be able to contact me after I'm Keyed.'

She drew back to look hard into his eyes. 'So, they expect you to travel all the way to Rogha, somehow negotiate a new Hidden One cell while only having half a mind, and then find your way back to us.'

'It's not half a mind! Gerion and I will travel aboard the Kerestra with Lumas and Igert. You know they'll bring us safely home again.'

'If the Myrrghin fleet doesn't find you first!'

'The Kerestra can sniff them out a league off.' He knelt back by the chest. 'Did we put my heavier shirts under the blankets in here?'

'Yes, I think so.' She pushed him aside. 'Let me look.'

He lifted the blankets out and she began angrily pulling various pieces of woolen clothing from the chest, abandoning some to the floor and tossing the more useful items onto the foot of the bed. She knew he was right, she knew they had no choice, and she must let him go out into the dark sea, alone but for Gerion and the Talae brothers.

'Will you remember me?' she asked. 'Or will they destroy all your recent memories?'

'Keying doesn't destroy anything. It just locks it away.' He lifted the lid of the chest and indicated she should move away from it, and then dropped it with a thud of wood on wood. 'Just like that. When the Key is removed,' he lifted the lid. 'It's all still there, untouched.'

She gave him a glare. 'Or so you hope.' She grabbed the lid and slammed it shut again with a much louder, more satisfying thump.

He stood, went to the window and gazed out at the sea. 'Nothing, *nothing*, could ever make me forget you. You are my heart. If you hadn't come to me when you did . . . .'

He returned to sit on the edge of the bed and gather her to him. She leaned her head against his shoulder and he kissed her forehead. Silently, they watched the lowering, entwined moonbeams slowly crossing the floor, the soothing hiss and boom of the big breakers on the beach easing the tension between them.

'You think this might help you find Bren,' she said at last.

He nodded against her hair. 'Somehow, yes.' He turned and regarded her solemnly. 'While I'm away, do what you can for me for Sean?'

'I'll watch him and I'll be sure he always has someone to talk to. When you do have to leave?'

'I'll go to the Grove first, for the Keying, but no time soon by the sound of that twin-moon tide.'

'Then we still have tonight, at least. Or what's left of it.'

She began drawing him back onto the bed with her, but suddenly, he straightened up, shaking his head.

'Outside,' he said, with a slow smile. 'Let's try out the magic of SilverNight. If it unites us as it's supposed to—'

She managed to return his smile. 'No harm in trying.'

'No harm and much pleasure,' he said with a wink.

She dared not remind him that to complete the so-called magic, he'd need to sing.

But she needn't have worried. He dedicated his new love song to her with soul and body in the still warm sands of the dunes about their home as the golden full moon completely covered its smaller, soft blue companion. Their combined light glittered on phosphorescent waves and painted all with eerily beautiful color as m'Connor and Rhyssa, too, made love, united in a rhythmic dance as old as the tide.

CHAPTER FOURTEEN

Electric tension rippled through The Grove with enough power to stun m'Connor should he come into physical contact with any of the Akkarra. Fortunately, Gerion—who'd have felt it simply by walking on the grass—was safely in the Lodge, sleeping off his Keying. He wouldn't wake until after he'd been carried onto the Talae ship, The Kerestra, waiting to take both he and m'Connor far from Sanctuary toward Rogha. Now, it was his turn.

After much discussion, Cantrell had agreed to m'Connor's new, more personally dangerous strategy but one that might bring them a greater, more abiding success. The Leader had worked on the crucial military aspect of his Keying as well as that of m'Garran and m'Sharral who were also to go out again, to Khengha, not Rogha. But nothing remotely like the Keying intended for m'Connor had ever before been attempted and the Akkarra too, were unsettled and worried; which didn't help m'Connor's confidence in his ability to survive their planned savagely extensive manipulation of his mind.

Silsun appeared from out of the late afternoon tree shadows and walked toward him, slow and solemn, her face set more grimly than he'd ever before seen her looking. His heart thudded with fear.

This Keying could leave him . . . no longer him. Forever. And not even knowing it.

She drew closer to stand before him. Of course, she'd have Read his feelings accurately. She extended her hand, asking, and he nodded permission. Her touch, her Sharing, restored his strength with a depth of love that astonished him. He'd known the incredible unconditional love of the Akkarra and the Magi before, but this . . . this filled him with such a humble pride that he found he had to break the contact. It was too much. They shouldn't feel so deeply, care so much for him, for the terrible dangers of what he was setting himself to do.

'Of course we should,' Silsun said and he understood that with the Akkarra in this intense mood, everyone's thoughts were plainly visible.

He had nothing to hide, certainly not his perfectly understandable terror. Silsun, perhaps, was even more terrified. If there'd been anything at all that he'd prefer they didn't Read in him, it would only be his dread that he might fail them and in so doing almost certainly kill everyone at Sanctuary . . . . Flynn, Dierna, Sean, Bruska . . . Rhyssa. Everyone.

Taking hold of his arm without asking, Silsun told him fiercely, 'In this there can never be failure! No matter the outcome, Taran. Hear me? *There is no failure!*'

He nodded, understanding she meant victory would always be theirs simply in his willingness to sacrifice himself, perhaps utterly destroy himself forever, to save them. He didn't share the sentiment. She shook her head in scolding with a fondness that warmed him anew.

'I left the others that we could talk in private before it starts,' she explained. 'I can't let you do this without asking one last time—Are you certain? There is no shame in stopping now. None of us are sure if we even have the right to ask you to—'

'It's right,' he interrupted firmly. 'And none of you asked. It was my idea.'

They stood a long moment, drawing strength from one another, trying to quell some small part of the terror gnawing at the back of their control. What was about to be done to him terrified m'Connor in a way nothing else had ever terrified him.

'It won't come to the worst, Taran,' Silsun reassured, emphasizing the truth of it with another Sharing. 'There are plans in place in case something should go wrong.'

'Plans,' he repeated over a heavy sigh. That's what they called giving Gerion a set of questions to test him with when he came round somewhere far from Sanctuary. If he answered incorrectly it meant either there were gaping holes in his memory that shouldn't be there, or, possibly worse, the Keying hadn't taken effect properly, leaving him exposed to betraying them.

'I know you don't find the follow-up exam idea very reassuring,' Silsun told him, 'But much thought went into putting together those questions. We've covered every possible contingency, I'm sure of it.' As soon as she said the words, they both felt the hesitation. As sure as she could be, was a more accurate way of putting it.

'Marc will be checked out in the same way?' he asked, already knowing the answer, but wanting to hear it again.

'Yes. Since he speaks very little Talae, and there'll be no one else on board but you both and Lumas and Igert, he'll have to read a set of written questions.'

M'Connor nodded. 'And only after he's done will the Talaers supply the written answers. I understand. I just hope . . . .'

'I know.' Neither of them wanted to imagine Gerion discovering his memory faulty in such a way and then having to return home along with m'Connor.

Thunder rumbled and electricity cracked, making m'Connor jump, but it wasn't an approaching storm. Rather, the Akkarra were testing their joined circuitry, the same circuits they'd soon apply to following the pathways of m'Connor's memory, leaving some, blocking others. And hopefully,—as he'd demonstrated to Rhyssa with the clothes-chest, still leaving all of them neatly intact, exactly as they were before and ready for safe retrieval.

'They're ready for you,' Silsun said unnecessarily.

His mouth gone completely dry, m'Connor nodded and took a pace forward. Again, Silsun's touch, her hand on his arm, stopped him. He turned and looked direct into her eyes, knowing what she was about to say but letting her do it regardless.

'You're sure, Taran. Really sure? We might have lost Bren forever. To lose you, too . . . .' Tears welled in her eyes, a blue sea of sorrow. He drew her into his embrace and held her a moment, feeling the racing thud of her heart. Being a Magi didn't make her any less human.

Another bolt of lightning flashed and danced about the leafy Akkarra canopy. When its rolling thunder faded, m'Connor heard voices lifted in song. All the Magi, all the Weavers of Sanctuary, gathered in the Grove, would join with the Akkarra to sing his Keying.

Then, setting all the hair at the back of his neck bristling and running goose-bumps down his spine, more and more voices joined the harmony. Hundreds of them.

'They wanted to help and to deliver their thanks in a special tribute to you,' Silsun told him, pride making new tears brim in her eyes.

'They? Who, where—'

'The dead of Tol Eabah and Lellgha. They're all here, Taran. Waiting and wanting to help. Great strength will be needed to sing this intricate, all-night-long Keying correctly.'

Waiting. Waiting for the pathways of rebirth to be reopened by a miracle, for an end to the war that was destroying their homeland and warping their children.

'Come on, Taran. Time to wake up.'

Pain thudded through his head in beat with each word.

'Easy,' Gerion said in a softer, more sympathetic tone, probably having seen the flinch. 'Here. Drink.'

A strong hand slid under his head, propping him up. He opened his eyes and found, blessedly, the cabin was dark. The Kerestra rolled gently beneath him but even so small a swell was enough to make his stomach complain. He pushed at the cup Gerion was trying to hold to his mouth and leaned over the side of the bed. He hoped there was a bucket there somewhere as he emptied his stomach. Recovered, he slumped back against the pillows and lifted his arm to wipe away the sick on his lips, but Gerion swabbed his mouth with a dampened cloth.

'Damn. They really hit you hard this time, didn't they?' Gerion said, wiping away and sounding even more worried.

'. . . . fine,' m'Connor tried to assure him, but the first words were lost to his dry voice.

'Drink', Gerion repeated, then added hastily, 'If you can?'

M'Connor dipped his chin by way of a yes. Something wasn't right; he'd never felt as bad as this after a Keying. The cup returned to his mouth and he swallowed, immediately grateful for whatever Healer had mixed the concoction of peppermint and honey to disguise the medicines needed to combat the awful headache and nausea.

'It's all right, Marc,' he said, managing a smile. 'I'll live.'

'Glad to hear it. So, tell me, where are you?'

'The first question on the Magi list?' m'Connor guessed.

'Right. So . . . ?'

Pain flared bright and high as he locked into his instinctive navigation.

'No!' Gerion yelped, grabbing his arm. 'Don't try that! Not yet!'

'But . . . you asked—'

'Not where are we as in co-ords. Just where are we in general.'

'Oh.' The pain settled but he still found he had to concentrate for a moment longer than was comfortable for Gerion's anxiety levels. 'Somewhere on the Western Sea aboard the Kerestra? About a day out?'

Gerion exhaled relief. 'Right. Except we're three days out.'

'Three days!'

'Three,' Gerion confirmed and pushed him down gently as he tried to sit up and swing his legs from the bunk. 'Not yet. You're still too shaky. Just lie back and enjoy the interrogation. At least you've made it this far this time.'

'Huh?'

'You've already been awake twice before. Don't you remember?'

'No,' m'Connor said with some alarm. Then, hazy memory returned and he realized his slowness on that front had nothing to do with Keying and everything to do with having been ill. 'I do now,' he added so Gerion would start breathing again. 'Don't fuss. It was just the bloody headaches were killers.'

'You got that right. Taran . . . . Maybe they shouldn't have tried this with you. Not now.'

Not without Bren.

'So you argued back in the Grove, several times, as I recall. I'm all right. It's . . . not having his support to help bypass the affected neural pathways probably made this Keying impact me harder, is all.'

'All!' Gerion snorted skeptically but sounded reassured nonetheless. 'We haven't tried all the questions yet. I'd wait, but . . . .' He trailed off guiltily.

'You told the brothers to get ready to turn back?'

'Umm . . . We turned around about two hours ago.'

'What!?'

'Don't yell. You'll hurt yourself. There's no wind anyway so we're not going far.'

'Like that makes much difference to Lumas and Igert's sailing!'

'Aha!' Gerion exclaimed with evident pleasure. 'Their names was question two!'

'Good,' m' Connor said. 'So hit me with the rest. I'm game.' It was said lightly but it unnerved him; Keying always did. And this time, he'd gone into it only half a Weaver. The rest of his answers met with equal approval and the medicinal drink had eased the pain and settled his stomach enough that he felt hungry when 'the interrogation' was done. 'Do I pass?'

'You do.'

'I take it you got yours right, too?'

'Mine was harder,' Gerion said smugly. 'Mine was a written exam.'

'You never told me you could read!'

'Funny.' Gerion swatted him with a shirt, one of his own, left ready for him to dress. He sat up and tugged the shirt from his friend's hands then pulled it on and sat looking for his trousers in the gloom.

'Can you take some light?' Gerion asked.

'Please.' He tensed but found the flare of flint lighting a fish oil lantern didn't hurt. Gerion threw a pair of trousers at him and he sat pulling them on and wondering if he'd be back to a completely fish diet again for the duration of the voyage.

Gerion muttered a curse as he tripped on something concealed in the still shadowy cabin interior. 'Huh. Almost forgot,' he said, bending to pick it up. 'I have to ask you about these, too.'

'These what?' m'Connor asked, looking up to see his friend and Lieutenant holding up their two Stinger pistols with their beautifully crafted holsters complete with sleeves from which protruded red-tipped darts.

'I'm supposed to ask if you remember what they are. It's a question to test recent memory, Silsun said.'

'Stingers, to stun but not harm the enemy,' m'Connor replied. 'Given to us and to m'Garran and m'Sharral before we left on our separate missions.'

'Part one correct. Part two—why?'

M'Connor frowned at him blankly. 'To take prisoners alive and to avoid killing? But, since we also have these . . . .' He patted the sword and dagger that hung on the bedpost.

'I know, it doesn't make sense,' Gerion agreed. 'Oh,' he added, 'I was only joking about it being part two of the test.' He shrugged for m'Connor's exasperation. 'Sorry. I thought it might prompt you to give me some enlightenment as regards the doings of the higher echelons of command.'

Shaking his head with amusement, M'Connor reached up and took one of the holstered set of darts from his friend. The workmanship was truly beautiful, the pistols made from polished Akkarra heart-wood and the holster of some tough yet fine leathery material produced from their leaves and shaped to look like them. The Akkarra had created the venom for the darts, too, but from what exactly m'Connor was unsure. They had, however, reassuringly, also provided antidote darts that would wake a victim promptly.

'So, the darts will only knock the bastards down?' Gerion asked.

'And out.'

'Fast, I hope! Although I suppose, they're only relatively harmless Roghinners and we're supposed to win 'em over to our side.'

M'Connor had a niggling suspicion their mission was about more than just setting up a Hidden One cell in Rogha City, but he knew any further information on that subject would be well and truly kept from him by the Keying. Putting the holster back with the sword on the bedpost, he stood and clapped his friend on the shoulder. 'I have no problems with not harming the locals, but the Myrrghin officers at the Garrison are fair targets.'

Gerion scowled agreement. 'Silsun and Cantrell warned me . . . repeatedly, that the darts are lethal if you shoot someone twice.'

Laughing, m'Connor headed up the companionway into bright sunshine. He needed to tell the Talae brothers to turn around and set sail again for Rogha.

Little wonder coal shipments are down, Lerant understood, quelling the urge to turn and run his sword through the bastard Overseer who stood at his side. Lerant had emptied his stomach more than once when he'd first entered the mine, the stench of broken and rotting bodies overcoming him. And he'd thought it couldn't get any worse.

'Why haven't they been buried?' he asked, his voice sounding as chill as his mood.

'Beg pardon, Sir?' Chief Overseer Hugerka replied.

Glaring pure murder, Lerant pulled the kerchief down from over his mouth and nose. He was certain the Overseer had understood him perfectly. 'How long ago was the cave-in that killed them?' he demanded, fairly certain, too, that the relatively minor slippage he could see was not responsible for every one of the dozen or more dead piled here in the side shaft. He'd already inspected the disease-ridden and almost equally foul underground rooms in which the Lellghin slaves were imprisoned.

'A month or two, I think, sir,' Hugerka hedged.

'You think!?' Lerant snarled, his temper boiling over. If he had his way, everyone responsible would be hanged for the horrific neglect he'd found here. For one thing, someone had been selling the supplies of food that should have gone to the slaves. If not for the 'imposition' caused Myrrgha by the delayed shipments, no one would ever have known. Biting back sharper words, Lerant realized he'd need this brute's cooperation, and none in Myrrghin command cared for anything but coal. He'd need to play it that way if he wanted to have any chance of keeping his and Mancire's efforts secret.

'I repeat—why haven't these poor bastards been buried?'

Hugerka's brow furrowed as he weighed up how much of a threat Lerant might become to him. 'Buried, sir? No need, surely. They're already underground.'

'How soon do you think it will be before you all go down to the disease this will spread?' Realizing finer feeling was wasted on the man, Lerant added, 'I have been given orders from the Emperor himself to see coal shipments return to normal.'

Hugerka's dirty face tightened and eyes narrowed. 'There are ways I can employ to make these lazy Tree-suckers work harder—'

'Listen closely, Overseer,' Lerant interrupted, 'you won't be given another chance. One, you will not in my hearing refer to the slaves as 'Tree-suckers'. Two, you and your fellow guards will have every one of these bodies removed and properly buried—no mass grave! Three, you and your fellows will move all your belongings from the barracks and into the old loading station rooms. Then, we will both oversee the removal of the slaves from their current *quarters* into the barracks!'

'What!? Sir?'

'There they will be given hot water and fresh clothing and blankets. From this day forward they eat the same food given to you and your men or better if I can find it. Until such time as their strength is improved, I can't see any greater amounts of coal being mined, can you Overseer!?'

'Sir, I . . . We've been asking for a fresh shipment of slaves for some months now.'

'They are not an infinite reserve, Chief! Better you care for those you have than lose them and have General Rusark order you and your men to get in there and dig the coal yourselves!'

'Huh,' Marc Gerion muttered, squinting to take a closer look through the spy-glass he held directed on the slave-mine below him in the valley. His eyes did not deceive him; the bastard *guards* were digging individual graves. For dead Lellghinners. The living soon appeared, staggering and helping one another forward, some cowering in terror as if expecting they were about to be executed and placed in those same graves.

'Steady, steady,' Gerion urged. Charging down there to murder the filthy Myrrghin mongrels would only serve to get himself killed. Better to live and be certain of plans to rescue every one of the surviving prisoners. But it was hard, so very, very hard to sit up here and do nothing but watch, nothing but notice how skeletal his countrymen were, how they seemed no more than the jutting backbone, hips and shoulders, their arms and legs obscene sticks. And they were expected to dig coal?

The fingers of Gerion's left hand twitched against the hilt of the sword at his side. If he had a gun . . . . He sighed. Even a gun would be no use. He could perhaps have crept close enough to shoot the murdering Overseer and maybe even had time to kill the officer as well. But to what end? The hunt would be up and the Myrrghinners had plenty more soldiers to send to replace them.

'And . . . through there?' m'Connor asked politely.

As he'd expected, the silversmith suddenly lost his smear of a smile. 'Nothing of interest to the creation of our fine wares, Master Annderalt, I assure you. Personal quarters only. My close attention to the final smelting guarantees the high standards . . . .'

M'Connor let the weasel of a man babble on as he listened with less than half his attention. So, Videer, the man who had left messages that he wished to serve as Lellgha's friend in Rogha, was a silversmith . . . and a liar. That discovery had been of no real surprise. But beneath the small smelter workshop and the storefront proper something seethed, low and hungry, like a predatory animal watching its prey. M'Connor could only hope that whatever it was it wouldn't sense him through his false name and rudimentary disguise.

He'd left his closer examination of Videer's claim for last, going first to the list of families provided him by the Magi. All of those, thankfully, seemed legitimate, allowing him to begin putting into place plans for their evacuation from Rogha City's outer village, the squalid area referred to as Lowtown. Best that objective not be hindered by Videer's treacherous intent. Tomorrow night, M'Connor was to meet with Gerion, after his friend's return from scouting the coal mines. They'd make certain of more secure measures for the safety of their Roghin charges and, too, of preliminary plans for the later rescue of their people laboring to procure coal for Myrrgha's steamships.

It was cold in the abandoned warehouse. Wind whined through smashed windows and made loose boards creak and groan as it carried damp from the rolling swells on Rogha Harbor. M'Connor could just see the dark, oily water gleaming with reflections from lantern posts on the outskirts of the city three miles away.

He and Gerion had arrived in Rogha two weeks ago and immediately split up, knowing the enemy would be looking for a pair of Weavers. There were probably wanted posters showing their likenesses, although Rogha was so isolated and small an outpost that the local commander probably didn't think it likely they'd show up here. Gerion should be safe if he kept his head down. But . . . . It would be very difficult to watch and stay back and not let the slaves know help was being planned.

Come on, Marc, where are you?

Then, he Sensed it, Gerion's warm Presence coming closer. Looking in that direction, he could just see a darker blotch against the deep black of night-sky and more dilapidated buildings. Smiling in relief, he waited, hidden in the shadows until Gerion came closer.

'Hello?' Gerion called warily, careful not to use names in case someone else was with m'Connor.

'Welcome to my humble abode,' m'Connor greeted with a smile and they stepped into the rudimentary shelter of the derelict warehouse. 'You're all right?'

'This is where you've been staying?' Gerion asked. 'It's as cold as the hills.'

'Only tonight. I've been staying in different inns inside the city gates.'

Gerion snorted and shook his head. 'The privileges of rank!'

'Here. You won't get any of this at Sanctuary,' M'Connor said, gathering the laden rucksack he'd stowed and throwing it to his friend.

Gerion caught it and rummaged inside. 'It's warm . . . .'

'There's a vendor stall not far away, feeds the men coming off shift from loading the ships,' m'Connor explained, sensing his friend's momentary alarm that m'Connor might have used a quick Weave.

'Good. Oh. This isn't, it can't be . . . . It is! Beef and Mushroom pie! With potatoes! And cows' milk cheese and real bread!'

'Dig deeper, there's some sugar-cakes, too.'

'You've had it good, m'Connor. Now I know why you insisted on this job rather than the coal mine scouting.'

'Comes with being Captain,' m'Connor told him smugly.

'Ha!' Gerion could say no more with his face crammed with pie.

'Videer is a trap, probably a Myrrghin agent,' m'Connor told him, suddenly serious.

Gerion sighed gustily over his chewing. 'Figures. It was always too good to be true.' He bent his head to return to his meal, but paused to shoot m'Connor an accusing look. 'You waited to tell me when my mouth was full, didn't you? Bastard. Waste of good mushrooms!' He picked some off his coat and popped them in his mouth.

'The mines?' m'Connor prompted, knowing there were people back in Sanctuary who suspected family members were held there.

Gerion chewed a bit more. 'Worse than you can imagine, but improving.'

'Improving?'

'No hope of us getting them out,' Gerion added, although m'Connor well knew there was no real chance of an escape without more man-power, much greater preparation and most importantly, somewhere for so many to go. 'But there's a new commander in charge and he's got our people in new quarters.'

'Where?'

'The old barracks and they've been given warm clothing, blankets, hot food . . . .'

M'Connor frowned. 'Have the stupid bastards finally figured that people who are better cared for can work harder?'

Gerion shrugged, and looked away, his face suddenly tight with anger and grief that washed through m'Connor. 'They buried the dead a few days ago. Apparently, the former commander had left their bodies to rot in one of the closed off shafts.'

'The new man had them buried?' That, indeed, was strange. 'Maybe the others were refusing to work until their friends . . . .'

Gerion sighed. 'I just want them all out of there, Taran. The sooner the better. They're walking skeletons.'

'As soon as we're done here we'll come back for them with whatever it takes, no matter what the Circle says. Did you find anything that might help?'

'I think so. I've made sketches of some blind spots in their perimeter walls.'

'Good. I'll need to find other alternatives to help us with the deserters' families.'

'You need to keep your head down and stay away from Videer. You know they have those outlaw notices posted on us.'

M'Connor said bitterly. 'I'd like to slit that slimy bastard's throat.'

'Hmm,' Gerion grunted, swallowed, and said, 'Need to make it look like an accident if you don't want all Myrrgha to know we've been here.'

'Videer must have plenty of local enemies, too,' m'Connor disputed, but not with any confidence. Gerion was right, better they not draw any more attention than necessary.

'Look.' He pulled a tattered map of Rogha from the pocket inside his heavy great-coat and spread it on the barrel Gerion was using as a table. 'Best we change the location of the Kerestra to collect these families. I'm not sure how much Videer knows.'

'Good idea. But where?'

M'Connor peered more closely at the map of Rogha's rugged western coastline. Only one option seemed reasonable with winter closing in. 'Seelski?'

Gerion too, bent closer to the map, dropping sugar cake crumbs everywhere. He'd already finished off the pies. It was cold enough in Rogha City, let alone in the high hill country around the coal mines. M'Connor had to admit he'd felt a little guilty, settling to sleep in a nice warm bed while his friend was out in the elements. But the down side was m'Connor had the more dangerous job. Only m'Connor's Weaver Senses had kept him one step ahead of them thus far. Getting these people, some of them small children, out under cover would be difficult even with a few leaving at a time.

'It's well protected from both the north and south by these bluffs but has easier access to the beach. Seelski it is!'

'I'll need you to go back and tell the brothers to up anchor and meet us there three nights after you get back.'

Gerion nodded, holding m'Connor's gaze a long moment. They didn't need Empathy to know what the other was thinking—it would be very hard to leave their own people behind to endure slavery in the mines.

'There's no way we can get them out and they're too weak to make it right now anyway,' Gerion said on a long sigh. 'They should be stronger when we come back. The new man seems to be feeding them the same fare the soldiers are getting.'

'Least the bastard can do.' M'Connor looked away toward the cracked and dirty windowpanes beyond which the city lights glittered in the chill air. 'The people here aren't much happier about having slaves work the mines than are we. There's talk of an uprising against Myrrgha.'

'Once their garrison and the fleet is gone, there'll be rebellion,' Gerion agreed, hunting in the rucksack for more cakes.

'First things first. We get these three families out. They'll be ready to begin the trek soon. I hope the weather holds. If anything goes wrong, I'll take them into the hills and leave a message for you at Seelski as to where to try next.'

'Taran . . . .'

'Nothing else for it, Marc.'

M'Connor well knew his friend thought this mission badly planned right at the outset. Gerion had several times complained that it didn't make sense to Key and risk a Weaver just to get a few would-be deserters' families clear. M'Connor could only shrug and tell him the Magi and the Akkarra must have seen something in Rogha's future. At the very least, they would be aiming to free the slaves.

'Here,' M'Connor said, reaching for the second rucksack he'd brought with him.

'What?' Gerion asked as he handed it over to him.

'More food. It's a three day walk all the way back to the Kerestra.'

Gerion sighed. 'I still don't like leaving you here alone.'

'We've been over this before.' They couldn't risk being seen together, their orders were most specific on that point. 'It'll be all right. I'll stay well clear of Videer and I'll leave town by the North Gate; I've never been anywhere near there before.'

Gerion collected the rucksack and stood, holding m'Connor's gaze. 'I'll see you at Seelski.'

'If for whatever reason I don't show, leave a message for me and go on up the coast somewhere.'

'It's a big beach for a small message. Where exactly?'

'Make a stone circle, in line with two others. Put it under there.'

'Watch your back, m'Connor. Don't leave me having to tell Rhyssa you're not coming home.'

'You take care, too. Katya would be much worse!'

Gerion chuckled quickly but his eyes were darkly serious in the shadows. 'Seelski,' he said again and hefted the rucksack onto his shoulder, turned and left.

CHAPTER FIFTEEN

'Take care of little Parla!' Annalie Hollin called to the eldest of her sons, 'Don't let him wander off.'

'I'll look after him, Mama,' Alarn promised, his head held high and his jaw set proudly with the important responsibility she'd given him.

He's so like Parlan, she thought, feeling the familiar ache of loss. Hand-in-hand with his little brother, nine-year-old Alarn ran down the cobbled garden path to the small picket gate and the old man waiting there. Bundled in a tattered green coat and seated high on the driver's seat of his peat-cutter's wagon, Refallt greeted the boys with a gap-toothed smile in a wind-weathered, bony face. Reliable and gentle, Refallt was a good friend Annalie had known most of her life. The boys would have plenty of vigorous, muddy fun helping load the peat he dried and sold as fuel. More importantly, Refallt could deliver Annalie's urgent message to those living in Lowtown.

Alarn and Parla made first for the horse standing patiently in harness. The big brown gelding's ears pricked forward and his head lowered to them. Parla giggled as the horse's fat velvet lips snuffled up his offered carrots.

'I'll have them back before dark, Good-Missus Hollin,' Refallt said and frowned as she approached to speak with him privately. 'What's wrong?' he asked as soon as she was in earshot.

She cast a warning glance at the boys but saw they were busy befriending the horse. 'Nothing, I hope,' she replied. 'Lerant's been posted back here for a few days.'

'Why would they haul him away from guarding the mines?'

'Why, indeed. I overheard talk when I attended the birth of the Symmonds' latest child last night. Something's up; but no one down there will talk to me ever since . . . .'

Since Parlan had been killed in the line of duty. As far as everyone in Lowtown was concerned that put Annalie on the outer—she had her war widow's pension, her Uptown home, her sons safe at last. It hurt to see people, friends, for whom she'd acted as midwife for years whispering, rather than including her in whatever hoped-for rebellion they'd dreamed up. None of those had been of any substance until recently. Annalie was certain something had changed, that they were ready to move.

'You don't think?' Refallt asked, reading her expression.

She nodded. 'Tell them not to try anything at least until Lerant returns to the mines. I have a feeling Myrrghin Command are watching them more closely than usual. They must suspect something.'

'I heard a rumor . . . .' Refallt leaned closer still toward her. 'A pair of Weavers in town.'

The downtrodden of Lowtown were always talking of imaginary Weavers coming to rescue them and Refallt had always been as skeptical as she. If he believed it now . . . that would explain the urgent excitement she'd felt wherever she went in

Lowtown last night. She looked up at him, eyebrows raised in silent question.

'It makes sense they'd call the Commander back into the city,' Refallt finished.

'Right.' Lerant couldn't, *wouldn't,* tell her if it was true. Weavers! She gripped Refallt's thin arm hard. 'Tell them to keep their heads down. Now is not the time!'

'I'll do my best,' he said laconically and gave her a hesitant smile. Some of them were hotheads who wouldn't listen no matter how dire the situation.

Annalie sighed and shook her head. 'Just tell them.'

'We can help you cut peat!' Alarn announced excitedly, returning to her side, his brown eyes shining with excitement beneath a fringe of unruly chestnut curls.

'Load, not cut,' she corrected, tucking his scarf back in around his jacket collar and giving him a boost up to the wagon. She lifted Parla and Refallt leaned down to take the tiny, chubby hands and pull him up.

'We help you cu'pea',' Parla parroted happily. Cuddling his favorite soft toy, he added, 'Peko likes it up here, Mama!'

With both his small passengers safely aboard, the old man took up the reins and clucked to the horse. Annalie watched until the wagon rattled off around the corner at the bottom of the hill. She walked up onto the open wooden porch of her gray stone cottage that looked down over Rogha Harbor. Though the morning sun was slanting in warm and bright, the chill air told her winter was not far off. Clouds building high on the northern horizon heralded a storm by nightfall, possibly snow.

Parlan's brother had returned some weeks ago, barely given any leave, just a day or two to spend to mourn with his nephews and their mother and try to come to terms with his shattering loss. Having received word sooner, Annalie had had longer to grieve and begin recovering. But she was worried about Lerant who had returned believing he'd failed. He'd promised her he would protect her husband. She had told him then it was a promise he couldn't make, and now she was afraid he was punishing himself for it by staying away from a home and the boys he loved.

As it was, he was rarely in town, ordered to stand as Commander at the coal-mines. Then, yesterday, he'd suddenly been stationed back at Rogha Fortress, in the heart of the city. Annalie would ask that now he was in town and on a regular day shift, he, like the other officers, should come home when off duty. Perhaps she might even be able to wheedle some information out of him as to his new orders.

Rebellion was in the wind. She could smell it.

An unexpected storm-wind slammed the shutters of the Rogha City boarding house's tiny dormer window, startling Taran m'Connor. He left off shoving clothing into his carry-all to note the sun had disappeared and decided to wear his greatcoat after all. Everything was at last arranged. The three families who had chosen to flee Myrrgha's rule would escape with him tomorrow night after gathering at the selected forest grove on the outskirts of Lowtown. From there, he'd guide them on to the Kerestra at Seelski. A Sharing with each of them had ascertained their sincerity, though there would be further checks long before they headed at last for Sanctuary.

He shouldered the rucksack and made sure that his Stinger gun and dart-quiver, worn over his shirt, were safely hidden inside the buttoned-up coat. Downstairs, he settled his bill and stepped outside to find the street empty and rain falling in a steady drizzle. He hurried on, winding his way through the shabby harbor district and on uphill then down again toward the town square and the northern wall that circled about the rear of the city. He'd made several useful contacts among the ship crews about the docks. At the market square there were more people about, vendors at their stalls and farmers off-loading produce while more prosperous-looking citizens moved in and out of permanent shop-fronts. There should be no more than a bored pair of guards on duty at the Arch gate on the other side of the square.

Instead, after making his way closer, he saw armed soldiers about a low wooden barricade they'd erected to check everyone exiting the city. Standing watching them was a Myrrghin Commander, battle-ready in cuirass, black-red cloak, and flashy scarlet-plumed helm. Worse, at his belt hung a set of manacles and a methirri slave collar.

Armed with a mix of short-swords, knives and muskets, his militia soldiers meant trouble. And with those glittering, blood-red, diamond-shaped methirri bands centered above their eyes, they were expecting someone capable of Weaving. Not some poor escaped slave from the mines.

Him.

He'd been betrayed. Quickly, he retreated away from the square but came to a shocked halt as he heard the loud tramp of boots and the metallic clanking of weapons from somewhere just ahead. More of the militia, out hunting, searching thoroughly as they closed toward the Arch. The other access street was likewise under military control. At the barricade, the officer remained waiting, draped in the black of death as his hounds drove his prey to the kill. With every passing moment, the noose tightened.

Desperately, m'Connor looked about for some way out of the trap. He ducked into the nearest foul-smelling, shadowed alley-way, climbed a pile of garbage, and reached for a balcony railing. He scaled the unevenly set masonry and slid onto the tiled roof just as the militia squad jogged past in a clinking of swords and muskets. Two paused to check the alleyway then rejoined the main troop.

Relieved, m'Connor made his way from roof-top to roof-top, crouched low, and taking a circular route about the square and on to the city wall. There, he climbed out and sat perched precariously atop the decaying, crumbling masonry. Darkness was deeper now, and the gusting winds cut into him more viciously in his exposed position. High above Rogha, he had a view of warm cottage lights to one side and on the other a dull smear of murky river-moat, a perilously long drop into carnivore-infested waters. He didn't like what he'd heard of the results of an attack by a full-grown Roghin slargapent. There were no slargapents in Lellghin waters, the Akkarra made sure of that. Or they had once.

He stripped off his backpack and coat, throwing them toward the opposite embankment. The wind caught his coat and carried it clear, but his pack hit the muddy slope of the river-bank and slid into the dark water. He took a deep breath, braced himself to jump, and then hesitated. Was that a splash? Had he seen the looping, scaled back-ridge of a reptilian body moving on the surface down there? Anxiously, he looked back toward the square, brightly lit now by torches in sconces about the arch.

More militiamen came hurrying out of a blind alley and collided with a vendor cart. It teetered, and then toppled over, sending fragments of shattered pottery flying in all directions. The owner, a potter by the look of him, picked up his long-handled kiln spade and attacked the troopers. Some of the townspeople joined in, throwing garbage or cheering him on. Leaving one trooper on guard, the officer led his remaining men away from their post to restore order.

Taking his chance, m'Connor moved closer along the rampart and climbed down close by the Arch. Adding a barely discernible Cloaking Weave as protection, he made a smooth run by the unseeing sentry, vaulted the barricade and sprinted through the open Arch gate.

There were no travelers but for a single horse-drawn wagon approaching the bridge from the far side of the river. An old, sinewy man wearing a shabby green coat was on foot leading a big brown horse and two small boys were perched atop the driver's seat. Building strength, the icy wind screamed through the boughs of a dense needle pine that stood by the other end of the bridge. The horse shifted and snorted nervously, pulling at the reins as the old man urged it up onto the bridge.

With a mighty splintering crack, a gnarled limb broke free from the tree and crashed down immediately behind the wagon. Squealing in terror, the horse reared, knocking the old man aside and charging forward onto the bridge, dragging the wagon and bearing down on m'Connor. He swung up to straddle the stone balustrade and dropped back to the road as the horse and swaying wagon charged by in a clattering of wheels and hooves to disappear through the Arch. Men shouted and women screamed from within the town square. M'Connor broke into a run, hoping to reach the concealing shrubbery on the farther embankment before soldiers came looking for the wagon's owner who was lying unconscious and bleeding by the roadside.

The driverless wagon smashed through the wooden barricade, not slowing a fraction as the spooked horse charged toward the crowd about the potter. Busy settling the argument and soothing the potter's pride, Kerell Lerant looked up in alarm. Karatin, who was by far the largest of Lerant's squad, made a leap for the horse's head and grabbed the harness. Sweating and shaking from nose to tail, the animal came to a skidding halt, sending the wagon careening over onto its side. Peat spilled everywhere.

Peat! Refallt! He'd known the old peat-cutter since childhood.

'Where's Refallt!' voices among the crowd called, echoing Lerant's urgent recognition. Suddenly, Lerant spotted something else, something that made him sick to his gut. A soft toy. He hurried to it, hoping against hope that it wasn't what he thought. Cold through to the marrow, he bent and picked it up. A little brown rabbit with a blue ribbon askew around its chubby neck.

'Peko . . . .' he murmured. Parla never went anywhere without him. Automatically he straightened the ribbon and dusted debris from its much-petted fabric, his knuckles whitening against the small brown body, one sightless blue eye staring up at him.

'Parla!' he shouted, running toward the wagon. His men had already righted it, Karatin heaving it up onto its teetering wheels almost single-handedly. He could see its tray was empty.

'Sir?' the giant trooper questioned, frowning at him.

The gate sentry yelled. 'Old Refallt's fallen! Two small boys were with him when he left.'

So, it was Alarn, too. Lerant ran toward the man, shoving the broken barricade aside the better to try to see beyond the darkness of the Archway and the curving road that led out over the bridge.

'I can't see them . . . .' The sentry reported.

'Sir!' a trooper yelled from beyond the Arch-tunnel, 'It's the outlaw! I'll get 'im!' Hefting his musket, he fired.

'No!' Lerant thundered. 'Don't shoot!!'

He raced through the shadowy stone tunnel, his aging Second, Brant Wilgar, only a pace behind. Wilgar had known both Lerant and Parlan all their lives and was like a great-uncle to Alarn and Parla. His men and the crowd surged out behind them, united for the moment in the search.

The young trooper, Blakan, fumbled for his powder pouch, cursing as he reloaded. Either he hadn't heard, or he didn't care. Lerant snatched the gun from the startled youngster's hands. 'Orders? Take him alive, or else? Remember that?! And my nephews are out there!' He didn't wait for the reply, but turned to scan the road.

Out on the bridge, a dark-haired man regained his feet after ducking the shot. He pulled a strange-looking weapon from a shoulder-holster, his free hand drawing and loading something. Lerant ducked. The gate sentry gave a strangled cry, dropped and lay unmoving.

'Take cover and get these people back!' Lerant shouted and moved to aid the wounded man, relieved when he found no more than a small dart had taken him in the face. He was unconscious, apparently drugged. Carefully craning up from cover of the town wall buttress, Lerant could see Refallt lying unmoving on the road on the other side of the bridge but there was no sign of Parlan's sons.

'Keep the outlaw busy,' he ordered. 'Blakan, Sandor, with me. We're going after him. The rest of you aim wide, you hear me, aim *wide!* We need him alive! And for pity's sake, keep an eye out for the boys!'

M'Connor jumped from the road into the cover of some shrubbery beside the bridge-ramp. A shrill scream pierced the roaring storm-wind and the crack of musket fire.

'Help! Help!' A small mud-splattered boy screamed from the water's edge. He didn't seem hurt, but his cries broke to racking sobs and he pointed a desperate finger at the swirling river-water.

Squinting against the failing light, m'Connor saw a splashing figure, a smaller child, clutching at clods of peat that were water-logged and sinking. Water poured into the child's rounded mouth, and, eyes wide with panic, he vanished beneath the murky surface. The elder boy wailed in utter despair, helplessly watching the other's submersion and took a step toward the river. Another instant and he'd be in over his head.

'Stop!' m'Connor shouted. Startled, the boy turned and stared, his expression going rapidly from fear to joyous hope as m'Connor added, 'I'll get him for you, son!'

Dropping the Stinger, m'Connor dove headlong into shockingly icy water, using the bobbing peat clods as a marker. He hoped the slargapents were busy eating his rucksack.

'Bloody fool!' Blakan gaped. 'The slargapents'll 'ave him for dinner!'

Equally surprised by the dive into the river, Lerant came to such a sudden halt on the bridge that his two troopers almost ran him down. They joined him to lean over the railing and peer down into impenetrable darkness.

'He's from Lellgha,' Sandor said. 'He don't know about them.'

'Well, 'e's gonna learn in a big hurry!'

'Sandor, tend to the old man,' Lerant ordered. Refallt was unconscious, no hope of answers there. 'Blakan, take Karatin and watch that side of the river. He can't stay in that freezing water much longer.' They saluted and left at a run.

Lerant had only just gotten his other men into position along the town wall river bank when Blakan came charging back over the bridge, coming to a halt before him.

'A boy, sir!' he reported breathlessly. 'Says he's lost his little brother.'

'Alarn Hollin?' Lerant grabbed at the trooper's arm.

'Dunno, sir. Didn't give no name.'

Where was little Parla?! Lerant turned sharply to his Second who was craning to listen. 'Wilgar, keep the men on watch here. I'll be back in a moment.' He hurried up onto the bridge to meet the giant Karatin who put a struggling Alarn down close to where a now conscious Refallt was being treated by Sandor.

'The Weaver!' Trooper Howlett, the sharp-eyed marksman of the squad called. 'He's coming up! There! Toward the Arch!'

Lerant hesitated, torn by Alarn's hysterical sobbing and a waking Refallt's urgent 'Where's your brother, son?' But Alarn had heard Howlett's shout and ran toward the Arch end of the bridge. 'Steady, Alarn, steady! It's me, Uncle Kerell!' Lerant caught him and went down on his knee to hold him. 'Is Parla down there? Is that it?'

Alarn nodded urgently, his tear-filled eyes wide with terror. 'Th-the m-man w-went after . . . h-him,' he sobbed, struggling to break free, 'In th-the water. Let me go! He s-said he'd g-get him!'

'Parla fell in the river!?' Shocked, Lerant called urgently to his troopers. 'There's another boy! In the river!'

Howlett shouted, 'The Weaver's got him, Sir! Went in after him!'

Standing, Lerant saw a white shape against the dark water, a man swimming on his back toward the pool of torchlight, straight toward his would-be captors. He was making slow progress, only one arm stroking and the other clutched about a bundle he held to his chest. Parla!

'He's got him, Uncle! He's got him!' Alarn craned to look where the troopers were pointing and shouted triumphantly. 'I knew he would!'

'Wait here with Refallt,' Lerant said firmly.

'Slargapents!' Howlett cried warning.

Closing in on the Weaver was a series of unnatural ripples. 'Controlled fire!' Lerant shouted, knowing his pistol wasn't much use from this angle. 'Careful!'

From the bridge and the river-banks, the gloom was lit by flashes of musket-fire. The slargapents veered away but that was no guarantee of safety; they were not easily put off the scent of prey. The stranger quickly reached shallower water, got his feet beneath him, and began wading toward the steep-sided, rocky river-bank. He held little Parla high at his shoulder, clear of the cold water. The little body was still, silent. Dead?

Lerant ran down to them, uncaring of his footing. A trooper held on to Wilgar who leaned down, stretching out over the water to take Parla safely into his arms. 'Alive?' Lerant asked, arriving breathlessly and trying to keep to duty enough to watch the outlaw as well.

'I'm not sure,' Wilgar said. 'I can't see. Let's get him up to the road.'

Dripping water from dark hair, his white shirt wet and clinging, Parla's rescuer placed his hands on his head in a gesture of surrender. He looked half frozen to death. Several troopers had guns aimed at him and no one's methirri bands were burning bright with warning.

'Keep close watch!' Lerant ordered.

In the better light by the Arch, he pulled off his cloak and put it down for Wilgar to carefully lower little Parla whose tiny face was blue and white and so still. Unable to do more than watch, Lerant silently begged mercy as Wilgar refused to give up but repeatedly massaged the small chest. Parla coughed and vomited violently and Wilgar hurriedly placed him on his side to avoid choking. 'Mama!' the toddler cried, strong and clear.

'Uncle's here. I'm here, Parla. You're all right.' Overcome, Lerant half-fell to his knees and wrapped his crying nephew tightly within the folds of his cloak. Wilgar clapped Lerant on the shoulder, and called to the others, 'He's all right!' and there were cheers at the news.

'Guard the prisoner well,' Lerant ordered Wilgar and got to his feet, carrying a still-crying Parla. 'I'll be back in a moment.' The old soldier nodded grim acceptance, his expression losing all its elation.

Lerant signaled Karatin to release a sobbing Alarn who shrugged off the cloak the giant had wrapped warmly about him to run flat out across the bridge. Holding out his free arm to collect the hurtling boy, Lerant knelt down so Alarn could see his little brother tucked up warm and snug. 'He's all right,' he assured, 'See? It's over.'

Lerant drew back and allowed him to help hold Parla, smiling as the boy kissed his little brother's red and blue mottled face. The Weaver waiting for him at the river's edge, waiting to be collared in methirri, was responsible for the boys' heart-warming, miraculous reunion. Having followed Alarn, Karatin stood watching, relieved at Parla's survival. Lerant unclipped the slave collar and chains hanging heavy at his belt. Something else bumped against his hand as he reached for them—the little toy rabbit.

'Collar and chain the prisoner,' he ordered Karatin tiredly, handing over the ugly shackles. 'I'll follow when I'm finished here.'

'Thank you, sir!' Karatin exclaimed, eagerly accepting the duty.

'The man saved him, Uncle Kerell, just like he said he would.' Alarn said, thankfully too busy with his brother to notice the order to imprison his hero. 'I was coming for you, though, Parla, don't worry, even if I can't swim real good.'

Horrified, Lerant understood the Weaver had in fact saved both Parlan's sons. 'Come, we must get you home and out of this cold. Your mother will be worrying. Here, Parla, hush, here's Peko.' Parla gulped back a cry, sniffed and grabbed at his toy. Lerant called one of his troopers to his side. 'Rawlins, here, will carry Parla for you,' he told Alarn. 'It's a long way home, can you walk that far?'

"'Course I can!' Alarn said indignantly and released his precious cargo as Rawlins stooped, smiling reassuringly. Lerant gave orders for others to see that the wounded and Refallt were taken to the garrison and city infirmaries. He snagged the boy's jacket as Alarn turned in the opposite direction. 'Where are you going?'

Alarn said impatiently. 'I need to thank the man. Like Papa would want me to.'

'He would,' Lerant said with quiet pain and Alarn tugged at his hold, assuming his consent. 'I'll do it for you. You need to catch up to Parla and get him safely home.'

Alarn frowned, looking from him to the river and back again. 'All right. But tell him where we live so he can come visit. Mama will want to thank him, too.'

'I'll tell him,' Lerant promised, wincing inwardly.

He made his way to the riverside where his troopers were gathered about the prisoner. Long shadows shifted about them, cast by the steep bank and the overhanging bridge. A single guttering torch, spitting and failing in the increasingly strong wind and rain, did little to help. Elbowing his way through the group, Lerant saw the prisoner sprawled on his side in the mud. Karatin had chained his hands and slid the methirri slave collar into place, locking it with a snap.

'Here you go, sir!' Proudly, Karatin cut the Weaver's dart quiver and holster free and passed it up, trophy-like, to his commander.

Lerant indicated he'd examine the weapon later and took a step closer to the prisoner. 'I thank you for rescuing the child,' he said, adding stiffly, 'but you've not earned freedom.'

'Sir,' Trooper Howlett cleared his throat nervously. 'He's hurt, sir. Bad hurt.'

Wilgar and another trooper scrambled down the rocky slope, each carrying a bundle of flaming torches. Light pushed back the darkness, and Lerant found the Weaver's face terribly white, bleached by more than the sudden illumination. Alarmed, he squatted down closer, sudden concern swamping the stern, military stance he'd hoped to use to shield his private emotion.

'You're hurt?' he asked. The man was shaken but struggling grimly to hold to his composure. So this was the infamous escaped slave, Weaver Taran m'Connor.

'Slargapent,' m'Connor said clearly. His calm faltering, he added, 'My leg.'

For a long moment Lerant was frozen with disbelieving horror—he'd gone into the river for Parla knowing what was waiting?

'I've sent for the anti-venom, Sir,' Wilgar reported breathlessly as he came to a halt at their side.

'It got him just as Wilgar and I were pulling him out, Sir,' Howlett explained, sounding sick. 'Damn near dragged him back in.'

Tugging at his belt buckle, Wilgar went to his knees at the prisoner's other side. 'We need to get a tourniquet on that leg,' he said.

Lerant bent to help and to closely examine the man's wounds and drew a sharp, hissing breath, finding the sheer, raw savagery of the injury shocking. His stomach lurched in reaction and he swallowed hard. As his men gathered close to peer over his and Wilgar's shoulders there was a chorus of similar, sickened reactions.

'Bloody hell!' 'His boot's almost gone!' 'Would have been his leg if not!'

'Shut up and hold those torches closer!' Lerant snapped.

They obeyed and the flaring light made it worse, much worse. M'Connor's right leg from knee to toe was a mass of bloodied, gouged flesh and muscle embedded with shredded boot-leather. Blood welled and flowed, scarlet mixing with the mire of the embankment.

'Steady,' Lerant said, wincing as Wilgar twisted the tourniquet into a tight knot and m'Connor gave in to a strangled cry of pain. Orders to take him alive didn't rate at the top of Lerant's list right then. He just wanted to have the chance to somehow repay him for Parla's life. 'Hang on now, hear me?' he said and shifted to grip m'Connor's shoulder.

'You!' The Weaver gasped, his expression wide and startled, and strangely joyful. Elation touched Lerant, too, for a single moment, and he shook it off like a spider on his back.

'*Mi serraga,*' m'Connor said, using his old native tongue, the so-called Magi language. Fainting, he fell back.

The words resounded in Lerant's mind, hard to dismiss as much as he tried. An unwanted and confusing image of a small white flower came to him, from his nightmare about Parlan, he thought. Wilgar had stopped bandaging and was watching Lerant with the strangest expression etched in his wrinkled face, an almost comical puzzlement. 'He's only fainted,' Lerant assured. 'Better he's out of it.'

Regaining his composure, Wilgar returned to his work. The thick, white roll of bandaging in his hands became a dark, wet red as it was wound again and again about raw ribbons of torn muscle. But, as more layers were added, the blood grew less, the tourniquet was holding.

'Did he try to curse me or something?' Lerant asked, knowing Wilgar had many years ago traded coal for wheat with Lellgha and knew something of their customs.

Wilgar shook his head. 'Quite the opposite, some kind of ancient greeting.'

'The man's delirious,' Lerant said, pushing down the part of himself that insisted he'd understood those foreign words.

'Like as not,' Wilgar agreed and tied off the bandage. He got to his feet. 'That's all I can do for him. He needs a surgeon. Where's Larkin and that damn anti-venom?'

'It'll take him a while to explain and get back here,' Lerant said as he got to his feet, brushing mud from his knees. He saw that two of his troopers had found a rope net and some planks and were hurrying with the makeshift stretcher back to them. The others stood watching him, their youthful, newly appointed commander, from beneath methirri bands and helms, rainwater dripping from their faces.

'Put the stretcher down here. You two, lift him, carefully now!' Wilgar urged. He stripped quickly out of his cloak and spread it as soft bedding over the net of ropes. Awkwardly, they lay the man on his back with chained hands beneath. 'He'll freeze to death before we need worry about the poison,' Wilgar said worriedly. 'We need blankets. You, you and you. Your cloaks, come on, quickly!' They obeyed readily enough despite the growing chill of the closing rainy winter's day. Wilgar collected the damp garments and placed them dry, warm side down over m'Connor.

'Right, then,' Lerant ordered. 'Berial, Howlett, you carry him. The rest of you fall in about the litter. Stay alert.'

'Take him to the Civilian Infirmary?' Wilgar asked, straightening up after tucking the cloaks more warmly. 'Pearce and his man, Callay, are the best surgeons in Rogha.'

The garrison's military surgeon, Starran, was more butcher than doctor. Lerant nodded frowning agreement but knew he must first report to his superior officer. Wearily, he pulled out the small Connector he'd been given from its pouch at his shoulder. He ducked his head over it, sheltering from the wind and rain and trying to draw warmth from the glow as its mysterious power responded to his voice.

'Rogha Fort. Report.'

'We have captured the Lellghin outlaw,' Lerant said calmly though his pulse jumped. 'His appearance fits the description of m'Connor. End.'

'Good work, Kerell!' Chief Commander Gareck's booming voice cut off the operator. 'High Inquisitor Zaraxan himself wants this one. I'll relay the news to him.'

Lerant flinched. Zaraxan was a sadistic madman, everyone knew that. Everyone but Gareck who had already torn shreds from Lerant for the 'lily-livered, softness' of his treatment of the slaves at the coal mine and was suspicious of the incoming 'donated' Khenghin charity.

'There's more to report, Chief Gareck,' he continued. 'M'Connor was mauled by a slargapent as he saved a child from the river. He needs Callay, not—'

'No!!' Gareck interrupted furiously. 'I heard all about the slargapent from your man who came running for the anti-venom! Get m'Connor to me now, Lerant! *Now!* If we can get him to talk so much the better! The bastard escaped from within Myrrgha Citadel itself, burned the place to the ground! And you think Rogha Infirmary will hold him?' He snorted. 'Watch him closely, Lerant, you hear me? He's a murdering Weaver, full of deceitful tricks. We'll give him the slarga cure . . . eventually.'

Gareck snickered and his tone dropped to a secretive eagerness. 'They say the pain of slarga poisoning is worse than any torture.

He'll tell us anything we want to hear when he starts screaming for that cure. We've got something over him the inquisitors never had.'

Bile rose in Lerant's throat, forcing him to swallow before continuing and giving him time to reconsider his approach. There was no point in invoking m'Connor's heroism; Gareck didn't have the heart to appreciate it. Best try aiming for his ambition instead.

'He's dying, Sir,' he said bluntly, hoping it wasn't true. 'If he doesn't get that anti-venom right now, he won't be around to answer anyone's questions.'

'Are you hard of hearing, Lerant?' Gareck roared so loud that the Connector flared bright green. 'He's tough! He'll live! He'd kill us all without a second thought. I assume you do have him collared? It's as well he's working alone!'

'Of course, but—'

'Good! Then you know your duty! Bring him in, Lerant—*now!*'

The Connector-stone darkened abruptly. Lerant shoved it back into its pouch and swung furiously about to face his troopers. Their disgusted expressions proved they'd heard every word despite the storm. 'Move!' he shouted at them. 'Gareck wants his prisoner now!'

Formed up as he'd ordered, they moved off. Wilgar hesitated, his mouth set to argue. Lerant was in no mood. He glared at the old man and nodded for him to follow the others. Wilgar's blue eyes regarded him coldly before he gave a sharp salute and obeyed. It wasn't easy watching a man who had been like an uncle to he and Parlan stalk away in icy disapproval.

Lerant noticed Parla's mittens lying in the mud at his feet. Wilgar had pulled them from the child's tiny, frozen hands as he rubbed warmth into them. Lerant stooped to pick them up and stuff them under his belt. So small, so wet. The river hissed softly in the darkness and the slargapents slapped hungrily at its surface, scenting the blood on the embankment, angry, twice denied their food. Shuddering, Lerant turned away and hurried to catch up to his troopers.

CHAPTER SIXTEEN

'All right. Ready? Everyone down,' Rhyssa instructed, making certain the members of her new Arc, The Dancers, obeyed.

Old m'Hallon, watching, raised an eyebrow. They both knew her latest design was unlikely to succeed any better than its predecessor, but that if it did, the worse everyone would suffer without taking cover would be a drenching with seawater and they were already wet from their early morning practice dive with the Wavedancers towing them down to the reef. They'd stripped out of the upper portion of their diving suits, too hot under the noonday sun. The cleverly crafted breathers and air tanks had been carefully returned to storage in their little beach hut.

'Good,' Rhyssa said, as everyone took cover. 'Ready, Kyle?'

M'Hallon nodded and moved to stand arm outstretched toward the fuse but far enough away to avoid a drenching. How far back would he need to be when it was for real, and the mine contained enough powder to blow out a chunk of the side of a metal ship hull? Lighting the fuse could be the deadly part in their planned attack on the Myrrghin Fleet. M'Hallon knew that, but wasn't particularly distressed; he had no family remaining alive and his Brother would be waiting for him as he passed from life to death.

He might be sanguine about the process, but Rhyssa still couldn't quite bring herself to believe as did the Lellghinners. She was in no hurry to die, either way.

'Yes, I'm ready,' m'Hallon repeated, and gave her a gentle smile, able to Read her pensive mood and probably guess the cause.

'Right,' she said briskly, 'Here goes!'

She squatted behind the sand-bunker with the others, but unlike them, kept her head up to watch m'Hallon's efforts with the fuse that protruded from the mine weighed down beneath the gently lapping waves. The Weaver's arm began to glow with those disturbing green lines. Abruptly, a bright sparking flash leapt from his fingertips to the underwater fuse. It burned with satisfying gusto, staying alight despite the seawater. That invention alone had caused her sleepless nights, until the Akkarra had come to the rescue providing a mysterious waterproof material.

Tense, hopefully, Rhyssa waited as the fuse burned on under the seal on the mine detonator cap. She held her breath. Nothing happened.

'Well, damn,' she muttered, straightening up. With a thumping, whooshing bang seawater rained down to drench her from head to toe. A little startled by the force of the mine's eruption, she wiped saltwater from her eyes and laughed.

'It works! It works!' Tosharski, the youngest of her team exclaimed, the others joining in, equally elated.

Rhyssa joined in as they engulfed her in their group hug-dance. She'd become fond of her team, proud of their work and their courage in trying something that had been so alien to them. The thought that any of them might be hurt or killed suddenly drained away her happiness. Sensing that, they too stopped, looking to each other in some confusion as, again, they realized they couldn't Share their supportive feeling or reactions with her.

'It'll be all right,' Madierina told her awkwardly.

'Of course it will,' Rhyssa agreed, shaking off her mood and marshalling her confidence. It *should* be safe enough. For all but m'Hallon. He'd watched them happily but had now returned to their little cooking fire having, as usual, not returned from the reef empty-handed. Several tailor-fish lay roasting on the coals and there were lily-tubers as well.

'Just about done. Time for lunch,' he called.

'Take the afternoon off everyone,' Rhyssa told them, enjoying their surprised joy. 'You've earned it. Celebrate! I have to go, but I'll catch up with you later.'

They nodded and called thanks as she set off on her daily walk to join the Fetrins for lunch. Aside from Bruska expecting her, she'd promised m'Connor she'd keep an eye on Sean. His impatience for battle was tempered by her reports on her work, and today she'd have very good news for him.

As she approached Home Cove village, she caught some strange rising and falling sound, an eerie, sorrowful wailing. As she grew closer, it resounded from the cliff-tops behind the trees. 'Bruska,' she whispered, recognizing his distressed human-dog howling. It climbed higher, more and more agonized, utterly heart-broken. She broke into a run and met Flynn charging out to look for her.

'What happened?' she demanded.

'Nothing,' Flynn said breathlessly as he turned to jog back with her to the house. 'He's howling and howling and he won't settle.'

'How long?'

'A while.'

'Is Sean here yet?'

Flynn shook his head as together they stepped up to the front door and entered. Dierna was sitting on the floor, m'Fetrin's upper body cradled in her arms. She looked up at Rhyssa, her face strained and white. Rhyssa went to her knees at their side. 'Hush, Bruska, hush. What is it? What's wrong?'

His howling lowered to snuffles and he lifted his head. His eyes met hers full of confusion and pain and a desperate hope that she could make it all better, as she had done so many times in the past. Always before, she'd had some clue as to the cause of his distress.

'It's Taran,' Sean said at their backs, entering the door.

'What?' Rhyssa turned toward him, suddenly chill to the bone.

Sean looked ill, terribly shaken, an emptiness in his eyes somehow echoing Bruska's expression as he traded glances with his mother. 'Silsun will be here shortly. She's crossing the bay to come speak to you. She just Sent to me, to all of us.'

'Me? Silsun?' Rhyssa said, her mind trying to follow. Abruptly, like a kick to the gut, it hit her. Silsun was coming to Rhyssa because she couldn't reach a Myrrghinner the way she could anyone else at Home Cove. Rhyssa and m'Connor were lovers, yet she'd been last to know.

Terrified, she met Fetrin's grim gaze and, her voice thin and emotionless, asked, 'Dead?'

'Alive,' Sean assured hastily, reaching out a steadying arm. 'Captured, but alive. They don't know about Marc. The Severing hit her a little while ago. We all felt it.' He looked down at his brother's body and added darkly, 'Bruska must have felt it, too.'

'Captured?' Flynn repeated. 'But he said he wouldn't let them! He promised!'

'He tried,' Sean said and took his younger brother into a Sharing hug.

Dierna's hand slipped into hers, squeezing, and Rhyssa met her eyes, found pain beyond words. Perhaps it was as well she couldn't Share, but never had she felt so much an outsider. She missed her father, her brothers. She missed Taran.

After a moment, blinking tears from her eyes, she said, 'I'm going after him.'

'No,' Sean said, cold and sure as if he'd expected this. He stood. 'I go, you stay. You know why.'

'The explosive mines are working now!'

'They are?' he blinked pleased surprise but quickly added, 'They still need you. They don't know how to plant them or set them, or anything . . . .'

She swore and stormed away to the hearth, feeling an urgent need to move, to do anything, *something*. She must find him! Bruska crouched up on his haunches, watching her beseechingly, as if she'd have the answers. What exactly was he feeling from m'Connor?

'Can you . . . could you uncover anything about what's happened if you Linked to Bruska?' she asked Sean.

He nodded slowly. 'Maybe. But Silsun will have seen it all better for herself.'

Suddenly, Rhyssa was more angry than ever before in her life. 'She's coming here? Good! She has a lot of explaining to do! I told them it was madness to send him out there!'

'It had to be done,' Silsun said, quiet and cool into the fire of the moment as she entered the small room.

Silsun stood there, so calm, so . . . resigned, it stole all the angry words from Rhyssa's mouth. The look in Silsun's eyes took Rhyssa from anger to ice-cold hatred.

'You knew he'd be captured, didn't you?'

Silsun nodded, everyone in the room watching her, silent and still as she replied, 'So did Taran.'

People pushed and shoved, ignoring repeated shouts to stand clear, curious to see the prisoner just visible under the mounded cloaks spread atop the litter that swayed in his guards' grasp. One of them stumbled a little and the jolt woke m'Connor, dragging a surprised cry of pain from his lips. 'Be still,' Lerant urged, reaching down to steady him.

M'Connor peered up at him, squinting dazedly. His gaze followed up Lerant's body, taking in the Cross-swords insignia and up to the methirri band and the red-plumed helm. He groaned and closed his eyes a moment, muttering a curse, and looked up again to ask, 'The boy?'

'Alive.' Someone in the crowd pushed the front row of spectators, bringing them hard up against the litter. Enraged, Lerant bellowed, 'Get back or I shoot!' A hush fell, everyone staring at him and obeying fearfully.

Before he could leave the War Ministry, General Rusark had sent Lerant on an errand to the Inquisition Tower. He'd never forget the one glimpse he'd caught beyond an open interrogation room door. The desperate, agonized pleading in the chained man's bloodied face was forever seared into Lerant's mind. 'Nothing I could do! Not my doing!'

'What?' m'Connor asked.

Annoyed as he realized he'd been talking aloud to himself, Lerant glared down at the injured man. 'It's your doing! All yours and your foul witches! You should never have come here! You should—'

A deafening booming roar resounded ahead of them and the Fortress erupted in a monstrous fireball. Night was day, Rogha City engulfed in vengeful, devouring red firelight. The ground trembled violently and earsplitting blasts echoed from the burning fortress, black-powder and other munitions going up. A scorching shock wave raced down the tunnel made by the surrounding buildings and stonewalls in a rushing, howling turbulence that caught Lerant and his squad and hurled them from their feet. Lerant slammed to a stop against a low stone wall bordering a cottage in the curve of the street. Rubble rained heavily down or sliced screaming at high pitch past his head.

Dazed, he crawled into the inadequate, partial shelter of the cottage-garden where he could see two troopers dragging m'Connor's limp form. Dead? No. The man shook his head and, coming round, tried to focus on his surroundings. Pieces of timber, stone and shards of glass continued to fall, littering the frost-seared garden with dull thuds, clangs and sharp crashing. The cowering troopers covered their faces with their arms. M'Connor had no such protection. Lerant threw himself bodily over the injured man and together, they waited for the deadly hail to end.

Eventually an eerie silence replaced the noisy chaos. A cloud of dust and smoke whirled haphazardly in the icy, moaning wind. Nothing else moved. Then, as if at a given signal, rose a nightmare chorus of screams, shouts and agonized wailing.

Lerant sat up and stared disbelieving toward the fires of destruction. M'Connor propped himself on an elbow and craned to peer through the remains of the garden's picket gate. Utterly shocked, Lerant instinctively sought the other man's eyes. M'Connor's expression mirrored Lerant's reaction. His dazed green-brown eyes reflected the leaping flames, and in his wide-eyed shock there was also sorrow; a horrified, agonized compassion. In a moment of profoundly shared emotion, both he and Lerant were sick with the same despair for others like them, flesh and blood, and all too fragile.

Dust began to settle thickly over them. Lerant coughed and stumbled to his feet. Peering in the uncertain light, he searched for the men of his command. Every lantern in the street had been shattered, but the fires grew, giving off an eerie, flickering red light. Lerant found and waved a still burning torch. He cleared his throat and called, 'Rogha militia to me. All of you, over here!' One by one they staggered out of the gloom, most bloodied by minor cuts, but miraculously all escaping severe injury. Then, Lerant realized with dread Wilgar was missing.

'There he is, Sir!' Blakan exclaimed, pointing.

Gasping relief, Lerant spotted his old friend a little distance down the street, bent down, busy tending one of the wounded civilians. Somehow, he'd hung onto the aid kit. 'Everyone all right?' Lerant asked, moving among them. They trembled with shock, but each responded steadily. They stood in a circle about him, their faces gray-dusted and ghost-like in the uncertain light, all casting disbelieving stares at the shattered fortress.

The ruined street flowed beneath an ever-changing pattern of fire-lit shadows, and against that screen men and women appeared, some carrying lanterns as they emerged from their cottages. At the head of the road there was no sign that the two-floored complex of brick and mortar Fortress, walls and towers, had ever existed. A pillar of impenetrable smoke and fire roiled up over a monstrous pile of rubble and slabs of masonry, all that remained to give testimony to the ancient fort's past domination of Rogha City.

The townspeople too, had suffered. The Gateway Meeting Hall had been caught in the secondary explosion and completely demolished while neighboring cottages were severely damaged. Shattered walls crumbled and toppled, endangering those beginning to search for buried survivors and adding more debris to the already clogged street. Bodies lay pinned beneath timber and stone, tiled roofs hung by flimsy supports that swayed precariously in the wind, and flames sprouted everywhere, feeding on the wreckage.

The wounded screamed and begged for help, others shouted names of lost loved ones. More and more townsmen were gathering, joining the ragged figures staggering blindly from the ruins or carrying the dead and injured. Several troopers gave sobbing cries, and Lerant's heart was torn anew as he too, realized . . . .

Children. Two tiny, broken bodies thrown outward by the explosion that had engulfed the Hall, lay twisted and limp, scattered like abandoned, broken dolls on the bloodied cobblestones. Tomorrow was Harvest Eve; they'd have been preparing their pageant . . . .

Alarn and little Parla were safe; they'd been excluded because of Annalie's changed status and her marriage-brother commanding the slaves at the mine. Lerant's mind raced, his thoughts tumbling one over the other, until one image remained—a man running, desperate, seeking escape from Rogha, needing darkness to hide him and hide his evil work.

Then, Gareck's warning returned: *'He escaped from within Myrrgha Citadel. Burned it . . . A murdering Weaver, full of deceitful tricks!'*

Slowly, Lerant turned and looked down at the prisoner whose apparent courage he'd so recently admired. Now he saw not courage, but fanaticism. 'Murderer!' one of the troopers snarled suddenly, whirling on m'Connor.

'Gareck was right about you!' Lerant snapped, cold as the grave, promising retribution. 'You destroyed Myrrgha Citadel with fire and now you've done it to us.'

'No. Rogha is friendly to us. Why would I—?' m'Connor spoke with a steady, almost believable calm, his gaze open to Lerant's scrutiny. All the more proof of his ability to deceive.

'Enough! Don't insult us with your lies!'

M'Connor struggled, tried to get to his feet and gave up. 'Be warned. This can only be Methaggar—'

'Shut up!' Lerant growled and lifted a fist. He stormed away a few paces as much to avoid attacking the man where he lay as to organize his men to aid the survivors. Bellowing his hatred in a wordless roar, Karatin bent and snatched m'Connor up by the shirt front, pinning him against the cottage wall. 'No!' Lerant shouted, moving swiftly back.

'Die! You filthy butcher!' Karatin closed one huge hand about m'Connor's throat. Cursing frustration, the giant altered his grip, and Lerant realized the slave collar had just saved m'Connor's life.

'I gave you an order, soldier!' Lerant tugged at Karatin's massive arm and he eased the pressure, turned wide-eyed to face him. M'Connor drew a wheezing breath. 'You won't honor your friends by giving their murderer a quick death.' Lerant hoped he was getting through, his other hand rested on his pistol butt. He'd didn't want to have to shoot one of his own troopers, but he must keep m'Connor alive. 'We'll deal justice to him later, my word on it.' Sanity edged back into Karatin's grief-crazed eyes. 'Come,' Lerant said more gently, 'if we move quickly we might find some of the children alive back there.'

Karatin nodded and dropped m'Connor as if he was fouling his hands with excrement. Falling on his mangled leg, m'Connor passed out. Lerant wondered who he could trust to guard the murderer. Wilgar had arrived and was standing at the broken gate, Lerant's now tattered plumed helm in his hands. He came forward to hand it over.

'Thanks.' Lerant buckled the helm back on his head. 'You stay here and guard this piece of filth. Blakan!'

'Sir?'

'Get down to the City Infirmary as fast as you can and give them this.' He pulled his notebook from his pocket and scribbled quickly, reading aloud as he did so in case the man couldn't read. 'Slarga anti-venom. By order, Commander Lerant.' He looked back up at the trooper as he handed him the written order. 'As fast as you can. If we don't keep this animal alive, all Rogha could pay the price.'

'Sir? But . . . They wouldn't, not now, not after this.'

'They would,' Lerant said, grimly certain. 'You haven't been to Myrrgha City, Trooper, I have. Move! Get that stuff back here and give it to Wilgar. He'll know what to do with it.' Blakan saluted crisply and took off at a sprint. 'Berial! Sandor! Run to Perrit's store and bring wedge-bars and shovels. Wilgar?'

'Yes, Commander?'

'You do know how to dose him with the anti-venom?'

'I do, Sir.'

'Good. Guard him well; there'll be plenty more around here who want to gut the bastard. Drag him back behind that wall.' Hearing m'Connor moan as he began to come around, Lerant cast him a murderous glare, and then was alarmed at how bad he looked. 'Don't let the mongrel die on me, Wilgar,' he snapped. 'See what you can find to keep him covered and warm. Cursed weather's getting worse.'

'Sir!' Howlett yelled from forward where he had been feeding the safety rope down to Karatin who had volunteered to crawl into the smoking, shifting wreckage of the Hall. 'He's found one alive!'

'Alive?' Lerant dared to allow hope to flicker back to life.

'Yes, sir!' Howlett repeated, a faint smile gleaming against the soot and dirt that coated his thin face. The smile faded as he added, 'Maybe this one will make it.'

Lerant nodded, unable to speak, choked by the memory. The last child Karatin had pulled from the rubble had died shortly afterward from horrific injuries. Lerant had been impressed when the big man had turned silently, grimly to get back to his knees and crawl down through the narrow shadowy gap into the still smoking, shifting rubble. Karatin was terrified of cramped, enclosed places. Only his great affection for small children could have pushed that terror down to a whimper. Nonetheless, Lerant couldn't imagine how he was managing down there in the dark, his massive strength shoving at beams and masonry no one else could have shifted.

'They've found someone alive?' Rankin called up as the message was relayed down the mountain of rubble where Lerant was standing exposed to the icy wind, anchoring the rope that was tied off about his waist. Rankin was Rogha's Archman, or mayor, and was working with his own team of townsmen who were trying to dig a tunnel through from the rear of the hall.

'He thinks so, yes!' Lerant yelled back. There was an outcry, a hopeful clamoring, mixed with some cheering and the onlookers as well as some of those who had been digging surged forward as if to run to Lerant's site. 'Tell them to stay back!' Lerant warned. 'They'll cave it in on top of my man! It's unstable up here!'

'Where's the Archman?' Another voice bellowed from below. 'Let me through, damn it!'

'Fogard? Is that you?' Rankin yelled back, one hand sheltering his eyes as he peered into the torchlight down slope.

'Sir!' the aide called breathlessly. 'The Connector! It's Myrrgha Command! They want to speak to the Commander.'

Rankin exchanged a sour look with Lerant. 'They must've finally realized the one at the fortress is never going to answer,' the Archman said.

'I can't leave my men!' Lerant snapped, the rope tightening about his waist.

'He says pull him up!' Howlett relayed. 'Slowly!'

Lerant tightened his grip on the rope and obeyed, feeling the weight of the big man on the other end working with them. It would be very difficult for Karatin, burdened by an injured child, trying to edge his way backwards up again through the rubble.

'They can wait,' Rankin agreed and bent to grab at the rope and help take the weight. His aide didn't call again from below, apparently made aware of the situation by the onlookers. Gradually, Karatin emerged, a great dust-caked mammoth appearing from a murky treacherous cave, one powerful arm holding a small child to his chest.

'A little girl!' Howlett called jubilantly. 'She's crying!'That was very good news. If she could cry her ribs were not collapsed onto her lungs as had been the case with the last rescue.

'I'll get her to her parents and on to the surgeon,' Rankin said, already edging downward, urged onward by the little girl's trembling cries for her mother who had broken free and was trying to climb up the slope.

Lerant nodded, distracted as he felt a tug on the rope he still held. Karatin was heading back into the rubble and Lerant wasn't sure he should let him. The fire was spreading further, feeding on wreckage that was sheltered from the rain. 'Could you speak to Command for me, please, Archman?' he pleaded. 'Tell them I'm needed here and I'll be there as soon as—'

'Understood,' Rankin said, preoccupied as he very carefully allowed the mother to take the crying child. Lerant knew Rankin had had repeated heated arguments with Myrrgha Command in the past. 'Remember,' he added, having to shout over the wind. 'We need them.'

'Since when?' Rankin shouted back.

'Their ships can carry doctors, supplies—.'

Rankin's expression was dubious at best beneath the flaring light of the torches gathered about the lower slope. Lerant couldn't make out all of his reply but caught the word 'coal'. Rankin was no fool; he knew as well as Lerant that there was no compassion in Myrrgha. They would fear only the loss of their fuel shipments. He was glad he didn't have to talk to them himself right now. It would be hard to keep a civil tongue.

At the end of the street where the cottage wall gave some shelter from the icy wind, m'Connor and his aging guard could do no more than watch the rescue effort. Ever more bodies were laid in a line down the center of the street and draped with blankets. Choked by emotion as he saw the smaller forms of children added to that terrible toll, m'Connor began softly chanting the words of The Ellaran, the ancient Lellghin prayer for the dead.

'Sen riata set T'rassa en venar, Al ana . . .'

'From the one sacred light we come, And to that . . .'

M'Connor stopped in surprise as he heard the old soldier translating and repeating the prayer in the common tongue. Noting the pause, the Roghinner turned his head to look at m'Connor and await the next line. Something in the man's expression made m'Connor sure he already knew it by heart but was being polite. Swallowing back surprise and growing pain, m'Connor began again, his words echoed by the translation.

'As sparks from the One Sacred Light we come,
And to that Hearth-Light we must return.
May the Holy Light grant that our souls shine brighter,
As we are welcomed Home.'

After the customary respectful silence, m'Connor nodded his thanks. His guard held his gaze a long moment then bent down and carefully eased m'Connor up to sit with his back supported by the wall. 'My name's Wilgar,' he said, 'Brant Wilgar. And I'd shake your hand, if I could.'

M'Connor stared at him and the old man snorted gently, apparently finding his consternation amusing.

'We're not all fools, man,' Wilgar said, his amusement settling to a look of sincere gratitude. 'Nor are we all totally lacking in basic good manners. My thanks, m'Connor,' he said intently. 'Thank you for saving the little one from the river. I'm sorry I can't do more for you and that you're so cold. They wouldn't spare me any blankets and I can't go looking and guard you at the same time. I've lost my cloak or you could have it. But here, this might help a little.' Quickly, he stripped out of his jacket and bent to tuck it about m'Connor's trembling shoulders, leaving himself exposed to the chill night in only his shirtsleeves.

'Thank you,' m'Connor said, further surprised by the kindness. With the cursed methirri collar blocking him, he couldn't Read the man, but he was somehow certain it wasn't only a desire for self-preservation that had him concerned for his health.

'There,' Wilgar said, as he stood back. 'That'll help until Blakan gets here.'

'Blakan?'

'Trooper Blakan. The Commander sent him for the anti-venom.'

'Oh. Good.' m'Connor added dryly, 'The Inquisition will be grateful.'

Wilgar flinched, but tilted his head in acknowledgment of the gallows humor. 'He shouldn't be much longer and then he can get some blankets for you from somewhere. Meantime, that tourniquet should be loosened if your leg's not to go bad.'

'I'll be all right,' m'Connor said, making Wilgar snort immediate disagreement. 'Leave the blankets. They need them more.' He peered curiously at the aged-lined face. 'You know the Old Tongue?'

'I traded with your people once. But that was a long, long time ago now. I'll do what I can for you but I can't endanger my friends.'

'Second? Where are you?' Someone called from out in the street.

'Over here, Blakan!' Wilgar yelled. 'Did you get it?'

'I did, but I 'ad to do a lot of talkin' first. It's somethin' awful back there. How is he?'

M'Connor squinted blearily upward to find a young, good-looking curly-haired youngster in a Roghin Militiaman's jerkin looking down at him.

'About frozen.'

'You gave him your jacket?!' Blakan demanded, obviously scandalized.

Wilgar sighed. 'Give me the drug.'

Blakan hunted in a pocket and handed it over. 'The doctor said you just jab it into his thigh.'

'Can you go find some blankets? Don't let on they're for him.'

'Shouldn't have told me that. I thought you wanted them for yourself!'

'Just do it!' Wilgar snapped.

'Only jokin', Second! Only jokin'!' Blakan bent down to say low and intent, 'I don't think he did it, neither. Don't make sense now do it? I was thinkin' about it on the way up here. I mean why would he save the one kid and—'

'I'm glad you have some brains, Blakan,' Wilgar interrupted acerbically. 'Now, hurry! This tourniquet must be released and he's likely to pass out. He'll need those blankets. And when you're done here, I need you to report to the Commander for me.'

'So much fer getting' a breather, or any thanks!' Blakan grumbled but hurried away again back out into the rain.

'Karatin deserves a medal 'r sumthin',' Blakan said as he arrived breathlessly at Lerant's side wearing a great grin as he observed the joyful reunion below in the street. Karatin had found another child, a small boy this time, conscious, but suffering a broken leg and severe gashes to head and arms.

'He does,' Lerant agreed, but couldn't find a return smile. They'd found four, only four of twenty alive. 'Tell him I said, 'No'! He's not to go further in! The fires have spread too far!' Lerant shouted down to Howlett and Sandor. 'Damn it! He's going to get himself killed! Haul him up! All of you, pull for all your worth! Pull!'

Blakan grabbed the rope and lent his strength to the task. Karatin didn't resist for more than a moment. The tautness in the line slackened as at last as he gave up, admitting it was hopeless. 'We got the remedy into m'Connor all right, sir,' Blakan said, able to let go as he saw Karatin's head appear in the hollow below them.

Lerant grunted. He couldn't say as he cared much, if not for the penalty Rogha would be made to pay for the man's death. Blakan looked disappointed in his less than impressed reaction, so Lerant added sincerely, 'Good work, trooper,' and clapped him on the shoulder.

'Thanks, sir. Oh, and the mayor says to tell you Myrrgha won't talk to him anymore. They want you, sir.'

'Tell him I'll be there as soon as I've secured my men!' Lerant peered forward into the shadows to see Karatin had again refused to return empty-handed but was carrying yet another limp and bloodied bundle in his arms. At least the parents would have a body to bury.

'Sir,' Blakan added. 'Almost forgot. He says to tell you it's the Lord High Inquisitor?'

'What does he want?' Lerant asked as he ducked beneath a low, heavily beamed lintel and stepped through the doorway. He squinted against the bright light of the foyer and stumbled further inside, following Rankin into a reception room. The world inside, away from the storm, away from the cold, the horror and the blood, seemed impossibly clean and ordered.

'He wants m'Connor,' Rankin answered tersely. 'Refuses to talk about anything else.'

'Welcome to him,' Lerant growled. 'Believe me if I could bundle him up and fire him down there from a cannon, murdering bastard to murdering bastard, I'd do it in a heartbeat.'

'And I'd light the fuse, if it would get the madman's attention away from Rogha. Damn it, we need them to send a hospital ship up here, not those Inquisition lunatics!'

Lerant frowned. 'Surely Myrrgha Command had made him understand what's happening here?'

Rankin shook his head distractedly. 'I haven't had any luck getting through to him—or anyone else.' His shrewd gaze went to the insignia on Lerant's filthy sleeve. 'But you're one of them; maybe they'll listen to you.'

Lerant sighed. Right now he didn't feel like 'one of them', he felt only the terrible suffering of the town in which he'd grown up. 'I'll try.'

'Thank you. It's through here.' Rankin led the way into an inner room, much smaller than the first and much warmer, heated by an over-sized blazing hearth. Through a window on the other wall, Lerant could see the dark night and see the glow of the partly subdued fires on the battered skyline. Sleet rattled against the windowpane and wind whistled about the eaves. It was hard to believe that a large chunk of Rogha's heart had been torn to pieces out there, that the garrison was gone, so many children dead . . . .

'Sit down before you fall down. You've been working out there a long time,' Rankin said kindly and took his arm to move him in the right direction. 'I do thank you, and your men, for all you've done to help us.'

'Least we could do,' Lerant mumbled tiredly. 'The bastard was aiming for us.'

Lerant collapsed into a cushioned, winged armchair someone had dragged close to a big heavy dark wood desk with drawers on either side of its wide tabletop. There the Connector Stone sat blinking sullenly at him, surrounded by tidy bundles of books and papers to one side, and a littered mess of scrawled notes and other unrecognizable bits and pieces on the other. The Connector was not much smaller than the huge one in Garek's office, about the size of a man's head. Or rather, it was like the one that had *been* in Garek's office. No, he realized numbly, Connector Stones were indestructible, as near as anyone could tell. The thing would still be there. Somewhere, buried under . . . .

In a flash of vivid memory, he saw Garek's corpse, or what they'd assumed was his corpse when they'd dragged it out, judging by the remnants of burned uniform. The face was unidentifiable, reduced to a charred blackened lump contrasted by bared pieces of astonishingly clean white skull and patches of burned hair. Bared teeth grimaced accusingly up at Lerant amid scraps of raw red flesh where the mouth, nose and lips . . . .

Suddenly, he saw another very familiar corpse, his first mother, her throat an ugly gaping gash from which blood spurted, splashing Lerant's clothing. He wiped at his tunic, saw an arrow embedded in the same uniform, heard Parlan choke for breath, the thud as his body hit the ground.

'Stay with us, now, son,' Rankin said, and shook Lerant's shoulder gently. 'You've been working out there hour after hour without rest.'

Lerant blinked back to the moment, realizing he had been drifting, staring blankly at the Connector Stone. The warmth, the incredible peace in here, combined with the chance to sit down, to rest and he had almost been asleep. A sleep full of horror.

'Down this. It'll help you deal with speaking on that.' Rankin held out a goblet of wine and nodded toward the patiently blinking Connector Stone.

'Thanks,' Lerant said, his hand shaking as he accepted. He peered at the red liquid swirling in the cup a moment, hearing Fallon's voice saying much the same thing in what could only have been a different lifetime altogether. He downed the wine in one long gulp, then coughed and choked a little, discovering it was not wine but rather some kind of brandy fermented with cherries. He put the goblet down on the desktop and lifted his hand to wipe away the stinging tears brought by the unexpected burning of the liquor. The jolt of heat in his stomach spread quickly to clear his head and warm his tired limbs. Not really wanting to, but knowing he had no choice, he reached a gloved hand toward the Connector Stone, wary of what he might find hiding amid its sullen, greenish yellow light. He kept his hand from shaking, but it was filthy, covered in soot, mud and blood. The flashing stopped as he made contact.

'Commander Lerant reporting as requested,' he said tonelessly and told himself to get it together, he needed to think clearly to list everything Rogha would need to aid its people.

"Reporting as requested" a sneering, petulant voice mimicked. 'I've been waiting far too long, Commander! Far too long! Where have you been?'

'Sorry, sir, but—'

'My Lord High Inquisitor,' Zaraxan corrected, the chill in the words accurately conveying threat.

'My Lord High Inquisitor,' Lerant tried again, anger and the brandy combining to renew his energy and clear his thoughts. 'Rogha is honored that Command has seen fit to bring her plight to such august attention. All possible medical assistance is of—'

'Gareck reported you had captured the Weaver Slave, m'Connor?' Zaraxan interrupted.

'Gareck is dead, My Lord, and the garrison with him.'

'So I was told. A terrible tragedy caused by Rogha's stupidity.'

'I—' Lerant bit back a snarl and felt his fingers find tight purchase on the rim of an open desk drawer. 'I'm not sure I understand, My Lord.'

'How long do you suppose that murdering Weaver went undetected in your midst, Commander?' Zaraxan's tone was insulting, that of someone prompting an idiot.

'He *is* a Weaver, My Lord,' Lerant gritted out, 'and thus capable of concealing—'

'Do not lecture me, Commander! I know better than any the treachery of these sorcerers, and particularly that of the filthy savage, m'Connor!'

'I did not intend—'

'He murdered my beloved Rhyssa!' Zaraxan continued, having paused only long enough to take in air sufficient to fuel a second bellow of outrage. 'Can you even begin to understand what he has stolen from me, Commander?'

'His fiancé,' Rankin whispered for Lerant's bewildered and silent entreaty.

Lerant resisted the urge to sigh impatiently. Any woman who would choose to share a bed with the cruelest sadist in all Myrrgha, despite stiff competition for the title, would surely not be mourned by its populace. 'I didn't know, My Lord. I am grieved to learn of your great loss.'

'A very great loss, indeed!' Zaraxan huffed. 'We were planning our wedding, thinking of the children we would have, the coat of arms we would design for our new aristocratic House, the glory of our nation!'

'You show courage and selflessness in continuing your work during such a time of mourning, My Lord. Many would not be able.'

Rankin snorted in what sounded like, Lerant hoped, approval of his tactics.

'Well and good,' Zaraxan sniffed. 'You see why justice deems that m'Connor be returned to me at last.'

'Rogha has cause to hate him, too, My Lord.'

'They should have thought of that before they invited him in!'

Rankin leaned forward to refute that loudly and directly into the Connector Stone. Lerant hurriedly blocked him, mouthing, 'Don't!' and adding aloud. 'Rogha's suffered enough.'

Rankin surrendered angrily and marched across the room to stand by the eerily red-lit window. The house shuddered as a howling gust of wind, stronger than any thus far tonight, roared and whooshed overhead. Tiles snapped free of the eaves beyond the window, startling Rankin who hurried away from the glass. The Connector Stone trembled on the desk, its light flickering. The storm was worsening. Lerant relayed that news to Zaraxan, its truth evidenced by interference with the transmission.

'It is near freezing outside,' Lerant continued. 'There are many wounded and homeless. Some of our men were terribly burned by the explosion and are deserving of Myrrgha's—'

'It's late, man!' The Inquisitor snarled. 'Spare me the tale of woe!'

Rankin muttered a curse from the other side of the room. Lerant cast him a desperate glance. There must be some way to reach the madman and convince him to send aid! If all he wanted or cared about was m'Connor . . . .

'My Lord, I regret to inform you that the prisoner was badly injured by a slargapent—'

'What! See to it that he stays alive! I will have him made to answer!'

'We've given him anti-venom, but his injuries are severe and we've nothing more than a field aid kit. The garrison surgeon is dead, the infirmary and its stores of medicines gone.'

'Then use your brains, man! Take him to the civilian surgeon!'

'My Lord, I've already spoken to the man. He's outraged about the wounded children. I fear he might—'

'This surgeon has a family?' Zaraxan asked coldly.

Lerant slumped in the chair. He hadn't intended to cause any trouble for the man. 'He has no one, My Lord.' Lerant, in truth, had no idea whatever about the surgeon's personal circumstance.

'A pity. Hostages are always the best recourse.'

Lerant set his teeth. 'M'Connor needs independent medical aid, My Lord.'

There was a long silence. Rankin came over to squeeze Lerant's shoulder encouragingly.

'Very well!' Zaraxan snapped. 'I'll have my surgeon accompany me and bring all necessary medicines and equipment.'

'Accompany you, My Lord?' Lerant's blood suddenly ran cold despite the liquor and the heat of the blazing hearth.

'My battleship is prepared to get underway before dawn. The Emperor recognizes the importance of my work with these savages. M'Connor holds answers Myrrgha must have! I'm coming up there for him, Commander. Your job is simply to keep him alive. Can you manage that?'

'I will certainly do my best, My Lord. But I have only a handful of troopers to guard the man against attack or rescue. Weavers never work alone.'

'M'Connor does,' Zaraxan corrected. 'At least I've made him pay a little, there.'

'He works alone, My Lord?' At last, the Inquisitor had mentioned something of use. If there were no other Weavers in the area, that was one less worry.

'Yes, yes, m'Fetrin is as good as dead. He might have Gerion with him, though. Do not relax your guard, Commander!'

'No, My Lord. Rogha will gladly wait when they learn m'Connor faces a much more severe punishment at your hands.'

Zaraxan snickered, a lusting, low chuckle that set Lerant's fingers digging deeper into the wood beneath his grasp. It was exactly the same sound Gareck had made, when considering his obscene plans to make m'Connor suffer. 'Be sure there is no lynching, Commander! Where are you holding him?'

'I've taken him into my personal custody, My Lord. I give you my sworn oath to guard him well.' If anything went wrong, Lerant could hope that he alone might be held responsible.

The house shook again under the onslaught of the storm and the Connector Stone link failed momentarily then flickered back to life. Which gave Lerant another hope. If m'Connor was the source of trouble, it would pay to get him as far from Rogha as possible.

'Are you there, Commander?' Zaraxan demanded through increased static.

'Yes, My Lord. The storm worsens. I fear it will tear off rooftops and collapse walls. I'm concerned for your safety at sea. Allow me the honor of bringing the slave to you. There are coal ships in harbor. They'll be heading back to Myrrgha and—'

'A clever thought, Commander,' Zaraxan complimented smoothly. Then, he snarled furiously, 'And just what m'Connor would enjoy! How do you think he got to Rogha in the first place?! With his friends, the pirates! They took him from me once before, they will not do it again! Coal ships!' He snorted derisively. 'They travel at a snail's pace and are prone to sinking!'

'Yes, My Lord.' Lerant replied wearily. 'It's a long way from Myrrgha to Rogha.'

'The Emperor demands I make the journey! He asks I put aside my personal grief—again—to protect his precious coal shipments, and more importantly to learn where the other Weavers are hiding. Be sure you make a note of anything the slave says, especially if his injuries render him delirious. He might let something slip that will be of use in our hunt. And as for Rogha, it will have no aid unless the slave and our coal is secure, Commander! Tell them! My wrath upon them if they hinder my mission in any way! My very great wrath!'

'Yes, My Lord.' Lerant's fingers spasmed about the wooden drawer rim, making it creak in protest.

'Report to me again when I'm out at sea, Commander. My ship is well equipped.'

'Yes, My—' Lerant didn't finish the words before the Connector Stone blanked out, the transmission ended.

'Bastard!' Lerant cursed and beneath his fingers the drawer snapped, splintering into several pieces with a loud crash. He sat glaring at the wreckage a moment, and then muttered without much contrition, 'Sorry about your desk.'

'I spoke to him before you.' Rankin couldn't muster the sarcasm warranted as he pointed at the floor not far from Lerant's boots. Looking, Lerant found a broken mess of wood and ceramic pieces.

'A table lamp,' Rankin explained with a shrug. 'Cut my dammed hand.' He looked away from the wreckage to meet Lerant's eyes. 'You handled him well, Commander. He'll bring a surgeon who'll have medicines.'

Lerant shook his head in adamant disagreement. 'I couldn't stop him coming here.'

They both sat a moment, heaving identical weary sighs.

'Self-serving fool!' Rankin broke the defeated silence. 'Does he truly believe he can threaten a worse fate to people standing up to their kneecaps in their children's blood?' He sighed again and watched as Lerant climbed back to his feet. 'But he has a point about prisoner security. There will be plenty want m'Connor dead.'

'I can keep him on the move, go from place to place.' Lerant stopped as Rankin held up a hand and interrupted sharply.

'The less I know, the better, Commander. They know you've been here with me. You disappear; they come ask me where you are.'

'Right.' Lerant agreed as he turned and walked toward the door. 'But give it some thought; I'll need help finding shelter somewhere.'

'Very well,' Rankin accepted heavily.

Lerant looked back at him. 'Rogha needs us, Archman. Let's not fail her.'

CHAPTER SEVENTEEN

A painful, shaking yank on his hair roughly roused m'Connor to wakefulness. He gasped, finding the terrible pain in his leg hadn't lessened, shattering his hope that the anti-venom might've begun to take effect. Bleary-eyed, he found the Myrrghin officer standing over him. The smoky light of oil torches held by the troopers painted the officer's angry expression with shifting shadows. Unaffected by the filthy glare m'Connor gave him, Lerant's gray eyes set like ice. M'Connor too, had seen more than his share of mangled bodies twisted under blood-sticky rubble. He didn't need Empathy to understand exactly how brittle was the officer's mood.

'Get to your feet!' Lerant snatched away the blankets.

M'Connor had no idea how long he'd been unconscious, but the storm was much worse, howling and roaring about them like a horde of demons. The militiamen's eyes shone bright beneath their flaring torches, full of accusing, calculating hunger; like predatory cats hoping the mouse would try to run from them.

'I can manage,' m'Connor told Wilgar quietly as the man looked set to protest. He pressed his chained hands against the cottage wall for support and began pushing himself up. He wanted to stand tall and proud, meet the man eye to eye, but sickening pain shot through him and he swayed, began to fall. Wilgar and Blakan grabbed him and held him upright.

'Sandor! Berial!' Lerant ordered. 'You know what to do. Blakan! Howlett! Give Karatin your swords then stand ready, either side of the prisoner.'

A tall, sandy-haired trooper and another stockier man stepped forward, each carrying a length of longer chain. The giant bearded trooper stepped closer, one massive hand outstretched to take the weapons. 'What?' Wilgar asked, his eyes narrowed in suspicion as he regarded his commander.

'We need to be able to move fast if we're attacked. No stretchers. Blakan and Howlett can take an arm each and prop him up. Here.' He tossed a set of keys to his Second. 'Unchain him.' Lerant drew his pistol.

'That's gonna help,' m'Connor heard Blakan mutter as the youngster took a grip about the prisoner's waist, allowing Wilgar access to m'Connor's manacled hands. The other trooper, Howlett, was also one of the younger, fitter men of the squad. If the two men were to haul him around all night, they'd need to be. M'Connor let out a muted sigh of relief as at last his hands came free and he stiffly moved his arms from behind his back, stretching them a little. He didn't get further chance as each of the assigned troopers grabbed a wrist and secured their piece of chain to a manacle.

'Oh, you've got to be joking!' Blakan complained as Sandor began wrapping the other end of the long chain about Blakan's waist. Berial was doing the same to Howlett.

'It's only for a short while,' Lerant told him. 'None of his friends will get away with him like this.'

'Not unless they want all three of us,' Blakan muttered under his breath, not happy as the chain was locked in place.

'Right. Let's get moving,' Lerant said, suddenly sounding very tired and putting away his pistol. 'Be sure to keep the weight off that leg.'

'Where are we going, Sir?' Blakan asked the question on m'Connor's lips.

'Just . . . follow me,' Lerant replied heavily.

They turned a corner, passing behind a row of half-wrecked cottages to enter a more open area where people were salvaging what they could. On a flight of low steps, a young woman sat huddled over a tiny body wrapped in a gaily-colored cloak. In one hand she clutched a small soft toy. The Roghinners looked toward the approaching soldiers, their eyes flaring and mouths muttering as they noted the prisoner in their midst. One man straightened up from where he'd been helping others tend the grief-stricken mother. A chain of gold squares circled his broad chest, its red-stoned clasps secured to a blue brocaded vest. Rogha's Archman, the Mayor, Rankin. He was a squat chunky man, bald and gray-skinned, with keen, intelligent eyes.

'Honored Archman,' Lerant said evenly though fatigue echoed in his voice, 'Again, I thank you for your assistance and for the use of your Connector Stone. Now we must ask shelter.'

'I'll not force my people to share their homes. They decide.'

Someone began pushing through from the back of the crowd, and as they gave way, creating a corridor, m'Connor saw it was the same woman who had sat grieving her dead child. She strode closer, eyes swollen and red, ash-blackened cheeks streaked by tear tracks. Hatred ignited eyes that bored into him, tearing at him with heartbroken accusation. 'Murdering savage!' she screamed.

Drawing back her arm, she slapped him with all the strength she could find. He stumbled back, staying upright only because the troopers held him. She stood, blazing hatred, but also silently begging some response, some reason why her child should have been so cruelly taken from her. Her grief pained m'Connor to his very soul. He ached to Share comfort but had been robbed of the ability as surely as he'd been bound against lifting a consoling hand.

'*Mi nienta su*—my heart is yours,' he said softly but clearly, using the ancient phrase of mourning and looking long into her eyes.

'Murderer,' she repeated tiredly, as if all the life had drained from her forever. She turned her back, walked away, and the crowd closed about her. 'Murderer!' They took up the chant, raising fists or bending to pick up stones and lengths of wood. Nervously, the troopers shifted, casting glances to their young officer.

'Stand!' Lerant commanded calmly over the growing clamor. Nevertheless, several hands fidgeted with muskets and swords.

'Stop!' Rankin bellowed, climbing the steps to glare at them all. They muttered and tried to stare him down, but flinched as they met his fierce eyes. 'There has been enough killing! If you will not give these men shelter then so be it. But think hard on this, if any one of you attacks a Myrrghin prisoner or his guards, we'll all pay the price in blood when that warship arrives!' He paused then said more gently, 'Show the good sense I know each of you possesses. Go. Pray for those who are dead or dying.'

Bowed heads and a clattering as makeshift weapons were dropped proved most were willing to heed him. But, from the back of the crowd, half a dozen raggedly dressed, unkempt-looking men blocked those who tried to leave, scowling and cursing them for cowards. Their leader, was an unshaven man, so skeletally thin that his eyes burned like fiery pits in his bare skull, increasing an impression of predatory hunger. He pushed forward and climbed atop a mound of rubble, raising his bony hands to reclaim the attention of the crowd.

'So, Rogha don't have its own justice no more? Is everythin' for Myrrgha now?' He lifted his harsh voice above the wind. 'Our laws promise our kind 'o justice. Were it Myrrgha's children butchered tonight or Rogha's?'

'Rogha's!' Prompted by his followers, the townspeople readily picked up the chant. 'Rogha's children!'

'Yes!' he urged. 'Look at him! Standing there breathin' easy while your little 'uns r'dead. Lellgha be cursed!' He spat, and about him the crowd seethed like a cauldron about to boil over.

M'Connor's skin crawled, tingling beneath the methirri collar as his paralyzed Weaving called to him in angry, urgent alarm. *Methaggar!*

The thin man reeked of it, even if possessed from a vast distance. M'Connor struggled to call up a greater Reading of his foe, but there was no response. Physical weakness combined with the methirri collar and the Key to dampen his ability to almost nothing. But there was no mistake; the skeletal man was wrapped in a foul miasma so thick that he wondered no one else could sense it. This one had sold himself to the Methaggars and was more dangerous in the midst of these unseeing people than a rabid wolf. Already, he was enthralling them, leading them toward the Methaggar's bloody purpose.

Raising his arms and glaring at the rabble-rouser, Rankin waited until there was silence. 'We do have our rights.' Rankin turned to Lerant. 'When your prisoner is recovered, we will judge him under our law.'

'Take the murderer!' Jarrod and his companions pushed forward.

'We wait for the Commander's orders!' The giant trooper rumbled and stepped between them and m'Connor to shove them stumbling, back.

Until now, m'Connor hadn't really noticed just how massive a man the trooper was, a good head taller than the tallest among the crowd. His red hair gleamed in the fiery light of the torches, sending a stab of loneliness through m'Connor. Bren would have known the moment he'd been collared and would be even now running to the rescue. Gerion would come after him, m'Connor knew. It would just take longer. And he might not have longer.

Lerant didn't want to use force against his grief-stricken countrymen. They seemed set to obey a legal precedent if only he could find one. He studied his troopers' equally unhappy faces. Then, he looked to the prisoner. M'Connor's face was ashen and bruised in the uncertain light, but his eyes showed only weary courage. Holding that calm, intelligent gaze, Lerant found something there, something searching keen and sure, something hidden and begging Lerant to remember its importance. Whatever it was, it rattled him badly.

He turned back to the crowd where cheers and vengeful cries had welcomed Rankin's demand. Lerant knew they were both playing for time, to keep m'Connor alive, get he and Zaraxan away from here as fast as possible.

'I agree the prisoner should be tried by our justice, also,' Lerant called truthfully. 'But you must wait. We must ensure that more of his kind didn't come with him to Rogha. I'll question the prisoner.'

'You're gonna get a double dose of torture, scum!' someone yelled.

'All right!' Rankin bellowed above the noise. 'You will be notified of the time and place of Judgment. Go, take shelter.'

Noticing the rain was heavier and looking set to become snow, they obeyed, hurrying away for the shelter and warmth of their hearth-fires. Jarrod and his lackeys, however, remained unappeased. Lerant caught sight of a wickedly honed, double-edged dagger in a sheath at Jarrod's belt, his long, bony fingers stroking its ornate hilt.

'You men will be wantin' y' sleep,' Jarrod wheedled, his head lowered, but his eyes never losing their hunger. 'A night with me 'n the swine'll be squealin' whatever y'want t' hear!'

'Torture is Myrrgha's way! We will have none of it!' Rankin snapped.

His hand ready on his pistol, Lerant blinked and shut his mouth, realizing he'd been about to say the same thing and glad the man had gotten in before him. 'There will be no torture under my command,' Lerant agreed as Jarrod waited on him to have the final say.

'Then y'll never get yer answers.' Jarrod cast a murderous glance at m'Connor, 'Let me—'

'One more word,' Lerant promised, soft and sure. He leveled his pistol and took aim straight between the cruel eyes, suddenly itching to kill the creature. The yellow shadows vanished from Jarrod's eyes and he backed off, tripping over himself in his haste. Lerant's hand trembled and his fingers squeezed down on the trigger. A fraction before he fired, sweating with the effort, he jerked the barrel skyward. He stared at his hand as if it belonged to another man. When he looked up, Jarrod and his henchmen were disappearing at speed into an alleyway.

'Good work!' Rankin chuckled, nodding approval.

Lerant lifted his head, drawn to meet not the mayor's eyes, but m'Connor's. The Weaver looked worryingly ill, but his expression revealed only a surprised, deep thoughtfulness. With sudden cold terror, Lerant wanted nothing less than to further prompt m'Connor's understanding.

'Uncle Kerell?' A thin, high voice called, sounding afraid, lost.

'Alarn!' Lerant recognized, holstering his pistol. The boy appeared suddenly out of the darkness to charge breathlessly forward and throw himself into Lerant's embrace as he went on his knees to him. 'What are you doing here? Where's Parla?'

'Safe. With, Mama.'

'It's all right, Commander,' Wilgar said. 'Old Refallt is with him.'

Lerant looked up to see the old man, his face bruised and cut, watching them from a few paces away. 'Sorry, he got away from me,' Refallt explained, coming a little closer.

'Why in all the fires would you bring him here?' Lerant demanded, his anger flooding back as he got to his feet, one arm still holding Alarn protectively close.

'I didn't,' the old man said, calmly confronting him.

'I had to come!' Alarn cried, breaking free of Lerant's grasp to step forward and frown accusingly up at him. Lerant took a sharp breath. In that moment, he might've been looking direct into Parlan's angry, hurt eyes.

'Refallt told us what you all were doing to him! Why are you hurting him!? He saved Parla!' Tears stood in Alarn's eyes as he looked at the chained and injured man.

'It's not—I don't want—' Lerant stumbled, and then said simply. 'It's my duty.'

'He saved Parla!' Alarn repeated, shouting as if he didn't think Lerant could have heard him the first time.

'He did what?' Rankin asked.

Suddenly noticing the mayor's presence, Alarn turned pleadingly to him. 'He saved my little brother from the river, Sir. Can you help him, please?'

'I might,' Rankin replied. Smiling gently, he went on one knee to grasp the boy's thin shoulder with one hand. 'If you calm down and tell me what happened.'

While Alarn involved himself in a hurried summation of the river incident, Lerant turned back to Refallt. 'How did he follow you? His mother will be worried sick! And for that matter, why are you here?'

'She wanted me to give you her message,' Refallt explained. 'I was half way here when the boy appeared, telling me his mother had sent him after me because I'd forgotten my jacket.'

'Annalie sent you here?'

'I was on my way direct to her when half the town went up in fire. I turned back and helped out a while and I saw your troopers with him.' Refallt jerked his head toward m'Connor who was watching, listening with groggy but keen interest.

'And you told Annalie it all,' Lerant surmised with a muted groan.

Refallt lifted his head indignantly. 'She wanted to know what had happened to her son's rescuer! I didn't know the boy was listening at the door.'

'He'd have found out sooner or later,' Lerant said heavily, and reminded, looked back to find Alarn watching him with absolute betrayal in his tear-filmed eyes.

'Why can't you just let him go?' Alarn demanded immediately.

Lerant went back to one knee to look the boy direct in the eyes. 'Because he will hurt more people, Alarn. He killed many here tonight.'

Alarn frowned and turned back to look up at the prisoner. 'Did you?'

M'Connor shook his head. 'I have harmed no one.'

Alarn swung back to Lerant, eager to defend the man. 'He didn't do it, Uncle. He wouldn't.'

'He's lying,' Lerant said bluntly.

'He's not!' Alarn exclaimed hotly. 'He saved Parla! Why would he hurt anyone?!'

'Alarn—'

'A good question,' Rankin interrupted and gave the prisoner a fresh appraisal. He noted the injured leg, the signs of illness, and the wet clothing that had the man shivering violently. 'I didn't know he saved your nephew, Commander. Is that how he was hurt?'

'Yes, a slargapent.'

'Then all this makes even less sense than I thought.' Rankin stepped closer to m'Connor, and Lerant, frowning, followed at his side, Alarn tagging along, looking at them both with hope bright in his eyes. 'You gave up escape to rescue Alarn's little brother?' Rankin asked, sharply curious as m'Connor met his gaze. 'Did you know about the slargapents?'

M'Connor's lips twitched. He nodded. 'Almost m-made it.'

'He would have, if we hadn't slowed him down,' Howlett said, taking a better grip on the sagging prisoner. 'The thing hurt him bad, Sir.'

'We did the best we could for him under the circumstances,' Lerant said tersely as Rankin and Alarn turned about to regard him expectantly, joining forces against him. 'The first man we sent for the remedy died in the explosion.' It was probably a good idea he didn't mention Gareck's plans for m'Connor. 'I sent another runner to the City Infirmary for more. I've been busy trying to save as many of his victims as possible.'

'He didn't do it!' Alarn objected instantly, and Lerant knew he'd best set himself to hear that often.

'Well, it sure looked like that way, Lad! Makin' as fast as he could t' get out o' town, he was!' Karatin put in, apparently thinking his commander needed some help. Lerant gave him a stay-out-of-it glare and he subsided.

'Well, of course he was running!' Rankin snapped. 'He saw you, and he is an escaped slave, after all. A murderer does not use sleep-darts against his hunters.'

Lerant had to admit Rankin's logic carried weight—why take elaborate measures to avoid violence if you intended to murder an entire garrison? A dart gun would aid a quiet escape, but if that had been m'Connor's aim, then why turn back for Parla?

'It doesn't add up.' Rankin probed further. 'An anonymous informant knew enough to tell you how to trap him, but said nothing of the planned murders?'

Lerant noted Sandor and Berial, posted to keep a look out, had moved a little closer and were craning to listen. Judging by the lessening of hostility in the veiled glances they were directing at their injured prisoner, they too, were doing some rethinking. 'The fact remains,' Lerant said firmly, 'we've identified him as the man responsible for—'

'Uncle!' Alarn cried. 'He's sick!' Bent double, his wrists tugging at his chains while his props tried to steady him, the Weaver was ill, dry-retching as if to turn himself inside out.

'It's all right, Alarn.' Lerant crouched down again and gently drew the boy away from the suffering man and back to his embrace. 'It's just the anti-venom making him sick to his stomach.'

If only that were true. Wilgar gave Lerant an alarmed raise of an eyebrow; they both knew the drug didn't cause nausea. But the venom, if left go long enough, certainly would.

M'Connor drew a great shaking breath and managed to straighten up, but was terribly white-faced. Blakan offered some water from his canteen and, nodding thanks, m'Connor allowed the trooper to place the bottle to his lips. He tried to grasp it with the hand that rested on Blakan's shoulder and the muscles in his forearms spasmed viciously. Another bad sign. Both troopers looked worriedly to Lerant and lowered their gazes in silent question to the manacles.

Lerant shook his head. He must not risk losing the prisoner to either the mob or a rescue. Zaraxan's threat had been all too clear.

Rankin bent down to take a closer look at the bloodied bandage that was beginning to unwind from about the wounded leg. 'This doesn't look good. He was given the anti-venom later than you would have liked?' he demanded.

'I gave him extra to cover for that, Sir,' Wilgar told the man and held up an empty glass bottle he'd taken from his pocket. 'The whole lot. Should've done the trick.' He eyed m'Connor worriedly, 'But it doesn't seem to have helped him at all. I can't figure it.'

Lerant dropped down next to Rankin; m'Connor's leg was a mess, showing every sign of advanced slargapent poisoning. Without a word, Lerant stretched his free hand up toward Wilgar. His Second handed him the empty bottle with a sour look. 'It all went in,' the older man said. 'I have done this before, Sir.'

Lerant had to let go of Alarn to open the bottle. He sniffed it then stuck a finger in the neck, shaking the few drops of liquid left in it onto his skin. Removing the finger carefully, he sniffed the droplets again, and then stuck his finger in his mouth. 'Water,' he realized, with just enough of the bitter anti-venom taste to indicate that the little bottle had once held the medicine. 'Looks like there's more than we thought want him dead.'

He shot a glance at Blakan, and the trooper shook his head, denying that he'd been the one who had made the deadly switch. Lerant believed him, not the least because Blakan couldn't manage to lie any better than a small child.

'Missus Hollin was right on target, then,' Refallt said disgustedly, coming closer. 'She knew he wouldn't be safe here in the town, so she sent me to fetch him back to her.'

Lerant looked up in surprise. 'Annalie wants him taken to her home?'

Refallt nodded. 'That's the message. She says she'll look after him, and you and yours in the bargain, Kerell.'

'Mama's a good healer,' Alarn encouraged, his arms going around Lerant in a pleading hug. 'She can help him.'

Wilgar and Rankin exchanged looks, but said nothing, leaving it to Lerant. 'He's dying, Alarn,' he explained as gently as he could. 'He needs the medicine, and someone has destroyed it.'

'Mama can help him,' Alarn insisted.

'People in Rogha survived slargapent attacks before Myrrgha brought the anti-venom here,' Wilgar reminded him. 'If anyone will know the old cures, it's Annalie.'

Lerant shook his head. 'It's too far gone; the anti-venom is his only hope. There must be a supply somewhere that hasn't been corrupted. Wilgar, take Sandor and find one of the surgeons, see if there's any supply of the stuff that's still good. Bring the doctor back with you, regardless.'

'Doctor won't want to come,' Wilgar warned.

'I don't care what he wants!' Lerant snapped. 'Put a gun to his head if you have to. Bind him and lug him like a pig for market, but get him there!'

'Sir!' Wilgar saluted and turned to call to Sandor who had already heard.

'You'll need every man you've got to get safely through to the Hollin's home,' Rankin pointed out, resting a staying hand to Wilgar's arm. 'Jarrod and his lot aren't done, not by a long shot if I know the little bastard. I'll take your one trooper and get the doctor to you; you get home and get dug in. You aren't safe here, not as long as he's in your custody.'

'I won't risk Annalie and the boys. We'll take him to the coal mines,' Lerant decided. 'We've got supplies and food there.'

'Too far, he'll never make it,' Wilgar reminded him.

Lerant countered angrily. 'We'll go to one of the old warehouses, then, by the dock.'

'We'll be blind in there,' Wilgar objected truthfully. 'And it won't help. Annalie will be down here, searching for you. She owes m'Connor, and she's as stubborn as you are.'

Lerant hid his face in his hands, the better to swear foully without Alarn hearing.

'We can't count on finding the anti-venom,' Rankin pointed out. 'Annalie may be the last hope Rogha has.'

'The Hollin homestead is on a height, with good stone walls,' Wilgar prompted, his eyes alight with amused sympathy as Lerant left off his swearing and looked up at him. That was true, Lerant knew. He and Parlan had built them together. 'A small band of well armed men could hold the place against a mob,' Wilgar continued. 'And the weather coming in will make the road impassible by morning.'

'All right, we take him home, then,' he agreed heavily. 'Let's get moving before he freezes to death.'

'He's cold and his clothes are wet!' Alarn accused. 'There's a blanket over there.'

Lerant nodded at Wilgar who hurried back around the corner to where he'd stood guarding the prisoner. 'Sandor! Go with Rankin.' The lean trooper saluted and left.

'You'll get Alarn home safely? I'd like to go with them,' Refallt asked Lerant and added with a sour frown. 'You know, make sure there's no more dirty work afoot.'

Refallt was gone before Lerant could answer. Looking back, he found the boy watching Wilgar who had swiftly returned and was knotting the thick woolen blanket about the prisoner's shuddering shoulders. Lerant ducked his head into the now much sharper wind and rain and called to his troopers, 'Form up around the prisoner. Wilgar take point. Karatin, rear. Keep a sharp eye.' Which left only Lerant and Berial as free-moving flank guards and Howlett and Blakan chained props; not exactly the best guard duty he could've wished.

Catching Lerant's worried frown, Alarn tugged his hand and said, 'It'll be all right, Uncle Ker'. Mama will make him better.'

'She will if anyone can,' Lerant agreed with a smile. 'Take us home to her, Alarn.'

They followed their diminutive guide back across the main avenue, heavy with the smell of blood and smoke, then into the streets behind the ruined garrison. Here they began to climb, the roads winding wetly up the hillside between long rows of shoulder-high stone fences bordering cottages dark and quiet. They rounded another corner and saw, high against the storm-dark sky at the top of the hill a single, lantern-lit porch. Inside the house it would be warm and Annalie would be waiting for them.

Whatever strength m'Connor had held in reserve was fast fading as the slope became steeper and the stony paths more uneven, slick with mud and ice. His labored breathing could be heard over the roar of the wind, and he sagged and slipped more often despite his props' work to support and keep him from jarring his leg. 'Sir!' Blakan called. 'He can't go on! Let me carry him?'

'We'll never get there like this,' Lerant agreed. Yet, these dark, narrow, walled streets were the perfect place for a rescue attempt by m'Connor's friends or an attack by the many who wanted him dead. 'All right, then,' he decided. 'Change off with Howlett when you reach . . . .' He trailed off as shadowy movement caught his eye. Close by the next walled corner a cloak flapped in the wind. Reaching to stop Alarn, Lerant said. 'There's someone up there. Karatin, come forward and—'

A man-shaped figure suddenly came flying, bat-like, through the storm-wind toward them. It landed in the middle of the road less than fifty spans ahead, blocking their path. An oddly hued light flared then settled into a glowing, blue nimbus that writhed and pulsed about the sorcerer with threatening power.

'A Weaver!' Karatin cried.

Lerant lifted Alarn up and over the nearest wall. 'Stay there, Lad! Keep down!'

'Illker!' m'Connor shouted, sounding alarmed, rather than pleased by a rescue bid. 'It'll kill us all!'

Confused, off-balance, Lerant barked, 'What?'

M'Connor met his gaze, eyes intense with warning and desperate frustration. 'The Possessed! Your weapons are useless!' His arms jerked as he struggled to pull his hands free of his guards' grip, but the strength in his voice hadn't reached his body.

The blue-shrouded figure gave a hissing, gurgling sound that could have been laughter. 'Kill him! Kill the Trees' foul spawn!'

Several black-cloaked and hooded men emerged from the shelter of the cross street and charged down-slope toward Lerant's group, their faces hidden beneath sacks. The blue fog clung luminously to them, glowing brighter about spears and knives.

'Cut them down!' Lerant ordered, drawing his pistol. 'Wait for—'

His voice wrenched away, strangled, and his fingers froze, refusing to pull the trigger. He couldn't so much as twitch a muscle; he could only move his eyes. He tried to shake his head, throw off the paralysis, blink, anything. His troopers were equally afflicted. Those he could see wore expressions of utter terror, their limbs as stiff and useless as stone, their mouths straining wide, but no words escaped. So much for the alleged power of a methirri band to protect him!

Chains rattled and sidelong, Lerant saw m'Connor tug his arms free of his guards' numbed grip. He began chanting some kind of counter-spell. Maybe it was holding back his paralysis. Wary dread and iron determination set his face, his stance resolute as it could be when he had only one leg beneath him and his hands chained to guards at either side. Yet there was enough slack in those chains to allow him to bring his right arm forward.

It shouldn't have been possible for m'Connor to grasp Lerant's sword hilt, and it wasn't. Abruptly, the sword fell free and slapped into m'Connor's palm. In a humming of steel through rain, the blade arced upward in the Weaver's hands. M'Connor shouted defiance that challenged the cloying fog about them.

Undaunted, the attackers gathered speed, something all wrong about the way they moved: awkward, wooden, stiff as puppets whose master had unsteady control of their strings. Regardless, the sure promise of death flashed savage and keen from their blades, each and every one aimed at m'Connor. Lerant and his men might not exist so completely were they ignored. Immobilized, frozen like statues, they'd all be slaughtered as soon as m'Connor was felled.

But he wasn't about to surrender though desperation and strain were thick in his chanting. Hindered by his chains, and unable to move forward or back on a crippled leg, he stood his ground, facing down six armed assailants. M'Connor's chant became a song, though that was too simple a word to describe so stirring a sound.

Lerant had never before heard anything like it. And yet, he had. Somewhere, sometime, long, long ago . . . . Defiant and proud, it touched his heart with its compelling call, igniting something that stirred deep within him, something he didn't want to know. He shoved the feeling away, grasping the bitter present instead.

All m'Connor's courage would not save him. Not to fight alone, wounded, bound by methirri. His attempted Weaving of the Song drained strength from him and drew no more than a pale glimmer of white light. It failed even as it was called forth, sucked up and into the ravenous slave collar as fast as it emerged. His arm trembled with the weight of the sword. The Song fell silent and he gasped for breath, sweat and rain streaking his face as the first of his enemy reached him.

Bracing himself with one hand on Howlett's shoulder, m'Connor lifted his uninjured leg and kicked out hard, slamming his booted foot into the foremost attacker's groin. The man screamed shrilly, doubled over and fell. Closing fast, two others tripped over him in a jarring tangle of arms and legs that jolted their weapons from their hands. Three down without the aid of a sword!

The remaining three slowed, spreading to outflank their prey. M'Connor's dark eyes flashed as he tracked them warily, able to turn his head but not his body. Limping, he backed away, trying to get the garden wall behind him and prevent them encircling him. But the chains brought him up short and he simply could not move fast enough. The two men who had tripped reclaimed their weapons and got to their feet.

'Akkarra!' m'Connor shouted, and in a reverberating clash sword met sword. M'Connor's blade flowed in a series of thrusts and parries, smooth and fast as water about river-stones. Two assailants went down, their faces and chests bloodied by fatal wounds. But the third, hefting a solid quarterstaff had gotten behind m'Connor. He struck, slamming the staff hard into the man's bandaged leg.

Lerant heard the bone snap and m'Connor screamed in agony and went down on one knee. The chains tugged at his wrists and he dropped the sword. Behind him, the hooded man lifted the staff again; honed and sharpened into a spear. The killer paused as if listening, and braced to drive the point through m'Connor's back, deep into the heart.

Lerant concentrated all his will on moving. He and his men, and then Alarn, would be next to die. His fingers moved a fraction, tightening their grip on the pistol. Struggle as he might, he'd be too late to save the Weaver.

A fourth attacker rushed forward. M'Connor ducked, turning a thudding, killing blow to a stunning glance to the side of his head. Unconscious, he toppled face downward, his arms pulled up and back behind him, straining against the chains. It was too late for the spearman to alter his aim. The point flew home high and wide to tear through the muscle of m'Connor's upper shoulder. Cursing, the spearman straddled m'Connor's body, struggling to wrench the weapon free and set it again for the heart. His companion stepped closer, lifting the club ready to smash the Weaver's skull.

'He dies!' the Sorcerer hissed from within his shielding mist, laughing, ripe with pleasure.

Whatever m'Connor's Song had stirred within Lerant, it erupted in sheer, molten rage. 'No!!' he roared.

The attacker collapsed and dropped the club. To his own astonishment, Lerant lifted his pistol, aimed and fired toward the sorcerer despite his attention being all for his sword lying in the rain at his feet. Dropping the gun, he bent and retrieved it. The evil blue fog recoiled. The Illker-sorcerer vanished. Alarn yelled wordlessly, jumped from the garden wall and smashed the spearman's head with a huge rock. The henchman fell atop m'Connor, snapping off the still-embedded spear shaft. About them, the troopers too, were responding.

'Hold!' Lerant called urgently, but the militia had seen the boy, held their fire.

Suddenly, there was no further need of violence. The last two attackers dropped, as lifeless and crumpled as unstrung puppets.

'Karatin, Berial, stand guard, point and rear,' Lerant ordered breathlessly and stooped to pick up his pistol with his left hand and scabbard the sword.

'What in all the fires was that?' Karatin growled and obeyed, musket at the ready. Everyone looked to the commander, expecting he'd have the answer.

Ignoring them, Lerant holstered his pistol and pulled Alarn away from where he was trying to kick the dead spearman from off m'Connor. He took the boy hard by the arms, barely resisting the urge to shake him as he glared down at him. 'I told you to stay down!'

Alarn's lower lip trembled and he began to shiver. 'They stabbed him! Let me help him!'

Sighing, all the unreasoning anger leaving him with the breath, Lerant drew the boy close to his chest and hugged him reassuringly. 'You did well, Alarn. You certainly have courage, and you might've saved the prisoner's life, but . . .' He tightened his grip. 'You could've been killed. If your mother finds out about this . . .'

'You won't tell her, will you?' Alarn wailed, his eyes widening in a terror more vivid than any supernatural onslaught could ever hope to cause.

'I won't, if you make me one promise?'Alarn nodded eager agreement. 'From now on, you do exactly what I tell you!' The second nod was more reluctant. 'Good. Stay away from those bodies.'

'Sir?' Howlett said, and he and Blakan lifted their arms to remind him they were still chained to the fallen man. Lerant found the keys and freed them from what might yet be a dead body. 'Sir?' Howlett repeated unsteadily. The flesh of his face was a pasty white and his hand trembled as he dropped the chain and took a step back from the bodies at his feet. 'What was all that about? Why would another Weaver try to kill him?'

A disgusted grimace added more wrinkles to Wilgar's face as he shoved the spearman's body from atop the Weaver and bent to tend him. Blakan, who took a certain pride in his reputation for being incorrigible and carefree, somehow kept his hands steady but his face was just as drained as he touched his fingers to the methirri band on his brow. 'What I want to know is why these things didn't protect us. Mine didn't even get hot. We all stood here like statues!'

Berial and Karatin cocked their heads, waiting with equal interest, and Lerant drew breath to tell them he was just as mystified.

'They didn't work because it wasn't a Weaver attack,' Wilgar said. 'Illker, that's what m'Connor called it, and that's what it was. I've heard of them, but . . . .' He sighed heavily.

'But what?' Lerant squatted down, watching as Wilgar eased m'Connor over to lie on his back on the rain-slick road.

'I thought they belonged only in myth.' Wilgar touched a hand to the sticky trail of blood seeping from a cut above m'Connor's left eye. Those eyes remained closed, the face ash-gray and splattered with blood and mud. The broken-off haft of the rough wooden spear protruded from ugly wounds both front and back having sliced through the thickly corded muscle of the shoulder above the collarbone.

'Is he dead?' Alarn asked fearfully.

Lerant reached up and squeezed the boy's shoulder, turning him away from the sight, and felt Alarn's gulping, relieved breath as Wilgar answered, 'He's alive, Lad. He's still breathing. Someone hold that lantern closer so I can tend his wound.' Lerant held it to throw maximum light on the wounded shoulder and Wilgar announced with grim determination, 'I'll get this thing out of him while he's still unconscious. Hold him steady for me, Blakan.'

The trooper swallowed hard and bent down to take a grip under the Weaver's arms. Wilgar took a tight hold and gave one sharp, clean tug and the spear slid smoothly, quickly all the way through the wound. M'Connor shuddered and gave a loud moan. There was a surge of bright blood, but it settled, Wilgar using wadded bandages tight over the wounds.

'How bad is it?' Berial spoke up from where he was nervously standing guard, watching one street corner while Karatin watched the other. 'We need to get moving.'

'He'll live,' Lerant replied tersely and surveyed the dead assassins. 'What did he do to them is the true question. If he can kill like that in spite of his collar . . . .'

'No,' Wilgar said, looking sharply up at him. 'He didn't do this. His Weaving failed. He had no defense whatever, other than that sword.'

'The sorcerer disappeared before those last two died! Who else but m'Connor could have killed them without so much as touching them?' Lerant demanded.

Wilgar frowned at him. 'He was unconscious. You saw that. As for his attackers, they were as good as dead before they entered this street. An Illker poisons and uses its victims to do the fighting; their hearts can beat only under its dominion. They died the moment it left. I don't know what chased it off.' He grunted, pausing as he knotted the bandage in place.

'Maybe it thought m'Connor had been killed?' Lerant suggested. 'Maybe it was only after him?'

Wilgar shrugged. 'His Song-spell could have weakened it. But, by all I've heard nothing should have stopped it. Only a Magi can equal an Illker's power.'

Lerant stared at him, very glad Alarn wasn't able to hear any of this over the lashing rain. Wilgar eyed his disbelieving expression. 'Take a look at their faces, if you dare, and you'll see the poison drove them mad,' his Second suggested.

Feeling a thrill of dread, Lerant moved to look, Howlett and Blakan following. They watched over his shoulder as he bent and lifted the flap of one of those sacks. Howlett gagged and turned hurriedly away. The dead man's face was black and swollen, the tongue protruding, the lips pulled back in an animal snarl, froth white and thick where it had foamed about the mouth. The eyes were completely white, no pupils, no color, nothing.

Sickened, Lerant dropped the sack, straightened and returned to Wilgar. 'You're absolutely certain m'Connor had nothing to do with this?'

The old soldier gave him an exasperated look. 'You think we could have enslaved any of them if they could kill like this while wearing methirri collars?'

Seeing Alarn's shoulders shuddering with silent weeping while he obediently stood face to the wall, Lerant gave up the argument to go to him. He took him in his arms and held him until the crying eased. 'Easy, Lad,' he murmured. 'It's over. We're safe now. That thing's gone, it won't be back.' He hoped he wasn't lying.

Alarn gave a huge sniff and looked back at m'Connor. 'Let me go to him? Please?'

Overhearing, Wilgar indicated the wounds were covered. Lerant let him go and Alarn hurried over, dropping to his knees and sitting back on his heels to lift the wounded man's head onto his lap out of the mud puddle. 'Is he going to be all right?' the boy asked, touching gentle fingers to m'Connor's bruised face.

'He's a tough one,' Wilgar said. 'The spear wound won't kill him and the crack on the head only stunned him. He should come round any moment now.'

There was no time and no material to construct another litter. 'Karatin. You carry him the rest of the way,' Lerant ordered firmly.

'Steady, steady!' Wilgar urged as m'Connor moaned, gasped and began struggling feebly as if to resume the fight. 'It's over.'

'He's awake, let him walk it!' Karatin snarled. 'Damn good idea t' try killin' him, if you ask me, except a spear's too quick for the likes 'o him!'

'I'm not asking you, Trooper!' Lerant snapped. 'We need him alive, and the sooner we're off these streets, the better! You carry him, and you make sure he gets where we're going alive. Understood?'

'Sir!' Karatin grumbled. He looked down in time to catch Wilgar's glare. 'Give me the mongrel,' he said to him, noting that a white-faced Alarn Hollin was cradling the Weaver's head. 'Easy, lad,' he said, his voice suddenly kindly. 'I don't mean no harm.' With an awkward gentleness, the big man bent down and tousled the boy's head.

'We're not far from home now, are we?' Lerant put in as added distraction. Gently, he guided the boy away from the wounded man. 'Berial, go back and find Rankin and report this attack. He might want to send someone up here to collect these bodies.' The trooper saluted and started off and Lerant called after him. 'And make sure that doctor brings a full surgical kit for the prisoner.'

Wilgar and Howlett eased m'Connor upright, and he peered at them groggily. His expression registered dawning astonishment to find everyone alive and undamaged while the foe lay dead all around them. All but one. 'Where's the Illker?' he rasped.

340

'Gone,' Wilgar said. 'We were lucky.'

'But . . . Who? How? An Illker doesn't just—'

Karatin abruptly heaved the Weaver up and roughly flung him over his broad shoulder, driving m'Connor back into unconsciousness.

'It would've been useful to hear what he had to say, don't you think, Trooper!' Lerant roared, absolutely furious. Regaining control as he saw Alarn watching, he said, 'Come on. Your mother will be worrying herself sick.' He tugged gently on Alarn's small hand and the boy fell into step at Lerant's side.

'She's worried about you, too,' he confided. 'She thought you might've got killed when we heard the explosion.'

CHAPTER EIGHTEEN

At last certain that little Parla was not in danger of succumbing to cold-sickness or pneumonia, and was sound asleep, Annalie Hollin prepared to go in search of her other son. She pulled on her coat and crossed the living room, checking that the hearth-fire was burning well and didn't need more fuel. She walked into a small, slate-tiled foyer just as the front door flew back and banged against the wall. Her oldest son heaved the door shut again, then turned to her.

'Alarn!' She fell to her knees to pull him hard into her arms and hold him tight against her.

'Mama! They're coming!' he announced agitatedly, his words muffled as she swamped him in a hug. 'They're bringing him!'

'Alarn!' She held him back at arm's length long enough to look him sternly in the eye. 'Don't you *ever* do that again!'

'You said Refallt would need his coat, and I—'

'Don't! You know I did not mean for you to go out there!'

'I had to!' he pleaded, his eyes filling with tears. 'The man got hurt when he saved Parla, and the soldiers don't care! They say he killed people, but he didn't! I know he didn't!'

'Hush, now, hush.' Annalie pulled him back against her and asked, 'Where is Refallt?'

'He's gone with one of the soldiers and the Archman to get medicine.'

'The Archman?' Surely he'd have enough to do with finding shelter and aid for the survivors of the explosion. 'Who's the medicine for?'

'The man who saved Parla; m'Connor.' He drew a great breath. 'Uncle Kerell says he's dying from the slargapent! And he got stabbed by the spear, too. He's so white and sick . . . . But you'll save him, Mama, won't you?'

'I'll try.' Refallt had told her the man had been badly hurt, his leg bloodied by a slargapent, but Wilgar was tending him when he'd left and said he should be all right. A spear? What had her son witnessed? She heard tramping boots on her front path and porch steps and Alarn turned to let them in. 'No! You're soaked and shivering. Go to your room and change into dry clothes.' He stood, face turned to the door. 'Alarn! Do what I tell you! Now!'

'Yes, Mama.' Reluctantly obedient, he turned away toward the living room, his head lowered. 'Papa would want us to help the man, too,' he said earnestly.

'Yes, he would. Go. Change your clothes. Then, bring the goose-down cover from your bed. If the man's hurt and cold he'll need it.'

She unlatched the heavy door and ducked against a swirling, icy gust of sleet and snow. Leaning on the door-frame, exhausted and dripping rainwater, stood Kerell Lerant. His uniform and black leather cuirass was splattered with mud, ash and rust-colored smears of what could only be dried blood. Carried under his arm was the helm, its red plumes tattered and soaked flat.

'Kerell!' She gripped his arm. 'It's good to have you home safe.'

'My thanks for your caring, Annalie,' he said, stiffly. He looked away as his small band of troopers crowded up onto the porch, intent on the last man who came slowly up the path. He was huge, much taller than Lerant, and as he stepped into the light, she saw he carried the wounded man, Parla's rescuer. Unconscious, his dark head lolled and his arms swung limply. Wilgar stepped closer to say. 'He needs your care, Annalie.'

'Brant! I'm glad you're here.'

'So am I,' he said with a heavy sigh. 'It's been quite a night.'

'Well, everyone,' she said with forced cheer, allowing her smile to encompass them all, 'don't stand here freezing to death in my doorway. Come inside and welcome.'

'Are you sure?' Lerant asked her, deadly serious. He waved his men back, stalling them as they crowded closer, and so grim as he regarded her that she felt colder than any storm could cause. 'If I had anywhere else to take him . . . . This is very dangerous for you and the boys, but you're the only hope he has left. There're a lot of people who want him dead and—'

'I'm not afraid of them,' she said, meeting his eyes with a steady resolve that instantly lightened his load. She looked down at the wounded man. 'Get him inside now, to the fire.'

Lerant nodded permission and the giant went on through the door, ducking a little under the lintel. 'Alarn says he's dying?' she asked, leading the way and hearing the troopers' relieved sighs as finally they got out of the brutal night.

'Someone dumped the anti-venom and replaced it with water. We thought we'd treated him for the poison. Refallt and the others have gone to find more but he's out of time. Is there anything you can do for him?'

Appalled, Annalie frowned up at him. Slarga venom caused such terrible suffering, the pain alone could kill. 'He was attacked just before dark?' There were older remedies that had saved lives before the days of the anti-venom but they'd been effective because they'd been used immediately. She knew Lerant knew that, too.

'There's no hope? Nothing?' he asked.

'The old remedy might hold him until the other is found, I'm not sure it will do more. It's in my kit, in the kitchen. I'll get it.'

They all tramped into her living room, leaving muddy boot-prints on her newly polished floor and its blue and green diamond patterned wool rug. She hurried on into the kitchen, calling to Wilgar, 'There's food in here for the men. Make some tea, you know where everything is.'

'I do,' he said, following after her. 'They've not eaten since noon. Thank you for your thoughtfulness.'

She collected her kit from the high shelf in the pantry and quickly checked its contents. Then she took a cup and filled it with warm water, honey and peppermint. Wilgar busied himself placing cheese, bread and apples on the table and putting the kettle back on to return to a boil over the fire. 'Karatin!' she heard Lerant roar from out in the living room, so furious it made her flinch. 'What the Fires do you think you're doing?!'

'Oh, no,' Wilgar groaned. 'Not again!' Annalie returned with him hurriedly to the living room, aghast to find the giant trooper had chained the wounded man to the door post between the living room and entry hall instead of taking him to the warmth of the hearth. Putting the cup of tea down on a low table but keeping the kit, she went out to them.

Brought awake by the rough handling, m'Connor bit down hard, choking back any sound of pain. Bruises, mud, and blood darkened his strong-boned face and his clothing was reduced to bloodstained rags. He wore only one boot and his bare right leg and foot were horribly mangled and swollen, wrapped ineffectually in a scarlet tangle of tattered bandaging. With disgust, Annalie recognized the band of ugly red-black metal circling his throat. A slave collar. So, this was his reward for the rescue of her son.

'You were told to handle him carefully, Trooper!' Lerant bellowed, drawing m'Connor's bleary attention. 'How long do you think he can stay alive left like this?' Startled, Karatin came to a crisp, frightened salute as Lerant stepped around the chained man to stand in front of him. The other troopers stood around the room, most having drawn close to the fire, and all watching the show with interest.

'Stand back!' Wilgar snapped at them, pushing his way through. 'Here; I have the keys.' He went to the Weaver's side, crouching down and reaching back to the manacled wrists.

Ignoring the confrontation, Annalie squatted down closer to m'Connor. Blood oozed from a swollen bruise high on his brow, trickling down over an equally bruised cheek and mouth to drip from his jaw. Far more blood steadily soaked through the clumsy bandaging about what could only be the spear wound in his upper left shoulder.

There was something so odd, so out of place, in the emotion on m'Connor's face as he watched Lerant dressing down the big trooper, that it drew Annalie to want to see what he saw. He seemed to be transfixed by Karatin's profile. Tears brimmed in his eyes, and unable to wipe at them, he blinked them away, then turned his head sharply from the sight of the giant trooper, which left him looking directly at Annalie. He tried to avoid her gaze, but she reached out a gentle hand, wiping the blood from his jaw onto her fingers as she lifted his head back to her.

'I lost my husband,' she told him softly, her chest tight with renewed grief. 'I know how it hurts when something reminds me of him.' Steadying him, she took a swab and very gently cleaned some of the muck from his face. 'Who is it for you?'

'My Brother, Bren,' m'Connor admitted, his bleary gaze finally meeting hers.

'I understand,' she told him quietly. 'I'd have lost our boys, too, but for your courage. Thank you.' Whatever he might have said in answer was choked back in a gasp of pain as Wilgar at last managed to free his arms from the manacles.

'I was thinkin' o' the danger t' the lady and the little ones, Sir,' she heard the big trooper plead. 'The slave did fair right enough with that sword out there, chains 'n all.'

'When none of us could move to stop him and before he was further injured!' Lerant took a threatening step closer. 'There'll be many more at risk should he die! How many times do I have to explain! Pick him up! Put him on the rug in front of the hearth where he can dry off. And go easy or I'll have your scalp!' Glowering darkly, Karatin obeyed, putting m'Connor down very carefully on the thick rug on the floor immediately in front of the blazing hearth-fire.

'As soon as I've given him this, we'll get him into Alarn's bed,' Annalie said and sat on the floor beside him. The big trooper went to the kitchen and Lerant came closer to watch as she measured the potent herbs to mix into the sweetened tea. 'Your trooper is an idiot,' she told him.

'He is,' Lerant agreed, softening the words with a half-shrug and the shadow of a smile. 'But he's my idiot. They all did well out there tonight. But he was amazing. He went in under the wreckage to rescue some children despite being afraid of cramped places.' In the kitchen he could see his men were gathered in a quiet group that would at other times have been marked by banter and laughter. 'Most of us have had someone die in their arms tonight.'

Annalie had had patients die, but she couldn't imagine this kind of horror, this deliberate taking of life in the most savage manner possible. 'Go, eat, get warm. Rest.' She called Alarn who stood hesitantly in the entry to the bedroom hallway, watching them, the goose-down bed-cover draped over his arms and hiding the tossed together clothing he no doubt wore.

'Will he be all right, Mama?' Alarn asked anxiously.

'Don't worry, son. I'll live,' m'Connor whispered hoarsely, surprising them both as he answered. His eyes opened again and she noticed they were an unusual green-brown, dark with pain that overlay a bright intelligence and curiosity.

'You will,' Alarn agreed, flashing a great smile that earned a flicker of something like it in return. 'Mama's the best Healer in the whole world!'

'That's because my patients do what I tell them,' Annalie warned dryly, making the hint of a smile twitch on m'Connor's face. 'I have something for you that will help keep the venom at bay, if you can manage to swallow it.' She slid her free hand beneath his damp hair, propping him up, and holding the cup for him with the other. He sipped carefully but gradually downed the whole cup. She placed her hand to his heart in the manner Parlan had told her was the Lellghin fashion. 'I owe you my sons' lives. I swear, I will do all I can to help you.'

'I must not stay here,' he said, barely audible. 'The little one . . . ?'

'Safely asleep, thanks to you. Rest now.' She got to her feet, looking for Wilgar and saw that he was busy carrying some cheese and bread to Lerant from the kitchen.

Stepping closer, Lerant said, 'What do you think of his chances now?'

She heaved a considering sigh. 'He might just make it. He's tougher than I thought.'

'Oh, he's that all right,' Lerant agreed with feeling. 'M'Connor is a Weaver Captain, an escaped slave from Myrrgha Citadel.'

'He used a spell? Refallt said you were shooting at him but he went after Parla anyway?'

'*Something* happened,' Lerant corrected, frowning thoughtfully. 'When he was still in the water, maybe an attempt to chase off the slargapents . . . Stupid bastard, knew they were there,' he muttered with both admiration and exasperated pain in his tone.

'I owe him,' Annalie said intently.

'*We* owe him.' Lerant lifted his head to meet her eyes and she saw the pain she'd heard in his voice. 'I promised Parlan I'd keep you all safe. But m'Connor did it for me tonight, and he's paid a very heavy price. I can't save him, Annalie, anymore than I could save Parlan.'

Her sigh echoed his. 'I'll go get the boys' room ready for him.' She called to Wilgar to help her set a fire in the bedroom hearth. Alarn sat half-asleep, his head nodding on his chest, but one hand rested protectively on m'Connor's arm. 'Come along,' she said, reaching out to draw him to his feet, 'It's long past time you got to bed. You'll sleep in my bed with Parla tonight.'

'Can I help get my room ready for him first?' he pleaded over a great yawn.

'Very well,' she agreed, mussing his hair. 'But then, bed for you.'

As mother and son left the room, Lerant took his chance to ask questions. He squatted at the Weaver's side. Judging by the tightly controlled pattern of his breathing, all his efforts were going into keeping any sound of pain at bay. 'Captain?' M'Connor squinted up at him, suspiciously, wondering why he hadn't been addressed as 'slave'. 'After we were attacked out there, you wanted to say something about the person who led them?'

'Person? Illker. I tried to warn you.'

'Why was it after you?' Lerant demanded hurriedly. Annalie was already on her way back, carrying a bowl of steaming water while Alarn lugged some towels. 'Will it try again? Attack us here?'

'Safe for tonight. It can't . . . needs time . . .' A full-throated groan escaped him, every muscle suddenly tightened. The venom was breaching Annalie's safe-hold.

'But why?' Lerant asked, all the frustration of the night hitting him. Annalie was looking daggers at him, wanting him to leave off. 'Why attack you? Aren't you one of them?'

'No,' m'Connor whispered, 'Illker . . . hunts us . . . .' He gasped against another surge of pain and Annalie elbowed Lerant aside. Giving up, he took a seat nearby in the big chair by the hearth, wondering if he could believe the reassurance.

'So much for Gareck's plans,' Wilgar commented tersely, returning from his mission to set the hearth fire and collecting his still steaming mug of tea. 'He can't talk for the pain.'

There was a loud rapping at the front door. Howlett, who was closest, went to answer it, Lerant following. As the door-latch released, a howling whirl of snow slammed it open, the blizzard arriving in full force. Refallt, Trooper Sandor and his companion stumbled inside and Howlett and Lerant struggled to close the door. The third man held a very welcome, bright red-banded medical kit in his gloved hands. He pushed the hood from his face, and Lerant recognized him as Rogha City Surgeon, Callay. He looked none too happy.

'We got it, sir!' Sandor announced with a great grin.

'There was some left in a personal emergency kit in a back room,' Refallt explained, looking even happier than Sandor who carefully produced a small glass bottle from his pocket and took it to Annalie as she called him urgently to her.

'Good work. Where's Rankin?' Lerant asked. Annalie didn't wait for the doctor but busied herself making preparations to administer the drug aided by Wilgar.

'Organizing a burial detail for those bodies up here in the street,' Sandor answered, returning to him with a worried frown. 'What happened?'

'Oh, that's a tale!' Blakan complained, drawn from the kitchen by the newcomers.

'Blakan!' Lerant snapped. That was all he needed, to have Annalie overhear a lurid description of mythical monsters ready to devour her son.

'You have the drug, and you have a competent Healer. You don't need me,' Callay interrupted. 'I don't know why you forced me here, but I'm leaving.'

'Shut up and sit down,' Lerant ordered, turning a glare on the man. 'I have some questions I want answered, Doctor.'

Callay deigned to look down at the Weaver whose limbs were cramping violently. 'Careful. You don't want to break that needle point off in a blood vessel. But you're too late. You shouldn't have him so close to the fire.'

'Why not?' Lerant asked suspiciously.

'The warmth,' Callay said. 'That's why he's cramping. It's caused a sudden outpouring of the venom; the pain will cause shock and rapid death.'

'Shut him up!' Annalie snapped. Aided by Wilgar and Refallt's firm grip on the arm, she administered the anti-venom and then found a vial of painkiller and injected that, too. She gave Callay a cold glance. 'Left just a little longer and it *would* be too late.'

'He's cramping because he was given water instead of the anti-venom,' Lerant growled. 'Someone switched it when I sent Blakan for it. Could that someone have been you, Doctor?'

'I've had enough of these accusations, Commander! I don't care if he dies, true, but I'm not a killer. You can't hold me here. There are people dying back there for need of my skills.'

'More will die if we can't save him!' Lerant warned, keeping his voice low. He took the doctor by the arm and hauled him into the privacy of the mud-porch. 'Myrrghin High Command order that I deliver him alive.'

'Oh. Well, then they'll be disappointed.' The doctor shrugged, turning to leave.

'If they're disappointed there won't be anyone left to bury the bodies in Rogha!'

Callay turned back to him, frowning. 'Even the Myrrghin Military can't be so insane as to blame all Rogha because one man died of slarga poisoning.'

'The order comes from Grand Inquisitor Zaraxan, directly. He has a personal interest in this man and says he's coming here to collect him himself. Do you know anything about why he didn't receive the anti-venom when I sent for it the first time?' Lerant demanded.

'Obviously, your trooper destroyed it.'

'That's done,' Annalie said, arriving at their backs and making Lerant start. 'Now we get him into a bed and you can sew up his leg and shoulder wounds, Doctor.'

Callay spared her a glance. 'I'm not wasting my time sewing up a dead man!' Annalie glared and he sighed, 'You know it as well as I do, Widow Hollin. He's dead either way.'

'That leg needs a surgeon,' Lerant insisted. 'Get in there and get to work.'

'That leg needs a saw!' He put his hand on the door knob. 'I'm Rogha City Surgeon first. There are people dying back there, some of them no older than your sons, Widow. Let me go to them, I beg you, Commander.'

'My duty is to Rogha, too,' Lerant said, putting his hand on the man's arm to draw him away from the door.

'Let him go,' Annalie said, wearily. 'I can do what needs doing.'

Lerant stared at her aghast at the thought of her performing an amputation. Taking advantage of the distraction, Callay flung open the door and disappeared into the howling snow. 'Damn!' Lerant squinted out into the stormy dark, hugging his arms to himself over the cold.

'Want me to go after him?' Wilgar asked.

'No, I suppose we can manage.'

'Have your men carry him to Alarn's bed,' Annalie instructed, already moving in that direction herself. 'Get him out of these wet clothes. There are warm blankets in the closet behind the hearth.'

'I thought . . . wouldn't the table be better for . . . ?

'That leg can be saved,' Annalie said tersely, looking back over her shoulder at him, 'especially if he were to return to his own people.'

'Annalie . . . .' Lerant sighed. 'He's not going back to his people.'

She turned about fully to face him, her chin lifted in the stubborn manner he knew so well. 'I'm not giving up on him. I won't forget what he did.'

'Nor will I.' Lerant gave orders for his men to stand guard duty, taking shifts. He looked down again at m'Connor, flinching as he saw how badly the man was suffering. 'Annalie, I'd like Karatin to watch from the window in your room. It has the best view to the rear lane.'

'Missus?' Karatin asked. 'Might I crack the window open, t' rest my gun on the sill?'

'Of course,' Annalie said, aware of the man's fear of enclosed places. 'Just be sure to keep the fire burning and the room warm for the boys.'

'No child could be safer than with Karatin,' Lerant said, catching a surprised and pleased climb of eyebrows on the giant's weary face. 'Wilgar, you know some of the Lellghin tongue. We'll stay by the prisoner.'

He left Annalie to sort through her store of towels and bandaging while he collected and carried the warm blankets to the bedroom. The tiny cottage Lerant had known from his childhood was outwardly no different to most in Rogha. Yet Annalie had filled it with handcrafted furnishings that renewed the air of warmth and welcome it had known before Lerant's foster parents had died. Alarn's room was small but cheery with its warmly glowing hearth, bright blue curtains, embroidered quilts, pillows and toys.

It was somehow a blasphemy to Lerant to find grim duty waiting him here, too, the bed surrounded by troopers, Wilgar carefully stripping the wounded man of his filthy, damp clothing. 'Blakan, Howlett, get some sleep,' he ordered. 'Then change off with the others.'

'You think he'll make it?' Blakan asked over a huge yawn.

'I hope so,' Lerant said heavily.

'Me, too,' Howlett murmured. 'That was a brave thing he did at the river.'

'We'll do the best we can for him.'

The two troopers left the room and it was suddenly silent and still but for the crackling of the hearth fire. Lerant faintly heard a low moaning from m'Connor. It was the same awful sound he remembered hearing one winter's night from a starving dog he'd found, standing leaning against a wall with a badly broken leg. If not for m'Connor's selflessness, he'd have carried Annalie's dead sons home to her tonight—if he'd been lucky enough to retrieve the bodies. He couldn't imagine that Alarn might never have returned to his cozy room.

'He's hurting bad,' Lerant observed. 'Do you think someone's interfered with the kit?'

'No, we checked everything before we left,' Wilgar shook his head. 'It's been too long. We can only hope he can fight his way through it.' He moved to the bedside and bent to cover the man warmly from chest to feet.

Annalie entered the room carrying a basin of steaming water, ready for her grisly work with a white apron tied over her blue skirt and her hair pulled back beneath a red silk scarf. The sight put Lerant again at his brother's side in the hot, bustling markets of Myrrgha City.

'Red is Annalie's favorite color . . . earned it stabbing people through the guts with a bayonet.'

Alarn came in, carrying a stack of towels that he set down on the foot locker. His eyes darkened and his brows furrowed as he caught m'Connor's muted cries of pain. 'It'll be all right now,' he assured, hurrying to him. 'Mama will make you better.'

The two had certainly formed a strong bond in those first dark moments by the river. Lerant must surely lose the boy's affection forever when he gave his hero over to the Inquisitor. But better to have Alarn alive and hating him—alive because m'Connor had saved him.

'Alarn, could you go get me another pillow, please?' Annalie said, and, as he obeyed, shared a grim glance with Wilgar and Lerant. 'We put an end to this pain before it exhausts him beyond saving,' she said. 'I'll give him more of the pain-drug. We need him fully asleep before I can begin sewing that leg, anyway.'

Lerant waited tense until at last m'Connor's involuntary moans began to fade. It was a great relief to see the agony wash from his face. Taking a warm washcloth, Annalie stroked bloodied hair back from the man's brow until his eyes closed.

'I got the pillow for you, Mama,' Alarn whispered.

'Thank you. I'll need it for his leg when I'm done bandaging it. Come; let's get you tucked in with Parla in my big bed. He'll be frightened if he wakes alone and sees that big trooper by the window.'

'I have to go,' Alarn told m'Connor, touching his hand. 'But you're safe now. Mama won't let them hurt you.' He gave Lerant a look full of accusation and turned to leave the room, set to leave without so much as a good night for his uncle. Once, there'd have been a real laughing, bear-hugging tickling routine. Nothing now, and that hurt.

'Alarn?' Annalie prompted. 'Aren't you going to say good night to Uncle Kerell?'

'Good night, Uncle,' Alarn said dutifully and allowed himself to be stiffly enveloped in Lerant's quick hug.

'Good night, Alarn,' Lerant said, wanting desperately to add, don't worry. I swear I'll keep him safe for you, too. But he'd already given that promise to his nephew and failed—Alarn no longer had a father.

'That's the worst of it tended,' Annalie said, straightening up and rubbing her neck. 'If you could move him for me, please, I'll clean the wound in his back.'

They'd found m'Connor's leg was indeed broken and Lerant remembered the awful snap of it beneath the fearful blow delivered in the street battle. The smaller bones of foot and ankle however, had been crushed in the slargapent's jaws. M'Connor wouldn't be standing on that leg any time soon. Now, hidden beneath splints and neat white bandaging and propped with pillows, it at least looked better. Carefully, he rolled the wounded man toward him and held him steady.

Annalie bent to swab m'Connor's wound but suddenly froze. 'Look at this,' she said coldly. 'You don't believe it when Parlan and I tell you.'

He shifted awkwardly to see over m'Connor's shoulder and cursed in disgust. The Weaver's muscular back showed a regular pattern of upraised white scars. Torture like that could drive a man to cause the carnage in Rogha tonight. But a man pushed so far beyond the bounds of his own humanity would never have turned back to save one small child in an enemy city. Something didn't tally here.

'Myrrghin work!' Annalie snarled. Then, gathering her composure and steadying her hands as she collected new thread, she asked, 'This wound was caused by a spear, or so Alarn tells me. What happened?'

'Most of Rogha wants to tear him to pieces,' he replied, determined to avoid the details. 'Jarrod could have been behind the attack—he wanted him lynched.'

'Jarrod's always been a low-life sadistic bastard! No stray animal is safe from that collection of knives of his,' Annalie said, her mouth turned down in a sour scowl.

Suddenly, Lerant remembered his inability to control his actions as Jarrod taunted m'Connor. He'd never before fired a gun when he hadn't intended to. None of the dead faces beneath those masks would be recognizable, but Lerant would give odds Jarrod wasn't among them. The mongrel was probably plotting some new attack right now. Maybe he shouldn't have pulled that shot.

'Alarn was out there,' Annalie added darkly, 'He saw it all?'

'No! I put him behind a wall.'

Annalie raised a disbelieving eyebrow. 'And he stayed there?'

'It all happened very quickly. It was finished when he jumped over the fence.' He met Annalie's eyes to admit, 'He'd found a great hunk of rock for a weapon.'

'That boy!'

'He's Parlan's son, all right,' Lerant agreed, a smile escaping him.

'And your nephew,' Annalie said tersely. 'There, it's done. You can lay him back again.' She drew up the warm blankets and said with weary pride. 'At least he looks more comfortable.'

Lerant found a chair and pulled it up to the bed to sit watching as she began thoroughly and gently washing the mud and blood from the Weaver's face and hair. Haloed by the soft lamplight, Annalie's concerned frown as she tended the man revealed the caring heart of a gifted healer. Lerant folded his arms on the edge of the mattress and gave in to the urge to lower his head and close his eyes just for a few moments.

Taran m'Connor dreamed. He was with Rhyssa, relaxing on the warm sand of the beach near Home Cove. The tropical sun beamed hotly down, making the lapping blue-green water look cool and inviting. Abruptly, the sun expanded, filling the sky, becoming hotter and hotter, until he could feel his skin burning. He wanted to get up and plunge into the soothing, liquid depths of the lagoon, but it was no longer there. Instead, the desert plains of Myrrgha reached to the horizon. Volcanoes spewed smoke and ash, choking the air, and making breathing difficult. Lava spilled from craters and fissures, flowing in an inexorable tide of molten red-black, coming ever closer, the radiated heat scorching, deadly.

He felt his skin peel back, blistering raw, red and stinging. He struggled to get up, and terror filled him as he found he couldn't move. Something invisible, an unseen malevolent power held him captive. Gloating, reveling in his suffering, it forced him flat on his back, exposed his upturned face to that searing, white-hot light in a blood-red sky. About him appeared several black-robed specters, their faces no more than bleached, empty skulls, their fleshless mouths full of gaping, grinning stumps of teeth.

Then, someone broke through their ranks. Young and fair-haired, his was a pleasant countenance but for the eyes. Ice black, cold and lifeless, The Void itself beckoned from within.

'Hail, Master!' the specters chanted, bowing low. 'Hail He Who Commands the SunFire!'

The one so-named smiled; a terrible, twisted, leer of pleasured cruelty. He raised a fist and blood red flames flickered about his fingers. Using Shadow, he pushed someone forward.

'Rhyssa!' m'Connor cried in helpless anguish. Forced to move to the slave-master's side, she carried a silver tray laden with a crystal decanter of chilled water. M'Connor watched, dying of thirst, as she gave it to the Master to drink.

Suddenly, miraculously, something cool and wet brushed over his face, blocking the searing sun. Surprise broke the last thread of the nightmare, sending it whirling away. He was safe in bed, but was so sick, so feverish, that he couldn't remember why. He forced open heavy eyelids to find the glare eclipsed by the figure of a woman standing by his bed.

'Rhyssa? It's so hot here . . . . I wish we were home.' He drifted back to sleep, mumbling 'There'd be snow . . . .'

Annalie moved the lantern close to check for further bleeding, her patient struggling so much in delirium that she feared he'd tear open the wounds. The words he babbled were at first barely decipherable, but now were clear though none of it followed any logical progression. Undaunted, Lerant wrote it all down, even the most innocent-seeming, personal comments, obeying, as he'd finally confessed, an order from Inquisitor Zaraxan himself.

'Rhyssa? It's so hot here . . . . I wish we were home. There'd be snow . . . .'

Turning to put the lantern down, Annalie started a little to find Lerant frozen, his mouth open in surprise as he stared at the wounded man, his writing forgotten. Shaking himself back to his work, he muttered, 'Coincidence.' He looked up at her and asked, 'Did he say, 'Rhyssa?'

'I'm not about to confirm something he said so you can use it against him when he's handed to the Inquisitor.'

'Annalie . . . .' Lerant sighed. 'I'm not trying to find . . . I don't want to help them. But I have my orders and Rogha at stake.'

'Orders!' She slammed the lantern down, making the light flicker and Lerant's hand jump and the pencil tear across his page. He sat on the small chair he had pulled up close to the bed, the better to hear, a blue wax-covered notepad on his lap. 'How can you even think of giving him, hurt like this, to that bastard Zaraxan!'

'Gareck already sent word about his capture,' he said wearily, not looking up at her. 'The mongrel Inquisitor called me at Rankin's. He's coming for him, Annalie. I can't stop him, and I can't help m'Connor, especially not after what happened out there tonight.'

'And if he had nothing to do with that?'

'He's done the same thing before. He destroyed a large part of Myrrgha Citadel.'

'Good for him! You put a slave collar on this man, Kerell. Will you learn to condone torture and murder, next?'

'You know I will not!' He met her gaze, his jaw set defiantly, but his face flushed and his eyes shadowed. 'For pity's sake, Annalie, think! They're a people who put their trust in a tree that supposedly talks to them after they drink its nectar? That same kind of superstitious fanaticism killed my birth-mother.'

'Bren! They're burning them!' m'Connor cried, his eyes flying open, bright with delirium. 'We must save them! Bren! Where are you?' He lifted his head from the pillows and looked direct at Lerant, reaching toward him with his good arm, the fingers straining in desperate pleading. 'I've got to find him. Help me! Please! I must find him!'

Lerant dropped his notepad and pencil and took the straining hand in his. 'I'll help you. It'll be all right. We'll find him.'

'They took him,' m'Connor explained, tears spilling from his eyes. 'I couldn't stop them. I tried . . . .'

'We'll get him back. It's all right. We'll find him,' Lerant took hold with both hands around m'Connor's. 'It'll be all right.' Reassured, m'Connor settled back, his eyes closed.

Suddenly, Lerant looked sharply around as if he'd heard or seen someone approaching from behind. 'Do you see that?'

'See what?'

'High up, in the corner . . . It's gone. I thought . . . .' He looked up at her, embarrassed. 'I thought I saw something like the thing that attacked us in the street. Except . . . this light seemed friendly, somehow.'

'I told you hours ago you need to sleep. But you should eat first.'

Packing the plates onto a tray after an improvised meal, Annalie dropped the cutlery and the noise brought m'Connor partly to wakefulness. He stirred, his eyes opening a crack before sliding shut again as he called faintly, 'Rhyssa?'

Lerant was sure now that m'Connor was calling for the same woman—Zaraxan's supposed bride. Rhyssa wasn't a common name, a Myrrghin tribal name. It had to be the same woman. She hadn't been murdered by m'Connor, she'd run off with him, become his lover. The question was, did Zaraxan know? Of course he wouldn't admit to being a cuckold, would prefer to play for sympathy, but either way, he'd want m'Connor's hide.

'Who is this Rhyssa he keeps calling for?' Annalie asked.

'I'm not sure . . . I think she might be someone Zaraxan believes is dead.'

'Safest for her, then. Bren is his Weaver Brother?'

'Yes, or was, according to his lordship.' Lerant replied. Rhyssa—one murder m'Connor had been falsely accused of. How many other lies underpinned Zaraxan's hatred of the man?

'Look, he's sleeping,' Annalie said. 'You won't get anything more from him tonight. Please go to bed. You look so tired.'

He didn't answer and, shaking her head at him, she left him alone as she returned the plates to the kitchen. Lerant couldn't rid himself of the terrible image of Zaraxan entering Annalie and Parlan's home, his childhood home, the boys' home. The Emperor had ordered Zaraxan to come all this way primarily to uncover the whereabouts of the other Weavers. If Grouda was given that information tonight, Zaraxan and his battleship would almost certainly be ordered to turn around and go after them, to leave his personal vendetta in abeyance until their enemy's last stronghold had been destroyed. Slowly, a hazy idea formed in Lerant's weary mind, and though he hunted, he could find no flaws in his strategy. It was worth a try.

'I thought you'd be gone to bed by now.' Annalie sounded exasperated. Sighing, she sat in the extra chair at the other side of the bed.

'Annalie,' he spoke up nervously. 'It seems to me that if m'Connor would give me the answers Zaraxan wants, there'd be no need for the ship to come all the way up here. Its captain would be issued with new orders and Rogha would be safe. M'Connor is very groggy and confused whenever he wakes a moment. He thinks he's with Rhyssa, with friends. If the lantern is turned very low, the room dark . . . If I can convince him m'Fetrin's been found but needs their Healers, maybe he'll tell us where his people are —'

'And when you tell Myrrgha where they are, his family and friends will all be killed!' Annalie cut him off, standing, eyes flashing pure fury. 'Parlan told you what Myrrghin cannons do to people! Children included! Just like what you saw out there tonight, I'd think! Might as well light the fuse yourself!'

'If it's Rogha or them, my duty is to Rogha!' Lerant snarled.

'Oh? You're wearing a Myrrghin uniform! Seems to me you're doing their work!'

Smothering the sting of her accusation, Lerant stood and turned the lantern down to throw deep shadow. Bracing himself to do what was necessary to keep Rogha safe, he moved closer to the bed and placed his hand to m'Connor's bare shoulder. As gently as possible, he began shaking the wounded man to wakefulness.

M'Connor mumbled protest but opened drug-heavy eyelids. His brow furrowed in confusion, his eyes lacking focus as he squinted about him.

'M'Connor?' Lerant said, 'We got you out. You and Bren.'

'Bren?' m'Connor lifted his head fractionally and swallowed hard. He tried to lift a hand to rub at his eyes but failed. 'Bren?!' he said again. He struggled to push himself up on an elbow. The eager hope in his eyes cut Lerant to the bone. 'Where is he?'

'Not far.' Lerant had to grit himself to continue the lie despite the shame that burned through him. 'He's hurt. We must find a Healer for him, fast.'

'Hurt?' m'Connor's brow creased further, but in alarm, not an effort for focus. He looked ready to get out of bed and go to his friend despite his own injuries.

'Easy! You're hurt, too. There was an explosion . . . .' Lerant prompted carefully.

'The Citadel?' m'Connor asked in confusion. 'Bren wasn't—'

'No. Rogha Garrison.'

'Oh . . . .' He paused, concentrating.

The moment the words were out of his mouth Lerant could have kicked himself. What difference did it make, just so long as he led Zaraxan away from here.

'Methaggar!' m'Connor growled, hoarse but so vehement it made Lerant flinch. 'Killed the children . . . . The garrison, too. Bren . . . .' he mumbled with the last of his strength, his hand outstretched, trembling. 'Take me to him.'

'I can't. He's not here,' Lerant blurted, stunned. He didn't do it. Someone else murdered everyone out there tonight. M'Connor collapsed back into semi-consciousness, his eyes closed.

Lerant stared at the wounded man a moment, and then recoiled away from him, away from having to admit this ugly new reality. He saw again the utter shock in m'Connor's eyes moments after the explosion. He'd had no more forewarning than Lerant, was just as appalled, just as horrified. Just as innocent.

'Satisfied?' Annalie whispered, daring to step a little closer.

Lerant waved her back, took a deep breath, gathered himself, and tried to reclaim his focus. He might tell himself he was protecting Rogha, but in his innermost heart, he saw plainly two little boys, so like the brother he'd loved, and their mother. Zaraxan would never take them!

He took a step back to the bed and shook the half-conscious man again, urging him to stay awake. 'You're Bren's only hope. You must know where to find your Healers?'

'No. The Key,' m'Connor mumbled, his eyes opening a crack then closing again. 'Can't remember . . . . Talaers might . . . .' His voice a whisper, he sagged back.

Damn. That was no use. Lerant knew no one who could communicate in the sea nomads' language even if they could be found and made to cooperate. Frustrated, Lerant shook him much harder, making m'Connor gasp in pain. 'We can't wait! Bren is dying! Where are they?'

'Steady. I'll try. Where's Marc?' M'Connor suddenly sounded alarmingly clear-headed, the pain and the need to aid his Brother bringing him more awake.

He lifted his head, his gaze blinking but focused sharply against the shadows. He took in the narrow cot, his white-swathed and splinted broken leg raised on pillows, the hearth-fire, and the small room. He gasped and tensed and his eyes darkened with despair. His arm shook, but lifted, his fingers reached, found the methirri collar at his throat. His lips curled in fury and disgust over a low growl of outrage before his arm dropped back to the bed.

Then, he looked up at his captor, and Lerant flinched. The man's eyes flared green with fury. If he were still able to Weave every methirri in Rogha would be melting.

'You bastard!' he snarled, his fist clenching. Realizing he couldn't retaliate, he merely turned his head away in disgust.

Lerant felt more regret than shame. He'd failed Rogha, failed to protect his family. Again. 'You'll tell us, eventually,' he told m'Connor. 'Better to tell me than the Inquisitor.'

'No,' m'Connor said with an utter certainty that shattered Lerant. The truth of the denial was all there in the wounded man's eyes as he met Lerant's gaze again, angry but not shaken.

'You don't understand, you bastard! I don't *know* where they are! They're safe from you butchers! Safe!' He struggled a moment to sit up, grunting with effort and pain. He didn't make it to half way before collapsing back to the pillows, short of breath. He tried again, his arm and hand pushing against the mattress, but it was too much for him and he lost consciousness, his breathing shallow and ragged.

Alarmed, Annalie came to his side, pushing Lerant back. She checked m'Connor's pulse and waited, tense and listening until his breathing settled into a steady, strong rhythm once more. She tugged angrily at the blankets, pulling them warmly up about m'Connor's shoulders. Then, she turned about, her glare set to cut Lerant in half. 'Happy now?' she snapped.

Lerant set his teeth and returned her glare with equal measure. 'I was trying to save my people from a madman. I failed! No! I am not happy!' He moved away from her, taking an unsteady step to the window where the storm still raged. He'd almost forgotten it.

Annalie went to the fire and bent to collect the stained clothing. 'Well,' she said at last. 'At least now you've proved he had nothing to do with the explosion.'

'There are other crimes marked against his name.' He sat down again, slumped forward and letting this hands hang limp between his knees. 'If Military Command was in charge, there might've been some hope that his rescue of Parla could earn some mercy. But Zaraxan . . . .'

'Mercy? You saw the scars on his back! To Myrrgha he's just an escaped Weaver slave with information vital to their plans of war. And Zaraxan's cruelty knows no bounds!'

Lerant knew that better than she. Garek's intent had been vile, but it would have given m'Connor the release of death within an hour or two. But Zaraxan . . . Zaraxan was renowned for keeping his victims alive through months of torture. He looked across at where m'Connor lay completely defenseless, badly injured because he'd answered Alarn's plea for help. Damn it, damn it, *damn* it!

'I'll talk to him again when he's stronger,' he said, looking hopefully up at her. 'This storm will slow Zaraxan for days. It's his choice. He knew what he faced should he be captured.'

'Yes, he knew that when he turned back for my son! For Parlan's son! He'll be tortured to death, but you'll still have your nephews!'

'That's unfair, Anni!' His head jerked up to regard her, hurt flooding his eyes. 'I tell you there's nothing I can do if m'Connor won't listen to reason!'

'Reason? You think it's reasonable that he tell you all you need to know to have everyone he cares about slaughtered?'

He ran his hand over his burning eyes and climbed to his feet. 'I'm tired,' he said. 'I'm going to bed. I suggest you do the same.

I'll have Wilgar sit with m'Connor. You won't be any good to him if you're out on your feet.'

She regarded him more calmly and gave a brisk nod, checked her patient again with a glance, and turned to the door. Lerant grasped her arm gently. 'I'm sorry things have to be this way,' he said.

She pulled her arm free. 'So am I,' she said and left the room.

The attic trapdoor creaked upward. Lerant lifted his small lantern through and put it down on the rough, dusty planks. He climbed off the drop-down stairs and stepped inside, crouching low to avoid bumping his head on the rafters. This place had seemed so much bigger when he was a boy. Now it was just cold and lonely. Very lonely. This had been his and Parlan's winter fortress, their pirate ship, their castle . . . . Their own private, special refuge.

Shuffling with weariness, he went to the narrow bunk bed and sat down, put the lantern on a box table, and fingered the woolen blanket Annalie had thoughtfully left for him. Composed of many gaily-colored knitted squares stitched together, it was one she herself had made from the left over yarn.

Sighing, he lay back and unfolded the blanket over himself. The storm screamed and crashed, washing over the roof like waves pounding against an exposed headland. Some of the shingle edges flapped, threatening to tear away completely. Beneath the roar of the wind came the faint plink-plinking of dripping water. Lerant sat up and peered into the long, flickering shadows cast into the attic corners where numerous boxes and chests were stored. Yes, there was a puddle forming over there, endangering their contents.

Cursing, he got up, took the bucket left as a chamber pot and placed it to catch the leak. When the storm was over he'd need to go up there and repair that roof. When the storm was over, he'd have an entire garrison to rebuild . . . . He stood a moment, looking around the attic, hunting for more leaks and found none. He and Parlan had done a good job repairing the roof during Lerant's last leave here, but the winter storms always took their toll. Unbidden, the memory came to him as fresh as if it had happened today.

'Are you sure you're well enough?' Lerant's hand had grasped Parlan's wrist firmly, helping him up onto the sunlit shingles.

Mischievous brown eyes danced with laughter and Parlan grinned, heaving himself up to sit by Lerant. 'Quit trying to take all the glory, Engineer, and hand me that hammer.'

'You've had glory enough, Trooper!' Lerant returned, his smile forced as the bandaging about Parlan's shoulder reminded him of how close it had been. 'You're wounds are still healing. You sit there and watch me work this time.'

The memory winked out and grief cut at Lerant's heart. There were other memories, too. How many times had they had played together in this attic? Played at soldiers, sparring with mock wooden swords, laughing as one or the other fell down, pretended to be wounded. Or dying heroically. They used to make a competition of it, to see who could come up with the most dramatic, gory ending. Then, as adults, this was the place they'd come to discuss Myrrgha army's offer of employment when they no longer had the coal mines to provide work.

Tears flooded Lerant's eyes and he crumpled to sit on one of the boxes, covering his face with his hands as he fought the sobs rising in his chest. 'I miss you so much, Parlan!'

Something scraped and thumped across the floorboards, something very heavy. Wiping his eyes, Lerant looked up and blinked in disbelief. His iron-bound storage chest, the one in which he'd placed the few personal possessions he couldn't store at the garrison, was dragging itself ponderously toward him. It stopped then began again, grating closer, leaving scrapes in the soft timber.

'It's drafty up here, the wind is moving it,' he told himself.

There came faint, gently mocking laughter, filling his mind and sounding hauntingly like Parlan. *'Always an explanation, m'Lord Logic!'*

Lerant shook his head, his eyes gritty with exhaustion. Indulging himself and answering as if Parlan were present, he replied, 'I'm out on my feet and now I'm imaging I can hear you, brother. I don't believe in spirits, Parlan, let alone chests moving all by themselves. There must be a cause, I'll find it. Maybe the explosion at the garrison unsettled the cottage foundations and now the storm is rattling it further.'

He got to his feet, collected the lantern and went to the chest, kneeling beside it. But instead of checking the slope of the floor, his hands moved of their own volition to lift the iron clasps. He threw back the lid, held the lantern high. Golden light glowed from within and Lerant gaped a moment before realizing with delight that it was the inlaid sunburst on the hilt of his sword and scabbard throwing the lantern-light back at him. He'd almost forgotten he'd had it delivered here. He reached in and closed his right fist about the familiar hilt. It was like renewing acquaintance with a much-valued old friend. The sword called to his aching heart, soothing away the pangs of grief.

He lifted it out, scabbard and all, cradled it in his arms and carried it back to the bunk. He lay down with it against his side atop the blanket as had been his habit in Khengha. His thoughts turned to his days on the open tierdrun—the freedom, the honest work, and the beauty of the clear sky arching high over endless rolling, grassy hills. Maybe he should go back there, leave Rogha.

And what about the slaves in the mine? His imaginary Parlan demanded abruptly.

'Someone else could take over there easily enough,' he answered, glad there was no one present to see him talking aloud to himself. 'Mancire would choose the right man.'

So, you're going to leave Annalie and the boys?

'I'm not sure they'll want me here after I give m'Connor over to the Inquisitor. And I can't bear seeing Alarn looking at me like I'm the enemy. Maybe I should go back to Khengha. I'm an engineer there, not a slave overseer. I help people, not put chains on them.'

In Khengha you build bridges and railways that bring Myrrghin soldiers to enslave more people. That's no solution. It's time you faced up to what you're really doing, Little Brother, and who you're really helping. Parlan paused then added grimly, *Remember the monster slargapent? Someone wants you dead. Be careful.*

'A Seeker.' Again Lerant heard Fallon's sure warning. Then overlaid with that memory came another much more recent. He was bent over m'Connor, tending that mauled leg in the shadows by the river. *'You! Mi serraga!'*

He'd tried to block m'Connor's cry forever from his thoughts, finding something about it more unsettling than all the rest of the day's horror. He sat up suddenly and the sword glowed as the lantern-light reached it again. Determinedly, Lerant concentrated instead on the problem of Alarn and Annalie's coldness toward him. If only he could've talked Zaraxan out of coming up here . . . .

'You could try contacting the bastard again tomorrow,' Parlan's voice suggested in his tired mind. *Maybe you can tell him m'Connor is talking in fever, he should wait, there might be news.*

'It's worth a try,' Lerant agreed doubtfully. 'But he really hates m'Connor.'

'M'Connor is a good man,' Parlan said with soft insistence. *'Listen to him.'*

Lerant sighed. 'He's a Weaver, Parlan. You need to be careful listening to them; they can make you think whatever they want.'

'He's collared, and they don't,' Parlan rejected flatly.

'If I get that information, maybe Zaraxan will settle for sending m'Connor to the mines,' Lerant said aloud, trying to convince himself. Satisfied that he had at least some strategy at last, he snuffed out the lantern flame and lay back, in the darkness, listening to the storm and feeling the sword warm at his side. 'I'll wear you tomorrow for luck,' he decided, giving the blade an affectionate pat.

'Wear it <u>always</u>,' Parlan urged. *'It will keep you safe.'*

Lerant rolled onto his side and drew the soft blanket warmly about him, the memory of his brother somehow a comfort now rather than an agony. Parlan had loved this place so much. He could almost believe he was still here. Sleep came, gently soothing away his fears.

CHAPTER NINETEEN

Pallid daylight filtered through m'Connor's eyelids, distant unfamiliar sounds echoed, and dull pain vied for his attention. Above it all, one sense took precedence the chill, smooth touch of metal about his throat. Evil, cloying methirri, stealing away his link with the world of the spirit, with his Weaving, with the singing of life about him . . . . The enemy had made him one of them, enslaving his soul as much as his body; trapped inside the cursed Severing-Stone collar.

Again.

So much for his promise to Rhyssa and Flynn. He hoped they'd understand he'd had no choice. He couldn't have turned away and let the little brothers die.

He knew he'd had fever-dreams and he struggled to remember as much of them as possible. It was an Akkarra teaching that in dreams the soul could wander from the body to Travel the paths of time, see the future or the past without aid. Vital markers could be uncovered from such visions. But only the Magi were truly adept at unraveling them.

Gathering his will, he opened his eyes, expecting to find Myrrghin guards watching him. Surprised, craning to look around, he saw he was alone in what was an incredibly comfortable prison. He was warmly covered in a soft bed in a room adorned with a child's playthings. Cheerful blue and gold patterned curtains about a box-paned window opposite the foot of the bed failed to improve the bleakness of a wintry Roghin morning. A more encouraging, warming, glow radiated from the hearth on the left-hand wall. Flames crackled and spat greedily, devouring peat clods on a bed of purple-red coals. On the right hand side of the bed stood a small table and chair. An open door allowed a limited view of an empty hallway. He could hear soldiers' voices down the hall somewhere.

He wondered at his chances of escape but the reminder provided by the pain of his wounds brought that to a standstill. Quilted blankets hid most of his body, but his injured leg, propped high with pillows, was splinted and wrapped in thick, white bandaging. He'd certainly been given gentle, thorough treatment. Yes, they needed Weavers alive, but this . . . this was unnecessary to that purpose. Then he recalled the Myrrghin Commander's attempts at confusing him, the comfortable surrounds must have been part of the plan. The Key had saved him there, but what else had he said while he was fevered?

'Oh, you're awake!' a child's voice announced from the doorway. He looked up to find Alarn shyly smiling at him. 'I'll go tell Mama.'

Soon, the boy's mother entered carrying a laden breakfast tray. She wore a black skirt embroidered with delicate but realistically vivid flowers that also adorned the neck of her white blouse. Raven-dark curls escaped the no nonsense twisted knot of hair held at the back of her head by a long wooden pin. The lines about her eyes showed the weariness of one who had had much labor and little sleep. 'How are you feeling this morning?' she asked and put the tray atop the bedside table.

'Much better than last night.' He had to clear his throat to get rid of its rusty, hoarse sound. 'No doubt because of your care. My thanks.'

'You've been here since the night before last,' she corrected, turning to him with a shy smile the mirror of her son's. 'You slept yesterday all through.'

'Oh.' He must have been bad to lose track of an entire day and night. The Pig-man would be on his way. Vaguely, he remembered being fed water, tended when he needed to piss . . . But he thought one of the soldiers had done that. 'You have your children to run after without me keeping you busy,' he said.

'I owe you my sons' lives, Captain m'Connor. Tending your wounds is the least I can do . . . for the moment.'

Surprised, m'Connor recognized the offer of an ally. 'You have my name,' he said. 'I hope I didn't give away too much else while I was fevered?'

'You said little. An informant had already given the Commander your name.' She looked him straight in the eye with pleasing frankness and added with a certain satisfaction, 'You only told him enough to prove that you had no knowledge of the planned attack on Rogha Fortress.'

'I did?' Again, he couldn't prevent surprise escaping him. Relieved surprise. 'I tried to explain before, out in the street, but he'd have none of it. How—?'

'The circumstances of your telling left no room for doubt,' she explained as she turned and began briskly arranging things on the tray.

Trying to remember, m'Connor frowned, and then caught her meaning. 'You mean I told him when I was ill?'

'When he had you believing he was a friend. Yes.' She turned back to him, the lines of her face hard with a disgust that eased as she added, 'Some good came of it.'

His chest tightened as again, he heard Lerant lending him hope at last, but alarming him, too. *Lying. We found him, but Bren is hurt, dying.* Closing a fist about the bed clothes, he muttered, 'I hope the bastard never knows what it's like to lose a brother who's half of you.'

'He knows. He knew how it would hit you, and he did it precisely because of that,' she said bitterly. Gathering herself, she added softly, 'He is my late husband's brother. He was an orphan, an adopted brother and twice as dear for that.'

Wincing inwardly, m'Connor looked up at her. 'I'm sorry. I didn't know.'

'Believe me, I've had words with him about what he did.' Annalie paused, her lips pressed together in stern disapproval, one hand smoothing her skirts. 'It's no excuse, but he was trying to protect the boys and me. We're all he has left of Parlan.'

They'll never come here. They'll never find you. I promise. M'Connor could still see Flynn's trusting eyes and hear himself pledging protection he might have betrayed. Any man would do anything to protect a family he loved. Grudgingly, he admitted, 'I can't say as how I can claim I would've done it differently to save my own family.'

'It was wrong. Causing another to suffer in your place is never an answer.'

'True,' m'Connor agreed, knowing of the Empathic Atonement common among his own people. Somewhere, at some point,

377

someone had to have the courage to break the vicious circle and make a stand; saving your own family while destroying another's was no solution.

'Well,' he said, letting out a breath, 'maybe now he'll listen when I tell him who the real killers are.' A flashing image of those tiny bodies, sprawled broken in the rain-lashed street, made his stomach knot. If their deaths didn't fulfill its purpose, the Methaggar and its agents would strike again.

'You know?' Annalie asked keenly.

'I can point him in the right direction, but I'm not certain of names.'

A shadow in the doorway caught his eye, an achingly familiar profile. But it wasn't Bren, it couldn't be Bren. Rather it was the huge, red-haired, red-bearded militia guard glowering at him with evident dislike. So, not everyone was convinced.

His nurse took the covers from dishes, freeing several delicious aromas, and m'Connor's empty stomach grabbed at him. 'I hope you like eggs and tirrin fish, Captain m'Connor,' she said, looking pleased as she caught him hungrily staring at the food.

'I do, thank you,' he said, remembering the raw, sometimes stinking meat of Myrrgha dungeon. 'Please, call me Taran. And you are?'

'Annalie Hollin.'

She gathered spare pillows and propped him up. She placed the tray on his lap and he reached for the butter knife with his left hand. There was a loud click from the doorway and he looked up to find Karatin with the barrel of his musket aimed directly at him. 'Don't try anythin',' the red-bearded trooper growled.

'Afraid he might hop across the room and strangle you with the sheets?' Annalie demanded, making m'Connor splutter a laugh choked by his first mouthful. 'Eat,' she ordered, turning to him with a Healer's gentle sternness.

Karatin's ruddy face reddened further at the reprimand. 'Take care, Good Missus Hollin, don't get too close.' She blinked in pure disbelief, then, shaking her head, pulled a chair as close to the bed as possible and sat down.

M'Connor had to force himself to chew rather than gulping it all, it was so delicious and he was starving. There was honey, hot spiced bread, cheese and tea, as well. Not much later, with the meal finished, he leaned back. For a moment, he thought of hiding the knife under the covers, but no chance of that with that great red-headed hawk watching him from the doorway.

'I feel much better with some food under my belt. My thanks,' he said, adding with ironic humor as he remembered he was naked. 'Or wherever. Tell me, how is your youngest boy this morning?'

She moved the tray to the bedside table then sat down again. 'He's back to normal, busy teasing his brother. His name is Parlan, after his father.'

'A coal miner?' m'Connor guessed.

'Originally, yes. Both brothers were. Until Myrrgha brought slaves to work the mines and forced our men to become soldiers.' Noticing that her hands were tightly clenched, she very deliberately unfolded her fingers and relaxed them again. 'My husband was killed at Tol Eabah.'

'I'm sorry. I wish he could have come home to you all. I saw the massacre of Tol Eabah,' he added in solemn remembrance.

'You were there?' she asked sharply, and he felt the flicker of hope, the yearning that perhaps she might win another moment of her husband's life, another memory.

'I didn't step foot on the place, but I and several others were Linked with the mind of the Magi there.'

'So many have died since Myrrgha invaded your land,' she remarked sadly, sounding puzzlingly accepting of his description of Traveling. But then, she was a Healer, and most Healers had some small experience of it, at least.

But he could sense her disappointment at his being unable to tell her more of the battle in which her husband had died. He tried to recapture the fleeting glimpse he'd had of the beach where Myrrghin troopers were running closer, and was able to tell her truthfully, 'Some of the soldiers were reluctant to slaughter the defenseless, then . . . the Methaggars drove them to it.'

'Yes,' Annalie said softly, 'Parlan spoke of something, a dark will, shadowed sorcerers, filling the men with blood-lust. He practiced shutting them out, resisting their will. He said it was murder and he would not be part of it.'

'I wish I could have met him,' m'Connor said.

'He was a good man, a gentle man,' Annalie whispered with pride.

'Sympathy for us will get you killed, and fast,' m'Connor warned, making it apparent he meant her. She felt indebted to him, a dangerous sentiment in the circumstances. She only lifted her head and gave him a grave smile that said she understood the risks as well as her husband had done and she would not change her path anymore than had he.

She told him seriously, 'We knew he was in terrible danger. Kerell finally succeeded in getting him a transfer for home.' She braced herself and looked away down at the fire, before she could explain, 'But the order arrived a day too late.'

'Damn,' m'Connor murmured, knowing that kind of agony all too well. 'Kerell?'

'Kerell Lerant. He's the last of his tribe. The Hollins respected that and had him retain his name when they adopted him. He became a military engineer in Khengha, while Parlan saw some of the worst of the slaughters. First it broke his heart, and then it killed him.'

'He's finished with eatin'!' Karatin said, startling them as he tugged a set of heavy manacles and chain from a clip at his belt and tossed them with a loud rattle-clank onto the floor by the bed. 'Chain him. The Commander's orders.'

Annalie turned to confront the big man. 'I will not! As if that collar isn't bad enough!'

'Then I'll do it,' Karatin decided. 'He's lucky t' have that bed if y'ask me.' He checked the hammer wasn't cocked, preparing to put the musket carefully down, and leave it behind to be certain he didn't give m'Connor any opportunity.

'Stay away from him!' Annalie snapped and picked up the iron manacles as distastefully as if they were vermin.

'Where is Commander Lerant?' m'Connor asked, silently agreeing with Karatin that it was a wonder they'd left him the bed. Annalie, by contrast, steamed with anger. Lerant was in for a tongue-lashing from his marriage-sister.

'He went out earlier to contact Myrrgha over Rogha City Connector-stone again. I don't know what happened when he spoke to them yesterday, but he came home in a foul mood. And he won't be any happier when I tell him what I think of this!' She grimaced disgust as she locked one metal cuff of the manacles shut about the bruised wrist of his good arm and secured the other to the bed frame.

'I'm glad to see you looking better, Captain m'Connor. You'll need your strength to finish answering my questions.' Lerant stood framed in the doorway, his gray eyes stern beneath his methirri band. He'd removed his black cloak and folded it over his arm. He wasn't wearing armor but did have sword and pistol at his hips.

'How is Bren?' m'Connor said, calmly looking up at him, 'Still dying?'

'This isn't paint,' Lerant said tersely, touching his fingers to one of the red stains splattered over his black jacket sleeve. 'I did what I had to.' Turning to Annalie he said, 'I must ask you to leave us now, please.'

'This is my home!' Annalie rebuked. 'I will stay where I wish!'

'Right now this room is the Myrrghin Garrison,' he countered, firm and heavyhearted. 'Do I need to ask Karatin to escort you out?'

Annalie stood with smooth dignity, her hands straightening the folds of her skirt. She looked coolly up at Lerant and said, 'We'll discuss this later.' That was a warning m'Connor knew well, the female promise that this battle was far from over.

She strode from the room and Karatin shut the door at her back. Lerant hung his cloak on the back of the chair by the fire and brushed melting snow from it. M'Connor recognized a stall for time when he saw it and decided to get in the first blow.

'You're in trouble,' he observed.

'Not nearly as much as you are,' Lerant stated flatly, turning to face him. 'Zaraxan's already on his way here. He wants to collect you personally.'

'I'm not surprised,' m'Connor returned, shooting down the hoped-for shock tactic. It was always going to be the inevitable outcome of Zaraxan learning of his capture. But, little wonder

Lerant had thrown everything he had at m'Connor the other night. 'We're old friends. Though it is a long way to come and he does hate being uncomfortable.'

'You've brought Rogha to his attention,' Lerant said with harsh accusation. 'The people here might yet pay with their lives.'

'That wasn't my intent,' m'Connor replied seriously, knowing The Inquisitor's unbridled hatred of him made him a danger to all within reach.

'Then what was your intent, m'Connor? Why are you here?'

'I was invited. Rogha wants to help us.' He met Lerant's gaze and added with sorrowful grimness, 'Or it did.'

Holding that gaze, noting more than the blue-gray eyes and the lightly tanned fair complexion, m'Connor remembered Lerant was no Myrrghinner. He flinched as some memory tried to force its way around the methirri collar. He rubbed at his temple, scrubbing away the pain and then wincing anew as his fingers found a swollen bruise and cut.

'Are you all right?' Lerant asked, taking a pace closer to the bed.

'What?' m'Connor blinked up at him, catching genuine concern. 'Nothing. Just a reminder I should learn to duck faster.'

Lerant stepped back, saying,'They walloped you a good crack to the skull.'

'Lucky it's solid rock, then,' m'Connor muttered, silently admitting he did suddenly feel dizzy. 'Or so they tell me.' He could swear he'd felt a brief thrumming of power as Lerant had leaned over him, aiding m'Connor's extra sense despite the methirri's shadow for a fleeting moment. He held the man's gaze intently, and his collar tingled about his throat, blocking him from picking up all kinds of information from what must be an unusually vibrant, open Ea.

Lerant crossed to the hearth and picked up the iron poker. Prodding at the fire, he built it to a new blaze, apparently needing the warmth after enduring the bitter cold outside. M'Connor couldn't help but flinch, feeling the skin of his back and shoulders twitching in reflexive memory of terrible agony. Forcing control, he managed to stop himself from cowering back against the headboard, as far away as he could get from the thing, as, still holding the poker, Lerant turned back to him. That glowing red and white iron tip carried nightmares that made m'Connor's mouth dry and his heart race.

Reading his prisoner's reaction, Lerant's mouth twisted in utter revulsion. 'Inquisition animals!' he snarled. He threw the poker back into the grate and moved away from the fire. 'Believe me, m'Connor, if I could lose you in the paperwork, I would.'

He'd seen the scars, m'Connor realized, wondering what it must be like to be in those boots right now, stuck between the proverbial rock and a hard place. 'There's no way of stopping this now without paying the price in blood. Hand me over fast and get the madman away from your family.'

'Not so easy. There's a whole city out there who want to kill you. Just tell me, damn it! He'll torture it out of you anyway! Tell me, I protect you, protect Rogha—'

'You ask me to murder all my people to save yours!'

'Zaraxan will force you to betray them! We can't save your people but we can save mine! You got yourself into this saving my nephews. Now you want to see them dead?' Points of red showed high on Lerant's cheeks. It shamed him to strike so low.

M'Connor didn't give a damn. 'There's a boy just like Alarn waiting for me at home! And many other families relying on me to keep them safe!'

'Well, maybe you should've thought of that before you went into the river, idiot!' Lerant yelled.

'I suppose you'd have just stood there and let them drown!'

'You're a damn fine swimmer, m'Connor. I'd have gone under, too.'

'Which would make you the bigger idiot!'

Lerant drew a slow breath, calming down. 'Bigger idiot, yes. More selfless, no. I'd only have lost my life.'

A point.

'I only hoped there might be some way out for us both,' Lerant admitted, all the anger gone. 'I'd like to see you go home, m'Connor, a fair return for you giving me back my nephews. The boy at home is your son?'

'No,' m'Connor said, surprised by the sentiment despite it being, as Lerant said, a fair return. 'He's Bren's youngest brother.'

'We have that much in common, then,' Lerant said, but his heart wasn't in it. 'Trying to protect the families our brothers trusted to us.'

'Yes.' M'Connor hesitated a moment before saying, 'Annalie told me about your brother and Tol Eabah. I'm sorry.'

Lerant nodded brisk acceptance and seemed to opt to continue the personal conversation to avoid going back to the other. 'Parlan's family adopted me when he was seven and I was five, or so. He found me, somehow, starving, alone, up in the mountains in a snowstorm.' He shook his head in affectionate pride, then, smiling, added, 'Instant big brother, and a bossy one, too.'

'Still am.'

M'Connor started a little; sure he'd heard someone else speak as clearly as if he were standing right beside him. What was going on here? The voice had identified itself as Lerant's brother. Was Parlan's Ea still holding to his family? Or was it simply Lerant broadcasting a memory? Regardless, how was m'Connor picking up on it?

Apparently, Lerant had heard, too, though no doubt he'd tell himself it was a memory rather than believing in—as these people called them, 'ghosts'. Whatever he thought, he began to smile, slow and sad, but it was like the sun emerging from behind a dark cloud, changing his face entirely and making him look much younger.

'We grew up together in this house,' he murmured in soft reflection, 'played games in the streets out there with the other children, Annalie among them.' He went to the window to draw back the curtains and peer out at a white wall of whirling snow. When next he spoke, his tone was dull with defeat. 'Zaraxan will tear any answers he wants from you when his warship gets here in a day or two.' He moved away from the window to glance from one injury to the next along the length of his prisoner's battered body, settling on the slave collar. When his gaze reached m'Connor's bruised face, his gray eyes locked on, full of desperate hope.

'Look, m'Connor,' he said, 'I respect what you did at the river. Parla would be dead if you hadn't gone after him and probably Alarn, too. Thanks are all I can give you. I wish it was more. I don't want to see you hurt. If you tell me instead, there's at least some chance the army can claim you as its prisoner rather than the Inquisition taking you. General Rusark will order Zaraxan to back off.'

'Back off of me, maybe, but not you,' m'Connor warned, unsurprised at the officer's hoped-for evasion of the ugliest of all duties. 'Do you really believe Myrrghin soldiers will come all the way up here just to protect Rogha from Zaraxan? And even if so, they couldn't protect you or your family.' Holding Lerant's troubled gaze, he added, 'We all have to accept the consequences of our choices, Lerant.'

'I can only try,' he returned with great weariness, a weariness that to m'Connor seemed to echo and echo down through the ages.

'It's all any of us can do,' m'Connor said in heavy agreement. 'The fact is I can't answer you because I don't *know*. The memory's gone, taken from me when I was Keyed by the Magi and the Akkarra before I set out to come here.'

Lerant slumped to sit on the chair by the bed and run a hand through his already bedraggled hair. 'The Inquisitors must know about these Keys?' he asked.

'Zaraxan's been working on trying to break them for years. He never will.'

'So, they'll just keep on questioning you until you're dead.'

'Yes.' M'Connor hoped he sounded as casual about it as he intended over his body's terrified whimpering in the back of his mind. He could still smell his own flesh burning in his nostrils. 'They killed two more of our Weavers that way not long ago.'

'Your Brother, Bren?' Lerant asked, his gaze going evasively to the floor.

'No.' Suddenly angry again at that reminder, m'Connor replied coldly. 'Worse. They used him as an experiment and left him nothing more than an empty shell. His body breathes but he isn't there anymore to recognize us.'

Lerant let out a wordless sound of pure frustration and paced back to the window. He stood watching the pristine whiteness of the snow-mantle growing ever deeper on the windowpane edges. More and more flakes alighted ever so gently to blend invisibly with its soft blanket. M'Connor knew just what he was thinking—The seasons would go on turning, running one into the other, never altering their rhythm, uncaring how much butchery humankind inflicted on itself. Neither of them said anything, and the long silence was filled only by the roaring of the gale and the opposing cheerful crackling of the fire.

'I'd feel a lot better if I could get my hands on the bastards who killed those children,' m'Connor declared, finally. 'Doesn't look like I'll get the chance any time soon, but I can give you a good idea where to start hunting.' Lerant turned to him and he indicated his bandaged shoulder. 'The same mongrels did this, and tried to kill you all to cover it, because they'd failed to kill me inside The Fortress explosion.'

Lerant frowned. 'I thought you said the sorcerer came for you because of your . . . .' He seemed unable to say the word.

'Weaving,' m'Connor said firmly, 'I used it to help me find Parla in the river.'

'The men said their methirri warned them though I felt nothing,' Lerant admitted. 'They talk about being afraid a Weaver can turn them into pillars of fire, or something. There are several of our soldiers in Lellgha who've given sworn evidence of such.'

'Well, then, they shouldn't be there, butchering and raping my people!' m'Connor spat, the terrible images of Lellgha City burning through him again. 'Your Emperor's Methaggars and their Seekers do worse!'

'The Emperor knows nothing of any so-called Methaggar Seekers!' Lerant countered, 'If such creatures exist, they're a Magi created illusion!'

'What? You think that Illker out there was illusion? An *illusion* and its puppets tried to hack me to pieces? Why would a Magi—illusion or no—attack me rather than rescue me?'

Lerant stood glaring and m'Connor glared back, waiting an answer.

'That thing out in the street was a rogue creature, insane, beyond control,' Lerant reasoned. 'It was too far gone to know better than to attack indiscriminately.'

M'Connor gaped at him in disbelief. 'It came straight at me and paralyzed the rest of you first to do it! You saw that.'

'It could have had its orders mixed up if it was driven insane by something messing with its mind. Like maybe a *Keying* gone wrong?' Lerant threw back at him.

So that was the kind of excuses the enemy were making for themselves. Searching deep in the man's eyes, m'Connor sought the truth he was sure was buried there. Lerant turned away.

'Is the truth so painful?' m'Connor asked softly. 'Will you deny it like this the next time a Methaggar kills your people? It'll be too late to admit the truth when there are no Weavers left alive to help you stop them.' Back turned to him, Lerant simply heaved a weary sigh. 'I need to know exactly what happened after I was knocked unconscious out there the other night,' m'Connor said. 'I can't understand why any of us are still alive.'

Lerant sat down again. 'One of them drove a spear through your shoulder and another was set to pound your skull to mash. Lucky for you the thing in charge of them ran off and they all dropped dead.'

M'Connor frowned. That didn't make sense. 'An Illker doesn't give up without a fight. Did any of your men say anything or manage to move, even a little?'

Lerant avoided his gaze but admitted, 'Frozen like statues, the lot of us.'

There was a moment's silence as m'Connor continued to hunt for an answer and Lerant grudgingly added, 'I might have yelled and little Alarn came leaping over the garden wall and clouted the spearman on the back of the head with a great hunk of rock. The lad has more courage than any . . .'

'Alarn?' m'Connor interrupted in surprise. 'The boy could still move?'

Lerant shrugged. 'I dropped him over the wall where he was shielded.'

'It doesn't work that way,' m'Connor told him. 'I don't understand it, but I'm glad we won.' He leaned back into the pillows, his shoulder and leg thudding at him with hammer blows.

'Whatever that thing was, it didn't scare Alarn,' Lerant said with a flicker of a proud smile, 'He's more afraid of what his mother will say if she finds out.'

M'Connor snorted tiredly. 'Remind me to thank the boy. He has the makings of a fine man.'

'He reminds me of his father,' Lerant agreed quietly, then asked, 'Is there anything we could do to defend ourselves if this thing attacks again?'

'Yes,' m'Connor said with fresh annoyance, 'take this collar off me. A fully armed Weaver might drive it off.' Lerant gave him an equally annoyed look and m'Connor sighed. 'Practice Shielding. The stronger the mind, the greater the chance of resistance. Better, find the person who Summoned the Illker and kill him. You could start with the bastard who wanted to save you the effort and make me talk himself.'

'Jarrod?' Lerant said. 'He was certainly hungry enough to get his hands on you. Could he have . . . . ?'

'More than likely. I felt the stain of Methaggar about him.'

Lerant shook his head, dismissing that idea. 'There's no hard evidence or I'd arrest him.'

'Someone gave you information that told you where to find me?'

Lerant hunted inside a pocket beneath his tunic. 'A note, left at the Fortress. I still have it. Here, take a look.' Opening a little notepad, he unfolded a piece of paper so deeply creased and stained that it was falling apart.

M'Connor had to strain against the wrist manacle, but he took it carefully and read, his lips curling in disgust. 'It's Videer's hand, just as I thought. He's the only person in the city who'd know to have me followed.'

'Videer? The owner of the silverware store by the docks?' When M'Connor nodded, Lerant spluttered, 'But . . . He's one of the most prosperous men in all Rogha!'

'Right. That only added to my suspicion.' Lerant cocked an eyebrow at him and m'Connor explained, 'Videer is the avaricious kind and not one for moral causes yet he claimed to want to help my people.'

'Why would Videer want to trap you?'

M'Connor eyed him wearily. 'Do you think there's a Roghinner left alive today who still has any sympathy for Lellgha?'

Lerant gave him a sour look and tilted his head toward the door through which Annalie had departed. 'Oh, you'd be surprised. The one solid piece of evidence implicates Videer. I'll go speak with him before the trail grows colder.'

'If he leads you to Jarrod you'll need to be very careful,' m'Connor warned, 'A methirri band won't be any protection against a Methaggar, quite the opposite.'

'I'll take all the men I can spare with me.' Lerant picked up his cloak from the back of the chair and paused to ask, 'Would Jarrod risk trying to make another move against you here?'

M'Connor shook his head. 'He'll have orders to wait for Zaraxan to come for me.'

'He has no way of knowing Zaraxan's on his way here,' Lerant disputed irritably.

'He knows. He knows Zaraxan would have his guts if he robbed him of his prize. You forgot this.' He reached up to hand over the note-page.

'Thanks,' Lerant said as he accepted it and admitted slowly, 'I tried telling the bastard that you were dying and he might save himself the trouble of coming up here. He had a fit, says your dead body would be the first of many in Rogha.'

M'Connor shrugged one shoulder. 'He's pissed that he needs to keep Weavers alive.'

'You destroyed his Citadel,' Lerant said, matter-of-fact. He began carefully folding Videer's note and tucking it back into the little notepad. 'You made him look very bad.'

'I planned to kill him. I failed.'

'He says you killed his fiancée.'

M'Connor started a little in surprise, and then realized that naturally, Zaraxan would have played that card for all the sympathy he could milk from it. 'She's dead?' he said carefully neutral. 'She'd have been his ticket to aristocratic standing.'

'The Lord Inquisitor spoke . . . at length . . . 'about his great loss.'

M'Connor wondered what Rhyssa would say to that. 'I'm sure he did.'

'You find that amusing?'

'I had the opportunity to meet the Lady in question,' m'Connor said. 'She despised the man. She would have considered death a better fate.'

Lerant eyed him for a long moment, his expression sharply knowing. Somehow he'd guessed the truth and that unsettled m'Connor. It was vital to Rhyssa's and her family's safety that Zaraxan went on believing her dead.

Turning the little notepad over and over in his hands, Lerant said, 'You called to Rhyssa repeatedly while you were fevered.'

'Did I?' m'Connor managed a casual tone despite his suddenly dry mouth. 'Wishful thinking. She was very beautiful.'

'So Zaraxan said. You don't have a lady waiting for you back home, m'Connor?'

He didn't answer, his expression, he hoped, clearly telling Lerant to leave it alone.

Lerant watched him another moment, then said, 'Zaraxan is a sadistic bastard. I'm glad the Lady escaped him . . . no matter how she did it.' He looked long and hard into m'Connor's eyes and added, 'I never heard you mention her name and I'll tell Annalie she didn't, either. And as for this . . .'

He held up the little notebook. Pulling Videer's note free and shoving it into his pocket, he turned and tossed the notepad into the fire. He watched it burn then turned back and said, 'You were raving so incoherently and in such a mix of strange languages . . .' He shrugged. '. . . I couldn't understand a word of it.'

'Thank you,' m'Connor said intently, deeply grateful and more surprised than ever. That name would have bought a great deal of favor for Lerant at the highest levels of power.

'No sense giving the mongrel any more excuse to be pissed at you,' Lerant said.

M'Connor snorted sour amusement but never broke the eye contact that he hoped told the man just how much the erasure of that information meant to him.

Lerant sighed heavily and looked away. 'If I get anything out of Jarrod or Videer I'll let you know.' He paused at the door, though he didn't look back. 'The wrist manacle and chain is Zaraxan's direct order. Anyone else and I'd tell 'em to shove it.'

Setting his jaw over the pain of shoulder and leg, m'Connor gritted out, 'Believe me, I know what it's like to deal with the madman.'

Looking back at m'Connor one final time before he left, Lerant added, 'I'll let Annalie know you need more of those pain medicines.'

She appeared shortly after, carrying another tray which she put down to give m'Connor a quick check. Satisfied, she held out a small glass tumbler full of some dark brown liquid. 'Drink this down. It'll help keep back infection and ease the pain.'

M'Connor reached for it but was brought up short by the manacle. Annalie scowled and moved closer to put the tumbler in his grasp. 'Where does he think you could get to on that leg?'

M'Connor downed the medicine in one quick swallow. He looked up at her as he gave back the glass. 'He's trying his best to protect you . . . and even me in a way. He's . . . *forgotten* anything I said while I was fevered. Zaraxan will never know.'

Annalie only snorted dismissal and tugged angrily at the pillows, making room for him to lie down again. 'Yes, he asked me to forget it, too. I told him, loudly, that I'd never heard it in the first place! I wasn't the one taking notes!'

M'Connor lifted an eyebrow, smiling with some bemusement. 'A little blue covered paper pad?'

She straightened. 'You saw it? You were aware of what he was doing?'

'No.' He met her eyes. 'Only now, when he threw it in the fire.'

Her mouth opened a little in surprise, but quickly recovering her annoyed expression, she said, 'Good for him, but not before time!'

M'Connor yawned hugely. Whatever was in that stuff it certainly worked fast.

'Parlan always said Kerell would wake up to the truth some day.' Annalie spoke as if to herself, her voice dropping to grim reflection. 'I just wish my husband hadn't had to die to make it happen.'

Chapter Twenty

Lerant sighed in frustration and ran a hand over the ridiculous, tattered plumes on the helm clasped under his arm. Why couldn't it ever be easy?

They'd searched all morning and found nothing. Lerant had left some men digging through the rubble, searching for survivors. How many might yet be found alive if he deployed all his limited resources there rather than wasting time looking for murderers who had probably long since left the city? He swept his gaze around the silversmith's display shelves, hoping for inspiration. They'd had no luck tracking Jarrod, though someone had reported he seemed to come and go here regularly, often using a back exit.

'There now, you see, Commander?' Videer waved an arm toward the emptied cabinets. 'Nothing. As I said, you will find no illegalities on my premises. Smuggling, indeed! As if such a prosperous merchant as I need resort to such desperate means!' He patted at the fine gold-thread embossed, blue silk short cloak about his rounded shoulders. Gold and silver rings glittered on his fleshy fingers. Except for a chubby appearance of over-indulgence, Videer's narrow-eyed and self-satisfied expression reminded Lerant of nothing so much as a sewer rat. 'Our wares are locally crafted and fetch a tidy profit. Famous in Myrrgha now, you know . . . . despite their near-crippling tariffs on Roghinner goods.'

Lerant started along with Videer at a resounding crash from the rear of the store as some shelving toppled. Videer whirled about and hurried to collect and examine the fallen goods, Lerant following at his heels. 'Kindly call off your troopers before they do further damage!'

Ignoring him, he put his helm down atop the cabinet and helped Wilgar tap along the exposed wall, searching for possible hidden cubbyholes.

'You may be sure I will send to your High Command about this outrageous treatment!' Videer's snarl absurdly and suddenly twisted into a smile as a bell tinkled and the elegantly lead-paned glass front door popped open. A well-dressed couple entered, the man taking the woman's elbow. She adjusted a brocaded, velvet cloak and shook snow from its folds. Both stared as they saw the troopers, and the flustered silversmith hurried to reassure them that it was business as usual despite the mayhem.

'I fear the good Commander is overwrought,' he said, ushering the gentleman and his lady into a quieter corner even as both of their heads turned to keep track of Lerant. 'Distressed by the loss of his garrison.'

'No doubt,' the man nodded, removing fur-lined gloves. 'Terrible thing, so many deaths. But this . . . ! This ransacking of your property, Videer! It's unpardonable!'

'True. Rest assured I will give full report to Myrrghin Military Command and demand the man be demoted, at the least.' He leaned closer and said conspiratorially yet deliberately loud enough to be overheard across the room, 'Perhaps that sorcerer-slave prisoner has warped the poor Commander's mind? They can easily do such things I hear tell, collared or no, if you are with them long enough.'

'Truly?' the lady gave Lerant a startled glance.

Overhearing as he was intended to, Lerant gave Videer a glare. The remark had hit a sore spot. He'd just been thinking the same thing himself. Whatever could have possessed him to so readily believe the Weaver's theories? M'Connor could only be seeking some vengeance against Videer, surely. The man had admitted to being Keyed, his memory affected—wasn't it possible the Magi witches could somehow have set him to destroy Myrrgha Fortress without his awareness?

Something that would make the Weaver more a victim than any of them and more dangerous, unpredictable; maybe Lerant should have left more than Karatin on guard at the cottage. He rubbed a hand over his eyes and resisted the urge to immediately run back to the cottage. Videer was watching him, smirking, aware his remark had done its work. The silversmith was so cursedly smug, so slyly sure of himself that Lerant wanted to throw him through the nearest window.

He'd given Videer the story of suspected smuggling rather than level charges of involvement in mass murder and high treason. The man was indignant about Myrrghin taxes, mentioned them repeatedly . . . could that be a motive? And just where did the funds arise to purchase so much raw silver? That wasn't mined locally but came from the Smoking Mountains. Shipping costs alone would be exorbitant. Lerant itched to prove something, anything, even a minor infraction, if only to have the satisfaction of wiping that smirk from Videer's eyes.

'What's through there?' Lerant asked, noticing a curtain screened side door, a narrow slit in the wall behind the main countertop. He moved toward it and Videer's scowl deepened, silk rustling as he hurried after Lerant, leaving his customers.

'My sleeping quarters. I work long, late hours, Commander. Sometimes I find myself too weary, the hour too close to dawn, to bother journeying home. I snatch what sleep I can before the new day.'

Lerant nodded irritable dismissal of the man's whining. He pushed aside the screen and noted disappointedly that it was indeed no more than a small alcove containing a single untidy bunk and a wash stand and looking glass in one corner. He was about to turn away and re-enter the shop proper when a sudden chill enveloped him. Like a dousing of snow sliding from gable-tops, it shocked and froze him from head to toe.

'Where's that draft coming from?' he asked suspiciously, trying not to let his teeth chatter. 'It's freezing in here.'

'Freezing?' Videer sounded genuinely surprised. 'Why, this is a particularly warm room. It backs on to the smelter next door, as you are well aware. If anything, it grows too hot in here at times.' He squinted up at Lerant. 'Ahh, you're fevered! That explains your irrational behavior.'

Despite fighting against it, Lerant shivered harder, his skin crawling, and the fine hair bristling at the nape of his neck. Deliberately, he turned back to the storefront, but . . . . Again, he swung about, eyes narrowed as he peered into the shadowy interior of the small room. The cold remained, unnatural, unsettling, and completely alien.

Bracing himself against terrors that had lingered since childhood, Lerant forced himself to approach the exact spot from which he could feel that awful chill emanating. There. The center of floor bordered by the foot of the bed and the washstand wall.

'Come, Commander, some wine to warm you?' Videer sounded unnerved, anxious. 'Bad enough your troops continue to overturn my goods, but now you invade my personal quarters?'

Lerant turned and gave him a shrewd, calculating regard. Videer flinched and avoided his eyes. He was definitely hiding something here. Smuggled silver?

Something evil. Instinct warned, using Parlan's familiar voice.

Suddenly, he could feel it, a waiting abomination, it set all Lerant's nerve-ends to screaming at him to run, leave this room, and never return. Flesh tingling, ears ringing, pulse pounding, Lerant gripped hard at the sunburst sword-hilt, knuckles white, jaw set.

In his clenched fist the sword felt warm, seeming to echo his anger. Through the curtained doorway he could see a small brazier, its coals glowing red. The sunburst scabbard of his sword reflected the firelight in a coruscation of red rays. Something was here. Something very wrong. But where? Closing his eyes, Lerant followed the feeling closer. He took a pace, another, and stepped deeper into icy filth.

Suddenly, the chill fled, warm air and comfort, reassurance rising about him. Time stood still, all was deathly silent. A figure was forming in the corner by the wash-basin, a drift of smoke. It swirled once, became more substantial, hovered, rose higher, then suddenly seemed to merge with the glass of the looking-mirror. There it began to take on definite features.

All the blood drained in a rush from Lerant's face, his knees wobbled and he grabbed at the door frame for support.

Parlan!

There, smiling wryly back at him was the familiar face of his dead brother, brown eyes wide with delighted surprise at his own cleverness. Parlan's face glowed with a golden, incandescent light it had never possessed in life. But the smile faded, the expression becoming solemn, foreboding. Parlan's arm emerged like watery fog from the glass. Palm turned down, he pointed an urgent forefinger. Stabbing again, he repeated the gesture, indicating the floor at Lerant's feet.

Your proof is there! Be careful! Parlan whispered in his mind.

Licking dry lips with an equally dry tongue, Lerant glanced at the irritable silversmith, and realized he had not seen the spirit. Lerant looked back, found the glass wavering like the surface of a pool. He was dizzy, seeing things, imagining help he desperately wished could be there. Annalie was right, he hadn't had enough sleep. He was starting to hallucinate. It didn't help when he thought he heard the echo of a too familiar snort of laughter followed immediately by a repeated, stern, *Be careful, m'Lord Logic!*

Videer was muttering about him being out of his head. Lerant might agree, but could feel only the hollow place in his heart, the renewed surge of grief. The wash-basin suddenly wobbled on its narrow stand, toppled and crashed to the floor, spilling water across Lerant's boots. Startled, he jumped back. The liquid flowed down slope slightly and leaked into a gap Lerant hadn't noticed before, the edge to a hidden trapdoor? He stamped hard and the floor echoed hollowly. There had to be a cavern, or room beneath.

'Wilgar!' Lerant called, already dropping to his knees to better examine the planking. 'In here! I've found something!'

Alarn brought little Parla in to meet the man who had saved him from the river and urged him toward m'Connor's side with gentle prompting. The toddler, his round, blue eyes full of curiosity, closed his chubby fingers about m'Connor's big hand in a well-rehearsed move, and said a solemn, 'Thank you f'saving me, Cap'n.' He frowned from the bruise to the small mountain of splints and bandaging about m'Connor's broken leg and asked, 'Does it hurt much?'

'No. I'm glad to see you back to playing with your brother,' m'Connor replied. After they'd left, he met Annalie's proud but amused gaze and smiled. Even knowing what he faced as a result, he wouldn't have changed events at the river. His rescue of little Parla had borne witness to a compassionate, life-embracing spirit that gave enduring hope against the darkness of men like Zaraxan.

'Commander Lerant wants to know if the slarga venom has done much damage to the muscle strength of your good leg,' she commented. 'He doesn't want Zaraxan coming here to the house.'

'Nor do I. I'll be able to walk.'

'No, you will not.'

'Don't worry Missus, I'll carry him again if I have to, anythin' to keep you and the boys safe.' Karatin added in a mumble over his meal, 'Shouldn't've been here in the first place, if you ask me.' The guard's bushy red beard was stained with the gravy dripping from the bread he'd sopped over his dinner plate. He'd carried a kitchen chair to the door and now sat astride it, pleased that Annalie had prepared a meal for him as well as for m'Connor.

She pulled up the bottom of the blankets to test m'Connor's good foot. Resting the palm of her hand against his bare sole, she said, 'Push back as hard as you can.'

M'Connor obeyed her instructions, keeping part of his attention on Karatin, desperate for a more private moment when he could ask her what she was up to. He didn't need Empathy to know she'd lied about Lerant wanting the leg checked.

'Look at this one! It's the best! But it got broke,' little Parla cried, and m'Connor saw the small boy hurrying to Karatin's side to display yet another toy.

M'Connor leaned closer to Annalie as she checked the muscles of his forearm. 'What are you up to?' he asked in an urgent whisper. 'You can't—'

'Mama!' Parla called, rushing to her side. 'Mister Kara fixed it! Look!'

'That's wonderful, darling,' she said, quickly looking at the toy. 'Go show Alarn.' Parla rushed away, giggling happily, and Annalie looked back to m'Connor, both of them aware Karatin was now watching them again. The opportunity was gone.

'You're a very fit man, Captain,' Annalie said with a knowing lift of an eyebrow, 'There will be no problems when you need to leave. Meantime, get some rest.'

'Won't be doin' much of that after the Inquisition gets yer!' Karatin snorted.

Annalie sighed heavily and, crossing the room, snatched the plate from his hands. M'Connor wished the guard would disappear so he could get some answers. Could she somehow have contacted Gerion? Surely, not. She didn't know where he was, and he couldn't even try to walk back to the city in this storm.

'I have some errands to attend to,' Annalie told him meaningfully, 'but I'll be back before it's too late. It's important that you try to sleep while you can.'

Grimly determined, Lerant studied the coffin-length opening in Videer's floorboards. Bright light from the room above illuminated only the first two stone steps leading down into a pit of blackness. The shadows writhed, the darkness as impenetrable, thick and threatening as the depths of a storm-cloud. 'We'll need lanterns,' he said, holding hard to his anger to stifle the fear. He glared at Videer who stood slightly to one side, face deathly white and jaw set with unconcealed malice. A different man entirely to the gentleman he played in the store.

Lerant drew a deep breath, curled his fingers about the Sunburst sword-hilt, and in a ringing of steel drew it from its sunburst scabbard.

Videer flinched and cowered back, looking as if he wished he could fade into the wall. Wilgar, Howlett, Sandor and Blakan followed Lerant's example, drawing their own weapons. In the heat of their arguments over politics, Parlan had often reminded Lerant he'd never faced combat or had to lead men to their deaths. Lerant didn't want any of these men to die and the sudden terrible responsibility of it made him hesitate. There was something lurking, waiting down there, waiting its chance to kill.

'There's only room enough to go single file,' he said, wondering at the calm of his own voice and thinking, not good tactics. It's the perfect set-up for a trap. He cast a sharp glare at Videer, and said, 'You go first.'

He lifted the sword threateningly and its reflected red light washed over Videer's furtive eyes. Abruptly the merchant looked very unsure and the terror pressing on all their minds eased. Raising his chin in ineffectual haughtiness, Videer stepped forward and climbed down onto the first of the narrow, spiraling stairs in their rock-hewn tunnel.

Following, Lerant told his men, 'It's a steep descent; you'll need one hand for balance against the wall. Howlett, you take the rear and carry the lantern. The rest of you keep your weapons at the ready, and check your methirri bands!'

'Sir!' they chorused, remarkably willing to trust him with their lives. One by one they entered the spiraling stairwell. Boot-steps echoed hollowly, water trickled somewhere, and harsh, rasping breaths filled the emptiness. There was not another sound. Stealthy, patient silence surrounded them.

The rock wall was rough and slick with patches of moisture, the air impossibly cold. The men's nervous breathing puffed visibly about them, like steam from a Myrrghin engine. Down they went, ever deeper into the bowels of the earth. Lantern light floated on before them in a gradually fading circle of pale yellow, faintly illuminating some kind of chamber at the bottom of the stairs. A long way down, a lethal drop. The stairs continued to twist about, spiraling first out then in, and Lerant thought he caught sight of some kind of upraised stone table centered on a dais below.

Childhood terrors reached for him, awful memories bordered in blood. His left hand shook as it touched the stone wall, seeking balance. Another step down. Videer's back gleamed blue-gold silk, leading the way, the balding spot on his scalp pink and gleaming with sweat. The stairway gave a sudden sharp turn inward and Videer disappeared. Lerant expected to find him again around the blind curve, but the silversmith was gone, seemingly vanished into thin air.

Lerant swore foully and at his back Wilgar asked, 'What?'

Before he could answer, there came an ominous rumbling from deep beneath the rock steps. Peering down into the gloom, they all saw it, felt it. The darkness about the chamber floor had thickened and was roiling like a heaving sea of ugly, sooty smoke. It engulfed the foot of the stairway and began climbing, slow but sure as the tide. With it arose an ever-louder, moaning wail. A thousand agonized, dying voices, screaming, tearing, lunging, raced ahead of the shadow.

Icy air blasted upward, flinging hair back from their faces, grabbing at tunics and jerkins. The lantern light snuffed out. Blackness took them, pressing down, suffocating. Only the glowing methirri bands proved the troopers were still there. Above the deafening screams clearly came the sound of the trapdoor slamming shut overhead. Lerant felt the panicked urge to run and knew his men were feeling it too.

'Hold!' he roared over the unnatural, howling wind. Red-gold light suddenly blazed forth. He squinted, amazed, as his sword flared fierce and bright, living fire, driving back the dark. The wind died out and the smoking fog recoiled as if mortally wounded. Lerant looked hard at the glowing sword, immensely relieved and unnerved all at once.

'Where did you find that light?' Wilgar asked, coming closer, his voice hoarse, badly shaken. Then he gasped, 'The sword!'

'Yes.' Lerant's own voice sounded unfamiliar to his ears, steady, sure, unafraid, and much older. As if he'd done this a thousand times before. 'There's sorcery here all right. Look.'

He held the flickering blade high and gold light washed over the slick, wet rock-face. Shimmering there, etched like a tangled mass of cobwebs, was a blood-red, shifting, crawling network of shamanic symbols. From further up the stairs came a cry of pure relief as the lantern light re-ignited, apparently of its own accord.

Lerant and Wilgar glanced backward and the secret of Videer's sudden disappearance was revealed. The silversmith hadn't stepped forward and down with the curve of the wall but rather out into what moments before had appeared to be empty air. Videer had found solid wooden stairs, invisible before.

But the true illusion had been the steps Lerant and his men had been set to follow. Shock coursed through him as, suddenly dizzy, he looked down into the nothingness where he'd been about to put his foot. The false stone steps hugging the rock wall wavered in his sight, as insubstantial as shimmering heat above a desert sand dune. He turned his head, and found the real stairs led to the left, out from the wall. Solidly timbered, they gave access to the chamber below; rising from its flagstone floor to join with the stone section one step lower and to Lerant's left. A few more panicked steps in the darkness as they obeyed his order and followed along the wall and he'd have led all his men to their deaths.

Fury raged through him.

These lives are in my care! he challenged, silent, vehement, a warning to the darkness.

As if responding to his murderous mood, the sword flared brighter in response. Its clean, gold light burned defiantly against the crimson murk seething across the chamber below. There, Videer stood leering up at them. His narrow eyes were dark, glittering slits, and his lips drawn back in an animal twist of vile hatred. Like the faces of the men the Illker killed, Lerant realized.

'Follow me,' he said, suddenly feeling an urgent need to hurry. Where was Jarrod?

In a thunder of boot-heels over timber, they charged as quickly as they dared down the remaining stairs and out onto the level footing of the flagstone floor. Videer stood unmoving before the onslaught of their anger as they circled him, weapons ready, eyes searching the gloom for accomplices.

Oval-shaped and larger than the store-front above, the chamber disappeared into shadowed caverns at the rear, bordered on one side by a row of sandstone steps leading up to what was indeed an altar. Long, red smears trailed down its front surface, and atop it gleamed a neatly ordered series of silver knives. Every blade was marked with a grinning deaths-head.

Lerant took a pace toward it and Videer suddenly lunged at him, a dagger flashing in his fist. As impossibly fast, the Sunburst sword blade came up, blocking the downward thrust of the barbed knife. Steel met steel in a tremendous, ringing shock coursing up Lerant's arm. An eruption of jagged white light from about the blades blinded him and he turned about, squinting and blinking, and expecting Videer to come at him again.

His gaze cleared and he saw the silversmith collapsed in a shuddering, moaning, disheveled heap close by Lerant's feet. Videer cried like a frightened child as the troopers surrounded him. Thrown across the floor by the jolt of Lerant's sword, his dagger had fallen against the dais steps. Speechless, Lerant studied his own blade. No longer shining, it was plain, ordinary steel, unmarked by blood. The sullen, crimson murk that had surrounded the altar had vanished in that blinding explosion of white light. Plain, homely lantern-light filled the chamber and somehow made its horror even harder to grasp.

'Did you wound him?' Lerant asked, turning to Wilgar.

'None of us touched him,' the old Second said, and flicked an annoyed glance at the sobbing merchant. Wilgar frowned suspiciously at his surrounds. 'What is this place?

'A shaman's lair,' Lerant answered coldly, 'for the plying of so-called sorcery.' He scowled up at the stained altar. 'Supposed power paid for with human blood.'

His troopers stood about him, white-faced and shaken. Time to command.

'I'll examine those knives,' he said, forcing down the sickness in his stomach. 'I want to collect all the evidence I can. Wilgar you keep an eye on this . . . thing.' Videer was still sniffling and crying. 'Howlett, take a look back there and see if there's anything stored further back in the cavern. Sandor, you take the other side. Blakan, go on up and open that trapdoor, we need some fresh air. Then stay there and guard it.'

They saluted and dispersed. Lerant looked down at the silversmith. 'As for you, Videer,' he said, 'you'll have a civil trial with the Archman and the people of Rogha as your judge. The penalty for murder is death!'

Videer propped himself on one elbow and lifted the other sleeve to wipe his nose. Blood-shot, hate-filled eyes regarded Lerant. 'Traitor!' he snarled. 'The penalty for high treason is also death, and for you the inquisitors will make it slow and lingering.'

'Treason?' Growling angrily, Wilgar grabbed a fistful of silk and hauled the man to his feet. 'What do you mean?'

Videer's cheek twitched and he cast a nervous glance around the chamber. Smiling and dropping his voice to a secretive whisper he said, 'Myrrgha has—'

Wilgar grunted with sudden strain and took a stumbling step forward, still clutching to the silversmith. Had Videer called his dagger back and wounded the old soldier? But, no, it still lay where it had fallen at the foot of the altar.

'Are you all right?'Lerant asked, taking the old Second's arm. The muscles were trembling, as if holding a heavy weight.

'He's dead.' Wilgar said. He opened his fist, let go his grip and let Videer's corpse thud to the stone floor.

Lerant took a moment to examine it. There wasn't a mark on the body. 'Poison?' he asked, looking up at his aged Second.

Wilgar sighed heavily, sounding very tired. 'I don't know. Sorcery, more like. I doubt he was the Master here. Someone else was using him.'

'That's what m'Connor said, but—'

'Commander!' Howlett called suddenly from the rear of the altar. He sounded stunned, sickened. 'Over here. Look at this!'

M'Connor woke, startled by a loud clang from the direction of the doorway to see Karatin sprawled unmoving on the floor. He hoped to find Marc had felled the guard, but the collar and his common sense killed that desire. If his friend had been here he would have made himself known. He struggled to sit upright, his muscles trembling with pain and his body's surging readiness to fight. He drew a deep breath and prepared to roll out of the bed, where he could at least use his good leg and the limited reach of his chained arm in a fight.

'Don't move!' he heard Annalie snap.

He squinted toward the doorway to find her frowning at him, then assured he was staying put, she crouched down to Karatin. She put her fingertips to the pulse in the big man's throat. Her body relaxed its tense stance and she gave a relieved breath. 'Good,' she said with false calm. 'I haven't killed him.'

'What?' m'Connor demanded.

She looked up at him even as her hands found the keys at the giant's belt. 'He's a very big man. I put four times the amount of drugs into his tea that I gave you.'

410

'You knocked him out!?' m'Connor's jaw dropped open, and he wondered if he was still asleep and dreaming.

'Here,' she said, hurrying to the bedside. She crouched down and tried a key in the lock of the chain about m'Connor's wrist. It didn't fit and she reached for another. M'Connor put his hand over hers, stopping her, and she flicked him an irritated, questioning glance.

'Wait,' he said.

'We don't have the time,' she said, pulling her hand free to try the next key.

'Don't,' m'Connor said urgently. 'Have you thought this through? You help me and they'll—'

'Ahh!' she exclaimed as the key turned in the lock and the chain fell free of m'Connor's wrist. 'Done!' She looked up at him, smiling, but her eyes dark with the danger of the moment. She lifted a hand to touch the methirri collar at his throat. 'I'm sorry I have no way to remove this. Refallt is waiting outside for us. You won't have to walk far to his sleigh.'

'The risk for you all is great,' he objected.

'I'm getting the boys out of here. We just happen to be taking you with us. Parlan and I planned this months ago, during his last leave home, when we found out Kerell was trying to get him stationed at Rogha Garrison.' She sighed impatiently. 'Come on!'

'You had this planned . . . ?'

'Yes. Now, hurry and get dressed. Alarn!' she called, looking back to the door. The boy, who must have been waiting in the hall, appeared immediately, a great bundle of clothing in his arms forcing him to go slowly, peering around the pile. 'Put them down there, please,' Annalie instructed, waving a hand at the footlocker.

Alarn obeyed, and then looked up at m'Connor, to flash a great, excited grin. 'We're getting you away from them!'

M'Connor could see so much of Flynn in that smile that his chest tightened. He turned and gave Annalie a stern regard; 'You can't travel with me, I'll draw deadly trouble.'

'You can't walk. You come with us. It's the only way out for you.' She turned again to Alarn. 'Go get the crutches for me, please. Oh, and the overcoat and gloves.' Alarn turned and left at a run.

M'Connor rubbed his face in frustration. 'My friends will have moved their ship further up coast. Another Illker or worse, might attack and I can't Weave. There's nowhere to go.'

'Another Illker?' she asked, frowning and halting her sorting of clothing.

'It channels Shadow to paralyze then kill. It tried it on our way here to the house. We should all be dead.'

'But you're not,' Annalie reminded him stubbornly after a moment's startled pause. 'All the more reason why we should get out now. It must know, or will soon find out, where you are.'

'Sheer luck saved us the other night. I can't risk you and the boys like that.'

'There must be some way to fight these things, other than Weaving?' she asked

'There are some things, yes, but we don't have them. Daylight will protect us from Illkers if not Seekers, but when night falls we're sitting targets,' m'Connor told her.

'But we'll find your ship by then,' Alarn said.

Annalie held up a flannel-lined woolen over-shirt. 'This should keep you warm. Come on.' She pulled back the blankets.

'Without that ship, we're stuck out in the dark, without protection,' he warned.

'Papa found us a place. We'll be safe,' Alarn assured, laying the gloves on the bedside table. 'I've been there. It's really good.'

'It's an old mine and well supplied,' Annalie explained, giving him an impatient frown as she stood holding the shirt, waiting for him to duck his head to put it on.

'A mine?' m'Connor considered. 'That could work. The enemy might not sense us there.'

'If your ship is gone, we can be there by nightfall.' Annalie didn't wait for his co-operation but pulled the shirt on over his head. 'We're dead if we stay here.'

M'Connor pushed his head through, wrestling with the sleeve, and looked up at her. '*I'm* dead. If you gave Zaraxan what he wants—'

'Zaraxan will never have you!' Annalie spat. '*Never!*'

Her expression was so like Rhyssa's defiance it hurt to see it and he had to suppress a selfish desire to ignore all else, forget the danger to his new friends, and just take his chance now to get home. 'He won't stop hunting for me,' he reminded her.

'Good,' she said. 'Then we'll still have a chance to kill the bastard.'

He allowed her to help him get his arm into the sleeve. 'You're giving up your home, you're—'

'My sons are my home.' She stopped to look direct into his eyes, and despite her commanding manner he would swear there were tears filming her gaze. 'Do you understand what you gave me? You could have been on your way home right now if you hadn't turned back to save them. Do you seriously expect me to walk out of here and leave you to Zaraxan? It's not happening.

413

Now shut up and get moving.' She gripped his good arm firmly, pulling him slowly forward. 'Come on, carefully now, sit on the side of the bed.'

Awkwardly, painfully, m'Connor obeyed and with some difficulty, they got him sitting up and pulled on the specially prepared trousers. 'Alarn,' Annalie asked, 'can you get his boot, please? It's over by the hearth. Sit there and rest a moment. I have a surprise for you.'

She left the room and Alarn took her place, clutching m'Connor's rather worse-for-wear boot. 'Papa says that where your people live there are lots of parrots and beaches and jungle,' he said excitedly. 'And it's warm there all year round?'

'Where we live now, it is. It snows where I come from,' m'Connor said distractedly, watching the hallway. 'Do you know when your uncle is due back?'

Alarn shrugged. 'He said he had a lot of work to do and he might miss dinner.'

Sitting there, looking toward the doorway, m'Connor could plainly see Karatin sprawled unconscious on the floor. He didn't like the man, but he wouldn't wish Zaraxan on anyone. Then there was Lerant, a man m'Connor had come to respect and like as much as he disagreed with him. He'd be squarely in Zaraxan's sight, the focus of insane fury.

Annalie appeared, pressing a package to her chest with her right arm, her left hand guiding Parla at her side. M'Connor flinched at the sight of the toddler, not wanting to imagine the tiny child caught in a Seeker's attack. She must have read his expression. As he met her gaze he saw the same fear, a dark terror. But her mouth set, grimly determined. She put the package onto the table and lifted Parla up onto the bed beside m'Connor and the toddler gave him a happy smile as m'Connor wrapped his free arm about him. She collected the package again and unfolded the leather wrapping from about it to reveal its contents.

'You found my Stinger pistol!' he exclaimed, relieved and elated. Made of Akkarra wood it was resistant to Shadow-spells. It would only stun, but that could nonetheless make all the difference in a fight.

'Holster, darts and all,' she said, fighting a pleased smile for his reaction. 'I've known Kerell since we were children, and we all played in this house. He has no hiding places here that I don't know about.' She pulled something from a pocket of her coat. 'I almost forgot this.' She unfolded the leather that had surrounded the bundle and he saw it had the shape of a boot. 'You'll need some protection for your broken foot. Refallt made a leather slip-over for it.' She lay that on the pillows, then held up a long belt to which his Stinger holster was attached. 'I altered the holster so it will go round your waist. You can't put pressure on your wounded shoulder.'

She stood and leaned over him to circle the belt about his waist, settling the holster and gun at his left hip. She'd certainly prepared well, altering the trouser leg, too, fashioning it with an extra piece of material that had loops and buttons that closed about the bulky splint.

'Thank you,' m'Connor said sincerely. 'I'd never have thought of all this. Do we have any other weapons? We should take Karatin's musket.'

She stood back and checked him over, nodding satisfaction. 'Refallt and I will be armed. I have a crossbow waiting in the sleigh, and he has his hunting gun and knife. We'll put Karatin's musket and ammunition under cover with you in the peat sled at the back. No one will know you're there.'

'What about Lerant? He'll take the blame—and him,' m'Connor said and looked toward the unconscious trooper.

Annalie sighed heavily and looked down at the rolled sock in her hands. 'Parlan and I tried again and again to open Kerell's eyes to the reality of Myrrgha. He wouldn't listen and we didn't dare tell him of our plans. It broke Parlan's heart that we might have to disappear away from him, unannounced. Kerell has made his choice. He had no compunction about handing you over. We need to move fast to be safe by nightfall.' Annalie turned to Alarn. 'Help me get his boot on him.' The boy crouched down, eager to obey, but waiting until his mother finished with the warm sock first.

As they were helping get him ready, an idea blossomed in m'Connor's thoughts. If this escape failed, he could pretend Annalie and the boys were his prisoner-hostages. Still, no one was going to believe he'd managed to escape alone. They must leave as little incriminating evidence as possible. 'We have my Stinger,' he told Annalie. 'If we leave one of the darts by Karatin, and you stick a pin in him or something . . . .'

She looked up at him with an impatient frown until she realized what he was saying. 'Good idea. I wish I'd thought of it. I could have saved myself the trouble and shot him with it instead. Zaraxan might think Hidden Ones are responsible.'

'Nothing will stop him taking his disappointment out on someone,' m'Connor said.

'But he won't blame Karatin,' Alarn caught on, flashing a great grin up at his little brother in a way that said he, too, remembered just how kind the big man had been to him. Too, m'Connor had been told of the trooper's heroics in rescuing injured children from the burning rubble of the Assembly Hall. He deserved better than to be shot on the spot by an enraged Zaraxan. This could protect Lerant, a little, too.

'Right. Best get rid of that tea mug,' m'Connor pointed out.

Looking back toward the door where the mug still lay where it had fallen from Karatin's hand, complete with an accusing trail of spilled tea, Annalie groaned and put a hand to her forehead. 'Yes. Of course. I almost forgot.'

'I'll get it,' Alarn said and ran off to collect it.

'Here,' Annalie called to him and threw an m'Connor's old tattered shirt toward him, 'Mop up that spilled tea for me too, please, Alarn.'

'Yes, Mama,' he said obediently. Finishing his work, he touched a gentle hand to Karatin's shoulder and looked up at Annalie, to ask, 'He'll be all right, won't he, Mama?'

'Yes, darling. He's only asleep and he'll wake up soon just fine,' she assured, a little distracted as she struggled to get the leather protector to stay put about m'Connor's damaged foot. When she'd finished, m'Connor removed one of the darts from its sleeve and carefully gave it over.

'It has a safety cap,' he told her, adding with a wry smile, 'otherwise I'd probably have put myself to sleep out there on the bridge.'

Alarn giggled at that comment as he put the tea mug down on the bedside table. Picking up her medicine bag as well, Annalie went to Karatin's side. She took the dart, and very carefully removed the cap. Even more gingerly, she jabbed the dart into a roll of bandaging, emptying its contents to be sure that no close examination would reveal it hadn't been used. Looking relieved to have it safe to handle at last, she stooped down closer to Karatin.

'I can't say as he doesn't deserve this after all the horrible things he said,' she muttered and bending still lower, she jabbed the empty dart hard into Karatin's cheek, leaving a tiny trickle of blood.

'That should do it,' m'Connor told Annalie as she dropped the dart on the tiled floor near Karatin's head. With some difficulty and all the help m'Connor could give, they finally secured his boot and finished with coat and gloves.

'Now,' Annalie instructed, 'stand up very slowly and keep your weight on me. You'll be dizzy for a moment.'

'I know,' he told her dryly. He'd been hurt and gone through this routine more times than he cared to recall. Cautiously, he obeyed her, hoping he wouldn't fall flat on his face. He closed his eyes against the vertigo. 'I'm ready,' he said a moment later, opening his eyes. 'I'll take that now, thanks, Alarn.' He reached out his good hand and took one crutch, wedging it under his armpit. There was no point in taking the other when his left arm remained strapped to his chest under the loose shirt. That would be a major problem in a fight, but it couldn't be helped.

He hobbled on through the hallway and into the kitchen, Parla asking excited questions about where they were going, and hugging his soft toy to his chest. 'It'll be fun, Peko!' he told the little rabbit. 'Tell him we're going on a sail boat!' Alarn suggested, playing the big brother and holding Parla's free hand.

M'Connor plainly heard Annalie make a strangled sound of someone so tense they'd forgotten to breathe. They halted at the external kitchen door, and m'Connor took advantage of the bracing wall to move his hand from the crutch to touch Annalie's arm with some measure of comfort and sympathy. He knew what it was like to walk away from your home, possibly forever. He, Bren and

Gerion had been dragged in chains as the enemy threw burning fire brands onto the village rooftops. And left m'Connor's father, and many others, dead in the street.

Annalie pushed down on the latch for the last time. A gust of snow-laden air raced inside, as eager to gather the family to the storm's embrace as their home seemed forlornly reluctant to release them. A whirling funnel of stinging sleet spun into the room, tearing at the tablecloth, snatching it up and throwing it to the floor, and slamming the pictures hanging neatly in their frames about the stove.

The winter had won, claiming the house, the home Annalie and her husband had created and loved. Whatever her memories of it, she was not considering them now. 'I'm sorry, Kerell,' she said tightly and taking her sons by the hand, she stepped out into the stormy morning.

M'Connor would have said something if he could think of anything that would fit the occasion, anything that would match the woman's incredible generosity and courage. But he had no breath for words. The muscles in his right arm were threatening to turn completely liquid and give way beneath the weight as he took each hopping, jarring step. His vision blurred in time to the thudding of his heart, the pain in his broken, mauled leg and wounded shoulder tearing through him. He squinted into the whirling snow, relieved beyond measure to see a faint outline of horse and sleigh. Then the old man, Refallt, was at his side.

'Steady, now,' Refallt urged, taking his good arm around his shoulders and m'Connor let his screaming muscles release their hold on the crutch. Alarn took it, looking worriedly up at him. 'Almost there. Another three or four steps. I've got you,' Refallt said.

The sleigh consisted of two sections, driving seat and footboard in front, and the box-shaped sled for cargo with its not much lower walls at the rear. A prepared pile of peat lay on an animal hide spread nearby on the ground, ready to be lifted over m'Connor as concealment. With assistance, he climbed awkwardly in over the lowered, hinged side, lowering himself shakily flat on his back amid the softness and warmth of blankets and furs. The loaded Myrrghin musket lay at his side; Annalie must have relayed it to Refallt when she'd gone for the Stinger gun. She'd kept the powder horn and musket balls with her, knowing it would take two hands to reload the gun.

'Thanks,' he said breathlessly. 'Stop when we reach the crossroads . . . north, and I'll tell you . . . how to get to the ship.'

'The crossroads, north,' she repeated to assure him she'd heard correctly. Then, Refallt lifted the heavy hide cover and peat over m'Connor's hiding place and everything went dark. There was a small hole bored in one side to admit air and a thin beam of weak light. Exhausted, m'Connor closed his eyes and lay back, hoping and praying fervently that there would be no trouble, and soon they'd all be aboard the Kerestra, sailing south.

Sailing home.

The snowstorm had eased slightly by the time the sleigh left the narrow, walled streets and entered the maze of wooden slip-rail pens that made up the stockyards hidden behind the vendors' stalls bordering the market-square. Seated with her sons high beside Refallt on the driver's board, Annalie studied the empty mud-churned yards most with horse stall doors closed. No animal sounds came to her ears and there was no sign of activity. Refallt knew of a postern gate through the town wall, used by herdsmen it was seldom guarded at this late season.

'Stop! Right there!'

Annalie bent and grabbed the crossbow from under the seat. Five rough-faced, raggedly dressed men emerged from hiding to quickly surround the sleigh. All wore swords belted over sheepskin jerkins and coats. One of them also wore a set of knives marked with grinning skulls.

'Jarrod!' Annalie whispered in horror.

She twisted from the waist to loose a bolt at him. It burst into fire and something unseen snatched the weapon from her grasp. It flew to Jarrod's waiting hands and she heard Refallt swear and a dull thump-clink that could only be his gun falling to the cobblestones. They had been disarmed.

Jarrod stepped forward and leered up at her, his eyes twin burning shadows. 'That's no kind o welcome fer yer rescuers. We're here to save you from that murdering Weaver. Now, where is he?'

'Commander! Over here! Look at this!' Howlett sounded sick.

With Wilgar following him, Lerant hurried around the dais into the shadow of the altar block. The young trooper stood staring, white-faced, into a small alcove draped with a red-black Myrrghin flag. A simple wooden table and chair were pushed back against the curve of the rock wall where barrels and weapons were stored. Various parchments and maps cluttered the table's surface and were piled high about its centerpiece, a much larger than usual

Connector Stone. About it shimmered a faint red haze of energy, the like of which Lerant had never seen before. His hand trembling, Howlett handed Lerant one of the parchments. It bore the seal of Myrrghin Military Intelligence.

'There are traces of black-powder in those barrels,' Howlett told him. 'And the drawings on these papers . . . . It's a plan of attack on Rogha Garrison, Sir.'

Wordlessly, Lerant nodded, his gaze fixed on the diagrams. They'd been drawn up in the very precise hand of a Myrrghin engineering officer following protocol to the letter. Lerant could have drawn it in his sleep. This was it; this was what Parlan had tried to tell him. This was what being an engineer who served Myrrgha was really all about . . . .

'Sir,' Howlett's strained voice was barely audible. 'That can't be from Myrrgha Command . . . ?'

Lerant flicked a finger against the paper, the snap loud in the silence. 'It is, Trooper. But this drawing is the Assembly Hall. The children were the primary target. M'Connor was right. The garrison was just a cover.'

'They . . . what? Why?' Howlett's anguished question echoed in the chamber. 'They were only little children . . . .'

'What better way to keep us all loyal to Myrrgha and root out any Hidden Ones before they took any further hold,' Wilgar answered bitterly when Lerant said nothing.

He was too gutted for words. All he could see was m'Connor's face, the shock and sorrow as together, he and Lerant had turned toward the carnage.

'What do we do now, Sir?' Howlett asked, and Lerant realized the young trooper was looking to him for direction. Shouldn't Howlett know the answer to keeping his family alive was to pretend he'd seen nothing? Except if Howlett's child had been old enough to take part in the Harvest pantomime . . . .

'The Inquisitor will be here soon,' Wilgar reminded Lerant grimly.

'We need us much information as we can get before we act,' Lerant decided. 'There's a message waiting on that Connector. It's probably locked, but if I can get round it, we all need to hear this.'

Strength flooding back into his voice, Howlett asked, 'I'll get the men, Sir?'

Lerant nodded and a moment later, with the entire squad gathered, he presented the evidence of Myrrgha's treachery, inwardly flinching as each man came to understand the same horrible new reality.

'This Connector Stone is linked to High Command,' Lerant explained to them and put down the letter on the table beside the oddly threatening-looking Stone. 'It contains a message. If I can reach it, I want you all to hear, I want you all to remember it when the time comes for us to defend Rogha.'

To Lerant's surprise, the hand he reached toward the Connector Stone was steady, sure in its movement. For a moment, he hesitated to push his fingers through the murky red haze about the thing. For insurance, he drew his sword and took hold of the Sunburst hilt with his left hand. Then, he forced his right hand through. He breathed again as it didn't hurt and nor did some creature like that had attacked them the other night, suddenly rouse to protect its masters. He rubbed at the cold surface. Nothing happened. He tried again. Still nothing.

'It doesn't matter,' Wilgar said flatly, holding out the diagrams. 'We have all the evidence we need.'

Again, Lerant saw that neat engineer's hand, condemning Rogha's children as efficiently as he would design a bridge. 'I should have listened to Parlan,' he muttered, leaving his hand resting on the Connector Stone.

'You're listening now,' Wilgar told him.

'Too little, too late,' Lerant said bitterly, half-turning to him and hearing his sword give a musical clink as the blade bumped against the Connector.

'It's never too late,' Wilgar replied firmly, the familiar words sounding so much like Parlan that it threatened to overwhelm him.

Never! Lerant would swear Parlan was there, spitting the word defiantly. His fingers clenched so hard about the Connector that they hurt.

'Sir! Look!' Blakan cried. 'The Connector! It's working!'

An ugly yellow-crimson light leaked from between Lerant's fingers, burning him a little. A familiar, bland voice reverberated about the cavern. Lerant recognized it immediately as General Rusark, a man he'd spent several days with in Myrrgha Palace's War Ministry.

'Good, your success has been confirmed, Jarrod.' Rusark sounded satisfied, complacent. 'Congratulations. Those overly sentimental Roghin citizens who lend aid to our enemies would have no sympathy for dead soldiers, but dead children . . . yes; their deaths will purchase a good deal of hatred for Lellgha. Well done. I will commend your service at the highest levels. Myrrgha Command. Out.'

'Jarrod!' Blakan growled. 'I knew it. I'll kill the little bastard!'

'We'll kill the bastard,' Lerant corrected. 'Myrrgha will never betray us again.'

424

'Us?' Blakan asked and directed his gaze pointedly at the insignia on Lerant's Myrrghin jacket.

'Us,' Lerant confirmed. Slowly, aware every gaze was on him, he reached up to pull off the Myrrghin Commander's insignia from on his chest, something he'd once worn so proudly. Now it was just a damning reminder of how much and how badly he'd failed his brother.

'No!' Wilgar's hand closed around his wrist. 'Leave it!' Lerant stopped, blinking at him. 'We might need an inside man,—sir,' Wilgar told him shrewdly.

Lerant smiled, grim and hard, but feeling it stretch across his face as if he'd forgotten how. 'Right,' he agreed with a short nod.

He turned back to his squad, now his Hidden Ones. 'We're dead men if they find out about us coming down here. We'll work on our story later, but basically, we searched Videer's store while looking for proof to back his loyalty to Myrrgha. He was alive when we left. We don't know what happened later.'

'Sir!'

'For now we get rid of the body, hide all trace that we were down here, and then you all go home. If there's trouble when Zaraxan arrives, get your families and go to the coal mine. If the Inquisitor wants us, he'll get us, but not the way he expects. The former Lellghin slaves might like to join us.'

There was another chorus of 'Yes Sirs!' and Lerant clapped Wilgar on the shoulder. 'I need to get to Annalie. She might have her own plans.'

Wilgar frowned. 'She won't leave m'Connor.'

Lerant noted all the troopers were listening, hanging on every word. 'I know.'

'And he won't go with us,' Blakan said. 'He's a good man,' Howlett added. 'He wouldn't draw danger down on us like that.' Sandor nodded agreement.

'I'll talk to him; see what else we can come up with.' Lerant gave them all a stern regard. 'Which means I might not be back any time soon, Wilgar is in command until then.'

'I'll make sure we all stay low,' Wilgar promised. 'Let's see what we can find in Videer's stables. You can move a lot faster with a good horse.'

CHAPTER TWENTY ONE

'She's gone.'

Lerant knew it even before he pushed down on the front door latch and stepped inside. The house was empty. There was no challenge from Karatin, no small boys running through the living room to greet him, no harried Annalie chasing after and keeping a wary eye on the door. Nothing.

'Annalie!!' he shouted, knowing there'd be no answer and praying she and the boys hadn't been killed. Dropping the helm he was carrying under his arm, and drawing his pistol, he charged through the house into the bedroom hallway and came to a sliding, shocked halt, almost tripping over the big body at his feet.

Karatin. Unconscious.

Lerant glanced up and saw m'Connor's room was empty, the bed linen thrown back, the chain hanging from the bed frame, the manacle lock open. Lerant bent to check Karatin who lay on his side on the floor, but could hear his soft snoring before his fingers found a steady, even pulse. A red dart like those used against Lerant's troopers in the fight against m'Connor lay on the floor not far away. He'd been stunned, then. Hidden Ones? No, they surely were not armed with Stingers. Gerion? More likely.

'Annalie?!' Lerant called again, his hands shaking. Too late. Again. He hadn't been able to save his brother and now he'd lost Parlan's family. But . . . .

He frowned. Why would Gerion want to take a woman and two small boys with him? He'd have enough to do, keeping m'Connor moving. He drew a deep breath, fighting to steady himself and noted Karatin's gun was missing. On m'Connor's bedside table sat a tin tea mug, the one Annalie used for Karatin, not the pretty china one she used when she brought meals to her patient. Lerant picked it up, smelled it and ran his finger around the moisture still clinging to its inside. His gut gone cold, he didn't need the proof he found when he tasted the bitterness of its dregs to know what Annalie had done.

Zaraxan would kill her and the boys both for this.

He sagged heavily down into the chair by m'Connor's bed, Karatin's empty tea mug in his shaking hand. If m'Connor wanted to set up a new Hidden One cell, he should have come here first. 'Damn it!' Lerant threw the mug hard and it struck the water pitcher on the bedside table with a loud clang. The pitcher toppled and fell, the mug rebounded and hit the wall then dropped to join it.

Getting to his feet, Lerant returned to the mud-porch. Kneeling, he pulled out the loose skirting board and slipped his hand inside. He patted around and around but, as he'd suspected, found nothing. He should've realized Annalie would know every last one of the hiding places they'd used as children. She'd taken m'Connor's Stinger gun but had drugged Karatin, not shot him, despite the red mark on the man's face. Elaborate measures taken to make it appear to Zaraxan that Gerion and Hidden Ones had come to m'Connor's rescue.

Lerant needed to do all he could to back that impression. Getting to his feet, he stood thinking a moment. He'd chase after them; there would be tracks here somewhere, but what about Karatin? Returning to his unconscious trooper's side, he stood frowning down at the big man. He'd be left dead meat for the Inquisitor.

Lerant scrubbed a hand over his face and met the methirri band across his brow. He'd dropped his plumed helm back in the living room. He blinked at the mess he'd made with the water pitcher in m'Connor's room, an idea coming to him. At least Annalie had supplied Karatin with the beginnings of a good cover story—Lerant could use one, too. If he made it look as if there'd been a fight with m'Connor's rescuers, made it seem Lerant had returned in time to try to prevent them getting away . . . .

He took out some of his self-annoyance on the bed pillows, tearing them as if they'd been slashed by an errant sword strike. He tipped over the bedside table and turned the footlocker. He hurried back into the living room, shoved some of the furniture on its side, collected his helm and returned to the hall to place it close by Karatin.

'The cup!' he remembered. If he could find the sleep-drug and figure what Annalie had done, the Lord High Inquisitor certainly would. He went back to collect the tin mug and shove it beneath his leather armored breastplate. He'd dump it somewhere out in the street, far from the house. 'Sorry,' he said to the sleeping trooper and bent to grip his solid shoulder. 'Good luck.'

There'd been no tracks on the front porch, and Annalie certainly wouldn't have gone that way. Lerant ran into the kitchen, stopped as he found a pool of melted snow on the kitchen rug. He stooped to study it. Among smaller marks of Annalie's and the boys' footprints was one large boot-print and an odd mark like that of a walking cane or crutch, m'Connor. No one else. Good. He tramped around and around, making a mess of any tracks.

He lifted the door-latch and staggered as icy air snatched at him, reminding him of Videer and that pit of crawling filth. Outside he stood a moment gulping clean, wintry air. Snowflakes brushed his upturned face, cooling the heat of his frantic thoughts.

She couldn't turn to me. She's taken the boys and left her home and didn't dare ask me for help. What have I become?

M'Connor couldn't walk more than a few steps, surely. It took moments to find the remaining piece of the puzzle—Refallt and his sleigh. Returning to his horse, Lerant gathered the reins and vaulted into the saddle. He'd follow the sleigh tracks although he was fairly certain where they'd be heading; there was only one reasonably safe route out of town. But first, he'd make sure the horse destroyed the tracks he'd found and confuse anyone as to how many horsemen had been here.

From the darkness of his hiding-place, m'Connor felt the sleigh's sudden halt. He heard shouts and recognized Jarrod's voice. Refallt jerked at the reins, but m'Connor could hear other men moving, crowding in and grabbing the harness. He couldn't be certain how many attackers he must take out, but Jarrod was the lynch-pin—kill him and the others would weaken. Careful in the confined space, m'Connor shifted and checked the already primed Myrrghin musket. In almost total darkness, he felt around for the catch that would drop the side of the sleigh. He'd need to be fast . . . .

'Drop the reins!' Jarrod ordered. 'Or are ya in a hurry t' die, old man?'

Refallt cursed but must have obeyed as the sleigh steadied and m'Connor heard someone else trying to calm the horse. Jarrod's words were clearer; he must be standing by the drivers-board. 'Now why would anyone be in a hurry when they got such luscious company?' There were more boot-steps dull on the muddy cobblestones as he walked to the rear of the sleigh. 'What happened to yer friend, the filthy, murdering Weaver?'

Finding the latch at last, m'Connor gave it a hard shove and grabbed the musket. Daylight dazzled him, but he need only aim for the blot of shadow standing close, Jarrod. The sleigh side dropped, peat spilled out in a sudden flood, further complicating m'Connor's shot. He fired at the same moment the horse shied away from the thud as the wooden side hit the cobblestones and the shot went wide.

Jarrod cursed foully and jumped back, one of his knives at the ready. M'Connor heaved himself to his feet with a grunt of pain, his hand going to his Stinger, but tangling in the folds of the overcoat. Annalie turned on the seat, ready to give what aid she could, but hindered as she kept an arm about each of her boys. Pulling the gun free, m'Connor lifted it to aim. Its Akkarra-makers had insured it couldn't be affected by human Methaggar Seekers, but it required a reloaded dart for every shot and the Stinger venom had been designed for use on ordinary troopers, not someone like Jarrod. Ironically, m'Connor's methirri slave collar hummed warning in reaction to the Methaggar Lord Sending power and orders to its puppet.

From the corner of his eye, m'Connor saw one man holding Refallt at sword-point. He dared not look away from the more

431

dangerous Jarrod. His broken leg stabbed at him as he twisted, tracking a flash of sudden movement forward on the far side of the sleigh.

'Let him go!' Annalie screamed as another man snatched Parla from her arms.

'Well done, Ferag!' Jarrod's dark eyes glittered as he looked up at m'Connor. 'Drop that gun or we kill the boy!'

Annalie jumped from the driver's board and grabbed for Ferag's arm, using her falling weight to try to break his grip. But the henchman was tall, broad and muscular, and he shook her off. She fell onto the road and his haggard face split with a gapped-toothed laugh. Alarn jumped and attacked in a frenzy of kicking and swinging arms and legs. Ferag stepped quickly back, his laughter stilled. He shifted his grip on Parla, and shoved at Annalie as she got to her feet again, sending both she and Alarn sprawling back against the sleigh.

The horse snorted and tried to bolt. The other men fought to steady it, this time aided by Refallt, who called, 'Whoa, Rae, easy lad!' M'Connor somehow kept his balance, wedged into a corner of the box-like sled and kept the Stinger to the aim.

'Give it up, Weaver, or the boy dies!' The wind blew Ferag's hair back from his eyes as he turned to threaten m'Connor who tensed, expecting the sudden rush of Weaving in answer to his instinctive call, but it was swallowed by the methirri collar's greedy pull. 'Go ahead,' Ferag sneered. 'One shot, slave. Then I snap the runt's neck, and the other boy.'

Cursing, m'Connor hurled the weapon to the ground. Ferag whooped victory and dropped Parla to run round the sleigh and kick the weapon further from m'Connor. Annalie and Alarn hurried to Parla whose coughs were turning to wails of fear. Taking the blanket from the seat, Refallt defied his one remaining guard and climbed down to wrap the warm wool about the boy. Annalie held Parla tight, but her eyes remained fixed on what was happening to m'Connor.

'That's more like it, coward!' Jarrod spat, stepping closer. 'Get down here! This won't take long—'

'Fine by me,' m'Connor interrupted, concentrating as he leaned onto the sleigh wall to take his weight. 'First, you let these people go.'

'No, can't do that.' Jarrod licked his lips with a long, thick tongue. 'Can't deprive 'em of the pleasure of watching you die.'

Refallt and the Hollin family had been herded back against the stable wall on the far side of the sleigh. Two of the men who had been steadying the horse let go to draw swords but remained close. Ferag collected the Myrrghin musket and found Karatin's lead shot and powder under the driver's seat. Quickly, he reloaded the gun and stood close to Jarrod to aim it at m'Connor.

'They won't take you from me again, Weaver,' Jarrod threatened. He put away the plain throwing-knife and pulled out a ritual, sacrificial blade, its silver hilt wrought as a death skull. He turned it to the weak daylight and the skull seemed to grin hungrily, the razor-honed, wickedly curved blade flashing cruel intent. A smaller henchman came around the sleigh to join them, his eyes bright with the lust for blood.

M'Connor flicked a warning glance to Annalie. He knew she'd be looking for any chance to turn the odds, her first priority being to get the boys to safety. With an arm and leg out of action, and the slave collar blocking all his attempts to Weave, m'Connor was at a hopeless disadvantage. Nonetheless, the look he gave Annalie said be ready to run, he'd make a break for them. She gave him a firm nod of understanding.

He bent to pick up the crutch and took the opportunity to push some peat clods into his pocket. He straightened up and hobbled unsteadily down the peat-strewn ramp made by the sleigh side. He groaned and swayed dizzily, half-leaning, half-falling back against the sleigh, making a deliberate, exaggerated show of his weakness and hoping with all he had that Jarrod would take the bait.

'What a pathetic sight.' Jarrod fingered the blade and looked m'Connor over like a butcher displeased with the animal brought to him for slaughter. 'The cripple can't even stand!' Malicious inspiration lit his blank eyes with a chill, midnight gleam. 'You'd like me to let your friends go, wouldn't you, snake-belly?' M'Connor nodded obediently, head and eyes lowered. 'Speak up!' Jarrod took a pace closer, continually toying with the knife. "Don't forget yer manners.'

'Please, Master,' m'Connor said in the placating tone he and Bren had perfected against their guards in the slave pens, 'I beg you. Allow my friends their freedom.'

'Oh, nicely done! You learn obedience. Soon, you'll beg me to let you die!' He waved the knife point at m'Connor's stomach, then lower. 'Got your leg all mangled playin' the hero, didn't ya? Tell y' what, hero, show me you can walk and I'll let 'em go.' He turned, looking for a suitable marker. 'To that old tree there.'

Lifting the knife, Jarrod made a mocking bow along the road toward the tree fifty paces forward of the sleigh. 'Get goin', slave. No falling down or the deal's off. And you won't need that.' He jabbed toward the crutch and the small man came close to snatch it out from under m'Connor's shoulder, chuckling as m'Connor staggered.

'Don't!' Alarn shouted and stepped forward to aid his friend.

'No!' Annalie cried and Refallt pulled Alarn back, turning him away and holding him tight to his side.

Shuffling awkwardly to face forward, m'Connor took the chance to catch Annalie's gaze, willing her to be ready to take her chance to escape when he drew them all away from her. He only needed two steps; he could see the Stinger lying in the snow just forward of the horse.

Annalie returned his look, understanding immediately what he intended. She took the trailing corner of the blanket and flipped it up over her shoulder, ready to run with Parla in her arms. She knew as well as m'Connor that Jarrod's bargain wouldn't be honored and he'd turn on her next. The snow was falling heavily and the daylight fading. At Annalie's back, there was a narrow lane leading into a maze of animal yards and stalls.

Setting himself as best he could, m'Connor took the first step. He gasped and stumbled, a jolt of sheer agony searing through him as his weight briefly came down on his broken foot and leg. He hopped and paused in relief as his good leg came down under him, shaking with the strain. He drew strength from somewhere and took yet another torturous, limping step. This time the pain was much worse and he wavered and sagged to his knee before he realized it.

His captors laughed and began claiming the win, but m'Connor grabbed at the sleigh and heaved himself up. Some of the stitches had come free. Dark blood soaked the thick, white bandaging and trailed down the splints to leave a scarlet trail in the snow. He couldn't hold to consciousness much longer. Pain etched acid into every muscle, his sight tunneling and black around the edges.

He turned his head, looking over the horse's back and found the blur he knew was Annalie, Refallt and Alarn standing against the horse stall wall. Shifting his balance to his good foot, he grabbed the peat clods from his pocket and threw them at the nervous horse's flank. Squealing in fright, the horse bolted, running down the two guards and scattering the rest. With Parla in her arms, and Refallt carrying a struggling Alarn, Annalie disappeared at a run into the gloom of the lane. M'Connor fell heavily, consciousness fading into soft blackness for a moment.

'Ahh, let 'em go!' he groggily heard Jarrod shouting. 'I'll Cloak this place so no one can get in or out. We can take the woman later. It's time to carve a slave, nice and slow.'

'Look!' Ferag snorted and m'Connor got a whiff of foul breath. 'A Weaver! Stranded like a flapping fish.'

'They kick and jerk about when I cut,' Jarrod said, his voice thickening with lust. 'Kierjin, Therast, grab his legs. Ferag, take his shoulders.'

'Should I gag him?' Ferag asked, leaning closer and putting down the gun. 'They yell good and loud when you get started and we don't want those soldiers—'

'No. I like it better this way and the Cloak'll do the rest. Therast, wake him up!'

M'Connor had intended to fall but not as heavily. Nonetheless, he'd succeeded, had them drawn close about him and his friends were free. Too, he'd managed to reach and cover his Stinger. He fumbled one-handed beneath his coat, finding and loading an already uncapped dart.

'This is my best blade, coated with poison that'll keep you awake,' Jarrod said, slurring the words as he squatted close at m'Connor's side. The Methaggar Lord was honing in, taking fuller charge of Jarrod's body, wanting to see what was happening, wanting to share the butchering of a Weaver. 'I'll carve you a piece at a time, and the people here will thank me!'

M'Connor drew the Stinger clear of his coat but his aim at Jarrod was blocked as Therast leaned closer, pushing hard on m'Connor's good knee and laughing in anticipation. A shockingly loud retort of a Myrrghin pistol startled m'Connor. Therast jerked, his laugh becoming a gurgling sigh. Blood gushed from his mouth and he fell, sprawled atop m'Connor who was as surprised as the dead man looked.

Quickly getting to his feet, Jarrod turned toward the sound, his eyes narrowed and flickering with flame-like points. The Methaggar-Link had strengthened, allowing Jarrod to Summon Dark Power. He dropped the knife. His skeletal hands lifted, straining like hounds at the leash, lunging toward someone in the near distance.

Struggling to get out from under the dead man, m'Connor saw a black and red uniformed figure, his stance, his manner familiar. Lerant! With a Myrrghin pistol in his fist, he crouched low beside a winter-gnarled tree near the stockyard fence.

M'Connor kicked the dead body clear and aimed his Stinger at Kierjin. The henchman caught the movement and lifted his sword. M'Connor fired and Kierjin dropped the sword to slap at the dart in his face. He toppled and m'Connor rolled aside to avoid being pinned a second time.

An explosive clap and a searing flash accompanied Jarrod's release of a blue-white thunderbolt. Part of the wooden slip-rail fence behind Lerant disintegrated in a shower of timber shrapnel. Saved by his leather armor, he ducked away then came up on one knee, aiming and firing. Another henchman went down, dropping his sword and collapsing immediately at m'Connor's back, a neat hole bored in his forehead. M'Connor hadn't seen him and would have been skewered by his sword. Dazed, Lerant had managed a near miracle of accurate shooting with a notoriously inaccurate weapon.

Jarrod hurled a second lightning bolt, weaker than the first. It surrounded Lerant's weapon hand with a pulsing, burning orb of extreme heat. He cried out and dropped the gun and it steamed and hissed in the snow at his feet. Ferag left off trying to aid his master and came back at m'Connor to kick him hard on the elbow and jolt the Stinger free to slide across the slush-covered road.

'Don't kill him, Ferag!' Jarrod called. 'He's mine! But first, his soldier friend dies.' Apparently no longer having the strength to Summon Fire, Jarrod drew his sword and closed the gap between himself and Lerant.

M'Connor rolled backward and claimed the fallen short-sword. Ferag suddenly didn't care as much for Jarrod's orders as he did for defending himself. He brought his sword blade humming down in a savage arc set to cleave m'Connor's head from his shoulders. Throwing himself aside, m'Connor saw the steel chop into the cobblestones sending mud and stone chips flying, blinding him. He couldn't release his grip on the sword hilt to wipe at his eyes. Damning his useless arm and leg, he rolled over and over, trying to gain distance from Ferag who would be struggling to free the blade stuck fast between the stones. Giving up on that, the man threw himself atop m'Connor.

Powerful fists closed about m'Connor's arm, trying to wrest the sword away from him. M'Connor fought back, slamming his good knee hard into Ferag's stomach and winding him enough to take some of the strength from those grappling fingers. Locked together, they twisted and struggled. Ferag landed a weak kick to the broken leg and m'Connor cried out, but clung desperately to the sword, trying to bring its point up under Ferag's ribs. Using the sound and smell of the man's breath to guide him, he lifted his head and slammed it with a mighty crack against Ferag's forehead. He stunned himself a little, but had the satisfaction of hearing a loud grunt and feeling Ferag collapse limply atop him, unconscious.

Some distance away, he could hear Jarrod shouting taunts and Lerant crying out his own challenges amid the sharp ringing of blade meeting blade. M'Connor sat up, put the sword down, and wiped the mud from his eyes. Ferag was coming round, groggily reaching for a knife at his belt. M'Connor grabbed the sword again and slashed the man's throat open. Then, he turned to check on Lerant.

The Myrrghin officer was trading ferocious, clanging blows with Jarrod, and gaining ground as his military training and the protection afforded by his armor gave him the advantage. But the Methaggar-Link came to Jarrod's aid and a great gust of wind drove Lerant back and slammed him up against the slip-railed fence. Lerant's sword lowered unsteadily and, winded and gasping, he shook his head. Jarrod's voice changed to something barely human, a guttural snarling and spitting. The Methaggar Lord was now fully locked in.

The wooden fence rails came alive and like giant writhing snakes, waved sinuous lengths about Lerant. At the Methaggar's direction, they gathered and coiled again and again about the man's body. Lerant's armored breastplate began to buckle as the spell crushed and squeezed with slow, lethal, cruelty.

Lerant cried out in terror as much as pain. He twisted and kicked to break free, but the wooden arms only closed all the more securely, bearing down on the ribs beneath armor and flesh. He gasped and strained for breath, his pale face racked with pain and his gray eyes wide with disbelieving horror. His knees sagged, but the demon-driven prison held him upright as his Sunburst sword fell from his numbed hand.

The Methaggar lessened the power enough to allow his victim consciousness. Gasping and blinking sweat from his eyes, Lerant lifted his weary head to confront his enemy.

'So,' Jarrod sneered and took a pace closer, 'Videer was weak, yet even his poor trap nearly had you. Only the Weavers resist us and you destroy them at our command.' The Methaggar laughed, calling the sword from m'Connor's hand, and the very sky seemed to shudder. 'He struggles to save you who would give him death. Fool! He can watch you die!'

Jarrod's long, thin fingers lifted, directed at the leaf-bare tree growing against the fence, and suddenly it too, came to life, twigs and branches razor-sharp, gleaming teeth. The knots on the trunk blinked and opened, feral, hungry eyes circling a gaping mouth. The creature leaned down and sap ran like saliva as it set to swallow Lerant's head and shoulders. He kicked and struggled, desperately trying to reach his sword.

M'Connor continued dragging himself toward the fallen Stinger. 'Call your sword to you, Lerant!' he shouted. 'Use your Will! Call it!' But Lerant's ghost-white face was fixed, fear-paralyzed, on the monstrous mouth closing slowly down on him. 'Don't look! Fight! Fight for your family, for Parlan!'

Lerant's Sunburst sword flew, gold-radiant, to his hand. M'Connor reclaimed the Stinger and shoved a dart into the breach. Jarrod lifted his arms to Call Lerant's sword from his grasp. M'Connor fired. The dart flew true, hitting Jarrod in the back, and he staggered as the stun venom flooded him. But it didn't fell him, the Methaggar power melting it away.

Jarrod-Methaggar left Lerant and pivoted to confront the new threat. It hurled energy bolts at m'Connor who rolled hard into the scant cover of Kierjin's fallen body and pulled it over himself as a shield. A burning orb of raw energy struck the body, sending shock waves jarring through m'Connor's wounds. The Methaggar directed more and more fire, creating a veritable rain of flames. The shielding corpse erupted in an inferno of searing fire and m'Connor barely rolled clear in time.

With the Methaggar distracted, its power was gone from the tree and gave Lerant the chance to escape. He need only chop his way clear of the wooden arms of the distorted fence.

Beyond reach of any possible shelter, m'Connor lay exposed to deadly fire. Then, a sword came sliding hilt-first toward him across the cobblestones. He closed his fist about it and managed to deflect the next lightning bolt, but the searing shock numbed his arm and forced the weapon free. Jarrod pulled a knife into each hand and moved closer.

Dazed, his eyes stinging with sweat, m'Connor saw Lerant leaping free. He lifted his sword and it filled his hands like a living creature, no longer rigid, cold steel but rather molten, flowing, energy. And suddenly, the falling snow pulsed with a halo of red-gold light.

Sensing danger, Jarrod spun about only to meet that hungry, incandescent blade. It sliced cleanly through his throat, severing his head from his body in a spray of crimson blood. The body dropped twitching and jerking and the head bounced on the scuffle-bared cobblestones and rolled to a halt at Lerant's feet. The sword shimmered and became again solid steel. The red light vanished.

The Methaggar had been unable to flee, and now was as dead as its host, Jarrod. Weavers trained all their lives and still struggled to be able to overcome a Methaggar, but a Myrrghin officer had done it?

'M'Connor?' Lerant staggered toward him.

M'Connor fumbled one-handed to aim the Stinger gun at the man. It was empty, and he hoped Lerant wouldn't know he didn't have the time or the strength to find and load another dart. His vision was progressively more dark and spotted and his hand shaking. He'd have to bluff it out; he wasn't going back to Zaraxan now!

He shook his head, desperately clearing his sight; Lerant was much closer, much easier to see. When he saw the Stinger, he paused and lifted both empty hands in the air. 'It's all right, m'Connor!' he called. 'Videer is dead. I know the truth. It's over.'

'What?' m'Connor muttered, trying to understand and squinting hazily up at him.

'Videer is dead!' Lerant repeated. 'Where are Annalie and the boys?'

'Safe,' m'Connor tried to tell him, but his voice came out a hoarse whisper. He no longer had the strength to hold the gun, had to let it drop. His elbow went out from under him and he slumped heavily onto his back. Everything went black but he could still hear Lerant's boots over the cobblestones as he came running to him.

Then the man was bent over him, pulling back his coat. 'Did that animal cut you?' Lerant demanded as m'Connor managed to force the blackness down to a gray haze.

'No . . .' m'Connor realized Lerant had reacted to all the blood soaking the front of his coat. 'Not my blood,' he said, tilting his head vaguely toward the dead enemy lying all around them.

'Be still,' Lerant urged, pulling the coat open and making m'Connor shiver with the suddenly deeper cold. 'Annalie and the boys are safe?'

'Yes,' he replied hoarsely. 'With Refallt.'

Lerant let out a great frosty breath in relief and sat back on his heels to pull off his gory gloves and take an aid kit from his belt. He found some bandaging, bunched it into a pad and leaned forward. M'Connor hissed in pain as Lerant pressed the linen against his wounded shoulder. It had torn open and was bleeding again. Lerant's hands were blessedly warm, brushing against his cold neck and face.

'Your leg's a mess, too,' Lerant told him as he secured the bandage by closing the coat and doing up the catches over it. 'Annalie won't be happy when she sees all her hard work undone.'

Something suddenly burned and stung, circling m'Connor's throat and growing rapidly hotter. The slave collar hummed and vibrated.

'Get back!' m'Connor warned and tried weakly to shove Lerant away from him. 'The Death-Spell!'

'What?' Lerant demanded, ignoring m'Connor's ineffectual struggles. 'Easy, now, steady. I'll get you—'

'Get *back*!' m'Connor snarled, the pain about his neck much worse. 'The collar! It'll take you out, too! Damn it! Get *back!*' He shoved again, desperation and terror giving him strength sufficient to unbalance Lerant.

'The collar?' Lerant looked down at it.

'Methaggar . . .' m'Connor grunted, and clenched his teeth over the agonizing pain, he knew the collar would be beginning to glow red with heat now. 'Death-Spell. Go!' He kicked Lerant back, repeated, *'Go!'*

'No!' he heard Lerant say and then felt snow on his face, Lerant packing the wonderful coolness about his throat. But the relief was short-lived, the snow melting and hissing into steam.

'Nothing . . . you can . . . do!' m'Connor grated out, desperate to make the other man leave him. 'It'll kill you, too! Go!'

'There must be some way to get the fucking thing off!' Lerant growled, reaching out to take the glowing hot collar in bare hands. M'Connor heard the combined hiss-grunt of pain as Lerant got a grip on it and didn't let go. A sudden flaring energy jolted m'Connor, a bright essence pouring into him as Lerant's fingers dug deeper beneath the collar, pressing into his burned flesh, pulling hard, dooming them both.

With a loud click, the lock suddenly released, opening the collar at the back of m'Connor's neck and sending Lerant flying backward, the collar in his hands.

'Get rid of it!' m'Connor gasped.

Lerant didn't hesitate, throwing it as far from him as possible and immediately shoving his burned empty hands into the slush. In an eruption of bright red and yellow flames against the dull gray sky, the collar blew apart, raining down tiny burning fragments that hissed in scattered blotches through the white mantle of snow.

Buoyed by the energy still coursing through him, m'Connor propped himself back up on his uninjured elbow, his sight clearing and his breath heaving, fogging the air. He saw Lerant sitting in the snow staring at the steam-holes around the burning metal fragments.

'You did it,' m'Connor murmured, unable to believe it even as he said it. 'You broke the spell . . .'

'The lock was faulty!' Lerant snapped, turning back, 'The cold of the snow against the heat finished it off. I did nothing!' He stared, wide-eyed, appalled and wincing in sympathy at what must be an ugly burn mark about m'Connor's throat. 'Myrrgha!' He spat disgustedly and gathered more snow into his bare hands to carry to him.

Lerant intended to stand, but wound up crawling, his knees trembling and his face suddenly drawn, hollowed, and more exhausted than the battle warranted. Here, surely, was an untrained Weaver, a man with enough power to kill a Methaggar and overcome its Death spell. Had m'Connor really seen the sword shining in his hands? He looked to the sunburst emblem on the scabbard, obviously a powerful amulet.

The burst of energy faded from him, and m'Connor gritted his teeth hard against the pain that suddenly returned to pound him from head to toe. Shaking with cold and exhaustion, he let himself drop back down onto the frozen cobblestones and closed his eyes. His shaking settled into a deep muscle shivering that tore at his wounds.

'. . . not too deep,' he heard Lerant say and sighed relief as more snow was packed about his neck. 'We've got to get you warm.' Lerant shifted to take a grip under m'Connor's arms.

'No . . . .' m'Connor tried to pull away. He wouldn't lose his freedom again.

'It's all right,' Lerant said steadily. 'You're safe. I have you.' Oddly reassured, m'Connor let the darkness take him.

'Steady, steady,' someone said and the rim of a canteen pressed to m'Connor's lips. The water trickled into his mouth and he coughed, then swallowed, glad of the liquid's easing.

'Who . . . . ?' He tried to lift his head as the water was taken away. He sensed a strong, bright presence, and instinctively reached out to that strength but was overwhelmed by an unfamiliar, immensely powerful presence. Its clear, honest energy bristled with angry desolation and confusion.

'Who . . . . ?' Memory of the battle flooded back. The collar was gone! He was whole again! And . . . Lerant!? It couldn't be, but it had to be. Untrained, in denial, yet a Methaggar killed, and a Death Spell overcome. 'Lerant?' he croaked.

'Hold still, damn it,' the man said gruffly. 'I'm trying to get this bleeding stopped. Your leg's bad.'

'Oh . . . .'

M'Connor forced open his eyes to find himself lying on soft, warm hay and wrapped in smelly, bloodstained sheepskin jerkins. M'Connor's brows rose as he realized Lerant could only have taken them from the dead men. He hoped Jarrod's wasn't among them, for all their warmth. It was good to no longer feel the brutally cold, ice-hard cobblestoned road beneath him, nor be exposed to the storm beating him from above.

A rough wooden roof and stone walls of a cattle stall sheltered him. Lerant had managed to carry him to a shallow wooden stock feed trough, long enough to allow many animals to eat at once and more than long enough to make a narrow bed. The officer was on his knees at his side, his hands busy as he cut away the filthy, tangled bandaging from about m'Connor's leg, the pieces of broken splints gone.

'Thanks,' m'Connor told him, sincerely grateful. But, seeing the cross-swords and cog wheel insignias of a Myrrghin engineering officer on Lerant's shoulder, the gratitude was dampened by the knowledge of why he was being so well cared for. 'Keeping me all neat and shipshape for Zaraxan?' he asked bitterly.

'Fuck Zaraxan,' Lerant said succinctly, without looking up from his work.

M'Connor blinked, then realizing he'd heard right, he snorted. 'No thanks.' Unexpected pain stabbed at him and he jerked as Lerant did something to his leg.

'Hold still!' Lerant finished tugging off a sticky length of bandage that had been embedded in the wounds. 'There.' He took his canteen from his belt and washed away the worst of the dirt. After a moment he said, 'Annalie would do this better.' He paused, and added intently, 'She won't leave you here.'

'No,' m'Connor agreed. 'She'll get the boys safe and come back, ready to fight.'

'This was your idea?' Lerant asked tersely.

M'Connor shrugged. 'I needed some exercise.'

'Annalie talked you into it, didn't she?' It wasn't a question.

Lerant missed his grip on the next piece of bandage, his eyes not on the task, but scanning the area, desperate to find the family he loved. After all the violence of the battle, the surrounds were eerily silent and peaceful. Softly drifting snow was already hiding the ugly mutilation of the bodies scattered along the road. Soon there'd be nothing to show for the fight but several white-draped mounds.

'They got away from Jarrod all right?'

'Yes,' m'Connor assured him. 'Scared, maybe a little bruised, but safe.'

'Damn it! They should never have been out here!' Lerant thumped a closed fist down on top of the bale of hay at his side.

'No, they shouldn't have,' m'Connor agreed quietly, leaving Lerant and Annalie to sort that for themselves.

Lerant pulled more bandaging from the kit and wound it tight about the broken leg. M'Connor swore and almost broke the side of the old rickety trough, but when his vision cleared, he saw the worst of the bleeding had stopped. 'Thanks,' he said hoarsely.

Lerant sagged wearily to sit on a hay bale beside the trough. Sighing heavily, he said nothing, and just sat watching the snowfall beyond the open door.

'Videer is dead?' m'Connor asked after a moment.

'Yes. I think we've got them all. We should be safe for now.'

There was something in Lerant's voice, an emptiness, a bleak resignation. 'Are your men all right?' m'Connor asked sharply.

'Yes, they're safe, with Wilgar.' Some emotion, a niggling worry entered his tone. 'Except Karatin.'

M'Connor winced, remembering the big red-haired man sprawled unconscious on the floor. 'He'll get out of there as soon as he wakes,' he assured. 'So what exactly happened with Videer?'

Lerant drew a breath and let it out slowly. He rubbed one fist over the other hand. 'You were right, m'Connor. You were right about everything.' He frowned, surprised to see the burn mark on his hand. He ran his thumb lightly over the red mark crossing his palm. 'Rusark planned it, targeted the children. We have the proof.'

M'Connor couldn't imagine what it would be like to suddenly have all you believed in proven worse than false. He sighed, scrubbed a hand over his face, and said, 'I'm sorry.'

'I'll go check the road,' Lerant said and got to his feet, then disappeared outside. 'No sign of her,' he reported worriedly some moments later as he came back. 'Could Jarrod have sent someone after her?'

'No. I kept track and they were more interested in me. He had a Cloak on the area, it'd be gone now but it could have delayed her.' Something else occurred to him and he frowned up at Lerant. 'Come to think of it, you shouldn't have been able to get through to find us.' He shook his head in confusion. 'You shouldn't have been able to kill a Methaggar or take that collar off me, either. Thanks for that, by the way.' Lerant shrugged, his gaze still on the road. 'I thought I saw something,' m'Connor said, 'a light shining about that sword of yours . . . .'

'You were passing out, m'Connor,' Lerant interrupted brusquely, 'You lost enough blood to float a small navy. Of course you're seeing things.'

'Probably,' m'Connor had to agree.

'We need a drink,' Lerant decided.

'Do you have one?' m'Connor asked hopefully. He could use one—the pain was setting his teeth on edge.

'As it happens, yes,' Lerant said, turning to him with what could have been a smile. 'Very fine brandy. A gift from my brother.'

M'Connor watched as Lerant reached under his jacket and pulled out a small, flat silver flask. Lerant stood staring at it a moment, chewing his lower lip and his brows pulled down in a very boyish-looking puzzlement. Squinting hard, m'Connor saw that the flask was dented and much flatter than it should have been. Lerant ran his free hand over his armor, checking it for damage and finding it so badly buckled that it had torn free of its leather straps in two places and was hanging loosely on him. It was covered in sticky splotches of what looked like tree sap.

With some struggle for the warping of the flask, Lerant uncapped it and took a hefty swig before he bent down to help m'Connor. 'Here,' he said. 'Don't tell Annalie, she'll skin us both. Just a swallow, no more.'

'Yes, mother.' M'Connor waved off his assistance and took the flask himself. 'Don't ask me to make excuses to Annalie for you.' Lerant held the flask a moment, making sure m'Connor could manage before he let go. 'Of course,' m'Connor said airily, 'I could tell her that you needed it after nearly being eaten by a tree.'

'Trees don't eat people,' Lerant said, sitting down on the hay bale again.

'Well, that one gave it a good try,' m'Connor said, enjoying the stinging warmth of the brandy.

Lerant scowled down at him. 'Explosives, m'Connor,' he said, dismissively, 'Jarrod threw them and the concussion blew the tree apart on top of me.'

'Good story. I might use it. Sleep better.'

Lerant paused before accepting the brandy back, a pained look of nostalgia crossing his face. 'I had a Sergeant say almost exactly the same thing to me, once.'

'He tried to warn you of very real danger,' m'Connor said seriously. 'Refusing to admit Methaggars exist will only get you killed some day.'

Lerant just saluted him with the flask and took another swig. 'You and Fallon, both superstitious idiots. You weren't lucid, m'Connor, you're imagining things.'

The pain was easing, the brandy was good, and he was too tired to argue. 'If you say so,' he said. Light reflected from the sunburst scabbard at Lerant's hip as he turned to look outside and reminded, m'Connor commented, 'Nice sword. Where did you get it?'

'I found it in a Myrrgha City marketplace,' Lerant replied, unable to suppress a proud smile as he glanced down at it. 'But my brother gifted it to me. He says it looks like the emblem of my tribal clan, the Kartai. But he's wrong.'

450

M'Connor reached up for the flask. Lerant frowned, and then surrendered. 'You're going to get us into trouble,' he pointed out amiably.

M'Connor tried to cover his shaking hand giving away that the alcohol and the aftermath of the battle was hitting his injured body hard. He decided to forgo his turn and gave back the flask. Lerant got up and paced to the door. 'I'd go look for Anni and the boys,' he said impatiently, 'but I know I'd probably miss them in that maze out there.'

'They'll be here,' m'Connor said, thinking to ask. 'Where ever it came from, you're lucky you had that sword just now; it made all the difference. I swear I saw it glowing.' He tried to force his muddled brain to come up with some information about that sunburst emblem. He had the strongest feeling he'd heard of it before.

Lerant paced again, then came back to squat down and check m'Connor's leg. 'Look all right?' m'Connor asked when he remained silent.

'It looks bloody awful,' Lerant said truthfully. 'What do I do with you now, m'Connor? I can't take you into hiding in the coal mine with the others.'

'That's where Wilgar's gone?'

'Yes. If it comes to it. I hope Annalie will see that's where she must take the boys.'

'Into the coal mines?' m'Connor blinked, trying to force his tired mind to follow that reasoning. If Lerant planned to hand him over, there'd be no need for anyone to go into hiding. 'With the slaves?'

Lerant flinched. 'I've told Wilgar to free them,' he said.

'You what!?' m'Connor demanded, groaning with the pain of movement.

'Will you stay still! Yes, free them!' Lerant snapped. 'You think the people of Rogha will just lie down and let Zaraxan and his band of thugs butcher half the town?! We're going to fight!'

M'Connor stared at him in disbelief and then said, 'Bad idea. Except for the part about the slaves. You might win the first round, but eventually Myrrgha will make an example of your city. There won't be so much as a dog left alive.'

Lerant looked away and moved back a little, distancing himself from that ugly image. 'I figured the same,' he finally admitted quietly. 'There's no way out. I have to give you over to the murdering mongrels, m'Connor, but I'm going with you. I hope you're right about the sword. It'll come in handy when we escape.'

'We? Escape? From where?'

Lerant turned back with a twitch of a smile for m'Connor's elated surprise. 'Zaraxan invited me along to watch the fun,' he said, nonchalant. 'I'll take him up on the offer, give you over, stay on board ship with you, and then we'll escape together out at sea among the islands. Simple.'

M'Connor stared, trying to believe this was really happening and he wasn't drunk and imagining it. 'So, what, we just go over the side in the middle of the night?'

'Why not? You seem to like to swim.'

M'Connor shook his aching head slowly then began to grin. 'I like it! It has a certain . . . elegant simplicity.'

'Elegant,' Lerant said with a weary sigh. 'That's me all right.'

'Get away from him!'

Startled, m'Connor jumped at the sound of Annalie's sharp voice, then cursed at the pain that shot through him. Lerant swung

452

about, happy to see Annalie standing amid the snowfall beyond the open end of the stall. She took a step closer, appearing wraith-like in the swirling white wind that billowed her dark cloak about her face. In her hands she held the small crossbow, an arrow loaded and aimed toward Lerant. Peering into the shadowy stall, she recognized him with surprise and lowered the weapon quickly, locking the safety on the trigger.

'Where did you come from?' she exclaimed, moving into the stall.

'Anni'!' Lerant hurried forward, ready to embrace her in his relief, then drawing back as he saw her cold suspicion. 'I was worried there were more of Jarrod's men back there, but I couldn't find you.'

'It's clear,' Annalie said in a matter-of-fact manner that belied the urgency and anger at Lerant that m'Connor could feel radiating from her like an animal with its hackles up. It was good being able to feel again, the methirri collar not crippling him.

Stepping closer and moving to one side so the grey winter light from the doorway would reach him, she looked down at m'Connor. 'Are you all right?' she asked him, warily keeping Lerant in her peripheral vision.

'I'm fine,' m'Connor said expansively. It made her frown that disbelieving Healer's frown at him, but he just smiled at her, delighted to see her safe.

'You're fine, huh?' she said skeptically.

'Not good,' Lerant corrected, returning to his side. 'His leg's mangled again.'

'It would be,' Annalie said, angry and shaken. 'Jarrod made him walk on it.' Lerant drew a hissing breath in shocked sympathy. 'M'Connor used it as a cover for us to escape,' she explained, her free hand smoothing her skirt, the barest indication of the tremendous strain m'Connor could feel in her.

Lerant turned and met m'Connor's bleary gaze to say fierce and low, 'I owe you m'Connor, more than I can say.'

'I think we're even,' m'Connor returned, clumsily indicating the burn mark at his throat.

Annalie said crisply. 'We need to get moving.'

'M'Connor's not going anywhere with you,' Lerant refused and added with open hostility, 'Where exactly are the boys? Is Refallt taking them home? Are they all right?'

'They're close by, unharmed, and they're not going home.' Ignoring the glare Lerant leveled at her, she sat on the bale closest to m'Connor, doing a quick visual assessment. She gasped, seeing the burn mark at his throat. 'The collar's gone!'

'Lerant got it off,' m'Connor told her woozily. 'No idea how.'

'Kerell?' Annalie exclaimed in disbelief, resting a wonderfully cool hand on m'Connor's brow. 'You're fevered again,' she told him. 'Do I smell brandy?'

'Just a little,' m'Connor said, wishing Rhyssa was here to get angry with him. He watched with interest as Annalie's disapproval targeted his partner in crime. 'I was about to say you've done good work looking after him,' she added, giving Lerant the pinned-to-the-wall look, 'But . . . you gave him brandy?!'

'It's not my fault,' Lerant shrugged, gesturing at m'Connor. 'He used his Weaver cunning on me.'

M'Connor snorted amused approval of the parry and grinned up at Lerant. Annalie looked considering, at m'Connor then to Lerant and back to him again, a pleased realization of their changed manner toward one another settling in her eyes. She let out a breath and the tension eased from her as she got back to work, checking the tourniquet bandaging. 'I saw Jarrod, or what's left of him.'

M'Connor waved a vague hand at Lerant, indicating where credit was due.

'I couldn't have done it without m'Connor nearly getting himself killed distracting the bastard,' Lerant qualified.

'And what do you plan to do with him now he's saved your life?'Annalie demanded, looking up at him accusingly. Lerant remained silent, returning her challenging gaze, his jaw set. 'I'm not letting you take him prisoner again, Kerell,' she told him, leaving no room for argument.

'Annalie . . . .'

She stood. 'We don't need your help. I'll get Refallt.'

M'Connor intervened tiredly. 'S'all right, Annalie, Lerant has a plan . . . .'

She turned to snap, 'He what?'

'A plan,' m'Connor repeated. 'Hand me over while you and the boys get away . . . then we're taking a swim from Zaraxan's ship.'

She looked back sharply, seeking confirmation of that in Lerant's eyes. 'A lifeboat, actually,' he corrected and couldn't help but smile at her completely thrown expression. Seriously, determined, he added, 'I'll gut that bastard Inquisitor before I let him lay a finger on m'Connor. I'll gut him anyway. Zaraxan dead is the best safety you and I and the boys and Rogha can have.'

'Parlan was right about you,' she said quietly, her smile a mix of affection, respect and great sorrow. 'He said you'd see the truth eventually and act on it. He'd be so proud. So am I.' Stretching up on tiptoe, she kissed a surprised Lerant softly on the cheek. She turned back to m'Connor, her smile growing wider with shining relief and, behind her, he saw Lerant take the chance to wipe his brimming eyes.

'It won't work of course, his plans never do,' Annalie told m'Connor dryly, 'I speak from experience.'

'I'm not so keen on swimming as I was,' m'Connor admitted, knowing, lifeboat or no, Lerant's plan was almost certain suicide.

'We go with my plan.' She looked back at Lerant. 'Yours would only get the both of you killed, Kerell, you know that. Rogha will have to look after itself—m'Connor's not going anywhere near Zaraxan and neither are you. You're coming with us.'

In the silence that followed, m'Connor could hear Annalie holding her breath.

'If Rogha is to stand against Zaraxan, I'll need to get back to my men,' Lerant finally decided. 'But . . .' He sighed as he considered it, wincing as he ran a burned hand over the hilt of his Sunburst sword. 'You're making for m'Connor's ship?'

'Yes,' she confirmed, frowning as she noticed his pain.

'It'll still be there?' Lerant asked m'Connor.

'Gerion might've gone to cover but if so he'll have left a message as to when and where he'll be back,' m'Connor replied.

'If we must wait, we can go to Refallt's hideout in the mountains,' Annalie explained. Stepping closer to Lerant she took hold of his arm, and, avoiding touching the injured hand, she turned it palm up for her examination. 'We've been stocking it, there are plenty of supplies.' She shook her head as she saw the damage done to Lerant's hand and held out her own to indicate she wanted to see his other hand as well.

'You're sure the boys will be safe?' Lerant asked as he obeyed. 'It's a long way, and Zaraxan won't give up looking for him.'

'Safer by far than they would be here,' Annalie answered sharply. 'These should be kept covered. I'll wrap them before you leave us, but think about it, Kerell. Zaraxan won't hang around Rogha City for longer than it takes to ask 'Which way did they go'. The people here won't need you half so much as we will.'

'Maybe,' Lerant said uncertainly. 'It's how many might die until he gets the answers he wants or satisfies his temper that worries me.' He drew a breath and exhaled slowly, deciding. 'This storm will delay the bastard. I can stay with you until you're offshore or secured with Refallt and still be back here before midday tomorrow.'

Turning away quickly to hide her expression, didn't prevent m'Connor catching the backwash of exhausted relief that shook Annalie from head to toe. She said tightly, 'Good. I'll call Refallt.' She collected the crossbow and left the stall. He heard her give a shrill, loud whistle through her teeth, apparently the arranged signal that it was safe to come out again.

Craning stiffly higher, m'Connor saw a blurry shape appear from behind the opposite line of stalls. Eventually, it resolved itself into Refallt leading the horse, a sword grasped in his free hand. Up on the sleigh seat, Alarn sat cradling his little brother. 'Is everything all right?' Refallt called, noting Lerant's presence.

'Yes.' Annalie glanced back over her shoulder to add, 'Kerell, get him up but watch that leg. I doubt there are many stitches still holding. Refallt? Can you back that sleigh in here a little, do you think? I'd rather we just lift him straight inside.'

As the sleigh came to a halt partially inside the low-roofed stall, m'Connor heard Alarn demand, 'Did they hurt him, Mama? Did that man cut him with his knife?'

'No, everything's going to be all right now,' she assured, standing outside on the driver's board to circle his shoulders and give him a brief hug. 'Your Uncle Kerell saved the Captain and he's coming with us to help him get away.' She reached for something—probably the medical kit—stored under the seat.

'You are?' Alarn asked, his brown eyes round with elated surprise as he ducked low under the roof to regard Lerant.

'I am,' Lerant assured, busy dismantling the side of the feed trough to make it easier to move him and leaving m'Connor wondering at the strength it must have taken to carry him and put him safely down in here in the first place.

Alarn jumped down from the sleigh and ran to Lerant who, already down on one knee, happily accepted the boy's enthusiastic hug. M'Connor could plainly see Lerant fighting back tears and wondered hazily why he couldn't sense the man's emotions . . . or much of anything else. Exhaustion? Blood loss . . . Brandy . . . ?

Busy trying to find what she needed, Annalie spared a brief smile for her oldest son's exuberant greeting of his uncle. Leaving Lerant, Alarn came to m'Connor to check for himself. 'They didn't hurt you?'

'Your uncle saved me just in time. And he did this for me, too—look—no slave collar! I'm free, Alarn, and I'm going home!' Saying it, m'Connor felt himself smiling, felt the truth of the words only now sinking in.

CHAPTER TWENTY TWO

'Parlan wouldn't leave without saying good bye.'

Waking, it took m'Connor a moment to identify the man's voice as Lerant. His burned neck hurt, but the collar was gone! The world about him was again vibrant, alive with pulsing energies, although for some odd reason he still couldn't sense Lerant. The feeling of being again complete and whole and alive was a wonder. He had passed out when they moved him, he remembered. He was comfortable and warm, lying in the sleigh, well covered, and sheltered from the icy cold he could feel with each breath. Alarn lay curled at his side beneath the blankets.

'I'm not letting Myrrgha do to my sons what it did to their father!' Annalie said, sharp despite her efforts to keep her voice low and not wake them. 'We'd have been gone already but Parlan kept telling me that your eyes would open and you'd see what was really happening and come with us.'

'Parlan was like that,' Lerant said, his words heavy with a familiar sorrow.

'He had faith in you; he believed you'd figure it out.' There was a rustle of clothing and m'Connor knew Annalie had reached out to soften her words with a touch. 'He was right.'

'Too late. I almost got him home, Anni. We almost made it.' Suppressed grief and frustration trembled in the heartbreaking words. 'His transfer papers went through the afternoon of the same day his ship sailed. Half a day! I'd have had him safe!'

Uncomfortable for his unintentional eavesdropping, m'Connor tried to cough, but it came out a dry husk of a whisper.

'That's not happening to my sons,' Annalie repeated, her steady voice belying the added grief Lerant's admission had carried.

The sleigh had halted, Refallt stamping about forward somewhere, perhaps checking the harness. Craning his head painfully, M'Connor saw they'd reached The Crossroads north of Rogha, the dull, wintry afternoon fading further into evening. Snow drifted softly down, flowing in unbroken white over fields and forested hills.

A broad, smooth surface of snow overlaid the stone-filled, solid road in good repair, leading westward to the village of Cauvgha. Part of his inward journey had taken m'Connor through the more treacherous valleys and crests of the second choice, a rutted route that wound through boulder-strewn, densely forested hills to follow the rugged coastline and link Rogha's fishing communities. He'd never followed the third road, but had heard it was not much more than a rough track, climbing laboriously north into the towering mountains and its isolated mining and timber operations.

'Did m'Connor say exactly which way to go from here?' Lerant asked.

'No. He wanted to wait and see if we reached this far. I hate to wake him.' Annalie shifted again and Parla cried a sleepy protest.

'Stay there,' Lerant said and climbed down. 'I'll do it.'

'It's likely to be some smuggler's cove,' Refallt pointed out, 'which means no road that will take the sleigh.'

Squinting against the softly gleaming lantern-light, M'Connor heard Lerant climb up onto the sled's running board and lean over the wooden side to look down into the shadowed interior. Propping himself up as best he could, m'Connor said, 'We're at The Crossroads?'

'You're awake?' Lerant said, with relief. 'Yes. Do we take the coast road?'

'It might be best to send someone on ahead to check if the ship is there or not,' m'Connor said. 'It was to go to Seelski the day I was captured. But, by now, they've probably gone. They'll have left a message.'

'Seelski! Well, I can't fault your choice,' Lerant said with cheerful disgust. 'It'd take a battalion to search all these inlets and coves. What do you think, Refallt?'

The old man came closer, his craggy face shadowed in the lantern-light. He gave m'Connor a brief, friendly nod of greeting. 'Seelski is perfect for smugglers, but not so good for anyone else. We'd have to leave the sleigh to head down that final stretch.'

Trying carefully to sit up further, m'Connor woke Alarn who gave him a sleepy yawn. 'Thanks, son,' he said, 'You've kept me nice and warm. We've been traveling a long time. Are you getting cramped?'

'Oh, no, Sir!' the boy denied, a little too quickly.

'Well,' m'Connor advised with a smile, 'if we stay here a while maybe you should take this chance to stretch your legs.'

'Wait until we move off the road, Alarn,' Annalie warned.

'If your ship's at Seelski,' Lerant said, 'some of the crew will need to come back to help us. If they're not there . . . .' He shrugged. 'We go on to Refallt's mine.'

'I'll unharness the horse and ride on down there and see what I can see,' Refallt offered. 'I know this coastline well.'

'All right, then,' Lerant agreed. 'But we move the sleigh out of the open first. Over there, behind that grove of firs.'

With the sleigh in place, Alarn climbed out to relieve himself and m'Connor waited while Lerant went to aid Refallt with the horse. When they reappeared Refallt was already astride, riding bareback.

'We allowed for me being delayed,' m'Connor told them. 'Gerion was to leave a message beneath the second of stone circles directly in line with the south headland.'

'Understood,' Refallt said, stroking the horse's shoulder as it pawed at the snow. 'I'll find it if need be.'

'You'll need a lantern. If the ship is there, the crew will be watching for an all-clear code. Two short and one long flash.' Refallt nodded and m'Connor added, 'Be careful out there.'

'I will. There are oil torches behind the driver's seat.'

Lerant took the one Annalie found for him and set it aflame. Refallt took the lantern and dug his heels into his mount. The horse lunged up and over a snow-bank, dislodging more white powder from the laden trees surrounding it. He moved across the road and down the hill and the lantern light gradually disappeared behind the dark wall of the forest. Flaring shadows leaped about the sleigh in the yellow circle of torchlight, and the grove was very still and quiet.

M'Connor settled back, easing his wounded shoulder. 'All we can do now is wait. I'm not much good at waiting.'

'Me either,' Lerant said with a sigh. He stood staring off into the dark circle of trees, one bandaged hand on his sword hilt.

'In the meantime, we can drink the tea I packed.' Annalie sounded much more cheerful than m'Connor's sense of her indicated. She poured the tea into the cap-mug and handed it down to m'Connor. 'Sorry, it's cold.'

He took a thirsty swallow and gave the cup back. 'I could heat it for you . . . if I had the strength and if it wouldn't draw every Methaggar Seeker for miles down on us.'

Annalie checked that Alarn was safe and saw he was rolling stones down a slope into the small, ice-patched stream that ran through the grove. 'What is Weaving? How does it work?' she asked.

'I . . . .' M'Connor's brows rose as he realized he couldn't think how to describe the sensation of Weaving. 'That's like me asking 'How do you breathe?'' he replied. 'I just concentrate, look inward, release the neural Lock and Summon the source of the energy stored inside me. Then, I Weave it, direct it outward, reshaped as I need.'

Annalie gave him a sidelong glance and Lerant shook his head, plainly disbelieving. 'But where does the energy come from?' she asked.

'The sun. Plants do it every day. Long ago, before we came to this world, we were given the same ability; it was sewn into our blood.'

'Plants don't boil water,' Lerant said with a skeptical snort.

'What else is firewood but a way to release the power of stored sunlight?' m'Connor countered.

'So your people don't need coal or peat they just Weave heat?' Annalie asked.

'Providing a constant heat source would be too draining. A Weaver can ignite the flame easily enough, but we still need fuel, wood or peat, we have no coal mines.'

'They say a Magi has more power than a Weaver?' she asked.

'Yes. They can shape energy much more precisely, having the knowing of it over hundreds of years.'

Annalie frowned. 'They pass the knowledge from one generation to the next?'

'They retain their memory from one life to the next. Their Akkarra hold their souls—and their minds—for them between lives.' M'Connor sensed astonishment but, to her credit, no real disbelief.

'I can't imagine living like that,' she said.

M'Connor smiled. 'Yes. Sometimes they can be very . . . spooky, to be around. Especially when you're a boy and they scold you for not paying attention and say you haven't changed a whisker from when you were your great-uncle.'

'If you want to control a population through superstition, you have to start with the children!' Lerant interrupted. 'You'll note they always tell them things that can't be proven.'

M'Connor just shook his head tiredly; he'd heard that many times before from Myrrghinners. But, unlike them, the tension in Lerant's stance indicated an underlying, very real and very personal fear of the subject. It irritated him to observe it but not feel more through the Empathy he should have had with the man.

'I've had experience of things you can't see!' Annalie snapped at Lerant. 'I've seen spirits coming to help guide the dying—'

'When you'd been without sleep for how many days?' he cut her off.

464

'Oh, never mind! You never listen.' Dismissing him, she looked back to m'Connor, about to say something, but spotting something else, called, 'Alarn! You're too close to that stream!'

Looking back over her shoulder at m'Connor, she ordered, 'You. Rest.' She turned to Lerant. 'You, shut up and watch Parla for me.' She gave the mug of tea to Lerant and climbed down from the sleigh seat, leaving Parla asleep and warmly covered.

Lerant moved closer to the sleigh side. 'What are the chances of trouble?' he asked.

Taking a breath to fortify himself to hear more denials, m'Connor said, 'Our battle with Jarrod's Methaggar caused a stirring that will have reached all the way back to Myrrgha City.'

'You mean someone there already knows we killed him?'

'Yes. The other Methaggars will know one of their kind was killed and probably have reported it to the Emperor and through him, the military.'

Lerant winced as his bandaged fist closed about his sword-hilt. 'You're certain Grouda's in with them?'

'I've seen it. He thinks the Magi are immortal and he wants it.'

'He might believe they're immortal, but it's impossible.'

'His Methaggars and Zaraxan might just have found a way. A body will never last forever, but a mind? They want to do what they believe the Magi can for Grouda and the rest, but faster, immediate, taking a man's soul from his body and putting someone else in his place.'

Lerant shook his head. 'Impossible.'

'If I hadn't seen it myself, I'd agree. But, they took Bren, and . . . .' M'Connor swallowed hard against a suddenly tight throat. 'I know, Lerant. I tried to rescue him, and what I got was his body animated by the consciousness of a dog. It's just enough to keep the body alive and break Bren's family's heart.'

'So your Brother's dead, too,' Lerant murmured.

'Sometimes I wish he was,' m'Connor said, meeting his gaze levelly. 'But, no. He's still out there somewhere, trapped by . . . I don't know what exactly. But, I'll find him and the Akkarra will restore him . . . or release him.'

After a long moment's silence, Lerant said gently, 'Sometimes I imagine Parlan is here talking to me, but he's not, and he never will be. He's gone. I've seen men with their minds broken, reduced to no more than beasts. I'm sorry it happened to your Brother. Believe me, m'Connor, I'm truly sorry. But what you say they've done is utterly impossible.'

'I was there!' Simmering anger gave m'Connor's voice strength. 'It only works with Weavers! We're trained in leaving our bodies to Travel. That's why Lellgha was invaded,' he continued breathlessly, 'Not to defend Myrrgha's borders from 'witchcraft', not for gold or slaves, but for us! For Weavers! Because one warped old man won't let go of power!'

'I don't doubt The Emperor's mad enough to believe he can become immortal and that he's hunting Weavers because of that.' Lerant said in a tone of appeasement. 'You did well to get your Brother home. Maybe with enough time his mind can be healed.'

'I'll find him,' m'Connor repeated, adamant despite his breathlessness. 'The Akkarra and I will make him whole.'

Lerant moved closer to frown down at him in concern. 'Annalie's right, you need to rest. There's no such thing as a soul. Consciousness yes, but something you can trap like that? No.'

'There is,' m'Connor said, taking another deep breath against the fatigue that weighed him. 'The Akkarra can locate anyone by tracking the unique vibrations of their *Ea*, their soul, through the Void.'

'M'Connor, you're trying to tell me my sword glows, a tree tried to eat me, and someone's stolen your Brother's soul. My sword is designed to reflect light, the tree exploded, and . . . I'm sorry. Your Brother's mind is broken and no amount of narcotic tree sap induced hallucination will fix it.'

'So it's a shared 'narcotic-induced hallucination' every time you speak to someone using an Akkarra Amber . . . what you call a Connector-Stone, made from that same 'tree sap'?'

'Maybe the bastard Emperor will die soon and that will end the war,' Lerant sighed even more heavily, creating a halo of frosted air.

'The Methaggar will only use some other puppet,' m'Connor told him. 'If they succeed their madness will be unleashed on us all. And their—'

Lerant lifted a hand to override m'Connor's protest. 'Rest, m'Connor. And please, don't talk to Alarn about this. His father is dead. He needs to deal with that reality. False hope is cruel.'

'I'm sorry everyone,' Refallt announced tiredly as he returned some time later, the horse's huffing and thudding waking m'Connor with a start. He dismounted stiffly and gave Rae a proud pat and a cube of sugar then tied off the reins to the sleigh. He hunted about in his tattered coat, and, producing a small box, approached m'Connor, who with Lerant's aid, was sitting upright once more.

'The ship wasn't there, but I found the message container.'

Pulling his arm free of the covers, m'Connor gripped the old man's thin wrist before taking the box. 'My thanks,' he said sincerely.

The peat-cutter's eyes twinkled under his heavily ridged wiry gray brows. He accepted the mug of tea Annalie handed to him from her seat up on the drivers' board. 'It is I should give you thanks, Captain, he said with a chuckle that made him look much younger despite his weariness. 'I've not had the chance to do anything very daring or worthwhile in many a long year. It's quite a change from peat and mud, and I find it much to my liking!'

'You're a good man, Refallt. There'll be a warm spot for you in the southern sun any time you care to accept.

Lerant moved to stand close to Annalie and they watched with nervous impatience as m'Connor removed a coded message scrawled on a piece of parchment. Quickly decoding and reading it, m'Connor gave a gusty exhalation of relief.

'Everything will work out,' he announced to the worried group looking down at him. 'Gerion's gone to the lee of the island to see out the storm and avoid any Seekers. He intended snatching me from The Fortress itself if I didn't show when he drops anchor again.'

'So, when and where do we make contact?' Lerant asked.

'A little further north of here, Scalion Cove. He expects to be back late afternoon two or three days from now.'

'Zaraxan could be here by tomorrow morning,' Lerant frowned. 'Bad weather notwithstanding. We'll need to stay well hidden. He could have his scouts scouring these hills by afternoon.'

'You're staying with us?' Annalie asked hopefully.

'Not much point in trying to walk back now through the snow and the dark,' Lerant said. 'I'll see you safe.'

M'Connor refolded the parchment and tucked the box under the covers beside him, moving the Stinger that lay nearby. 'No one can know which road we'd take from here, and the snow will hide our tracks. I doubt they'll look for us so far north.'

'Let's get moving.' Lerant clapped Refallt on the shoulder, turning to help him with the harnessing of the horse. 'I hope you have plenty of peat fuel in this hide-out of yours, Refallt! I think my feet are frozen to the soles of my boots!'

CHAPTER TWENTY THREE

'M'Connor has a Magi with him now. The witch killed Apomerghia and the Jarrod-Link. Stay awake or she'll do it to you, too', Lurghiar said, low and angry. 'You take the lion-Seeker and watch the mountain road, and I'll take the other near the coast. Keep close watch and tell me if you see a group of people. He's taken a woman and children hostages. Apomerghia-Jarrod killed a Myrrghin officer who attacked him.'

'Good,' Varasaghir said, his voice husky with grief. 'At least he had that satisfaction.' He'd felt the enormous surge of Magi power humming into the upper cavern rooms, violent, honed to hunt just one, deadly and he knew Apomerghia was at the time in Link with a Seeker-human somewhere far away.

'M'Connor is crippled and of no use to us, the Magi, however, is most valuable. She might expect we'll have more Seekers hunting them. Be on your guard. We must take her alive, which means possessing her. Only I can do that—be sure to call me!'

'Yes, Superior.' The fine hair that covered Varasaghir rippled and tingled with fear.

'Afraid? Good!' Lurghiar sneered. 'It might help you concentrate! But, he'll be heading for the coast, meeting his sea-slime friends. I doubt they'll take the mountain road. If I thought otherwise, even as short-handed as we are, I wouldn't trust you with something of so great importance!'

That knowledge both cheered and irritated Varasaghir—he certainly didn't want to have to confront a Magi, or even a Weaver for that matter, but it was galling to know his Superiors thought him incompetent. Especially after all his long hours of work, and damn it, he *had* found the Seedling, even if they didn't believe him!

Silently, he collected the correct Blood-Code Link, a tiny thin slice of methirri. He pressed his thumb hard down on it, making the methirri hair part about the opening surgically created in his hand when he'd been recruited for this work. He closed his eyes, waiting for the blood in the small capillaries of the scar on his thumb to meet and respond to that implanted in the Contact.

Instantly, and a little disorienting, he was seeing and feeling along with the lion-Seeker. It had been implanted with a Seeker-tracker years ago to use as a guard on the slave mines. Several other creatures had likewise been 'recruited' as eyes and ears, and more importantly, noses. Sitting almost invisible in the shadows on another ledge across the cavern room, Superior Lurghiar maintained the other Link, his no doubt much more likely to succeed.

I could be helping find her, if they'd just let me direct my Seeker over there. But, no, Lurghiar wants all the glory. At least Apomerghia was fair. I can't believe he's dead! He was my Superior; I should have the right to find his killer—if I had the courage for it.

Hungry. Hungry. *Hungry*!

Is that all these creatures ever think about? Sighing, Varasaghir shifted on his stony ledge, vainly trying to settle more comfortably, his empty stomach grabbing at him. The damn Seeker-lion wasn't making it any easier, swamping his mind and body with waves of a driving need to eat. The Myrrghin Palace cavern-room was dark and warm. *If I fall asleep I'll really be in trouble! As if I'm not in trouble enough already.*

The lion paused in its tracking, disobeying Varasaghir as it set to return to the solid dark of the snowy pine forest where hunting deer and rabbits would be better. *No! Go on! Keep climbing, stay by the road!* Naturally, it didn't understand words such as 'road'; Varasaghir had to paint the image for the creature, show it what he wanted, direct its attention to the broad smooth empty space so unnatural to the lion's normal hunting ground.

'Oh no!' Refallt exclaimed, rousing Annalie awake as he brought the horse to a sudden halt. She lifted her head from Lerant's shoulder, surprised that she'd managed to fall asleep sometime during their journey. Night had overtaken them.

'What's wrong?' Lerant asked anxiously, peering into the darkness.

'Avalanche.' Refallt nodded grimly to the road ahead.

Annalie watched as Lerant took the lantern from its hook, climbed down and waded carefully through calf-deep, powdery snow that rapidly became deeper and more obstructive. A few spans beyond the horse, the level road disappeared abruptly, swallowed up in a forty-five to sixty degree incline of solid white. It was broken only by the dark patches of boulders, logs, branches

472

and other rubble torn free by the force of the avalanche. Its outline bleached the night sky like a mammoth white-furred beast sprawled asleep, blocking the pass immovably, and threatening death should its peace be violated.

'Between fifty and a hundred spans high and a quarter that wide,' Refallt concluded disgustedly. 'And we're so close to home, too.'

'There's got to be a way to get round it!' Lerant growled.

Shaking his head, Refallt waved a hand to either side of the steeply walled gorge. The rock faces were sheer, slippery with ice, the ravine maw crammed with packed snow to its teeth. 'This is the crest of the pass, high-country. It couldn't have happened at a worse spot. It's all downhill on the other side, only a quarter mile further on and it levels out at the mine entrance.'

'There's nowhere else to go.' Lerant ran a gloved hand over his brow as if trying to squeeze a solution from his weary mind. 'We can't get the sleigh over that. The rest of us could make it on foot, but m'Connor can't walk, let alone climb.'

'I'm not sure that the Captain and my horse friend are on good terms,' Refallt said, clapping a sinewy hand to Lerant's shoulder and guiding him back to the sleigh, 'but if I have a few words in his ear, I'm sure Rae will be willing to give it a try.'

'You think your horse can carry m'Connor over the slide'?'

The peat-cutter's shoulders heaved as he drew a long, considering breath. 'If you take the lantern and go ahead of us, sound out the firmest footing. It won't be easy, but Rae and I have done worse in the past. We'll get through.'

'We have to climb that on foot?' Annalie asked Lerant, shivering with cold as she pushed the blankets away.

473

'Yes. We'll get m'Connor up on the horse.' Lerant took a soundly sleeping Parla from her arms and helped her down. 'The mine's not far on the other side.'

'What's wrong?' m'Connor asked groggily, craning to look at them.

'Avalanche, cut the road,' Lerant told him as he handed Parla back to Annalie and reached into the sled to unload the bundles of supplies stored under the seat. 'Refallt's getting the horse ready for you. Do you think you can ride?'

'Ride, no; manage to stay aboard, yes. I've been on horseback hurt worse than this,' he assured.

'Tied over the saddle?' Annalie challenged. M'Connor just gave her a slow, sad smile that no doubt hid a dark story. 'Come on. I'll help you out of there,' Lerant offered

The procedure went more smoothly than Annalie had hoped, Lerant taking the weight as m'Connor cleared the sleigh and placed his booted foot into soft, slushy snow. He stood there, shaky and weak, but patently pleased to be upright once more, albeit leaning heavily on Lerant and unable to put his broken foot down.

'I've strapped some of those blankets up here,' Refallt said as he led the horse toward them, the animal's warm breath enshrouding him with a miniature fog in the chill night air.

'I could ride with him,' Alarn suggested. 'I'll hold onto him and keep him steady.'

Annalie and m'Connor exchanged considering glances. The footing on the slope would be treacherous and exhausting even for an adult. Alarn could easily fall and disappear where snow had piled up over a gap between rocks. 'I could use some help, thanks, Alarn,' m'Connor said, as she nodded. Alarn gave a happy smile and Annalie squeezed m'Connor's arm gratefully, letting him understand she was glad he'd said it like that, protecting her son's pride.

'What will you do with the sleigh?' Lerant asked Refallt, aware it was essential to the old man's trade.

'Hide it here under the trees and bury it a little in that snowdrift. It's deep enough that it won't melt anytime soon. We can haul it out later if we need it, and no one will find it.'

'Seekers might smell it out,' m'Connor warned.

Lerant shrugged. 'Nothing else for it,' he said, but Annalie, like m'Connor, could hear the dismissal underlying his answer. He didn't believe such creatures existed.

'They're real, Kerell,' Annalie prompted softly enough that Alarn wouldn't hear. 'We need to be ready to fight. I have my crossbow; I don't think I could carry the musket as well as Parla.'

'I'll take the gun,' Lerant told her. His pistol was no use, the barrel warped and he'd left it in the city.

'They won't be able to sense us once we're in the mine,' m'Connor said, by way of reassurance.

Hearing Lerant's disapproving sigh, Annalie whispered to him, 'I can't tell you how much I hope we don't get to prove to you that you're wrong.'

With Lerant's help m'Connor took one hobbling step closer to the horse and wound his fist tightly into the thick, shaggy mane, then took his weight from his good leg. Cupping the Weaver's booted foot, Lerant heaved. Boosted up to slide carefully into place, m'Connor could have felt only a slight jolt, but his already white face turned greenish-gray and he clutched the saddle horn, breathing through the pain. Impatient to help, Alarn mounted smoothly while Refallt continued to steady the horse that seemed to be accepting the situation readily enough.

'Keep your arms about Captain m'Connor,' Annalie instructed. 'But be careful.'

'Hold on very tight, Alarn,' m'Connor instructed, his voice terribly thin. 'The horse will have to jump in some places and he might not get time to warn us first.'

'It'll be rough going,' Lerant warned, sounding as if he wanted to find some other solution.

'Stop worrying,' m'Connor said, and managed to find a smile. 'Alarn and I have the best of it up here. You're all going to get very cold feet.'

'It's not nice to brag about it, m'Connor,' Lerant replied, glad of the banter. He aided Refallt in concealing the sleigh and returned to help tie Parla securely to Annalie's back. 'He's heavy and that snow is deep, Annalie. Maybe I should take him.'

'You'll have the worst of it out front hunting for the best path through this mess and you need to carry the lantern and the gun,' Annalie refused. 'I'll manage.'

Refallt led the horse forward and it took its first lunging stride up the slope. Tensing its hindquarters and leaping forward through the deeper drifts, the horse struggled valiantly upward.

M'Connor's leg would be jarred by each of the horse's successive leaps through the snow. It would be like riding a rack. Annalie hoped he could hang on.

Finally, through the gloom and floating snowflakes, a wider, deeper shadow became visible, and the steep, rugged ascent leveled off. 'We'll rest here a moment,' Lerant ordered. 'It'll be smoother, but trickier going down. I'll go ahead and see how solid it is.'

A few minutes later, he returned to report, 'It's not much of a path, but it's there. We'll need to take it very slowly.'

'*No!*' Varasaghir brought the lion-mind back into focus and concentrated again on the image of the flat white band, the road. He had shared its scent of humans there, but, with so heavy a snowstorm, it was impossible to say how old was that trace.

I'm so tired. They want to punish me and they want me to be on high alert as well. He'd been ordered to stand Seeker duty on double shifts, day after day. Ever since the disaster of his reported sighting of The Seedling—or at least of the Catalyst-sword, through the slargapent-Seeker in Khengha, he'd been on the outer with his people. He'd seriously embarrassed Superior Apomerghia who'd traveled all the way under cover of night into Khengha, going to Gallia, only to find no trace of the suspected Seedling.

Methaggars were badly handicapped in getting information because the humans' terror often rendered them incapable of giving reliable answers. Nor on this matter, could the military be asked for assistance. Varasaghir was certain that if he'd only been permitted to accompany his Superior, to take and use a human-Seeker such as the man, Jarrod, in Rogha, the mission would have been successful.

The Seedling's still out there somewhere, I know it! Now Apomerghia's dead, and he was the only one who believed me. Despondent, exhausted, Varasaghir struggled to maintain a close watch, the vast stretches of frozen night-shadowed landscape perfectly echoing his mood. *Rogha, what a terrible place; I'd freeze to death in an instant.*

Usually, the lion guarded the perimeters of the coal mine worked by Lellghin slaves, one such slave having been fed to it both as warning to the other slaves not to try escape and as training to the lion to associate the scent of humans with feeding.

Superior Lurghiar hadn't given him any warning before so coldly reporting Apomerghia had been murdered by a Magi. 'The cursed bitch must have gone to Rogha to aid her Weaver's escape. Took Apomerghia's head clean off his shoulders,' Lurghiar had said, an air of amazement the only emotion he'd let leak through the stiff words. 'General Rusark was terrified we'd think he'd killed him!' Lurghiar had added snidely. So, the General had been with Apomerghia, sharing whatever news of the battle Apomerghia had bothered to relay from Jarrod.

Huh?! What's that?

Lions had excellent night-sight and Varasaghir plainly saw as did it a great mountain of snow blocking the winding road. He had never personally seen snow, let alone such an immense amount in one place. He stared at it in astonishment while the lion stalked about its leading edge, sniffing here and there. An excited rush and Varasaghir plainly felt the surge of saliva in its mouth.

'Blood! It's found fresh blood! But is it human or animal? Varasaghir struggled to tamp down the urgency he shared with the creature. It was probably just some wounded deer, or something . . . . Although it had been trained to smell humans . . . . The lion bounded up the steep slope, revitalized, eagerly following the sharp tang of blood.

'A horse!' Varasaghir sensed, picking up the distinctive aroma along with the lion. He sagged, disappointed. He watched as the lion approached the crest of the rise, hoping—*'Ahh! What's that cursed light? People! Who . . . No!'*

They were halfway down, moving cautiously, when the horse picked up a scent on the wind and began pawing and snorting. 'Easy, lad. Easy!' Refallt urged.

'What is it?' Lerant called from forward of them. Lifting the lantern high to see beyond its glare, he juggled the musket into position off his shoulder. Her crossbow already in her hands, Annalie was not so hindered, sliding a bolt into its nock. She braced, waiting for Refallt's answer. 'There's something out there! I don't —'

A blood-curdling snarl drowned out whatever he'd said and a long, sinuous figure, darker than the starless sky, hurled itself at the horse, knocking him aside. He staggered and fell, losing his footing and going down, sliding from Annalie's view. All she could see of the thing was hate-filled hungry, eyes flashing red. No animal had eyes like that. She let off a shot that seemed to hit it but had no effect. Screaming in terror, Rae reared back, forelegs thrashing in a desperate effort to ward off his attacker and sending M'Connor and Alarn fallimg heavily to the snow.

Cold, gloved fingers slowed Annalie finding and loading another bolt. Racing upslope toward them, she knew Lerant couldn't risk a shot with the notoriously inaccurate musket. Rae succeeded in protecting his flank and belly, but the creature slashed at his upper legs and the horse screamed in agony. Off balance, Rae fell, sliding on the icy surface and gathering speed down the steep slope.

'Alarn!' Annalie shouted, seeing the fallen horse heading straight for the wounded m'Connor and her son. Shoving Alarn, m'Connor sent him skidding sideways across the ice toward a clump of avalanche-broken trees. M'Connor managed to throw himself the other way, a flaying hind hoof striking him a glancing blow on the back.

Steadying herself, Annalie got off a second shot that struck the lion high on the shoulder. Roaring outrage, it turned toward her, fangs bared in an ugly snarl. Then, as if compelled against its will, its eyes glazed and it turned away, back toward m'Connor.

'Get down!' Lerant shouted and she dropped out of his line of fire. She heard the crack of the musket and lifted her head to see the shot hit home, taking the Seeker in the gut. With a grunt, it staggered and crouched low, hissing angrily, yet despite its pain, remained focused on m'Connor.

Abandoning the empty gun and drawing his sword, Lerant scrambled upslope. Light suddenly blazed forth from the blade, illuminating the snow in red and gold. As uncanny as the lion's glowing eyes, yet utterly different, warm and brave, it pushed back the fear shaking Annalie. Glad of the light, she let a crying Parla slide from her shoulders, reloading her crossbow as she moved in toward the possessed animal, wanting to be close enough for a sure kill shot.

Below her on the slope, m'Connor grabbed at a branch of the shattered tree at his side, and somehow lurched up onto his good knee. The lion snarled and leapt toward him. Hampered by its wounds, it landed a few feet short of its target. Annalie caught a lungful of the awful, fetid odor of the beast and its challenging roar thrummed through her body. She doubted any mortal weapon could kill the thing but a shot through the eyes would blind it. The creature's fangs flashed in the dark, set to kill, to feed, as it stalked closer to the wounded man. Deeper snow and rubble tripped Annalie and the bow jolted free of her half-frozen grip.

Cursing in frustrated anger and terror, she hunted for it in the half-dark, catching a glimpse of m'Connor raising his unwounded arm. Steadying, he called something she didn't understand and abruptly, the winter night glowed bright and hot. Green-gold flames sizzled in a defensive line waist high above the snow, flaring up to engulf the Seeker. Its bellow ended mid-breath, climbed to a shriek, then fell to silence. Only the roar of flames filled the icy night, the scalding heat forcing Annalie back until she stumbled into Lerant.

His arms went around her and she was grateful, the embrace all that was holding her up. Together, they stared at the impossible. The outline of the beast was just visible, fallen on its side and wreathed in flames that licked at the snowy sky, embers and sparks swirling with the snowflakes in the wind as they consumed the corpse. M'Connor slumped limply forward into the snow, his grip on consciousness lost.

'Mama!' Alarn shouted, his voice thick with tears and terror. Annalie and Lerant swung about together to see him crawling out of hiding to go to m'Connor, but his sight fixed on the burning creature.

'Alarn! No!' Lerant shouted, suddenly more afraid than Annalie had ever heard him. 'Don't look at it! Don't look!'

'Get down!' Annalie snapped. He obeyed, dropping onto his belly, wrapping his head in his arms but still worming protectively close to the unmoving m'Connor.

Annalie turned back toward the stinging heat of the pyre, freezing as she saw something writhing there, growing to life, rising from the corpse. Swirling in the flames, a ghostly, black-robed man-shape emerged to drift like a wisp of somehow substantial smoke moving against the prevailing wind. Its face was a blur, two gleaming holes, pin point pupils blood red, locked onto hers, boring into her . . . . Piercing deep and cold, Seeking her heart, her mind, her will. She couldn't look away . . .

'Argat!' Lerant bellowed and suddenly, she could see only his back as he stood between her and the fire, swinging the Sunburst sword before him. Slicing through the smoke, the blade's edge scattered light in an arc of red-gold beams, protecting them against the thing living in the flames. Annalie could no longer see it, but she heard a snarling hiss. A thin trail of smoke drifted above Lerant's shielding form. No longer unnaturally solid, it thinned and dispersed, carried away on the night wind.

Annalie sagged, gasping for breath, trembling from head to toe.

'It's gone,' Lerant said, turning to face her, his voice seeming too loud in the sudden stillness. 'Are you all right?'

With a rush the real world thudded back into place, making Annalie aware of just how close it had been, how the thing had begun to drag her away . . . . She shuddered and Lerant moved to stand close at her side, wrapping his free arm about her back, his sword still held at the ready. It no longer glowed, and that, even more than Lerant's presence, gave her reassurance. Cold despite the still burning corpse, she dared to look down at the beast m'Connor had killed. The flames were low now, the blackened corpse visible, normal, just a dead mountain lion. Annalie shook her head and swallowed hard over a dry mouth. If not for Lerant's intervention . . . .

'I've found them!' Varasaghir shouted urgently to Superior Lurghiar, at the same time trying to marshal a defensive energy shield. He didn't have the power to take them on, of that he was certain. A loud bang, a shocking impact to the lion's gut drove Varasaghir back in reaction, slamming his head against the rock wall. *Musket fire!* He caught a glimpse of a sword and red-gold light suddenly penetrated into his very bones, eating, gnawing . . . . *The Catalyst Blade! The Seedling!? Again. Why me!'*

Fighting soaring agony, he forced the lion to attack. If it could kill m'Connor, Lurghiar would have a better chance at taking the Magi who would then be laboring under a Severing shock. Between them, they might then stun and take The Seedling, the man with the sword, a far more valuable catch. Vivid green Weaving-fire from m'Connor abruptly joined the agony flaring through Varasaghir, the burning heat as it devoured the lion unbearable. Gasping, grunting against the pain, Varasaghir struggled to maintain the fight.

'Dampen! Seek Anew!' he dimly heard Lurghiar snapping orders at his side. His welcome presence thrummed into Varasaghir, bolstering his battered strength. 'Dampen!'

Obeying readily, Varasaghir followed his training, avoiding the pain and the blinding of the Weave as he and Lurghiar hauled the Link high above the dead lion, completely clearing it.

'That woman is no Magi!' Lurghiar sneered. 'Concentrate! M'Connor's down. She's closer, easier, looking. Together, now! *Seek*!' Lurghiar took control, eager to claim the catch. Surely, he'd noticed The Seedling, too? Varasaghir dared not speak.

'Argat!!

The Magi kill command roared toward them, twisting, racing at Varasaghir, a thunderbolt. It slammed into him, cutting, digging, knotting his bowels, the ferocious agony of it robbing him of breath. He fell, blacking out, hoping that Lurghiar had heard, had seen, and must surely vindicate him—a *male* voice, delivering a Magi Severing!

The human who had escaped them over twenty years ago, The Seedling, still lived and had somehow reached Rogha. They must recapture him at any cost.

'Mama!' Alarn cried from where he sat in the snow at m'Connor's side. 'He's hurt again!'

'I'm coming!' Annalie cried, waiting only to scoop a crying Parla up from the snow, his cries carrying clearly above the crackle of the fire and the sighing of the wind in the pines. 'Hush it's all right, here's Mama, hush,' she soothed and kissed him, holding him tight against her and at the same time moving as quickly as the treacherous footing would allow to go to Alarn.

'He made the fire, just like this!' Alarn cried, looking up at her excitedly and throwing his arm out, the fingers pointed, just as m'Connor had done.

Annalie went to her knees and snatched him hard to her, engulfing both her sons in her embrace, her body shaking and her breathing coming in broken sobs. They could all be dead. Or worse. M'Connor had warned her—but . . . . She couldn't stop shaking or crying.

The warm familiar scent of clove soap came to her. Parlan! She could almost feel his arms around her and she let herself believe just for a moment, that he really was there.

'I'm all right, Mama!' Alarn complained, his words muffled against her chest and his small hands pushing her away. 'You're squashing me!'

'Refallt?' she head Lerant shout, and from somewhere further down slope came the echoing answer, 'Here! I'm going to fetch Rae.'

'Be careful!' Lerant called, the warning louder, closer. He was hurrying toward her and that gave her strength. She didn't want him to see her so close to falling apart. She drew a great heaving breath and let it out slowly. 'Mama!' Alarn protested, still struggling against her hold.

Annalie kissed the top of his head and let him go. 'Hold Parla for me,' she instructed and gave him over. She bent down and reached for m'Connor's throat pulse before remembering the burns. She slid her hand beneath his coat, checking the heartbeat. It pounded against her palm, racing erratically, indicating, if not shock, at the least severe exhaustion.

'Mama?' Alarn prompted anxiously.

Realizing she'd been frowning hard at her patient, she rearranged her expression into as much reassurance as she could muster. 'He'll be all right, Alarn, but we need to get him inside, out of the cold.' Alarn, too, was shivering, sitting in the snow, holding his little brother warmly to him. 'We need to get you all inside and into warm beds.'

I'd heat that tea; she remembered m'Connor saying only hours earlier, *if I had the strength . . . .* Just how badly had he drained himself to kill the Seeker? Was he dying? How many more of the things would they yet have to face? It was as well the mine was very close. There'd be no m'Connor to defend them next time, if the next time came soon, though it had been Lerant and that sword had finished the fight.

'Is he all right?' Lerant asked arriving at their side, his sword still upheld in case of further attack.

'Unconscious. His leg . . . the stitching is all but gone. The splints are shattered.' Her thoughts finished what she wouldn't say in front of her sons. Lerant's expression told her he knew it as well as she—the power needed to create the fire could have overtaxed his heart.

'He smashed his leg when he fell,' Alarn added sadly, 'It really hurt him, Mama, but he helped me anyway.'

'I know,' Annalie said, holding Lerant's equally worried gaze. That leg was already on the verge of going bad before Jarrod had forced m'Connor to walk on it. Callay had wanted to amputate . . . . How long ago now? It seemed forever but was only three days.

'I'll go get the lantern,' Lerant offered and walked away.

'Is his leg broken again, Mama?' Alarn asked, more quietly.

'I won't know for sure until we get him inside and I can take a closer look.' She bent, peering in the uncertain light, trying to judge how badly it was bleeding.

'There's a blanket, I'll get it,' Alarn said. Seeing him reaching out to snag it from somewhere very close-by, Annalie returned her attention to her patient.

'Dada! Dada!' Parla wailed abruptly. 'It's dark.'

'I want Dada, too,' Annalie replied hoarsely, trying not to weep. 'Mama's here.' She glanced up at Parla. Alarn had left his younger brother sitting on the blanket, and was hunting about for something else in the snow not far away.

Parla's small arms were reaching up as if someone was standing in front of him. All the hair stood up on the back of Annalie's neck. There was no one there . . . . Or rather, no one visible. The scent of cloves cut through her, more than just the soap now, it brought the essence of her husband.

'Dada,' Parla repeated, no longer upset, but sure of help, his hand held by another, unseen. 'Where's horsie?'

Cold through to the marrow, Annalie knew beyond doubt this was no enemy spell, no hallucination, no illusion. She knew her husband's touch. The whispering caress of his hand stroked her hair. Afraid to turn, not seeing him there would shatter this moment of having him back, the dreamed of reunion that had kept her going so long. Until death had stolen it. She hadn't even had his body to bury . . . .

It could not be. If Parla was seeing anything at all, he saw a ghost, and that hurt more than she could bear. It was not her husband, not the man who could laugh and chide her and take her in his arms, tell her it had only been a bad dream . . . . Make love to her.

The softest hint of a kiss on the top of her head, the same kiss Parlan had used to bid his sons good night. How many nights had she lain in the dark with her head on his shoulder and that kiss the last touch she'd known before the new day woke her.

'Refallt's gone for horsie, he's all right,' she said, almost weeping. She reached out and took her son's tiny, straining hands, bringing them down against her lips, kissing them as she wept silently. 'Mama's here, Mama's here,' she assured and he quieted.

'Dada gone bye-bye,' Parla told her sadly.

Taking a deep breath, she returned to carefully straightening m'Connor's leg and settling him more comfortably. 'Here, Mama. I found your bag,' Alarn startled her a little as he appeared at her elbow. Turning, she gave him a quick hug by way of thanks. 'Can I help?' he asked.

'Yes, mind your brother, please.'

'It's all right, Parla,' Alarn said, gathering his little brother up in his arms, standing, refusing the scant comfort of the blanket.

Glancing up at them, Annalie found Parla sucking his thumb, his eyes as wide and frightened as his older brother's as they both frowned off into the darkness. At that moment, Annalie wanted nothing so much as to have never left her home. But looking back at m'Connor, tallying his suffering, knowing what he'd given up for them . . . .

'Are there any more of those lions, do you think?' Alarn asked in a barely audible whisper, as if he were afraid to even admit the possibility. She caught him casting a doubtful frown at m'Connor. It had finally occurred to him, too, just how defenseless they were out here without the Weaver's protection.

'No,' she told him firmly and stroked his face. 'We won. They won't be back.'

'Here, I found the dry blanket we had rolled in the leather wrapping,' Lerant said, making her start again as he arrived back.

'Good. Put it over this one and help me slide him onto them,' Annalie said, not bothering to check m'Connor's shoulder wound any further. It was more important to get him out of the cold.

Lerant crouched down, arranging the blanket as she'd instructed. 'The lantern is no use,' he reported. 'The glass is shattered. Best secure that leg and get moving before we lose all the light from that fire.'

'Taran made the fire!' Alarn told his uncle, his pride in his friend overcoming his weariness and fear. 'Did you see him? It was green! It shot out from his fingers, like this!' Juggling an interested Parla, Alarn held out his right arm in perfect imitation of m'Connor but for the lack of those astounding flames. 'Did you see it?' Alarn demanded when Lerant said nothing.

'I saw . . . something,' Lerant admitted, and flicked an almost furtive look back at the fire. He shook his head and looked down at m'Connor in patent disbelief.

'Narcotic hallucinations, huh?' Annalie said curtly and gave him a sharp look that demanded a retraction of all his skepticism.

It was a stiff, cold and footsore procession that finally shuffled and limped into the shelter of the mine mouth. With her arms laden by the bundled medicine bag and clothing, Annalie carried an exhausted, sleeping Parla on her back. Ahead, their way was lit as Alarn carefully carried a fire brand Lerant had constructed from a torn piece of blanket, a green pine bough, and the oil from the smashed lantern. Alarn dragged himself soldierly onward, his tired gaze fixed immovably on the rough doorway that promised rest. The injured horse hobbled along behind them. Some distance to the rear, Lerant and Refallt struggled to carry an unconscious m'Connor.

'Keep going. It's just . . . round . . . that bend,' Refallt rasped out, probably as much for his own morale as for guidance. Annalie and the boys had been here a few times before with him. Turning slightly, she saw that every step was making him stagger now, under his share of the burden.

'Give him . . . to me,' Lerant panted. 'Take care . . . of the horse.'

Not having the breath for more words, Refallt nodded ready agreement and aided him in boosting m'Connor's limp body up until Lerant had him slung over his shoulders. There was no real door between outer stable and inner room, just some thick leather and wool covers held in place overhead by wooden battens. Annalie pushed them aside with her elbow to allow Alarn to precede her into the cavern room. It was a relief just to be out of the wind and have a roof overhead.

Alarn put the now weakly burning brand down in the hearth pit setting flame to the prepared wood and peat. He headed immediately to his hard-won goal. There were four camp beds, two to each wall flanking either side of a wonderfully large hearth set into the hewn rock of the rear wall. Annalie lowered Parla to join him on the bed and quickly pulled off the damp outer clothing from both her sons. Knowing they'd never again be tucked into their own beds at home was hard, very hard. She drew one of the neatly folded blankets up over them, and kissed them, more than grateful that they'd made it to some kind of safety at last. Alarn curled protectively about little Parla and was instantly asleep.

Straightening up, she found Refallt adding more peat to the fire. Flames leaped up, licking greedily at the fuel, smoke rising in a blue-gray mist to disappear up the rock chimney. Seeping warmth followed the dancing firelight that played over the bright colors of thick woven rugs laid on a sawdust-strewn, earthen floor. There were two cushion-filled chairs, a wooden stool, and a small table laden with pieces of leather work and saddlery. Further back were grain bins, water barrels, and shelves of cookware, cheeses and smoked meats.

'You've stocked it even more than since I last saw it,' Annalie said, relieved. 'We could stay here all winter if need be. Thank you.'

'Indeed I have,' Refallt agreed, enjoying her surprise. Both of them turned quickly to help Lerant who was staggering under his weighty burden as he came through the doorway.

Carefully, the three of them lowered m'Connor until they had him propped in a sitting position on the bunk. Annalie tugged at the

Weaver's coat buttons, removing the heavy, damp outer clothing. A moment later they finally had the injured man in bed.

'He doesn't look too good,' Lerant commented worriedly, 'We hurt him there a few times, trying to haul him down that slope.'

'Thank you, Kerell. I'm glad you're here with us.' Annalie hesitated and added, 'Parlan would be so proud of you.'

CHAPTER TWENTY FOUR

'You're not hurt. Wake up. Wake up!'

His Superior's voice echoed and echoed, each syllable adding to the pain that pounded Varasaghir's entire body. What—? The Seedling, the male Magi! It had attacked and cut the Link, striking back so hard that . . . .

'Wake up!' A cold hard hand slapped at his face.

'You don't have to hit me!' Varasaghir complained, opening his eyes.

'You've been sleeping for over a day.'

'A day!' Lying prone on one of the straw mattresses they used in the cavern rooms, Varasaghir squinted up at an angry Lurghiar. He felt terribly weak and parched.

'Yes! I've had to maintain the search all by myself!'

'Search . . . ? Oh, the escaped Weaver.'

'We had them, but you let them get away, and now they've vanished!' Lurghiar accused, stepping away from the bed.

'I—He had a Magi, and—'

'That woman was no Magi!'

'Not her, the . . . .' Suddenly, Varasaghir didn't want to talk about the Seedling, not to Lurghiar. He quelled the urge to shout are you blind or stupid or both. Who do you think took Apomerghia's head off, all the way from Rogha? Only the Seedling, the man named Lerant, and the Catalyst sword, could have commanded such incredible power.

'There was no Magi,' Lurghiar lied.

'Well, *something* hit us and hit us hard!' Varasaghir snapped in return. Damn it, he was tired of being subjugated, snarled at, humiliated. Obviously, Lurghiar assumed that Varasaghir knew little or nothing of the history of Lellgha, let alone had understood a Magi word of command. Good, let him stay ignorant, so much the better for ideas beginning to ferment in Varasaghir's waking mind.

'M'Connor is adept at such things,' Lurghiar said, offhandedly. 'Eat, and get back to work. We need to find them again.'

There was no doubting Lurghiar's frustration and need to track them again. Had he seen, did he know? Yes. He wanted the Seedling all for himself, always had. Perhaps it had been more than coincidence that Apomerghia had been killed, giving the command rank to Lurghiar . . . .

Varasaghir sat up, drawing his knobby knees to his chest and keeping still until a bout of dizziness subsided. There was very little light in their quarters, for which he was grateful. Then again, Lurghiar had caught at least a small amount of that energy recoil and would have a sore head, too. Someone had placed dried meat in baskets on a low table in the middle of the room and the sight of it made Varasaghir's stomach roll. He wanted to ask what kind of meat it was, but didn't dare. He'd already been taunted for his dislike of the kind of meat often provided here, taken from dead human slaves. The very thought revolted him—his people had never before needed to resort to what was surely a form of cannibalism, no matter what they said.

Shuffling across to the table, he hunted in the other baskets and found some fish and withered-up fruit. Lurghiar watched him impatiently, his long tongue curling in a sneer at the rejection of the meat. 'Hurry,' he snapped. 'I'm tired and must rest for a short while. I don't dare leave you on watch alone too long—we both know you can't be trusted.'

'That's not true!' Varasaghir cut his protest short knowing it was pointless; no one would listen, no one would believe—other than poor dead Apomerghia who had become a target of ridicule for it. The sensation of rebellion grew inside him, more warming and energizing than the bland, stale food. He knew what he'd seen, what he'd felt.

Lurghiar knew something more than a wounded m'Connor had attacked them, had heard that terrible male Magi word of attack. Perhaps he hadn't understood its import. Or rather, he was *pretending* he didn't understand. Varasaghir wondered at the means of Apomerghia's death—had Lurghiar had a hand in arranging for him to walk into that trap? Had he suspected the truth and made sure Apomerghia could not find The Seedling in Khengha?

Varasaghir had always had a keen interest in the history of the arrival of the Magi on this world, of how the male Akkarra seeds guided themselves to the fertile lands where they could germinate. The female seeds and all the male Magi and female Weavers they contained, had been thought to have perished in some unknown accident of the so-called 'Crossing'.

Only the Methaggar knew otherwise.

Exiled to the deadly methirri-saturated lands of the Smoking Mountains, they'd had to burrow deep to avoid the killing heat of the sun and sometimes too, of volcanic lava spills. A generation or more before Varasaghir had been born, that mining had uncovered something that only the Methaggar historians had been able to recognize—a female Akkarra 'seed'. With much work, they'd created a deep shelter where the seed had at last been forced to awaken, if not to grow to anything more than a small weedy thing. As a child, Varasaghir had once been taken to see it. Impressed by its tiny Kartai blood-soaked branches, leaves and soil, he'd been inspired then and there to become a scientist-historian himself.

It was so clever, how they'd learned to keep it alive with a blood-type that in some mysterious fashion protected it from the worst of the effects of methirri. The captured Kartai slaves had periodically been bled to provide both protection and nourishment to the precious plant with its tantalizing and aggravatingly well hidden information. Three of the human children born in captivity contained the linked energy imprints, the 'souls' of the Akkarra's male Magi and his two female Weavers.

'Stop daydreaming and get to work!' Lurghiar snarled. 'I know what you're thinking—Varasaghir the savior of our nation!' He spat, making his disgust plain in the saliva coating his thin lips. 'I saw that blade! Has it not occurred to you that the cursed Magi will have created fake Catalyst swords to draw our attention away from their true intent? Ha! How far did Apomerghia journey before he realized what a fool they'd made of him, or rather what a fool *you'd* made of him! His replacement will be here soon and I no longer need rely on your fanciful reports!'

'Then that will be a happy day for us both!' Varasaghir returned, surprising himself by saying it aloud, carried by the rush of blood he could feel making the fine hair of his arms and face bristle.

Lurghiar lifted a hand to slap him, but Varasaghir ducked away and scrambled quickly up to the Sentry ledge. There he sat a moment before remembering his lion-Seeker was dead and the Link severed.

'Make sure you do not fail us this time, Varasaghir! I won't be gone long; this work is far too important to entrust to the likes of you! Keep watch on the coastline, use my Seeker. Wake me if you see a Talae ship; it must soon return and lure m'Connor from his hiding place. Do not slacken, Varasaghir! Keep close attention! If he should escape us again, Grouda and Zaraxan will be looking to know why!'

'I'll find the ship,' Varasaghir said, quietly certain.

'Then you will report immediately to me!' Lurghiar snarled.

'Yes, Superior,' he said with a defeated sigh.

He searched along the ledge and soon found the Contact Lurghiar had been using. His fingers closed over the small piece of methirri instilled with the correct Blood-codes, a twin of that implanted in the tagged animal. He inserted it into his thumb and a sun-spangled blue ocean lined with small rocky coves and cliffs suddenly spun far beneath him. A wave of dizziness swept through him so powerfully that he very nearly toppled from the ledge, only a wild grab saving him and making him momentarily lose the Seeker—a sea eagle. Lurghiar might have warned him! He could hear his Superior's sniggering laughter.

Ignoring him, Varasaghir resumed Contact. He had to admit the eagle was a better choice for Seeker, giving him a panoramic view from high above a green-pine and snow-shrouded mountainous landscape bordered with rugged cliffs and blue sea. The weather had cleared and he could plainly see a long parading line of rocky ramparts about whose feet a still angry ocean churned, a sea-salt thick air and the exhilarating sensation of flying with the breeze beneath 'his' wings invigorating and lifting his mood.

And intensifying his resolve to rebel and follow his own mind, his certain knowing.

When Apomerghia's replacement arrived, Varasaghir would leave this place, collect the two friends he'd known since childhood, and together they'd go find the fair-haired human male, Lerant, who carried the Catalyst Blade. Varasaghir smiled, imagining how he would capture and return him, and see him forced to awaken and enslave more of his kind. Akkarra-Magi power would at last be made to serve and restore the Methaggars to their rightful place. No longer would they need to cower in the dark, no longer die before their time, poisoned by the prison the humans had created for them.

Varasaghir would be their savior, and better, he could finally ask Capadiccia to marry him!

Hands held him down. Zaraxan . . . ! Hot irons! M'Connor cursed, struggled. He burned, and his leg hurt badly.

'Steady! Easy! It's me, Lerant!'

The fog cleared for a moment and he remembered vaguely. The snowy mountainside.

'Seeker! Don't look!' He fought desperately to sit up, to save the boy.

'M'Connor! Listen to me! You must stay still!' A forceful bright power coursed into him, the words a command he couldn't resist, linking them like Magi and Weaver. 'We're safe. It's over. It's gone. We made it. We're in the mine. We're safe.'

'M'Connor? Come on, try. You must drink.' Annalie said.

He grunted, tried to open his eyes. A cool touch against his cheek, his lips. 'Here,' she said, and a hand slid beneath m'Connor's head, lifting him a little as something pressed to his mouth. 'Drink.' The familiar taste of sweetened tea laced with bitter medication trickled into his mouth. He swallowed. The cup was taken away, and then returned. Pure water. He drank thirstily, and they eased him back. A bed? There'd been snow, darkness . . . .

'Ann . . . Anna . . .?' He failed to force his thick tongue to form the name but couldn't lift his heavy eyelids to look up at her.

'It's all right. Hush. Rest.' Wonderfully soothing fingers rubbed firm, gentle circles on his brow. The thudding pain in his leg gradually faded and he drifted into a more gentle darkness . . . .

'You haven't slept in two days,' Annalie's voice came sharply into m'Connor's hearing, bringing him from his drugged sleep to partial wakefulness. 'You must sleep!'

'I need to know what's happening to my men.' Lerant's sigh was a swirling tangle of frustration and confusion.

'You can't go out there with those things hunting us!'

A pause.

'I wish I'd known this remedy before,' Annalie said. Careful, gentle hands did something to his leg, spreading a cool moistness over it.

'It's never been used like this,' Lerant protested. 'You can't rely on horse medicine to save a man's leg . . . and his life! I don't know, Annalie . . . .'

'If it comes to a choice . . . I'll do what needs to be done.'

'His fever's down,' Lerant said. 'You're exhausted. I'll sit with him.'

'Be all right,' m'Connor tried to say but they didn't hear him and he couldn't hang on.

There came a vague sense of more time passing, of bouts of fever shivering through him, one after another. Then . . .

'I hope we're doing the right thing for you, m'Connor. You might be better off without this leg crippling you.'

'Leave it!' m'Connor Sent in return, from the dark of his exhaustion, relieved someone was Sending to him when he couldn't speak for himself. He didn't know who was the vibrant, powerful presence close at his side. It sounded like Lerant, but that couldn't be. *'The Healers will save it! Find Gerion!'*

Starting as if in alarm, The Sender pulled away from him, and, with no Shielding to interrupt their Link, pulled a weakened m'Connor after him into his Traveling. The next he knew, they were both in the Void, or something like the Void . . . .

Cold and dark lasted a moment and then, together, they arrived . . . somewhere . . . .

A trembling wave of fearsome, shimmering white light towered over them both, threatening to drown them in its pounding power. Teeming voices cried out from within the light, begging for help, despairing of finding freedom. Overwhelmed, afraid, the Sender backed further away, unaware of a solid darkness, a dangerous hungry shadow behind him.

'No!' m'Connor warned, trying to use their connection to pull him back. But, not having the strength, he was dragged along into the maw. Abruptly they were blinded and engulfed in a dense, crushing cold nothing, methirri, but a thousand times stronger than any slave collar, incredibly powerful.

Desperate, he clawed for purchase, for something, anything to save him being utterly consumed and compressed into the same nothingness. Then, an eruption of warm light surrounded him, coming from the Sender, the one who'd dragged him here. At that moment, m'Connor didn't care how he was doing it, he was only glad to feel his Ea expand again, live again. Somehow he made a space for them both to exist, like an air-pocket in an avalanche, but he didn't know how to get them out.

Whoever he was, he possessed incredible power but lacked the training to use it fully. He'd brought them here; how could he be so completely unaware of what he was doing?

That unawareness had m'Connor trapped, had them both trapped. Knowing how dangerously weak his body was, m'Connor knew it would die if he didn't get back soon. He'd be stuck here like a fly in amber, his body dead, his ea trapped forever inside this bubble of light. The Akkarra could never find him, surrounded by that all that methirri outside . . . .

Just like they couldn't find Bren . . . .

Struggling to find a way out, he probed at the inside of the wall surrounding him like a womb. Somewhere must be the umbilical cord that would lead him back to his body, if it still existed. He could sense the methirri's cold threat waiting beyond the shelter. Following the wall further along, he came hard up against the bright strong life cord of the Sender. Vibrant, humming with energy, it fully connected him to his body, yet its owner seemed unaware of its existence. It was strong enough to survive the methirri and would last long enough for its body's demands to haul its owner back . . . eventually.

Seriously ill, M'Connor didn't have the luxury of that time. He searched in vain to find his own cord, every passing moment deepening his peril. Bracing himself, he extended his awareness as far as he dared into the methirri, hoping to see the glimmering cord that was his way out. Something blinked in the distant darkness, so dim, he wasn't sure it was really there.

Focusing on the spot, he strained to sense it again. Another blink. It wasn't a life cord, but wasn't part of the methirri, either. It blinked again, clearer this time, the tiniest pinpoint of white light, far, far off. The next blink was stronger, looking like a firefly on a moonless night. In the space of a heartbeat, it didn't blink anymore, and was instead streaking toward him like a tiny comet with a long, long tail. The closer it came, the faster it came, heading straight toward him like iron to a lodestone.

Drawing whatever strength he could find, he reached out further, something about it moving him, compelling him to go further than he should. The leading edge of its energy met his like hands plucking a lyre string. The vibration of it swept through him like music, setting his Ea singing as it always had in reply:

Bren!

He threw all he had into re-establishing the bond Zaraxan had shattered. There was no response. Bren's consciousness was so deeply buried and reduced to no more than the barest thread needed for survival, it didn't recognize him, couldn't recognize him. This was not Bren's waking mind. Driving this spark was the most basic part of a living soul, the mechanism that would keep someone alive in the deepest coma. It sensed the Sender's vibrant presence and lunged for it, seeing the way back to life, back to a body.

Back to what it thought was Bren's body. It would kill the Sender. If only m'Connor could find the faint thread of his own life cord, he might be able to attach Bren to it and draw him back into the Akkarra's awareness. But there was no time to search for it and he was too weak, regardless.

'Keep him back!' m'Connor urged, turning all his senses on his untrained companion.

Bren's essence ate deeper into the oblivious man's Ea, opening a great wound that bled life-light along the cord. Instinctively sensing escape, it was drawing strength, trying to restore itself, unknowing it was not its own, but another man's body he was attempting to claim. Bren would empty the man's presence to take his place in an unconscious, unthinking drive to survive.

'Bren! Don't! You'll kill him! Go back!' Terribly weak, m'Connor concentrated, focused, ignored the lack of their Bond, and knew somewhere, somehow, Bren *must* hear him. 'Bren! *Stop!*'

There was no pause. Bren's essence, starved for so long, engulfed more and more of the other's life force. If Bren succeeded, they'd all be worse than dead, left stranded here at the mercy of methirri, the man's bright life-cord broken by Bren's unseeing hunger. Bren gulped more and more, as ravenous as one of the giant terraketti he and m'Connor had fought in battle, but harder to stop.

'Bren! *No!*' Marshalling the last dregs of his strength, m'Connor braced then pushed outward against Bren's ever-brighter power. The recoil drained him, leaving him dazed.

Another light flared, a spirit, like a Magi coming to call a Tested one home, coming from behind and pouring itself into the unknown man, shielding him and aiding m'Connor's struggle to protect him. Vaguely, m'Connor thought he recognized this strange presence from somewhere . . . that day in the Grove, just before his Testing . . . .

'Parlan?' the man called to the newcomer. Broken, disbelieving, it repeated, '*Parlan*!' Finally, he was aware of something.

'Hurry*!*' Parlan ordered. 'Follow me! They're coming!'

'You're dead! This is just a dream!'

'There's no time for this, Kerell! You have to get out of here—now!

Kerell?! Lerant!? The untrained man channeling all this power was Kerell Lerant!? But, yes, it had to be, for even now he was refusing to accept the truth and denying the aid that would save him.

'If I wasn't dead I couldn't be here to save you!' Parlan insisted angrily. 'Listen to me or the Methaggar will take you! All will be lost! M'Connor?'

'Yes?'

'I need your help. Only you can make Bren let go. Even so deeply locked away he'll obey you.'

'I can't reach him. He doesn't hear me.'

'I'll give you the strength you need. He'll trust you.'

Energy poured into m'Connor, revitalizing him. He steeled himself to call to his Brother, to tell him to go back but hesitated, knowing what he was condemning him to, possibly forever.

'He's stronger now. We reached him once, we can do it again,' Parlan assured.

Knowing there was no other way to save them all, m'Connor took the offered sliver of hope into his heart and pushed away any other feeling. 'Bren!' he commanded. 'Hear me! Let go!! You'll kill him! Let go!' Bren's devouring Ea halted and hung suspended a long moment.

'I'll come for you, I swear. I'll free you,' m'Connor promised. With one last, heartbreaking effort, he severed his Brother's desperate hold and pushed him away, out again into the terrible dark of the methirri.

'Hurry!' Parlan ordered again and m'Connor felt himself pushed backward, down what was an almost impossibly thin thread of life-light. Parlan's warm presence swelled, wrapping about both m'Connor and Lerant, carrying them rapidly to safety. Abruptly, they emerged from the methirri to confront the waiting, trembling wall of trapped souls.

'There!' Parlan directed Lerant's attention to the blindingly bright, towering wave of Ea energies. 'You must free them, Kerell! If you fail, we all die forever! Now, go, back to yourself. Remember this and <u>believe!</u>'

Then, they were back in the odd Void, a fleeting, hurtling Travel through cold and dark, like yet unlike methirri, and m'Connor thudded heavily back into his body, shaking with pain and shock. Bren! He'd found Bren! He'd waited so long, clung to hope when even the Akkarra had failed. He'd found his Brother only to have to leave him behind. But unlike Parlan Hollin, Bren m'Fetrin was alive, and m'Connor had the key to finding him again—Kerell Lerant.

END BOOK ONE

CPSIA information can be obtained at www.ICGtesting.com
Printed in the USA
BVOW041459230413

318896BV00005B/14/P